HOLIDAY Rider

A SECOND CHANCE COWBOY ROMANCE

MAGGIE COLE

PULSE PRESS INC

1

—————

Willow Cartwright

"**G**otcha!" I shout, curling my arms around Emma and tugging her onto the sofa. "Time for the tickle monster!"

"Aunt Willow! No!" she screeches, her eyes wide, cheeks pink.

I barely flick my fingers over her belly.

She twists under my grasp, squealing louder.

"Willow! The phone's for you," Dad announces.

I don't give Emma any relief. "Who is it?"

Laughter peals out of her.

Dad replies, "Sheriff's office."

The hairs on my arms rise. I stop torturing my niece to pin my gaze on Dad. "What's going on?"

Emma wiggles off my lap and darts across the room.

A mix of amusement and disapproval fills Dad's expression. He answers, "Sounds like a few of your clients misbehaved."

"A few?"

"Sheriff said two of your guys got into it with some other bull rider at The Buck and Bruise. They're all in custody, waiting to be bailed out."

Irritation fills me. I blurt out, "They got into a bar fight on Christmas?"

Dad's lips twitch, but then his gaze sharpens back into disdain.

I groan and rise, brushing past him as I mutter, "I should let them rot until the New Year."

A chuckle escapes him. He calls out, "Hallway phone."

I shake my head, releasing a tense breath. The last thing I want to do is go into town on Christmas night. It's one of my family's favorite holidays, and besides, it's almost the kids' bedtime. I glance out the window, peering at the multicolored glow of the festive lights through the blanket of white snow, and pick up the phone.

My stomach twists, but I put on my professional voice and offer, "Merry Christmas. This is Willow Cartwright. How can I help you?"

"Merry Christmas, Willow. I'm sorry to bother you," Sheriff Lorall states.

"It's okay, sir. Which of my riders decided to be the prize idiots?" I twist the cord around my fingers. I've done it since I was a kid, always letting it dig into my skin until I can't take it anymore, as if it'll protect me from whatever is coming.

He lowers his voice. "Jericho Boone and Colt Remington."

"Seriously?" I'm surprised. Jericho and Colt aren't clients who normally get into trouble, especially not petty bar fights. They're experienced bull riders who compete individually and in the 5-on-5 team format. They take their careers seriously and, if anything, stop the younger guys on the team from making stupid decisions.

"Yes, ma'am," the sheriff confirms.

"Is bail the usual two grand apiece?" I question, stepping closer to the cold glass.

He clears his throat. "Yes, that's correct. However, we can waive it since it's Christmas."

"Really? What's the catch?" I ask, focusing on a red lightbulb on the fence that flickers before it burns out.

Sheriff Lorall explains, "Danny's offered not to press charges if he's paid sixty thousand in cash for damages."

"Sixty thousand!" I erupt, my pulse hammering in my throat, violent and uncontrollable.

"Unfortunately, yes."

"Isn't that a bit excessive?" I question.

"Umm... Well, in fairness, it looks like a bomb exploded. They broke a lot of tables and chairs. Shards of glass everywhere. And you know that mirror that covers the entire back wall?"

My gut drops. I close my eyes, gritting through my teeth, "What about it?"

"It's in a million pieces all over the floor. And that isn't a cheap fix," he states.

I take deliberate, slow breaths, trying to eliminate the building anger.

He clears his throat again, asking, "What should I tell Danny? He said the offer is only good for another hour."

I gently bang my head against the window and then hold it firmly against the chilled glass, squeezing my eyes tight.

Sixty grand.

They have a rodeo this week.

I should let them deal with the consequences.

If I do, they'll lose their sponsors, and I'll need to find two new clients.

"Ma'am?" the sheriff pushes.

I cave. "Tell Danny I'm on my way. But the roads are bad, so tell him not to leave if it takes me longer than an hour."

"Will do," he says.

I put the phone down and climb the staircase. I go into my closet and push my palm against the safe. There's a loud click, and the door opens.

My non-costume jewelry is on one shelf. Important documents are on the second. The bottom one contains one hundred thousand dollars in neat stacks of hundred-dollar bills.

Begrudgingly, I grab sixty thousand and try to stop my heart from slamming against my ribs, but it's pointless. I lock the safe, then grab an overnight bag. I stick the cash inside, and more anger festers in my chest.

"Idiots," I mumble as I step out of my room and rush down the hall-way, knowing Danny isn't going to wait too long. He's got my riders by the balls, and he knows it. I'm sure the damage is excessive, but sixty thousand has to have some extra padding for his inconvenience.

I can't really blame him.

He's being greedy.

They're lucky he won't press charges.

What in the world made them do this?

Jagger steps out of the game room and bumps into me. He teases, "Whoa. Where's the fire?"

"Sorry. I have to bail Jericho and Colt out of jail."

My brother's cocky smirk appears. "What for?"

"It's not funny," I reprimand.

"I'll be the judge of that. What did they do?" he prods.

"They destroyed The Buck and Bruise. Now Danny wants sixty thousand to not press charges and sweep it under the rug."

Jagger whistles. "Damn. Who did they get into it with?"

"I don't know. Honestly, I don't care. But Danny won't wait forever before he pulls the deal off the table, so now I get to drive through a snowstorm on Christmas. So if you'll kindly move." I flit my fingers in front of him.

He crosses his arms. "Think again, Willow."

"I don't have time for your games, Jagger," I scold, and try to step around his muscular frame.

He steps with me, creating a wall I can't escape.

"Jagger! This is serious!"

His eyes turn to slits. "How much wine have you had today?"

I freeze, think back, then wince, admitting, "A lot."

Arrogance floods his expression. "That's what I thought. You shouldn't be behind the wheel, especially in this weather. I'll take you."

"You've been drinking too," I point out, but I know he's right. I shouldn't be driving with or without the freak blizzard conditions we're experiencing.

"I had two beers today. All day. Haven't drank since dinner," he claims.

I reach up and touch his forehead. "Are you feeling okay?"

He chuckles. "Yes."

I peer closer. "Why haven't you had more than that?"

"None of your business. But you can thank me for leaving the warm house to help you save your ass." He smugly grins.

I tilt my head and glare at him.

"It's Christmas, so you have to be nice," he taunts, then grabs my bag, tossing it over his shoulder.

"Fine. Let's go," I mutter, then duck past him and jog down the stairs. I reach for the hooks, tug my coat off one, then yank open the front door.

A chill wind slices razors across my face. I jerk my head backward.

"Put your coat on, Willow," Jagger orders as he puts the cash down and grabs his jacket. He slips into it, reaches for the bag, and ducks out into the snow.

I obey, then follow him, fighting the flakes slapping into me.

He opens my door and then races around the truck.

I pull myself up into the cab and shut the door.

Jagger slides inside beside me, turns on the engine, then picks up the snow brush. He gets out, scrapes the ice off the windows, then gets back in. He accelerates down the driveway, gripping the wheel and asking, "What was the fight over?"

"How do I know?"

"You didn't ask?"

I huff. "No. When the sheriff told me I could pony up sixty grand or have my riders charged with disorderly conduct or possibly assault and battery, I didn't decide to have a gossip session about why they decided to be morons on Christmas."

"Touché," Jagger offers, then directs his concentration on the barely visible road.

"It's really bad out," I state, unable to see anything but the huge, wet flakes slamming into the windshield.

"Sure is," Jagger replies, then turns on a country music channel playing only Christmas music.

We barely talk for the rest of the ride. It takes over an hour to get into town. When we pull into the police station, my annoyance resurfaces.

Jagger parks near the entrance.

Eager to get this over with, I open the door, sliding into the icy-cold air. I move cautiously, each step pressing into the thin veil of snow that's crept back over the cleared path. My only focus is to get my riders out of the slammer and return home at a decent hour. More anger fills me, and I push the door open, barely feeling the warmth.

Lucinda, an officer I've known since I was a little girl, looks up from her desk. She comments, "Merry Christmas. Sheriff said to send you back when you get here. Assuming you don't need me to instruct you where to go?"

Sighing, I reply, "Unfortunately not. Merry Christmas."

She smiles, and a loud buzz fills the room.

I nod and push the metal door open, with Jagger on my heels. Stale air grows thicker the farther down the hallway I walk.

"I hate this place," he mumbles.

"Then it's good you've been staying out of it," I point out, remembering several bar fights he'd been in over the years, mostly with my other brothers.

A muscle jumps in his jaw. He points, directing, "This isn't about me. Besides, I'm an angel. Go pay off Danny so your riders can win this week."

I snark, "You're an angel with black wings," and turn the corner, stepping into an open area with several officers sitting at desks.

Sheriff Lorall stops talking and pins his stern expression on us. "Willow. Jagger."

Danny jumps up from his seat. He picks up his cowboy hat and points it at me, drawling, "Your riders destroyed my bar!"

A borderline toxic mix of guilt, shame, and rage churns in my chest, burning hotter with every passing second. Fire crawls across my cheeks, drowning me in further embarrassment.

These are my clients.

My riders.

This is a reflection on my agency.

"I'm sorry. I brought the money," I announce.

Danny glances at the bag in Jagger's hand. "Put it on the desk. I'm counting it before I leave."

"You think my sister would rip you off?" Jagger accuses, his voice laced with an unspoken warning, his eyes narrowing with fire.

I put my hand on his arm. "It's okay."

"No, it's not. Especially when he's ripping you off."

"Go look at my bar and tell me the value of the damage you think they did," Danny argues.

"Doubt it's sixty big ones," Jagger counters.

"Maybe I should make it eighty," Danny threatens.

"Now, now. There's no point making things more heated on Christmas. Sixty thousand was the price, and Willow's brought it, haven't you, sweetheart?" Sheriff Lorall says.

Revulsion coils in my gut, tightening into knots. I hate it when the sheriff or any man talks to me like I'm a helpless woman. Plus, he's my father's age. I'm not his sweetheart and never will be.

I fight through the disgust and force a smile. "Yes, sir. Can you release my riders, please?"

"I want to count it," Danny insists.

"You know where I live. It's Christmas, and I promised I'd read my nieces and nephews a story before bedtime. I assure you the money is all there, but if you find a discrepancy for any reason, you know where to find me," I state.

"You go get them. I'll stay here while Danny counts it just to make sure he doesn't try to rip you off," Jagger offers.

Danny fumes, "You're lucky I didn't press charges against you."

"Coulda, shoulda, woulda. Move on from the past, old man," my brother taunts.

"Jagger!" I scold.

The sheriff interjects again, ordering, "Danny, go count the money with Officer Tenpenny. Jagger, you sit in that chair and keep your comments to yourself." He points to a seat several desks away.

Both men follow orders.

The sheriff puts his hand on my back.

I do everything I can not to squirm away from him, knowing he'll eliminate even more space between us if I do.

That's the thing about a small town. Everyone tends to know everyone, and the sheriff is as dirty of an old man as any other. And it's not the first time I've had to deal with his unwelcome touches.

The moment to escape his grasp comes, and I rush through the door into the holding area, questioning, "What number?"

"Fifteen."

Catcalls erupt from the men locked up. They echo louder as I pass more cells.

"Shut up," the sheriff barks, but there's nothing he can do.

The noise increases. I get to fifteen, already thinking about what I'm going to say to my clients, and freeze, the air disappearing from my lungs.

It's not him.

A devil in cowboy boots lounges on a bench against the wall, owning the cell and reeking of sin. Denim covers his long legs, and a ripped, bloody white T-shirt stretches over his torso, half tucked into a belt buckle with a W on it. His wounded knuckles, full of ink and crossed peacefully on his taut abs, rise and fall with his breathing. A worn, brown leather cowboy hat tilts over his face, covering the bad-boy smirk I'm sure plays on his lips.

The dim light of the holding cell makes the inked sleeve on his forearm appear dangerous and majestic. Black lines etched into sun-warmed skin hint about stories you'd never unravel unless he let you close enough to trace them with your tongue.

He's the kind of man who'd wreck your plans, your bed, and your sense of right and wrong, without ever raising his voice.

And that's exactly what Wyatt Houston did to me.

Somehow, I forget to breathe. I reach for the bars, wrapping my fingers around one, trying to stop the adrenaline rush and chaos attacking me from every angle.

"Willow. Sorry to fuck up your Christmas," Jericho blurts out.

Wyatt's hands stop rising. His jaw clenches, and I don't miss the glint of his eye peeking out from the side of his hat. As if in slow motion, he raises a finger, pushes the brim of his hat up, and pins his dark eyes on me.

Flames flicker in the pit of my stomach, dark and reckless. The catcalls only intensify old feelings, giving life to something scarier.

It's been too many years since he's touched me.

Don't go there, I scold myself.

Wyatt's intoxicated, but the same challenging gaze that wrecked me all those years ago takes me in, undressing me with every passing second.

I don't move, scared of what I might do, even though there's a locked door and several men between us.

Ironically, Sheriff Lorall saves me, stepping beside me and unlocking the cage. He scolds, "You're lucky Willow is saving your asses. Call it your Christmas miracle. But you will lose your careers the next time this happens. Got it?"

"Yes, sir," Colt replies.

"Thank you," Jericho adds.

They shoot me guilty looks, quickly brushing past me.

"Well? I don't have all night, and this isn't a motel. Get up and out of here," the sheriff spits out, motioning toward Wyatt.

"You bailed him out?" Jericho whines.

"What? No. He's not my client," I assert, assuring the sheriff I'm not paying for Wyatt.

He shakes his head. "I can't keep him if Danny isn't pressing charges. Even if he did the most damage."

I gape at him and open my mouth to argue.

Lorall adds, "Plus, his agent fired him. So no one's coming to help him but you."

My head snaps toward Wyatt, and I hate myself.

His low, dangerous voice curls around my chest, suffocating me with promises I vowed I'd never allow into my life again. "Appreciate the help, sugar." He lifts his cowboy hat higher, his gaze dark with arrogance and pupils blown wide with want.

I'm torn between falling into his seductive trap and strangling him with my bare hands.

He makes it worse when he sits up.

My heart pounds harder. I stare at his quads, straining against dirty denim. After several seconds too long, my gaze drifts below his belt buckle, and whispers of the past dance between my thighs.

He shifts off the bench. His cowboy boots slam the floor with authority, causing me to jump.

I redirect my attention to the sheriff. "I'm not responsible for him."

"No one said that, but he's as free as your riders," he reiterates.

"What's wrong, sugar? Afraid I'll get you in trouble?" Wyatt drawls, his question laced with the same teasing dare I fell for when I was too naive and inexperienced to understand what a man like him could do to a girl like me.

I need air.

I turn away from him, blinking hard. Then I march past my riders and burst into the office, directing an order at Jagger. "Let's go."

"Danny's not done counting. He's slow as molasses," he jabs.

"I don't care. Let's go," I reiterate louder, stomping out into the raging chill that refuses to choke out the inferno blazing inside me. I get into the truck, reach for the keys my brother left in the ignition, and take the deepest breaths I can.

Stop letting him affect you, I tell myself repeatedly, but it's asking for the impossible.

Memories of my first everything flood me, and Wyatt's involved in every one of them.

Jericho and Colt appear at my window.

Jericho knocks on it with his knuckles.

I roll down the glass. "We'll talk about this tomorrow."

Their expressions are filled with guilt.

Colt offers, "I hope we didn't ruin your Christmas."

I glare daggers at them.

An Uber pulls up to the curb.

They wait.

"Just go. We're not discussing this tonight," I repeat and then shut the window.

They nod and almost disappear in the snow before getting into the SUV.

More time passes, then Jagger appears. Relief hits me, then dissipates into thin air.

Wyatt follows him and opens my door. "Scoot over."

I curse. I should have known my brother wouldn't leave Wyatt behind. They may not see each other often, but they've been best friends since their first day of preschool.

He pats the side of my thigh, close to my hip. "Come on, darlin'. It's cold out here."

I glare at him, snarling, "Don't touch me."

The driver's door opens. Jagger slides in and orders, "Willow, move over."

I turn toward him, locking my gaze on his.

"Why aren't you moving?" he questions.

What am I doing?

Wyatt Houston's my secret wound, and it's full of stitches. One pull of a thread and the entire scab will come off, creating a bloody mess I'll never be able to clean up.

Unable to do anything else, I slide closer to my brother, trying to breathe and not engage with Wyatt.

But I feel his lewd gaze, and one glance is all I need to know what he's thinking.

He's trying to decide if he's going to break me or make me beg him to do it first.

2

Wyatt Houston

eat ripples from the vents, driving me further to the edge. The alcohol in my system is wearing off, the throbbing bruises from the bar brawl aren't showing me any mercy, and I'm unprepared for my current predicament.

Willow Cartwright's the ruin that wraps around me in my sleep, all moans and memories I'd bleed to death to forget. But I never will. And here she sits after all these years, soft as silk, savage as sin, and hating me more than I could ever imagine.

How many years has it been?

"You going to tell me or what?" Jagger demands, tearing me out of my silence.

"What's that?" I ask, my eyes drifting from Willow's hand on her thigh to her brother's impatient stare.

"What was the fight about?" he pushes.

I shrug. "Nothing important."

Willow snaps, "You almost cost my riders their careers, and it was over nothing important?"

"*Your* riders?" I hiss in disdain, clenching my fist near the door with jealousy bubbling under my skin.

She glares at me with hatred. It's so intense, it chills my bones worse than the ice around the windshield. Venom laces her tone when she sneers, "Typical Wyatt. Destroy everything around you just because you can."

"Jeez, Willow. The guy just got out of jail. Don't be bitchy on Christmas just because they're your clients. You don't know what they did to provoke him," Jagger says in my defense.

She turns quickly, her sharp gaze pointed at him.

I chuckle, then shift in my seat to try and give some relief to the raging hard-on I've had since I heard her name earlier.

She orders, "Pull over."

"Why?" Jagger asks.

"I said pull over!" she insists.

"I can't. The snow's too high from the plows," he states.

She shouts, "Then stop the truck!"

Jagger groans but pushes the brake. The truck slows, and he asserts, "Stop being so dramatic, Willow. Your clients will survive, and so will your business."

She turns toward me. "Get out."

"Wyatt isn't getting out in the snow," Jagger states.

Willow jabs me in the chest. "Get. Out!"

I grab her wrist, my lips twitching with a cruel desire to press against hers and taunt, "You don't have to get violent. Unless that's the type of woman you've become?" My grin explodes, and I can't decide if I'd rather her try to beat me to death or cuddle me like I'm a baby she'll never let go.

Flames burn in her blues, anger exploding. "Fine. I'll get out." She leans over and reaches for the door.

The scent of warm amber and crushed jasmine terrorizes me. It's the kind of smell that clings to your skin, claiming you with a vicious hold. All you can do is keep breathing as deeply as possible. But the more I breathe, the more my demons won't stop torturing me. They tighten the shackles she wrapped around me years ago.

"Willow, you can't be out in this weather," Jagger declares.

I splay my palm on her spine. She stiffens, and I lean closer, reprimanding, "It's too cold to stomp down the road. I'm okay if you want to stay pissed at me the entire way home, but you're not freezing to death over my little bar fight."

She pushes off me. "Little bar fight? That *little bar fight* cost me sixty grand!"

I jerk my head back. "No way."

Her expression tells me she's not lying.

I glance at Jagger.

"It's true, bro," he affirms.

My gut sinks. "Shit. Willow, I'm sorry. I'll pay my share and make sure the others do too."

"How are you going to do that? Are you going to fight them for it?" she snaps.

I clench my jaw, wondering how quickly I can come up with twenty grand. I've made a lot of money bull riding, but I've been stupid with most of it. After too many losing bets, bar tabs, expensive toys, and my agent's cut of my winnings and sponsorships, the money ran through my fingers faster than I earned it. If I'd have been smart, I wouldn't have any money worries, but I've never considered myself intelligent. There's only one thing I know how to do, and it involves hanging on for dear life on top of a bull.

Her lip quivers, and her eyes glass over. She blinks hard, claiming, "I'm not sitting between you idiots. Let me out so I can get in the back."

My heart sinks. "I'm sorry. I didn't—"

"I said to get out!" she hurls, not breaking our stare.

"Calm down, Willow," Jagger orders.

"Get out," she repeats in a more controlled tone.

"I'll move. You stay here," I offer, and open the door.

A sharp gust tears through the cab, slapping my swollen face, but I deserve every ounce of pain.

I slip out of the front and into the back.

"You'll get your money back. No harm, no foul," Jagger says, trying to reassure her.

Willow crosses her arms, scoots closer to the door, and stares out the window.

He studies his sister for a moment, then shifts the truck into gear. We travel the rest of the way in silence, and the snowy road never seems to end. All I can do is stare at the back of her head, wondering how I'll ever make anything right with her.

The gates to the Cartwright Ranch finally appear. Ice glistens around the wrought iron. The sign is unreadable. Christmas lights glow under the wet flakes.

"Home sweet home," Jagger mumbles, glancing at Willow, who hasn't moved a muscle.

My stomach flips. I didn't leave things right with Willow the last time I was on this ranch. That was years ago. We were barely adults, but I should have been a better man. Yet I didn't know how.

I only saw two roads. Stay with Willow with nothing to offer her or go after my dream. Once I got my first big win and the sponsorships and checks started rolling in, I couldn't stay here. I knew I had to make something of myself, or I'd never be worthy of her. But everything went downhill after I made that choice.

I've avoided coming home every chance I got. What was there to come home to anyway? My father's always been a raging alcoholic. He used me as his whipping post. When I was three, my mother was smart and left as soon as she had her chance.

The Cartwrights took me in like I was part of their family. Jagger and I were attached at the hip growing up, and his siblings were like mine. Their mother, Ruby, always made sure I was fed and clothed. Their father, Jacob, taught me everything I know about horses.

If any of the kids got in trouble, I had to pay the consequences as well. There were more week-long punishments with barn duty than I can count. But I always showed up after school and completed the punishments next to the other Cartwrights. Call it solidarity if you want, but now, I'm pretty sure it was due to my fear I'd never be allowed back onto the ranch.

The day Willow went from a girl I saw as my little sister to a woman I couldn't stop obsessing over was the day I ruined the only good thing I ever had in my life. There was no way we could be together, and I knew it. Forget Jagger's anger. What would I tell Jacob? *I've been sneaking around with your daughter behind your back? I'm in love with your daughter but have nothing to offer her?*

I knew what kind of men Jacob raised his sons to be. I should have been just as honorable, but there were differences between the Cartwrights and me. I had too many demons. Yet it didn't stop me from secretly making Willow mine.

When I told her I loved her, I meant it. Then, her eighteenth birthday came, and everything got too intense. The reality of who we were glared sharper than sunlight. There was only one choice to make. When everything crashed around us, and I did what I felt I had to do, she made it clear there were no second chances.

It's why I've never returned to the ranch. I've seen the Cartwrights when I'm in town for a rodeo or other places if they happen to be there, but Willow never appears.

God, how I've looked for her. I've dreamed of her, imagined her, and picked up the phone too many times. After my initial attempts failed, I stopped having the balls to call her any more. But when her name was mentioned as I sat in that cell, I assumed I was still drunk and dreaming.

Now she's here. Willow's all curves and chaos, with hips that sway like sin and the same sassy lips that can slice egos or turn insults into art. She's kept her hair long, flowing like ink down her back, and I wonder if she did it to torture me. As if she knew about all the nights I curled my fist around vacant air, remembering how her throaty moan would rumble when I'd grabbed it.

Obsession only has one face for me—Willow's. And she's the only woman I'd sell my soul to mark as mine for the world to see.

Unfortunately, that's not my reality. I knew she hated me. Yet I didn't think it would run so deep.

The truck stops, and before Jagger can turn off the engine, Willow leaps out of the cab. She takes two steps and flies across the ice, landing on her back.

"Great," Jagger mumbles.

I push my door open, step forward, and slip across the pavement. I bump into Willow and fall over her, then push my palms on both sides of her head on the cold ground to stop my weight from crushing her.

She gasps, then her gaze moves slowly, unapologetically, over my face. It lingers on my mouth, like she's picturing it between her thighs. And hell, if that doesn't make everything between us real again.

"Jesus. Are you two alright? You almost crushed Willow," Jagger interjects, tugging on my arm to help me up.

I hold our stare for another second, then swallow hard, pushing off the ground and onto my feet. I reach down for Willow.

She rolls onto her knees and ignores my offer. She takes another step and almost kisses the ground again.

I tug her into me, declaring, "You're going to break all your bones if you don't slow down."

The front door opens, and Ruby exclaims, "Wyatt? Is that you?"

"Yes, ma'am," I reply, my heart aching for the only mother I've ever known. When I left the Cartwright ranch, I had no clue how much I would miss the entire family.

"Willow! Did you fall?" she frets.

"I'm fine," Willow claims as she tries to push away from me but slides again.

I tighten my arm around her, scolding, "Careful."

She lifts her face, and her blues slash me like knives. There's no warning and no mercy. It's just the two of us in a war zone, and she's already decided I'm the only target to strike.

I say through gritted teeth, "Get inside before you seriously hurt yourself."

Her glare intensifies, but she lets me help her onto the porch before wiggling out of my grasp and disappearing into the house.

Ruby holds her arms out. "It's been too long, Wyatt."

"Yes, ma'am, it has," I agree. I embrace her, then retreat. "Best to get inside. It's wild out here."

Jagger opens the door, and Ruby steps inside. We follow.

Where did Willow go?

I glance around, but the hallway and staircase are both empty.

"Jacob! You'll never guess who's here!" Ruby shouts.

As I stomp my boots on the rug, Jacob appears.

His deep voice has the same authority as when I was younger, but it's comforting. "Wyatt." He holds out his hand.

We shake, and he leans in and pats me on the back. "Son, what are you doing in town?"

My gut sinks.

There's the million-dollar question.

I open my mouth and then shut it.

Jacob arches his eyebrows, waiting.

I gather my thoughts, then stand taller, admitting, "I'm not sure, sir."

With a confused expression, he demands, "Meaning?"

"Don't grill him in the hallway, Jacob. Wyatt, have you had any dinner?" Ruby says, stepping between us.

My stomach growls, and I realize I don't know when I last ate.

Ruby laughs. "Come on. Let me reheat some dinner for you."

"Thank you," I reply and follow her into the kitchen, relieved to get a moment to try to figure out how to explain things to Jacob.

She opens the fridge and pulls out containers, nonchalantly asking, "How did you get that shiner?"

I touch my cheek and wince. I state, "Couldn't ever get anything past you."

Jagger interjects, "Nope. Never will. It's like she has a crystal ball and can see everything."

Ruby grins. "Don't forget it, my dear child." She pulls a plate out of the cabinet.

I grunt.

Jacob grabs three bottles of beer out of the fridge and opens one. He hands it to me and then sits across the table.

Jagger takes the seat on my right.

Circling back to the topic I'm dreading, Jacob prods, "Are you going to tell me what you meant when you said you don't know why you're back home?"

Home.

The place I couldn't bring myself to come back to.

My stomach curls, tying into thick knots that won't be easily undone. I sit back in my chair, taking in the Christmas decorations, scratched wooden floors Ruby gave up trying to keep perfectly stained, and mahogany cabinets.

The last thing I want to do is admit to Jacob my faults and failures, but I also won't lie to him. I did that when I slept with his daughter. And the day I left the ranch, I vowed I wouldn't ever deceive the Cartwrights again.

So I take a mouthful of beer, swallow it, and confess, "Kingy Altmonte broke his wrist. My agent wanted me to take his spot on the team for Whispering Junction's Boots, Bucks & Mistletoe Rodeo."

"You're a Texan. You shouldn't be competing on any other state team," Jagger grumbles.

I shrug. "I go where the money is, and that purse is huge." I don't add that Willow's riders represent Texas. There's no way she's ever letting me ride for her team.

Jacob leans closer. "So if you're supposed to be riding, why aren't you sure why you're here?"

My mouth goes dry, so I take another swig. The last forty-eight hours collide into me like a wrecking ball. Every second replays in my head, tearing me like paper until there's a pile of shreds in front of me, along with Jacob's unnerving stare. Every stupid decision I made and everything I've lost, including Willow, is in that pile, with no way to make it whole again.

Jacob crosses his arms, waiting.

Ruby sets a plate of hot food in front of me, scolding, "Let him eat, Jacob."

Jacob glances at her, then rises. He puts his hand on my shoulder. "Eat your Christmas dinner. We'll discuss things later."

Relief and dread fill me. I'd rather get it over with, but I don't know where to start. All I know is I've royally screwed things up, and Jacob isn't going to be too proud when he hears the truth.

"Eat," Ruby orders.

I focus on the steam drifting from the plate and then cut into the prime rib. I slide it through mashed potatoes and gravy before shoving it into my mouth. The concoction tastes like heaven, and as soon as I chew and swallow, I put a huge forkful of sweet potato casserole in my mouth.

I groan, wash it down with my beer, and say, "You don't know how much I missed your cooking."

She beams and pats my shoulder.

I finish two plates, and Jacob returns as soon as I take my last bite. It's like the old man could see me eating through the thick wooden door.

He cracks open more beers, distributes them, and sits back down.

Ruby sets down a plate full of pie—slices of pecan, pumpkin, and apple covered in homemade whipped cream. "I'll let you three talk." She throws another motherly smile my way and says, "It's so good to have you home, Wyatt."

My chest tightens. "Thank you, ma'am."

She disappears, and the claw in my gut reappears.

Jacob says nothing.

Time to pay the piper.

I blurt out, "I'm not going to lie to you, sir. I did some stupid things."

His face hardens.

I clear my throat. "Actually, I did a lot of stupid things over the last few months. My agent and I haven't been getting along too well. My sponsors dropped me, and he fired me."

"Oh shit," Jagger mutters.

I don't move. The ticking clock and my uncontrollable heartbeat pound between my ears.

Jacob doesn't flinch and he asks, "And what happened at The Buck and Bruise?"

The man always knows everything.

"I'm sure they had it coming," Jagger states, rushing to my defense.

Jacob pins his eyes on him, warning him not to speak with just a look.

Jagger shifts in his seat and takes a swig of beer.

Jacob returns his steely gaze to me.

Don't bullshit him.

The air thickens. I take a deep breath and admit, "I might have worked my anger out the wrong way."

He studies me with growing paternal authority that roots me to my chair.

My heart races as I wait him out.

He finally asks, "What do you plan to do to get your life back on track, son?"

I squeeze the bottle harder, wondering how to answer him. But I can't. So I admit, "Sir, I don't know."

Another cold stare lances through me, weaving around my lungs until I can't breathe.

I wanted to make Jacob proud when I finally came back.

I've failed miserably.

He rises, asserting, "Take a few days and figure it out. Let me know when you have some answers."

"Yes, sir."

He steps to the side of me and puts his hand on the table.

I force myself to meet his gaze.

His voice drops two octaves when he says, "Wyatt, you will pay my daughter back. Every last cent. Understand?" There's no room for arguing, not that I would. His words hang like a warning.

I nod. "Yes, sir. I already told her that."

He keeps his gaze on mine for another moment, then squeezes my shoulder. "Good to have you home, son."

3

Willow

"Goodnight," I tell my parents, trying to ignore Wyatt's sneaky yet clinging stare. It digs at the same feelings I reserved for him years ago and still can't seem to shake.

Our love might have burned as strong as a wildfire—reckless, scorching with hunger, and molten with secrets—but I'm no longer the girl who adores him. I'm a woman who sifted through all the ashes he left in his wake.

I survived.

I'm not looking for a repeat, I remind myself.

I refuse to do it again. I'm stronger now and no longer naive. So, no matter how many times he gives me his puppy-dog look, I'm not falling for it. Even if the wound he left me aches with or without him, I won't be a fool twice. I'll take the pain alone, where it's safer.

My determination doesn't get easier when he steps closer. He's just like a bull breathing heavily in the chute. His scorched-leather and storm-soaked dirt scent blends with hints of whiskey and beer, all raw and untamed, screaming of desire and obscene pleasure.

Goose bumps pop out on my skin and my knees shake. Everything is too familiar, yet it sits inside a shallow grave.

Does he remember the parts of me he used to love?

Get away from him and stop thinking these thoughts.

"I'm going to turn in soon too," he declares.

Panic, longing, and the memories of all the times we did this song and dance, only to sneak away once we were supposed to be sleeping, haunt me. I avoid glancing at him. I perfected it years ago, but that was so I didn't give anyone any suspicions about us. Now, it's to send him a cold message.

He's not getting in my pants ever again.

My mom steps forward and hugs me. "Merry Christmas, sweetie."

"You too, Mom," I reply, hugging her back, then cursing myself for not stopping myself from acknowledging Wyatt's stare. And once I do, his lips curve, all lazy and lethal, as if all he has to do is ask me to return to how we were, and I would.

And it scares me. I stayed far away from him out of hurt but also fear. I don't know what he's doing in town. I don't know how long he's staying. My only hope is that he leaves soon because those looks have haunted me for the last seven years. They've appeared in my mind, and I've desperately held on to them as much as I've wanted to erase them.

My heart stammers. It takes Mom retreating to cut our gaze.

My cheeks heat. I quickly hug Dad, then jog up the staircase, needing to breathe normally.

It's pointless. His scent hangs around me, as if stuck in my hair or woven into my clothes. So I pull off my sweater and jeans, jump in the shower, and try to wash him away.

When I'm done, I wrap a towel around my head and another one around my body, staring into the mirror, needing answers to all my questions.

It's not fair. Wyatt had no right to interrupt my Christmas or get into a fight with my riders. All was awesome until he appeared on the scene.

Why is he here?

The anger, years of heartache, and questions I want answers to win out over my need to keep my distance from him. I grab my knee-length red silk robe, tighten the belt, and storm out of the bathroom, running right into Wyatt.

"Just who I wanted to see," he drawls, his gaze drifting lower and setting my thighs on fire.

I cross my arms. "Why are you up here?"

"I'm staying the night." He steps closer, lowering his voice. "Actually, I might stay awhile," he taunts, sinking his warning deep under my skin.

My heart skips a beat, and I curse it. "Why aren't you staying at Jagger's?"

His lips twitch. "He's got overnight company already."

I roll my eyes.

So that's why my brother only had two beers all day.

"That's what I missed," Wyatt declares, his grin growing.

"What?"

He points at me. "What you just did."

"I didn't do anything."

He nods, insisting, "Yes, sugar, you did."

I press my thighs together, glaring at him. I glance past his shoulder and whisper, "Don't call me sugar."

His arrogant expression stays plastered on his face.

Suddenly, I want to drag his lips between my teeth just to watch his eyes darken with heat. Then, I'll be the one to leave him in pain.

I'm such a liar.

Stay focused.

I blurt out, "Why are you here?"

His smile grows. He claims, "We didn't finish our last conversation."

I tilt my head, trying to figure out what he's saying.

He leans closer, and the scent I scrubbed off in the shower penetrates me deeper. His breath hits my ear, and he murmurs, "When you figure something out, your face twitches."

I turn toward him, inches from his mouth, denying, "No, it doesn't."

"It does. You just figured something out about Jagger. Admit it."

I bite my lip.

His face falls, and so does his voice. He sternly orders, "Let's go into your room and talk, Willow."

A buzz flutters in my stomach, weightless with need and heavy with anticipation. My voice cracks. "No."

"Then let's go to mine," he says, then slides his arm around my waist and moves me down the hall.

"Wy—"

He puts his hand over my mouth. Then his lips brush against my ear. "We have to talk, sugar. Now, decide if you want your family to know about us or not."

Us?

I glare daggers at him, the blades sharper than before, while an entire sky of butterflies breaks open inside me.

He waits a moment, breathing hard and pinning me with a challenging stare, as if I'm a hand of poker there's no doubt he'll win.

Me.

My body.

My entire goddamn soul.

The longer he studies me, the bigger the urge to slap him and then kiss him until morning grows.

He finally lowers his hand, steers me past several more rooms, then opens the door to the bedroom adjacent to mine.

I step inside and turn to face him. He shuts the door, planting his body against it and flicking the lock.

"What are you doing?" I fret. I try to maintain that I'm in control, but I'm nothing of the sort. I've never been the one with the power when it comes to him. Wyatt's always had it and still does.

He steps toward me, and I back up until my knees hit the mattress, and I plop on the bed. He sits next to me and grabs my hand.

I yank it back, warning, "Don't touch me."

Something flashes in his eyes.

It takes me a minute to realize it's guilt. My insides quiver, and I close my eyes, begging, "Please. Whatever you want to say, get it over with so I can go."

"I shouldn't have made the choices I made."

Tense silence fills the air. My lips tremble. I blink hard, then turn toward him. "Don't."

He furrows his eyebrows. "Don't?"

"I don't need your sorries or your shoulda, coulda, wouldas. Not now. Not after seven years," I declare, then swipe at the tear falling down my cheek.

"Willow—"

"Why are you here?" I repeat, but with more strength in my tone.

"It's..." His jaw clenches, and he stares at me like the little boy who used to come to our ranch with bruises on his body and nowhere to go.

It hurts my heart. More than I ever thought it could, it cuts deep, stinging with a lasting bite. I wince, then look away, wishing my tears wouldn't fall.

He puts his callused hand on my thigh, and against my will, I lean closer to him, still looking away but unable to keep the boundary I told myself I wouldn't cross.

Wyatt touching me is a bad idea.

And now I remember why.

My brain tells me to leave, but my body betrays me, molding against him.

He slides his arm around my shoulders, admitting, "I fucked up."

It's the phrase I've wanted to hear for so long. Emotions swell in my chest. I allow myself to glance up, asking, "How?" before my gaze drifts to his lips.

His voice drips with shame. "I lost my agent. My sponsors pulled out. I was supposed to fill in for Kingy Altmonte, but I got kicked off the team, and it's my own damn fault."

I freeze.

He didn't mean he fucked up with me.

He meant he fucked up the precious career he chose over me.

I stare at the floor. Anger and hurt slowly unleash, taking over the quick burst of hope.

What was I thinking?

I rise and spin toward him. "I'm sorry to hear that. I'm sure you'll find another agent and more sponsors. You're a good rider."

He clenches his jaw, eyes wide, as if he's expecting something else from me.

I might have stayed away from him whenever he was here, but I know all about the infamous reputation Wyatt's built. Lots of women. Plenty of partying. Gambling debts and flashy toys.

I can't say he's any different from the other riders. It goes with the territory. So I need to stop thinking he's back for me.

He's not.

He's here for the rodeo.

Reality bites with sharp teeth, right into the wound I can't seem to heal. I turn and move toward the door.

"Willow," he calls out, his voice hollow.

I freeze, then slowly release a breath and turn back. "Yeah?"

"We need to talk."

"About what?" My heart bleeds further.

He swallows hard. "Everything."

Too many minutes pass. Wyatt's gaze locks on mine. Holy. Dark. Spinning with the past that's no longer ours.

"Too much time has passed," I claim, with my insides screaming it's not true.

His face falls. "So that's it? We're not going to discuss anything?"

A soft, sarcastic laugh flies out of my mouth. "What did you expect? You'd come here, and I'd run back into your arms?"

"No. Nothing of the sort," he claims.

"Really? Because I think you did. I think you remember the girl I used to be, and you know nothing about the woman I am now," I assert.

"You're right. So let me get to know you," he softly replies without hesitation.

But I don't consider his proposal. "Why? So you can run away when it gets tough? Then pick the next girl who's shinier than me?" Tears fill my eyes again.

"Willow—"

"Don't you sit there all denim and drawl like you own the sunset, then deny it. You no longer know me, but I know you. So let's be honest. The only reason you're here right now is because it's convenient for you," I accuse.

His head jerks backward.

Another tear falls down my cheek, and I scoff. "Go on. Admit it. I'll respect you more for your honesty."

He stares at me with dangerous, coiled-up hunger.

The quiver strengthens in my belly. I add in a lower voice, "We had our time. It was fun. But it was long ago. There's nothing left." I spin, take two steps, and he lunges at me.

He moves me against the wall, leaning over me, reeking of the scent that haunts me. His hand cups my cheek, rough, steady, and another reminder of all we were.

My breath hitches.

His words roll out of his mouth, dragging along my spine. "That's a lie, sugar." His gaze drifts to my lips.

My heart beats hard against my chest.

"Everything's still there. You just have to want it to be," he claims, his dark gaze challenging me once more.

I open my mouth, but nothing comes out.

He flicks his thumb over my chin, and I shudder. He murmurs, "I don't remember Willow Cartwright being dishonest."

"I'm not."

He arches his eyebrows like he caught me in a lie. "No?" He hovers closer, his breath beating into my lips so hot, I feel it in my thighs.

I stay silent, my pulse out of control.

"I wasn't the man you needed. I know that. But I can be better," he declares, and I almost believe him.

Almost.

It's just another one of his cowboy promises wrapped in barbed-wire heat, I tell myself.

I take a deep breath, lift my chin, and drag my finger down his cheek.

He presses closer, his body singing against mine.

"Want to know a secret?" I murmur, dragging my gaze to his.

"What's that, sugar?" he mumbles, pushing my silk robe aside and grazing his fingers over my collarbone.

A shiver runs down my spine. I squeeze my thighs tighter and slide my hand through his hair, knocking off his cowboy hat. It drops to the floor with a thud. I grip his thick, wavy locks and tug his head back.

He groans, keeping his eyes on me, pushing his erection against my stomach.

I let my tongue graze his earlobe, purring, "The only liar in the room is you."

He freezes.

I release his hair and step to the side, but he steps with me.

He pins his elbows on the wall, cages his body against mine, and slouches so his darkened face is an inch above my mouth. His drawl is as slow as honey sliding down a blade. "Sugar, the only person I ever lied to was myself."

"Oh?" I barely get out, doing everything I can to not move an inch. If I do, my lips are going on his, and I'll regret it.

He lowers his head, quickly shifting my robe and dragging his tongue over the curve of my neck.

I inhale sharply.

A monsoon of sensations comes flooding back. His lips. His breath. His tongue. It's all the same but more potent. More experienced. More lethal.

I blink hard, trying to stay focused, demanding, "Tell me."

He kisses the side of my neck, moving dangerously close to my mouth, then stops.

My knees wobble. I grip his biceps.

He pins a stormy gaze on me, pauses, then announces, "The lie I told myself is that I could survive without you."

Tense silence explodes between us. Neither of us move.

Minutes feel like hours until he runs his finger over my lips, breathing long, deep breaths. He murmurs, "Do you know how many tortured hours I spent reliving the memory of your lips?"

I close my eyes. Wyatt was always a lot to handle. But now? With all the history between us? He's a pack of dynamite waiting to blow up my entire world.

His lips hit my ear. "Don't go. Stay and let me show you how much I've missed you."

I open my eyes, and all the hurt and rage come back with a vengeance. "Is that what you think I'll do? Slip into your bed and sneak out before the others wake up, just like before?"

His face hardens. "No."

I push at his chest, needing space, and shake my head. "This isn't happening, Wyatt. Not tonight or ever. Understand?"

He reaches for me, but I duck around him. "Willow—"

"No. Like I said, you don't know me anymore. And I learn from my mistakes. I won't make the same one again," I seethe.

Pain fills his expression, crushing me, but I'm not falling for his old tricks. He asks, "That's what you think we were? A mistake?"

I scoff. "What would you call us?"

He pins me under his brooding gaze so long, I shift on my feet. Then he says, "We weren't a mistake. The way I handled things was, but we weren't."

I huff. "The way you 'handled things'? You mean running off the minute the going got tough?"

His jaw tics. He glances at the ceiling.

"Ah. There it is. The Wyatt Houston special!" I taunt.

His face turns red. "What does that mean?"

I jab him in the chest. "It means, there's no point in discussing any of this. It's done and over. *We're* over. Leave it at that. There's no point in stomping on old dust." I unlock the door and swing it open.

"Willow!" he calls out.

I pop my head back through the door. "Merry Christmas, Wyatt. Let's not ever discuss this again. From now on, forget about the past."

A mask I remember too well overtakes his features. One he uses when he's hurting. But it's no longer my job to console him. He made his bed, and he can lie in it.

I bolt into my bedroom, lock the door, and slide into my bed. I bury my face into the pillow, crying. All night, I want to go back to his room.

But I don't do it.

That train has left, and it's not one I need to chase after.

4

Wyatt

Wind whistles through the trees, violently barreling against me. I fight harder to trench through the thick carpet of snow, heading toward the barn.

The darkness hasn't lifted. The Christmas bulbs light my path, screaming cheer, but it's the opposite of my mood.

She hates me. And I don't blame her.

It's worse than I thought it could be. As the night progressed into the next day, every sin I committed against Willow played out in slow motion, mixing with the fresh scent of her shampoo still lingering on my stubble.

Her touch still burns me this morning, punishing me so much, I wonder if it'll ever go away.

I shouldn't have come here.

I clench my jaw, fight another merciless gust, and finally reach the barn. I open the door, enter, and slide it shut. I deeply breathe in the muted, sweet hay scent, trying to push my demons away.

"Was wondering when your pretty-boy, bull-riding ass would get out here," Mason jeers.

"It's four thirty in the morning," I point out.

"The horses like us here at four," he claims.

I groan. Jagger's older brother always liked to be the first in the barn. It's like his way of showing everyone he's a harder worker or something.

I glance around. "Where's Jagger? What about Alexander and Sebastian?"

Mason's lips curl. "I'm assuming Jagger's got his newest long-legged coed wrapped around him. Sebastian and Alexander have become pussies during the holidays now that they have their women."

"How so?" I question.

"They don't come out until at least five," he states.

Amused, I grunt. "Yeah. They're real pussies."

A black stallion in the stall next to me neighs so fiercely, I jump.

Mason smirks. "You ride bulls but are scared of horses now?"

"No. I'm hung like a horse, so he's my kindred spirit. What's your excuse?" I banter back, grabbing a nearby apple and then holding it out for the horse.

He chomps on it in one bite.

I stroke his mane.

Mason replies, "I'm not the one jumping from a hungry horse. By the way, that's Spitfire."

"That's a good name for you, buddy," I say as Spitfire nuzzles my chest.

Mason states, "Isabella wanted to call him Monique."

I arch my eyebrows.

Mason chuckles. "Thank goodness Jacob Jr. pulled the longer straw."

Nostalgia hits me like a brick. I smile at the memories, commenting, "Your dad still has the kids pull straws to name the horses?"

"Sure does."

Mason tosses me a brush, and I catch it. I groom Spitfire, and he does the same for a brown Thoroughbred. Then he asks, "So what's your plan?"

I groan. "You're just like your dad."

He chuckles. "So I've heard. Does that mean you have no clue what to do?"

A ferocious chill sweeps the barn. Jagger's booming voice interjects, proclaiming, "Damn, it's cold!" He slides the heavy wooden door shut.

Several horses snort in protest.

I taunt, "Did your new sugar turn you into a candy-ass?"

"She's a warm slice of pecan pie. You'd have to trade your saddle in to handle her, though," he says cockily.

"Why? Did you take up pegging?" I mock.

He grunts. "Only if it's a cold day in Hell."

Mason tosses a roll of white bandages to him. "It's too icy to run them this morning. Morning Glory needs her leg rewrapped."

Jagger's face falls. "I don't know if she's going to recover."

Mason's grim tone matches his. "Only time will tell."

"What happened?" I question.

"She cut her leg on barbed wire. The infection went deep and doesn't want to let up. Every time it starts to heal, the next day, it's aggravated again," Jagger answers, grabbing an apple and stepping in front of another stall.

A beautiful white-and-brown spotted Appaloosa limps toward the gate.

"Here you go, sweetheart," he coos, holding out the fruit.

Morning Glory chews it, gentler than Spitfire, almost graciously.

"Aw. You can tell she's not feeling well," I comment, reaching out and rubbing her mane.

"Yeah. Emma's going to be heartbroken if she doesn't kick this infection. The vet said there's a high possibility it'll attack her bone. If that happens, we all know what's next." Jagger adds, his tone sad.

"Emma named her?" I question.

"Yeah." He grabs another apple and offers it to Morning Glory. Then he says, "I know how to solve your problem."

My chest tightens, bringing me back to my harsh reality. "Yeah? Fill me in."

He looks at me like I'm a moron.

"What?" I push.

"Willow can represent you." His grin is laced with arrogance and mockery, undoubtedly about how simple the solution sounds to him.

"Surprised she didn't snatch you up last night when she found out you're a free agent," Mason chimes in.

I scoff. "Sure. Right after she found out I started a fight with her other riders."

"Not a big deal. You'd be a great addition to her client list," Jagger claims.

I shake my head. "I don't think that's a good idea."

Jagger's eyes turn to slits. "Why not?"

My pulse creeps up. I quickly claim, "She's pretty pissed at me. Or did you forget how she glared at me all night?"

He shrugs. "So what? You know it's not the first time her clients got into a little tiff."

I remind him, "I created a sixty-thousand-dollar problem for her. It wasn't just a 'little tiff,' and you know it."

"So what? You'll pay her back. And Jericho and Colt aren't innocent either," he replies.

I point out, "They didn't take the first swing. I did."

"When did you start falling on your sword?" Mason questions.

I pick up another apple, step into another stall, and hold it out for the horse so I can brush its mane. I sigh. "It's a bad idea, so drop it."

"Why? Because you have so many other options?" Mason retorts.

He speaks the truth, but Willow isn't going to represent me.

Jagger asserts, "Willow will do it. She's probably already cooled off. I bet she's already putting her pitch together for you."

My gut twists.

Doubt it.

He continues, "Anyway, she has to say yes. You're as good as a brother to her."

The twisting gets tighter.

I blurt out, "No, I'm not."

"Of course you are. Why would you say otherwise?" Jagger asks. And even though I'm focusing on the horse, I can feel the weight of his stare.

Panic hits me. I stroke through the horse's mane a couple more times, then turn, trying to look nonchalant, and shrug. "I haven't seen her in years. We're not kids anymore."

"So what? Family is family," he insists.

A tidal wave of guilt floods me. It's worse than seven years ago. Maybe time and age put my betrayal in a different light. But I broke bro code, and if Jagger or Mason ever find out, it'll ruin our friendship. They'll never call me family again.

The barn door grinds along the metal rails. Another rush of bitter cold floods the barn. Sebastian and Alexander enter with mugs of coffee.

Sebastian calls out, "What's the big debate?"

Alexander slams the door shut, cutting off the chill.

Jagger states, "Wyatt's going to ask Willow to be his agent."

"No. I'm not," I adamantly insist.

Sebastian glances at Alexander, who shakes his head and says, "I'm staying out of this one."

Panic shoots through me.

Does he know something?

I can't help myself and burst out, "Why?"

He pins me with a mocking gaze. "You want me to spell it out?"

The blood pounds harder between my ears.

Do I?

"Go for it," Mason answers for me.

I shoot him a dirty look.

"Super touchy this morning," he ridicules.

"Shut up," I spit back, irritated by this conversation.

Alexander takes a sip of coffee and then sets it down. He crosses his arms and leans against a pole. "Fine. Willow doesn't represent PR nightmares unless she's adamant the rider isn't a long-term liability. Right now, that's what you are."

I clench my jaw and close my hand into a fist.

"He's just telling the truth. Don't hit him," Sebastian taunts, glancing at my hand.

I don't speak, keeping my fist tight, unable to open it.

"It's going to take a lot of groveling to undo what you did last night," Alexander adds.

"She'll get over it," Jagger claims.

"Should she?" Alexander asks.

I stay frozen, the truth searing into my bones.

"Of course she should, and she will. Wyatt's family. And don't stand there and act like you two haven't been in plenty of bar fights," Jagger points out.

"I've never caused sixty grand in damages. Have you?" Sebastian asks Alexander.

"Nope," he answers with a smug expression.

"When did you two become angels?" I accuse, my panic turning to defense.

Sebastian taps his temple. "Use your head, Wyatt. This isn't about us. We may not see you often, but we all follow you and the headlines. You've been going downhill, and Willow doesn't take uncalculated risks when it involves her career."

Heat rises to my cheeks. I squeeze my fist harder, hating the taste of the truth.

Alexander asks, "Why should Willow step into your mess?"

"Don't listen to them. Alexander's brain isn't working since Phoebe agreed to marry him and decided against leaving his sorry ass. And Georgia must have accidentally put real sugar into Sebastian's food instead of the fake crap she uses for him," Jagger jabs.

Sebastian shakes his head. His eyes narrow. "At some point, Wyatt, you have to pivot. It looks like you still have a lot growing up to do if you think it's okay to put Willow's career on the line."

Guilt suffocates me. I reiterate, "I'm not asking Willow to sign me. So drop the subject." I toss Jagger a *don't push me* look.

He clenches his jaw, unhappy, but respects my wishes.

The rest of the morning moves along, with Cartwright banter and me trying to forget my problems.

It's pointless. All I can think about is my encounter with Willow last night, and my career turning to ash. I have to fix both problems, yet I'm as clueless as ever.

The meal bell rings, and Alexander's boys, Jacob and Wilder, shout, "Breakfast!"

I tug my collar up and hurry through the snow to the main house, close to the others. We stomp our snowy boots in the foyer, then head to the large dining room.

The Cartwrights' wooden table was custom-made and large enough for all the adults. The kids have another table since it's a holiday and all eight siblings are home.

More nostalgia hits me. The fireplace crackles with cherry wood. Excited voices fill the space. Delicious smells of bacon, eggs, pancakes,

French toast, waffles, and other breakfast items make my stomach rumble. The same faces, plus Georgia and Phoebe, beam around the table.

I grab an empty chair next to Willow. "Morning. Did you sleep well?"

Her head swivels toward me. She pins me with a gaze like broken glass, and slides her chair back with a chilling calm. She rises, picks up her juice, and walks around the table, selecting a seat as far away from me as possible.

"Still holding a grudge?" Jagger asks loudly, giving her a look of disapproval.

The room falls silent, and all eyes turn to Willow.

She glares at her brother.

"Leave it," I warn him.

But Jagger won't let it be. He points out, "Your riders get into bar fights. It's not a big deal. No charges. No long-term consequences. No one got hurt. You can't hold it against Wyatt forever."

Red rage fills her cheeks. She bursts out, "For your information, it is a big deal. So stay out of my business, Jagger."

"It's against the Cartwright code to not forgive and forget. So tell me how long you're going to stay mad so we can discuss the important issue at hand," he demands.

"Jagger, stop," I order.

Willow's eyes turn to slits. "What issue would that be?"

Jagger's cocky grin teases the corners of his mouth. His tone is just as arrogant. "Signing Wyatt and figuring out what sponsors to go after."

Her jaw drops, anger ready to explode from her.

Tension burns through the air, crackling harsher than the fire.

My mouth turns dry while my dick betrays me. Willow's defiance always affected me, and time hasn't eliminated my reaction to it. A flashback erupts where she's jabbing me in the chest, I push her against the stall door, and we fuck in the barn, only to finish a few moments before almost getting caught by Jacob.

Mason cuts in, "I heard Tough Rider is looking for someone for their new bull ropes."

I snap out of my trip down memory lane, and open my mouth to object, but Paisley interjects.

"Roughneck Armorworks needs one too. Their new vest came in, and it's supposed to give the rider 65 percent more protection without inhibiting movement." She turns next to me and beams. "I'm on the marketing team that just signed them on as a new client. So I could help Willow get a meeting before anyone else does."

"I'm not signing Wyatt as a client," Willow insists with finality.

Another round of sharp tension fills the room.

Ruby clears her throat. "Can I ask why?"

Willow takes a few deep breaths, then turns toward her mother, explaining, "He destroyed The Buck and Bruise."

"So did your other clients. Wyatt didn't do it on his own," Jagger adds.

My chest tightens. I shake my head at him in disapproval.

Willow exclaims, "Which is another reason not to sign him. He can't get along with my riders. I don't do drama, and I won't start now."

"I'm sure they already got over it and made friends during their time in the slammer. You kissed and made up, right, Wyatt?" Jagger taunts.

Willow's rage grows. "Even you aren't stupid enough to believe what you're saying. So stay out of my business."

"Wyatt's family. You have to sign him," Jagger insists sternly.

"No, she doesn't. Let it go," I warn again.

Willow anchors her gaze on me, but I'm not sure how to take it.

Jacob's raw-edged tone sears through the silence. "It's Willow's business, and therefore her decision."

She shoots him a grateful expression. "Thank you."

"However, don't be so quick to make a decision you might regret," he warns.

Her jaw twitches. "I won't regret not signing him."

"Are you sure? I understand you have some things to work out, but if last night hadn't happened, would you have signed him if you knew he was available?" Jacob questions.

More heavy stillness looms around the table with everyone's attention on Willow.

More guilt eats at me. "I've made dumb mistakes. Willow shouldn't have to pay for them. Can we drop this topic and eat before the food gets cold and breakfast is ruined?"

As if I'm a magnet, everyone's focus now turns on me. I force myself not to shift in my seat, keeping my attention on Jacob.

He studies me, and the uncomfortableness fills me like a balloon until I think I might pop. My only relief comes when he finally nods, answering, "We can. But you two should have a serious conversation before either of you writes the other off."

I will never write your daughter off.

Even if she wants to watch me burn in Hell.

A lump lodges itself in my throat, but I manage to get out, "Yes, sir. I understand. Sebastian, can you pass the waffles? I'm starving."

He picks up the platter and hands it to me. I don't know what to make of the expression that goes with it.

The rest of breakfast is normal for everyone but Willow and me. I sneak peeks at her when I can. A few times, I catch her looking at me. But it never makes me feel any better.

Willow would be great as my agent. She could turn my current situation around. She's done it for several riders. Yet there isn't a bone in my body that wants to sign with her. And the longer I sit at the table, far away from her, and watch her continue to be uncomfortable in my presence, the clearer it becomes.

Getting into a business relationship together is the worst decision we could make.

There's only one thing to focus on, and it doesn't involve contracts and deals.

The only thing that matters is finding a way for Willow to stop hating me and getting her back in my life, my arms, and my bed.

But the biggest problem still remains.

How do I convince Willow to forget about our past?

5

Willow - Age 15

Ten Years Ago

"**T**ruth or dare?" Hazel asks.

I debate for a moment, then say, "Truth."

Her lips twist. "Who do you have a crush on?"

I shake my head. "No one."

Hazel tilts her head and crosses her arms. "You're not allowed to lie during truth or dare, Willow."

"I'm not!" I insist.

"You are!"

"No, I'm not!"

She questions, "What about Brandon Murphy?"

I put my finger in my mouth and pretend to vomit, then declare, "He's gross."

"No, he's not," she says.

I wrinkle my nose. "Please tell me you don't think he's hot."

She shrugs. "He's all right. But I'm more into older guys."

My eyes widen. "Like who?"

She wiggles her finger in front of me, reprimanding, "Uh-uh-uh. You have to ask me the question."

I roll my eyes. Hazel can be a big pain in the butt. She's fun to hang out with most of the time, but she can sometimes be bossy and act like she's better than me. Right now, that's exactly how I'm feeling.

She fakes a yawn. "I'm getting bored."

"Truth or dare," I blurt out.

She leans forward confidently and states, "Truth," then smirks.

"Who do you think is hot?" I inquire.

"In this house?" she asks.

I cringe. "In this house?"

"Duh," she dramatically responds.

"It's only my brothers in this house."

"Well, Wyatt's here too," she points out.

My stomach flips. "Yeah. He's like my brother too."

Her lips twitch. "He's not mine. Neither are your brothers."

My gut stops flipping and starts to dive. "Eww."

She laughs. "Please. Grow up. Jagger and Wyatt are hot. So is Mason. But, honestly, I can't cross your older brothers off the list either."

My mouth drops open and I jerk my head backward.

She smirks. "Don't tell me you're going to be weird about this."

"They're my brothers. And Sebastian and Alexander are way too old for you anyway."

"Are they?" She squints.

"Yes."

She shakes her head. "No, they aren't. Any of them will do."

The sinking feeling pulls harder, and I think I might be swallowed by quicksand, but I can't help myself and ask, "Do for what?"

"Do I have to spell it out for you?" she scolds.

I stay quiet, wondering if I should answer her.

She continues, "To lose my virginity to."

"Eww!" I shriek, but I should have known. Lately, Hazel's obsessed about losing her virginity.

She rolls her eyes and rises. "There's nothing gross about your brothers or Wyatt."

"They're my brothers!" I argue again.

"And they're hot," she claims.

"It's not happening. Pick anyone else," I order.

Her eyes widen. "Sorry. I've decided it has to be one of them." She gets up and slinks over to the window.

My mouth goes dry, and my heart races. "Hazel, my brothers are off-limits."

She turns her head. "So you *do* think I have a chance, then?"

"What? No!" I cry out, feeling sick at the thought.

She spins, leaning against the window sill. "I bet I can convince one of them to take my virginity. The only question is when."

"Stop! You're just saying this to get a rise out of me," I assert, but my mind knows better. I've seen that look on Hazel's face before, and when she wants something, she'll stop at nothing to get it.

She snaps her fingers. "The perfect opportunity is almost here!"

"Did you just hear what I said?"

She smirks again, then sighs. "Willow, stop being a baby."

"You're out of line, Hazel!" I declare.

As if I didn't strongly object to her idea, she announces, "I'll give Wyatt my virginity next week at his eighteenth birthday party!"

My stomach pitches so fast, I put my hand over it and swallow down bile. "That's not okay, Hazel!"

"Don't be a Debbie Downer," she taunts.

Anger and a bit of fear wash over me. She's serious, and Wyatt...

Would he sleep with her?

Hazel's eyes brighten further, and excitement grows in her voice. "Unless you prefer I give it to Jagger? I can save Wyatt for yours? After all, we don't want sloppy seconds."

My breath catches in my lungs. I gape at her.

She holds her hands out. "Well? Do you want Wyatt for yourself?"

"Eww. No. Stop talking this way. I'm never sleeping with Wyatt, nor are you sleeping with him or my brothers!" I insist.

She snickers, then turns toward the window. She looks down and stills. "Well, well, well..."

My heart slams harder against my rib cage. I jump to my feet and race to the window, demanding, "What is it?"

"Looks like our boy has gotten into a bit of trouble," she states.

I glance at the yard and then swallow hard, feeling sicker.

Oh no.

Not again.

There's only one person who does that to Wyatt.

Blood stains his clothes. Two large rips slice across his T-shirt. A purplish bruise mars his cheek near a cut in his lip that's still bleeding.

Sebastian flies across the yard, yelling.

Wyatt closes his eyes, squeezes his red-laced knuckles, and winces. He takes a deep breath and slowly turns.

"Who did he fight?" Hazel questions, peering closer to the glass.

My insides quiver. I blurt out, "You have to go."

Shock fills her expression. "Why?"

"Sorry, but you have to leave," I reiterate, and move toward the door. Hazel's a big gossip. The last thing Wyatt needs is her running her mouth all over the high school.

"Stop being dramatic, Willow."

I whip open my door, square my shoulders, and lift my chin. "I'm sorry, but you have to go."

Rage fills her expression. She doesn't move.

"I'm not joking, Hazel," I assert.

She crosses her arms. "I don't have a ride."

"I'll find you one. One of my brothers—" I stop and take a deep breath.

She arches her eyebrows, and her mouth curls at the edges. She suggestively asks, "Which one do you want to drive me?"

"Wait here," I instruct.

"Where are you going?"

I exit my bedroom, shut the door, and rush down the hallway toward the muffled music. I open Ava's door, and she sings "Release me!" at the top of her lungs along with the new artist she's been listening to.

I turn the dial on her radio down. "I need you to take Hazel home."

She lifts her head from her college textbook and then turns it toward me. "Aren't you supposed to knock before you enter?"

"Please. She needs to go," I beg.

Ava's eyes narrow into those of my protective older sister. "Why? What's she done now?"

It's another thing about Ava. She doesn't care for Hazel, nor does Hazel care much for Ava. I'd normally keep them apart, but there's no way I'm letting Hazel ride in a car with one of my brothers.

"I can't get into it, but can you take her home? Please?" I plead.

Ava's eyes widen. She puts her book on the bed and grabs her keys off her desk. "Sure. But why don't you tell me what she's done."

"I will later," I lie, knowing I can't tell her what Hazel said. Even though I hate what she's insinuating, she's still my friend. I add, "Can you take her down the back staircase and out the kitchen door?"

Ava studies me closer. "Why?"

My insides quiver harder. I lower my voice and admit, "Wyatt's outside with blood all over him."

The color in her face drains. She squeezes her eyes shut, shakes her head, then sighs. "No problem."

"Thanks."

"Sure," she says, then marches past me, down the hall, and opens my bedroom door.

"Where's Willow?" Hazel snaps, but I don't bother to return to my room. My sister will handle it.

I take three steps, and Ava directs, "Get your stuff. I'm taking you home."

Hazel's muffled objections get quieter as I reach the bottom of the staircase. I step onto the wooden floor, and the front door opens.

"Dad!" Sebastian roars, pushing Wyatt inside.

My pulse throbs in my throat, as if trying to claw its way out. I grip the handrail, squeezing the oak so hard, it hurts.

Wyatt's swollen cheek hides his dimple and sharp jawline. His eye above it can barely stay open.

"Are you okay?" I fret.

"Willow, not now," Sebastian commands, then hollers, "Dad," in a rougher tone.

I lower my voice. "Wyatt?"

He slowly moves his head, peeking at me from under his cowboy hat. He strongly asserts, "I'm fine, Willow."

"You're not," I argue.

"Willow! I said not now. And go upstairs," Sebastian orders, warning me with his expression not to speak again.

"What's all the shouting for?" Dad asks, stepping into the hallway, then freezes.

A moment of tension fills the corridor. I ignore my brother's orders, trying to breathe, unable to take my gaze off Wyatt's bloody face.

Dad's words come out raw, stripped of warmth, and coated in steel. "What happened?"

"I'm fine," Wyatt declares.

"Like hell you are. Now, don't lie to me, son. What happened?" Dad demands, the weight of previous battles heavy in his question.

"Sir, I'm fine. Can I get cleaned up?" Wyatt asks, his tone begging for Dad to drop it.

Sebastian exchanges a glance with Dad.

He steps closer and removes Wyatt's cowboy hat.

Wyatt turns his face toward the wall, full of shame.

Dad lowers his voice even further. "Look at me, son."

Wyatt's chest fills with air. He slowly lifts his chin and stares into my father's eyes.

"Why were you there?" he questions.

Wyatt answers, "I went to get the rest of my stuff."

Dad asks, "Why didn't you take anyone with you?"

Guilt, self-loathing, and disgrace take over Wyatt's features. His jaw tics, and he clears his throat. "I'm eighteen next week, sir."

"Yes, we're all aware. What does that have to do with this?" Dad inquires.

Humiliation blooms over Wyatt's cheeks. He takes three short breaths, then stands taller. "I'm a man now. I should be able to handle my own affairs without involving others."

The air stretches tight until it's about to snap, with Dad keeping his gaze pinned on Wyatt's.

Dad finally says, "I see."

More silence coils in the hallway.

"I'm fine. Please forget about this," Wyatt implores.

"Like hell I will. Sebastian, grab the shotguns," Dad instructs.

"What? Dad, you can't kill him! You'll go to jail," I shriek.

He turns to look at me. "Why are you lurking in the background?"

Jagger steps inside, booming, "What's going on?"

Sebastian answers, "Come get the shotguns with me."

Jagger furrows his forehead in confusion, then turns and freezes when he catches sight of Wyatt. He stares at his friend, his anger growing hotter. He mutters, "I told you to wait for me."

Wyatt grinds his molars, focusing on the floor.

"Jagger. Now," Sebastian demands.

Jagger tears his gaze off Wyatt and follows Sebastian outside.

Wyatt starts, "Jacob—"

"What's the commotion out here?" Mom cries out, opening the door that leads into the kitchen and then stopping in her tracks. She gasps, "Oh my Lord! Wyatt!"

"I'm fine, ma'am," Wyatt insists, with a fresh load of shame.

"You aren't! Come into the kitchen so I can help clean you up. Willow, grab the first aid kit," she instructs.

"Ruby, not now," Dad interjects.

Mom glances up at him and puts her hand on her hip. "He needs medical attention."

"He'll get it when we return," Dad asserts.

"Where are you going?" she asks.

"Dad's going to kill Wyatt's father!" I shout in a panic.

Mom's jaw drops.

"Mind your own business, Willow," Dad orders.

"Jacob?" Mom questions.

"Shotguns are in the truck," Sebastian informs Dad, stepping through the doorway.

Dad grabs his hat off the hook and puts it on.

"Jacob?" Mom says again, tugging on his arm.

"We'll be back soon. Wyatt, let's get your stuff. Then you aren't going back there ever again. Understand?" Dad insists.

"Yes, sir," Wyatt replies, and brushes past Sebastian.

"Dad! Please don't kill him. You'll end up in jail," I plead.

He turns. "Willow, do what your mother says. Go get the first aid kit."

"Yes, sir," I reply, then suggest, "Why can't Wyatt stay here? Can't Jagger and Sebastian go in and get his stuff?"

"Mind your own business, Willow," Dad says, then kisses Mom on the cheek. "I'll be back soon."

"Don't do anything stupid, Jacob," she warns.

He says nothing as he steps outside.

Mom stares after him, then shuts the door and spins toward me. "Do what your father said, and also bring a pile of towels."

"Yes, ma'am," I reply, then run upstairs and into the bathroom. I open the cabinet, grab the first aid kit and towels, then meet Mom in the kitchen.

I set everything on the table and blurt out, "Why does Wyatt's dad hurt him?"

Mom's eyes narrow. "Because he's a drunk and a coward."

"Wyatt doesn't deserve that," I say.

Mom takes a deep breath. "No, he doesn't. I don't know what that boy was thinking going over there alone." She turns on the water and picks up a pot, then scrubs it with a steel pad.

I pace the kitchen.

She stops what she's doing. "Willow, go outside and do that. You're making me nervous."

I don't argue, heading for the door.

She calls out, "Hey. I thought Hazel was here."

I turn, telling her, "I had Ava take her home."

Surprise fills Mom's expression. "Ava? Is that a good idea?"

I shrug. "Probably not, but I don't want Hazel to gossip about Wyatt all over school."

Mom puts the pan on the drying mat, then dries her hands and puts one on her hip. "Why are you giving your time to someone if you can't trust them?"

"I can trust her," I say before I think, and instantly regret it.

"You trust her so much you worry about her spreading gossip about our family?" Mom questions.

Guilt gnaws at me. I soften my tone, confessing, "Okay. I only trust her with certain things."

"Like what?" Mom asks.

I open my mouth, but nothing comes out. I shut it and swallow hard.

"That's what I thought," Mom states.

I stare at her.

She adds, "If you can't trust someone, they aren't your friend."

My stomach dives. Is she right about Hazel and our friendship?

Mom returns to washing the dishes, and I go outside, taking laps around the barn and front yard until I hear a vehicle. My heart races again. I turn the corner, but disappointment hits me when it's only Ava.

She parks her car, gets out, and wags her finger. "You owe me."

"I did it for Wyatt," I claim.

"That girl doesn't belong in our house. She's a nightmare. You're playing with cyanide hanging out with her," Ava warns.

"She's not that bad," I protest.

Ava crosses her arms and tilts her head. "Keep telling yourself that lie. Don't say I didn't warn you when she burns you." She stomps off into the house.

I return to pacing the yard. It feels like forever until I hear the throaty growl of Dad's diesel truck.

Relief fills me when everyone gets out. Jagger and Sebastian grab items from the truck bed. They go into the house, and I follow them.

"Willow, this isn't your business," Dad declares when I step into the kitchen.

"I can help Mom," I offer.

"No. This isn't your business," Dad repeats in a sterner tone.

I glance at Wyatt's face, which has swelled even more, and my heart sinks.

His open eye meets mine. He mutters, "I'm fine, Willow. Go play, and stop worrying about me."

"Play? I'm not a little kid," I proclaim.

"Willow. Mind your own business like Dad told you to," Sebastian demands.

I cave, leaving the house in a sulk. I go for a long walk, thinking about all the things Hazel said, what my mom said, and Wyatt's bruised and battered body.

It's not fair. He doesn't deserve a nasty father, but no one has ever been able to do anything about it. Now that he's almost eighteen, at least he won't have to return to his house.

The afternoon sun begins to set. I turn the corner and catch Wyatt entering the barn. I make my way across the field and slip past the heavy wooden door, passing the dozens of stalls until I reach the final one.

He's sitting on a bale of hay with his cowboy hat on his knee. His head leans against the wall, battered fists clenched, and eyes closed.

I step closer.

He opens his good eye. "What do you want, Willow?"

I sit next to him. "Are you okay?"

"I'm fine," he grits out.

"Did he break anything this time?" I question.

Wyatt's jaw tics. He sarcastically mumbles, "Nope. I'm super lucky today."

I stay quiet, staring at his fist.

"Is there something else you need?" he asks.

I lean against the wall. "No."

"Then why are you still sitting here?" he questions, turning his head toward me.

Hazel's right. Wyatt's cute.

A warm flush floods me. It's sudden, chaotic, and seems to rewire me.

"Why are you staring at me like that?"

"I-I'm not," I stutter, my breath stumbling, two breaths behind every heartbeat.

What is happening?

"I don't need your pity, Willow."

The giddiness disappears. I put my hand on his forearm, confessing, "I'm sorry. I didn't mean to. I just feel bad for you."

"Well, don't," he barks.

Tension builds, full of silence and suffering, which seems almost appropriate due to Wyatt's situation.

I take my hand off his arm and return to leaning against the wall. I ask, "Why did you go there?"

"I wanted my stuff."

"Why didn't you take Jagger?"

"I already explained this to your dad. I don't need to explain myself to a kid," he sneers, spitting the last word like it tastes rotten in his mouth.

Hurt fills me. I snap back, "I'm not a kid."

"You are."

"I'm a freshman, and you're a senior. We're practically the same age," I argue.

He scoffs. "I'm eighteen next week, and graduating in three. I'm a man, and you're..." He glances over at me.

My heart slams into my rib cage. "I'm what?"

He turns and rests his head against the wall again, closing his eyes. He finishes, "You're a girl with everything. Go enjoy it, and stop fussing over me."

I open my mouth, but nothing comes out. I can't deny his statement. I am lucky.

He doesn't move, and neither do I.

We sit there for several minutes, our breaths in sync, the occasional neighs from the horses breaking up the silence.

He suddenly drawls, "Why are you still here, Willow?"

I reply in a soft tone, "I don't know."

He raises a brow at me. "You don't know?"

Heat fills my cheeks, and the funny feeling I had a few moments ago returns. I bite my lip and shrug. "I guess I just don't want you to be alone right now."

Something flickers in his expression, but then he gruffly states, "I may be bloody, but I'm not a wimp, Willow."

"I didn't say you were."

His look intensifies, and every nerve in my body braces for something. What, I don't know, but I hold my breath.

The meal bell rings, and Paisley shouts, "Dinner!"

Wyatt winces, rising off the bale, and puts on his cowboy hat. Without turning around, he mumbles, "Dinnertime," and leaves me in the barn, full of uncomfortable feelings and unanswered questions.

6

Wyatt – Age 18

One Week Later

Sun bakes into the barn's rafters, causing the early summer heat wave to ripple off the hay in smokelike curls.

I can't handle this furnace anymore.

I peel my T-shirt over my head, bunch it up, and swipe it over my neck and torso to absorb my sweat.

It's pointless. The shirt is already soaked, so I toss it to the ground. I dump another few hay bales down the chute, climb the ladder, and turn.

Willow barrels into me with no warning. Her hands smack my chest, and her blues snap up to mine like I just caught her red-handed.

"Whoa— Willow?" My hands grip her arms before she topples backward. "You all right?"

Her lips part, and a flush crawls into her cheeks. "Um..."

My brow furrows. "Did I hurt you?"

"No," she blurts. Her gaze drifts to my chest, then the loft, and back to my chest. She mumbles, "I'm great. Totally great."

"You sure?" I question, peering at her closer. Willow's been acting strange the last week, but I blame myself for our awkwardness.

"Yep," she insists.

I slowly release her.

She takes a giant step back. Then her gaze covers the same circuit as before.

"Why are you acting like a mouse who just got caught in a trap?" I tease.

Her cheeks redden further. "I'm not."

"You are," I taunt.

She shakes her head. "I'm not."

"I didn't mean to traumatize you," I offer.

"You didn't," she mutters, then releases an anxious breath and spins away from me. "I'll get out of your hair." She takes two steps.

I follow and reach for her. "Willow."

She freezes.

I step in front of her. "I owe you an apology."

Her eyebrows arch. "For?"

My gut twists. I hate thinking about the events of a week ago or any other encounter I've had with my father.

I suck it up and admit, "I was a total dick to you."

"You were?" she questions.

"Yeah."

"When?"

I grunt in amusement, but then the memory makes my grin fall. I shift on my feet, glance away, then stand taller. "After the incident with my sperm donor."

Her lips twitch. "It's okay."

I shake my head. "No, it's not. You were trying to be nice to me, and I took my anger and frustration out on you."

"You didn't," she claims.

I lean closer, teasing, "Since when are you a liar?"

Her mouth curls. "Okay. You were a dick."

I chuckle. "Yeah. So you'll forgive me?"

She nods, beaming. "Already forgotten."

I lower my voice. "Thanks. Now, tell me how big of a surprise party this will be tonight."

She gapes at me, quickly tries to recover, then unconvincingly claims, "There's no party."

I cross my arms and tilt my head. "You're lying again. Is this going to be a reoccurring thing?"

"Ah..." Her mouth hangs open.

I waggle my eyebrows. "If you tell me how many people are coming, I'll owe you big-time."

She pins her eyebrows together in frustration.

I wait her out.

She asks, "How did you know?"

I arrogantly grin. "Everyone gets a surprise party when they turn eighteen. And whatever your parents do for you and your siblings, they do for me."

She doesn't speak.

"Am I wrong?" I ask.

She chews on her lip.

"Don't bite your lip off. Some punk might want to kiss you tonight, and you'll be all scabbed up," I tease.

Her eyes widen, and the same nerves that filled her expression after she ran into me reappear.

I point out, "You're digging your teeth into your lip deeper."

"Oh. I-I...um..." She looks away and exhales a worried breath.

I chuckle again. "Willow, it's our secret. I promise I'll look surprised. How many?"

She meets my gaze. "Why do you want to know?"

My chest tightens. I shrug. "I guess I'm wondering how easy it'll be to sneak away for a bit."

Something flares in her expression. "Sneak away?"

I glance behind me to make sure no one else is in listening distance. Then I step closer to her, lean down, and tense.

A scent I have never smelled before flares around me, low and sweet, hitting me like dry wood. It's instant and unforgiving. Blood rushes south before I can stop it.

"Jesus. What are you wearing?" I choke out, rough and thick.

She tilts her head upward, meeting my stare. Another flicker I don't comprehend appears in her eyes and then disappears just as quickly. She asks, "What am I wearing?"

The scent intensifies, clinging to me. I'm already pulsing hard enough to ache.

What the fuck is happening?

The longer we stand staring at each other, the worse it gets.

This is Willow.

She's Jagger's little sister.

Jesus, she's like my little sister.

Why is my dick killing me right now?

She inhales slowly, her chest rising, as if trying to steal my attention.

I glance down at her cleavage.

When the fuck did Willow get boobs?

I drag my gaze upward, slowly lingering on her neck, then fixating on her lips.

Since when are they so plump?

I bet my cock would look perfect with her mouth around it.

Son of a bitch. What the hell am I thinking?

"I-I don't understand your question," she sputters, tearing me out of my sick thoughts.

I blink hard and then step back from her. In a harsh tone, I reply, "Nothing. Don't worry about it. So how many people?"

She takes a minute, recomposes herself, and admits, "Few hundred."

"Okay," I mumble.

"Is that good?" she asks.

"Good?" I question, still trying to shake off her scent, but it's like it's permanently seeping into my lungs.

She breathlessly answers, "You know. To um...sneak away?" She pins a look on me that makes me almost come in my Wranglers. Her wide eyes glisten with hope, lashes slowly fluttering just a few times to draw me further in, and her flushed cheeks don't relent.

Sneak...

I straighten up.

Chelsea.

"Oh. Right. Yes. That's good. See you later, Willow." I turn and hightail it out of the barn, passing Jagger on my way to the corral.

"Where've you been?" he questions.

Guilt hits me.

What just happened in there?

"Barn," I answer, continuing to walk.

"Doing what?" he asks.

"Chores. What else?" I snap.

"Touchy, touchy," he chides.

I stop and release a breath. "Sorry, man. Hey, why don't we ride down to the lake?"

He takes a minute, pretends to think, then says, "Sorry. Mom and Dad have a birthday dinner planned for you."

"Right. I forgot."

He glances at his watch. "You should go shower. They want to eat early," he lies.

"Sure. See you later," I say, happy to get away from him, still perturbed over my encounter with Willow.

I avoid the others, going straight upstairs when I get into the house. I head for the bathroom, and turn on the shower. I don't bother to warm up the water. My hard-on won't go away. I'm imagining too many things I shouldn't be. At least, not when Willow Cartwright is the center of my lewd fantasies.

I step under the frigid water, which barely eliminates my bad thoughts. If anything, being naked only makes it worse. Within a minute, I'm imagining Willow on her knees, sucking me off while I grip the back of her head.

I groan, hating myself and this current predicament, but there's only one thing to do. I pour soap into my hand, then jack myself off until I'm drained of every thought I should never have thought in the first place.

I step out of the shower, wrap a towel around my body, then put my hands on the counter. I stare at my reflection, muttering, "It's never happening. Think of Chelsea."

My eyes stare back at me, void of all the fantasies I used to have of Chelsea. And I don't get it. The girl's our homecoming queen, and every guy wants her. She's finally into me, and tonight was my big opportunity to show her what she's been missing out on.

Now, my mind won't stop returning to Willow's face and that damn look she gave me.

"Think Chelsea," I order myself.

Her face pops up next to Willow's, and I groan.

Nothing about Chelsea feels enticing anymore.

I rush into my room, pull out my phone, and study the photo I took of her. Her brown hair and blue eyes were the highlight and focus of my bedtime routine. I'd go to bed thinking about her and wake up the next morning immediately looking at her photo again. Right now, she seems ordinary.

"The heat has gotten to my head," I tell myself, then toss my phone on the bed. I put on a pair of clean jeans, a fresh T-shirt, and secure my belt buckle. I slide into my nicer boots, grab my cowboy hat, and descend the stairs.

Jacob appears at the bottom.

More guilt, along with fear, fills me. I love and respect the Cartwrights. They're the only family I've ever really had. I would never do anything to risk their acceptance of me.

I just jacked off to Willow's face.

I groan again, only this time, it's out loud.

"Something wrong, son?" Jacob asks.

I hold my breath.

Does he know?

His eyes turn to slits as he peers closer at me.

Snap out of it.

"It's just hot out," I claim.

He nods. "They say this summer will be a record high."

"Really?"

"Yep. Anyway, come outside with me. We've got an issue with Tibby we need to fix," he declares.

"Tibby? What's wrong with her?" I fret, forgetting about my dilemma. The Cartwrights got Tibby for me on my sixteenth birthday. She's a good horse, and I'm unaware of any issues.

"I think she's just overheated. Best if we hose her down. She's in the backyard corral."

"Okay," I agree as I put on my hat and follow him outside. I turn the corner of the house, then stop in my tracks.

"Surprise! Happy birthday!" a crowd shouts, and a band begins to play. Tents cover the lawn, smoke from a pig roaster fills the air, and several bars are set up.

I grin, then laugh. "You tricked me," I state, but it's true. I had forgotten about the party.

His lips twitch. He lowers his voice. "I'm sure you had some idea."

I shake my head. "Nah. You definitely took me by surprise."

He pats me on the back. "Happy birthday. You're officially a man."

"Thank you, sir. And I just wanted to..." Emotions hit me, and I have to pause.

Jacob pats my back again. "We're proud of the young man you've turned into."

"Happy birthday," Ruby sings, then reaches up to hug me.

I return her affection and offer, "Thank you. And this party is too much."

"Not at all," she says, waving her hand in front of her face.

One by one, the Cartwrights all step up to hug me, but all I can see is the one at the end of the line.

Willow.

My heart stops. She's in a yellow sundress, and I swear the sun looks dull in comparison.

The fabric clings to her, taunting me with a whole new set of fantasies I shouldn't be creating. But her bare shoulders beg for my lips. Her legs somehow seem longer than normal in her platform sandals, and all I want to do is run my hands up her thighs and past her fluttering hem.

Then there's that damn bow, screaming to the world "innocence," right between her breasts, and I'm convinced she glued it on her dress only to drive me crazy all night.

So I go through the motions, careful not to lean into her family members when they hug me. The strain against my zipper is relentless. I can't get the thought of hiking up that sundress and stealing her innocence until she gasps my name like a prayer and a curse all at once.

By the time she gets to me, I need another cold shower. She pins her soft smile on me like I'm more than I am or someone worth saving. The unfamiliar and unwelcome pull in my chest slowly twists, aching for something I should never have nor take.

"Happy birthday. Surprise," she teases, a slow flush in her cheeks appearing.

I'm imagining things.

I don't move or speak, afraid of what I might say or do. Yet today isn't my lucky day. Her presence only makes it worse.

Her torturous scent flares around me, dragging more buried desires to the surface. My gaze drifts over her body in slow motion, unable to linger in places I should never consider looking at or touching.

When I finally lock my eyes back on hers, hitched breaths flow between her parted lips. Her maroon cheeks highlight the unclaimed fire innocently burning in her blues.

She's pure sweetness with unspoiled grace, and my chaotic thoughts turn so clear, there's no denying it.

I want Willow Cartwright. But it's more than some high school crush.

I don't want a quick fix. I want to ruin her until the sun comes up, breaking her into pieces. And there's another truth I already know, which scares me more.

I'll watch her shatter around my body before putting her back together, only to do it again.

She inhales slowly, that bow I have to stop myself from pulling apart, moving with the action. She rises on her tiptoes and curls her arms around me.

Unlike the others, I don't keep my body away. I tug her closer, wrapping my arms around her waist. My lower body throbs against her stomach, and I murmur in her ear, "Thanks, sugar."

She stiffens.

"You smell good," I add before I can stop myself.

She slowly retreats, pinning an expression full of a million questions on me. A runaway wisp of hair falls across her cheek.

"There's the birthday boy." Chelsea's voice cuts in, causing Willow to tear her gaze off me.

My gut dives. I squeeze Willow's waist and release her, turning just as Chelsea throws herself at me.

Like with the other Cartwrights, I go through the motions, staring at Willow over Chelsea's shoulder, only to receive a sharp pain in my heart.

Hurt floods Willows's face.

It hits harder than any slap could. Buried in her expression is a question she won't ask, and a thousand things I might not be man enough to give.

Or worse...

Maybe I will.

I try to pry Chelsea off me, but she only hugs me tighter.

Willow's mouth curves into a tight smile, and she nods. Then she spins on her heel and walks away.

Chelsea finally retreats, gushing, "It was so hard keeping this a secret from you! How surprised were you?"

"Huh?" I question, tearing my fixation off Willow and giving Chelsea a cool once-over.

Everything I obsessed about for months morphs into the average. Her curled hair, polished and perfect, along with her bold, painted red lips, seem boring compared to Willow's flyaway hairs and soft, pink mouth.

She babbles, "On a scale of one to ten, how surprised were you?"

I stare at her.

What a dumb question.

Her smile grows. "You must still be in shock."

I clear my throat, admitting, "Yeah, I'm in shock." But it's not about the party.

How did I not notice Willow before?

She's Jacob's daughter.

Jagger and his brothers will kill me.

"Hey, Wyatt," a breathless female voice interrupts, and a hand wraps around my bicep from behind.

Chelsea's eyes narrow. "Hazel."

I turn my head and refrain from groaning.

Willow's annoying friend beams at me. "I wanted to come give the birthday boy a hug."

I have to get out of here.

"Can you two excuse me, please?" I say, tipping my hat. Then I glance into the tents, searching for Willow.

Jagger slides his arm around me and hands me a red Solo cup. "Thought you might need one of these."

"What is it?" I question, glancing at the fizzing cola.

"Drink it," he orders with mischief in his eyes.

I obey, grimacing as the whiskey overpowers the soda.

"Don't be a pussy," he taunts.

I down the cup's contents, hoping it'll cool the fire smoldering inside me.

"All you gotta do is make the rounds for an hour, then you can sneak off with Chelsea," he directs.

I clench my jaw.

"What's that look for?" he asks.

"Nothing. How do I get a refill?" I ask.

He grunts. "Mason has a flask. He'll fill you up."

"Great." I scan the party again.

"Jagger. Are you going to let the birthday boy have all the fun?" Hazel cuts in.

I groan, irritated once again.

Jagger turns and looks her over, his lips curling in approval. "Meaning?"

She giggles. "He shouldn't get all the hugs, should he?"

Jagger tosses me a sinister look, then steps closer to her, sliding his arm around her waist, and stating, "Darlin', I think a kiss on the cheek is appropriate too, don't you?"

She bats her eyes and flirts, "Well, if you want one from me..."

Annoyed and on a mission to find Willow, I leave them and enter the first tent.

The band is playing country music, and a dozen couples line dance. Guests fill tables, laughing, drinking, and eating. I know all of them, and every step I take pulls me into another conversation.

I'm halfway into the tent when I spot Willow. Our eyes meet, lingering on each other until Howard Stetson slaps my shoulder.

"Wyatt Houston, it's about time you came to say hello," he roars.

I turn and put out my hand. "Mr. Stetson. It's nice to see you."

He shakes my hand and declares, "It's Howard now. Once you become a man, we're on a first-name basis."

"Thank you, sir," I reply, then glance back, but Willow's no longer in the same spot.

My stomach sinks, and I curl my fist at my side.

I need to find her.

I excuse myself from the conversation, get stopped by more people, then spot her.

The entire night is a game of cat and mouse.

There's a flash of her bare shoulders, a curl of her innocent smile, a sneak peek of her sun-glazed legs.

I find her, only for her to disappear, swallowed by the crowd that never seems to dwindle.

She's a dare that I'm not sure I'll win, but I spend the night chasing her shadow.

Every circle of guests, every song, every too-loud laugh that isn't hers keeps me ignoring Chelsea's numerous attempts to grab my attention.

Then, I spot Willow on the edge of the dance floor. Her hips sway like sin to the song. I push through bodies, but she's vanished by the time I get there.

As my irritation hits a high, it suddenly dawns on me. She's been leaving me breadcrumbs all night. Between her lingering scent, lip gloss on empty cups, and the bow on her yellow dress taunting me all night, she knows what she's doing.

If she thinks she can avoid me all night, she's wrong.

If she wants a chase, then I'll give her one.

When I catch her, this game is going to end.

The only thing I need to decide is if it's her up against the wall or writhing underneath me.

Either way, Willow Cartwright's going to plead for me, my body, and all the things she's only imagined. I'll make her beg for the stretch, cry for more, and when she breaks around me, she'll never forget who made her a woman.

7

Willow – Age 15

gh. Chelsea Waverly, head cheerleader, homecoming queen, and every high school boy's wet dream.

That includes Wyatt.

The guests have bombarded him all night. Every time he gets a moment to breathe, she's there, offering him a drink or a plate of food, or flirtatiously brushing her hand on his bicep before squeezing it.

It all makes me queasy. I try to ignore it, try to stay busy and have fun, but it isn't easy. At the end of the night, I'm sure she'll be wrapped around his thighs, and Wyatt will be another mark in her book of sins.

Or maybe she'll be one in his.

That's the thing about popular girls and dangerous guys in denim. It's a game where it's a privilege to play. She's the queen of heartbreak, and he's the guy who can land his smirk on any girl he chooses and take what he wants from them. And in the aftermath, they miss him but never regret him.

Yes, I know all about what Wyatt and my brothers do. It's not a secret what Chelsea or her friends do either. And that's what makes my attraction to Wyatt even more dangerous.

Something is brewing between us. It sparked in the barn, and all my thoughts of him over the last week are either making me delusional or he's suddenly noticed me.

And I don't know how to stop it, but I need to figure it out. Wyatt Houston isn't meant to be anything to me but another brother figure, and I need to remember that. Plus, the last thing I'm going to be to him is another girl like Chelsea.

I grab a bottle of water. After taking several sips, I turn and catch my breath.

Wyatt stands ten feet from me, not staring at me but inspecting me. His slow, deliberate gaze drags over my body, causing an explosion of tingles and heat to race down my spine. He doesn't smile or blink. He just studies me, as if I'm a secret mission and he's deciding how to best approach his objective.

A shiver racks me, and I inhale sharply.

He sees it, and his smirk hooks at one corner of his mouth, like he's tasting trouble and enjoying the flavor.

Another round of heat floods my cheeks. I glance behind me to see if Chelsea is there, but it's only people my parents' age.

I must be going crazy.

He steps toward me, and, of course, Chelsea magically appears. She throws herself in front of him, causing him to stop in his tracks and grab her before she falls. His eyes break from mine to meet hers.

My gut dives, and my chest tightens. I push through the crowd, away from the party, and disappear into the darkness.

When I get to the pond, I sit on the huge tree trunk that's been there for as long as I can remember. I trace the heart with the E and C inside it, carved by my sister Evelyn when she was younger and met Clay, the man she married.

"What are you doing down here by yourself?" Wyatt's low, gritty voice scrapes across my skin, unraveling the ache I just contained.

I slowly look up.

His hat's tipped just enough to shadow the spark in his eyes.

My breathing stutters, and I can't come up with the words to respond.

Time stops. Music trickles through our silence, soaked in static and summer heat.

He finally sits next to me, takes off his hat, and puts it on his knee. His dizzying scent of leather and dirt mix with a touch of his sweat, seducing me deeper into the fantasies that'll never happen.

My heart kicks hard. Having him so near feels wild, reckless, and utterly exhilarating. But it's also scary.

It's Wyatt.

He leans closer, drawling, "Sugar, are you going to tell me why you're down here all by your lonesome?"

Sugar.

He's called other girls "sweetheart" or "darling," but he always eliminates those pet names when he's done with them.

Does him calling me "sugar" mean I'll be next?

Wyatt would never hurt me.

I bet those other girls thought that too.

My pulse throbs, hot and heavy, beneath my skin. I state, "I needed some air."

His lips twitch. He leans closer, teasing, "We're outside."

I crack a smile. "I know."

He scans my face, then inhales deeply before replying, "I understand. There are too many people up there."

"Where's Chelsea?" I blurt out, then silently scold myself. My face heats all over again, and I bite my lip.

He doesn't flinch. "Hopefully, heading home."

I arch my eyebrows, with hope blossoming in every cell of my being. "Why?"

His gaze drifts to my lips. "She can't get what she wants."

"You mean you?" I let the words slip out before I can censor myself.

Amusement lights his expression. "Maybe."

"Maybe?" I ask, tilting my head.

He grins. "Okay. You're right. But doesn't that make you happy?"

I gape at him with my heart violently banging against my ribs.

He lowers his voice further, sets my veins on fire with another lewd once-over, then murmurs, "Well? Tell me you don't care she left, sugar, and I'll apologize for getting the wrong impression."

My mouth turns dry. I barely get out, "The wrong impression?"

He nods, licking his lips.

I wait him out, unsure if I'm imagining this or if it's real.

He slides his callused hand on my thigh, caging his fingers around it and applying enough pressure to make me gasp.

With confidence, his words slide across my neck like smoke, then coil around me. He says, more to himself than me, "Yeah. I didn't get the wrong impression."

A kaleidoscope of butterflies riots inside me, trying to lift me off the ground.

He rubs his thumb on the inside of my thigh, asking, "Want to know a secret?"

"Yeah," I whisper.

"Your game of cat and mouse is driving me insane. But I've caught you now. So game over," he declares.

"Wh-what?"

"Don't act innocent, Willow Cartwright. You've been running from me all night," he accuses.

"What? No, I haven't! You're the one who had Chelsea draped all over you any chance she got!" I point out.

A wicked grin carved from trouble appears on his lips. He claims, "I think you're exaggerating."

"No, I'm not."

"Aren't you?"

"No," I insist.

He closes the distance. His breath hits my ear, thick with heat, and every word slides into my bones when he murmurs, "The only one I want draped all over me is you."

My mouth waters. The butterflies in my stomach wage a new, ferocious war. My heart races so fast, I get dizzy.

I'm hearing things.

"Are you going to look at me?" he asks.

I slowly turn, my face an inch from his.

He smiles. There's no smirk, no arrogance, no cowboy full of games this time. It's just a side of Wyatt few people see. It's soft, a bit vulnerable, and real.

He studies me for what feels like forever, then glances at my lips, declaring, "We shouldn't go down this road, Willow."

Disappointment hits me. I turn, blinking hard.

He takes a finger and turns my chin back toward him.

I keep blinking.

"You're going to be the demise of me, sugar."

I take a shaky breath.

"Do you understand what I'm saying?" he asks.

I furrow my forehead and admit with a cracking voice, "I don't know. I-I'm not sure, Wyatt. So make sure you're clear."

He presses his fingers deeper into my thigh. "You know we shouldn't cross the line, right?"

I blurt out, "Like putting your hand between my legs?"

Heat ignites in his gaze, and his lips curve. "Yeah, sugar. Exactly that." He moves his hand higher, keeping his gaze drilled into mine, challenging me to tell him to remove it.

I can't.

My breath hitches. I quiver.

He continues, "If anyone knew what was happening here between us..." His voice trails off, fading into the distant music.

"They won't," I offer. It comes out as a plea.

He groans. "Jesus, sugar."

I bite down hard on my lip.

He cups my cheek with his hand, stroking his thumb over my mouth.

I lock my gaze on his lips.

"Have you kissed anyone, Willow?" he asks.

Embarrassment washes over me. I try to look away, but he won't let me.

"It's nothing to be ashamed about, but I want to know," he claims.

I swallow hard. "No."

His expression tells me he approves of my answer before he says, "Good."

"Good?" I ask, confused.

A storm of arrogance washes over him. "I like knowing you're only going to be mine."

My entire body trembles.

He scoots closer, mumbling, "Damn, sugar… You don't play fair."

"What do you mean?"

"You're all innocence and heat, sweet and forbidden, and all you have to do is give me that look, and I'm done. I might as well have not even shown up tonight, because I couldn't enjoy myself. I kept fighting to get next to you, and you kept standing there, looking all pretty before running away from me," he says.

Happiness bursts from me. In a hushed tone, I let slip, "You think I look pretty?"

He pushes a lock of hair behind my ear. "Prettiest girl in all of Whispering Junction."

My ego skyrockets. I can't contain my smile.

Wyatt thinks I'm pretty.

Is this really happening?

He stares at me for so long, I get nervous. I ask, "What are you thinking?"

"I'm debating."

"About?"

He stays quiet.

In a sad tone, I answer for him. "About us."

He sternly replies, "No, sugar. That bull has come and gone. It threw me off, and I landed right in your world, so there's no getting out now."

Insanity, hope, and an ache for something I know nothing about lies in that statement.

"Then what are you debating about?"

His gaze drifts to my mouth, and his voice rolls through the air when he replies, "Whether I should kiss you now or wait."

Please kiss me.

My pulse shoots to the moon. I whisper, "Why wait?"

He graces me with a small, wicked grin before dipping his face to my collarbone. His lips flutter across my shoulder, up my neck, and land beneath my earlobe.

I whimper and squeeze my thighs together, pressing against his hand.

He murmurs, "I'm going to wait."

Disappointment flares inside me.

But then he kisses me across my jaw, and hope sparks anew.

He stops millimeters from my lips, stating, "Some kisses you don't care about, but this isn't one of them. You're a girl that needs to be savored, so I'm going to wait."

My heart melts. I take a shaky breath.

He leans back, keeping his hand pinned to my thigh, and looks up. He points to the sky and says, "It'll be a full moon in about a week."

Still in a trance of disbelief, a bit of frustration, but way more awe, I focus on the moon. "It's pretty."

"If it were the fall, the bulls would be battling it out," he says.

"What for?" I ask.

He pins a seductive grin on me. "To get their girl and breed."

"Oh." I nervously laugh.

A few minutes pass in silence.

I eventually break it, asking, "Why do you love riding bulls so much?"

He stares into the distance, then reveals in a tone mixed with romance and excitement, "It's the only place where there's eight seconds of chaos yet a peaceful quiet. There's no past or voices I don't want to hear or remember. There's only the bull and me, both determined to win. And when I hit the dirt, win or lose, I remember I'm alive, and he didn't kill me."

"That's..."

He turns toward me and arches his eyebrows. "Messed-up, right?"

I nod, wincing. "Maybe a little."

He chuckles, the sound quickly subsiding into silence. A moment passes, and he adds, "If it doesn't kill you, it makes you stronger. And this fight for survival is my choice, not forced upon me."

My stomach flips. I put my hand on his thigh, blurting out, "So it's like some sort of therapy from your dad?"

His face hardens. The air turns cold.

"I'm sorry. I shouldn't have said that."

His jaw twitches, and he shrugs. "It's fine. But don't call him my dad. He's just a sperm donor." He turns toward me and winks.

I softly laugh. "Sorry. I forgot."

"No worries."

"Wyatt!" Jagger calls out.

We both jump and look behind us. The silhouettes of Jagger, Mason, and Ava come barreling toward us.

Wyatt tears his hand off my thigh and rises. "Stop yelling. We're hiding."

Ava laughs and says way too loudly, "Are you trying to dodge Hazel too?"

The hairs on my arms rise. I roar, "Jagger! Mason! Neither of you two better have slept with her!"

"Eww!" Ava slaps Jagger's arm. "Don't tell me you touched her."

"Well, I could have," he boasts.

"Not a prize to brag about," Wyatt points out.

"Agreed. That girl is going to be a petri dish someday soon, if she isn't already," Mason states.

I put my hand over my mouth and giggle.

"Seriously. Can you stop inviting her over?" Ava asks as she plops down on the log, her drink sloshing over the rim of her plastic cup. "Whoops." She giggles.

Jagger unstacks the bottom cup from his drink, holds it out, and Mason pours something from a flask into it.

"Drink for the birthday boy," Jagger claims, handing it to Wyatt.

He takes a sip and grimaces.

"Pussy," Mason says, then chuckles.

"What is it?" I question.

"Nothing you can drink," Ava says, pointing at me like she's my mother.

"Why not?" I argue.

"Because you're too young," she declares, embarrassing me in front of Wyatt.

I glare at her.

Wyatt finally saw me, and now he's going to be reminded of our age differ-ence again.

"Drink your water." Ava motions to my bottle.

Wyatt steps closer and holds out his cup. "You can try mine, but I don't think you'll like it."

"What is it?"

"Moonshine," he answers.

"She's too young. Don't give that to her," Ava orders.

"Agreed," Mason says.

"You two are hypocrites. We all had drinks younger than Willow, so keep your opinions to yourself. She can taste it. Here, Willow," Wyatt offers, shaking his cup, then adds, "Just don't become a drunk. It's not very attractive."

I grab the cup, ignoring Ava's additional remarks, and take a large swig. I swallow it and immediately erupt into a coughing fit.

Wyatt chuckles and rubs my back. He hands me my water. "Told you it was nasty. Here, drink this."

I down half the bottle, then admit, "That's disgusting."

"Good. Don't drink," Mason says, sitting on the trunk next to Ava.

"So, what are you two doing down here?" Jagger asks.

Panic hits me. I nervously glance at Wyatt.

He slides his arm around my shoulder and teases, "Willow saved me from Chelsea. Didn't you?" He pins me with a look that's filled with our secrets that no one can see but me.

I nod. "Yep."

"Dude, I thought she was going to sleep with you tonight," Jagger says.

My gut dives. I freeze.

Wyatt steps away from me. "Decided not to."

"Why?" Jagger questions.

"Something about her isn't doing it for me," he claims.

Mason whines, "You could have told me that. I stayed away from her out of respect. If I'd known you weren't into her—"

"Eww. You're all so gross," Ava interjects.

"Agreed," I mutter, feeling a tad jealous and angry, thinking about Chelsea all over him all night.

Wyatt picks up a few stones and hands one to me. "Don't forget our bet."

I arch my eyebrows.

He turns to the others. "Willow thinks she can skip the rock more times than me."

Jagger groans. "You could've had Chelsea Waverly, but instead, you've been down here with Willow talking about skipping rocks?"

Wyatt puffs out his chest. "Yep."

"What does the winner get?" Ava asks, then gets up and grabs a stone. "I bet I can beat all of you."

"You wish," Mason retorts, taking a shot of moonshine right out of the flask, then wincing.

I look at Wyatt for help, and he rescues me again.

"Barn chores for a month," he states.

Great. I hate barn chores, and I can't skip rocks well.

"I'll join that bet," Ava announces.

Wyatt arches his eyebrows. "You sure?"

"Yep. You two first," she instructs.

Maybe Ava will lose, and I'll be off the hook.

Wyatt nods at me. "Go ahead, Willow."

I toss the rock, and it skips twice, then sinks. I moan. "Crap!"

"Well, this is predictable," Mason mutters.

"Shut up," I tell him.

Wyatt chuckles.

"It's not funny," I hurl at him.

He shrugs, then tosses his rock. It skips four times.

"Willow's out," Jagger states.

"Aren't you the genius," I grumble.

Ava tosses hers and matches Wyatt's skip.

"Tie-breaker," Mason declares.

Wyatt steps back. "Ladies first."

"No, you go first," she says.

He shakes his head. "No. I insist."

She rolls her eyes, takes a second to focus, then tosses it. The stone skips twice before sinking.

"Looks like Wyatt is the winner," Mason says.

"He hasn't gone yet," Ava declares, glaring at our brother.

Wyatt winks at me, steps up to the water, and tosses his rock. It sinks directly into the pond.

"What!" he cries out.

"Dude! That was pathetic!" Jagger taunts.

"Yes! No barn duty for me! Ha! Have fun, you two!" Ava cheers.

Wyatt tosses me a cocky grin, winks, then turns to the others. "Well, that sucks."

8

Wyatt – Age 18

Four Days Later

$\mathcal{M}$y history book falls from my locker, and I catch it just in time.

"Hey, I've been looking all over for you," Chelsea chirps in her overly-sweet voice.

I freeze, glancing at the metal locker, and release an annoyed breath. In my most neutral tone, I reply, "Hey, Chelsea, what's up?"

Desperate hope fills her expression. She bats her lashes at me and puts her hand on my arm. "Want to get together later?"

"No," I state, but I feel kind of bad. It comes out gruff, and I see her wince. So I sigh, grab her arm, and pull her over to the corner.

Dozens of kids filter past us, and I can see her hope rekindling. A wave of guilt hits me. But she has to realize the truth.

We're not an item.

She puts her hand on my chest. "I missed you this week."

I grab her hand and move it off me. "Chelsea, you're a great girl."

Her head jerks backward, and she gapes at me.

Just get it over with. Don't be a pussy, I tell myself.

I clear my throat. "Listen, I know I might have led you on."

"Led me on? What do you mean 'led me on'? You were all about me, and suddenly, you're just not. What's going on, Wyatt Houston?" she shrieks.

I inhale deeply, standing taller. "Look, it's just not going to work out between us, okay?"

Her eyes turn to slits. "Why not?"

I don't say anything.

Her face falls, and her voice shakes when she asks, "You don't find me attractive anymore?"

"Of course I do. It's not that," I say, trying to soften the blow.

"Then what is it, Wyatt? What made you go cold on me? Is it your training? Am I a distraction? Do I need to just back off for a few days and then we can get together this weekend?" she questions, her eyes widening with a desperation I find super unattractive.

"Chelsea, it's just not going to happen between us, okay?" I reaffirm. "You're a great girl. Tons of guys are dying to be with you."

"But not you?" she seethes.

I stare at her.

She demands, "Be very clear, Wyatt, so I don't waste any more of my time."

"It's not going to happen between us," I repeat.

Rage and hurt spark in her eyes as she glares at me.

I didn't mean to lead her on. But ever since I noticed the real Willow, I can't even look at anyone else.

Chelsea jabs me in the chest and snarls, "You're a lost cause, Wyatt," then she brushes past me.

I turn and lean against the wall, staring at the ceiling. When I finally look across the hall, my gut drops.

Willow stares at me, her books held tight to her chest, her face white as a ghost.

Jesus, my luck is horrible.

I move toward her, but she spins on her heel and saunters down the hall.

"Willow, wait up," I call out.

She stops.

I catch up to her and turn her to face me. "Hey."

"Hey," she softly replies.

"Nothing is going on between Chelsea and me," I assure her.

Her face hardens, and she averts her eyes.

I add, "I reiterated to her that she and I are never happening."

Willow meets my gaze.

"Tell me you believe me. One thing I've never done is lie to you," I remind her.

She bites her lip.

"Besides, sugar, she doesn't hold a candle to you." I wink.

Willow softly laughs.

Relief has the tension draining from me. "So, are we going to be able to do some barn chores together this week?" I waggle my eyebrows. All week, our timing has been off. Between riding practice and Jacob's sudden chores that I didn't anticipate, I've not done barn duty with Willow once.

"Depends. Are you going to actually be there when I am?"

I lower my voice. "That's the plan. But do me a favor."

"What?"

"Help me out."

"How?"

"Do your homework first, then eat dinner, then barn chores. I have practice, and I'll be devastated if I miss watching you toss manure all night." I grin.

She laughs, but then her expression turns serious. She asks, "Are you scared?"

"Scared?"

"Your new bull. You said at dinner last night that your coach is moving you up a level."

I puff out my chest. "Not scared. I got this!"

Her lips twitch.

"Don't worry," I tell her. I start to put my arm around her, then realize where I'm at and pull my hand back to my hip.

She pins her blues on me.

My heart stammers. I say, "Come on, I'll walk you to the parking lot."

"Okay."

We push through the thinning crowd and get outside. I lead her toward Jagger's truck.

"What time are you done today?" he asks me.

"I don't know. Coach Jax said it might be a little longer than normal," I reply.

"Gotcha. Maybe we can play poker before we go to bed tonight?"

Willow glances at me.

I shake my head. "I doubt it, man. I got barn duty, practice, and homework. Sorry."

He groans. "I'm sick of homework. I can't wait until we never have to do it again."

"Agreed." I nod, ready to never open another textbook again. Then I declare, "I'll see you two at home."

"Later," Jagger says and then gets in the truck.

I open the passenger door for Willow.

She flashes her semi-shy grin, and my heartbeat trips over itself. She gets inside, and I shut the door and then lean through the open window. "Have fun, and wish me luck."

"Have fun, and good luck," Willow says, beaming at me.

"Get it, bro," Jagger adds.

"I got this," I state again with a wink. I tap the hood and step back.

Jagger pulls away. I unlock my 1969 Ford Bronco. It's rusted and old, but Jagger and I rebuilt the engine. I slide inside and take off down the country roads, whistling. Today, everything good's happening. Tonight, I get to spend some time with Willow, and soon, I get to ride the next-level bull.

One more step, and I'm ready to compete professionally.

I turn up the country station on the radio, sing at the top of my lungs, and inhale the fresh air, feeling unstoppable.

The old windmill, grain silos, and battered wooden fence come into view. I pull through the rusted wrought iron gates, and zoom down the driveway. I park by the other vehicles and get out.

My coach, Jax McCoy, leans against a tree with ink-filled arms. His cigarette pack peeks out of his rolled navy-blue T-shirt sleeve, just like it does every other day. He turns his head, but his leather hat brim shields his gaze. His whiskey voice roars, "About time you got here."

I glance at my watch. "I'm fifteen minutes early, so I'm not late."

"Eh," he grunts, nodding.

Jax McCoy has a lot of qualities I admire. Besides Jacob Cartwright, he's the only other male I've ever had to look up to. And they're both everything my sperm donor isn't.

He orders, "Get stretching and warm up."

I don't argue. I move over to where the other bull riders are, and we exchange hellos.

There are eight stretches Jax makes us do, just like the eight seconds we're on a bull. I hold each stretch for the eighty-eight seconds he requires, adding "Texas" after each number to ensure it's a full second. Then, I run eight laps around the outside of the bullpen before stopping to stand against the fence.

Jax steps beside me, challenging, "Are you sure you're ready for the next level?"

"Of course I am," I arrogantly declare. I can't say I'm good at most things, but I know bull riding is my talent. If I work hard, I know I can win the world championships someday.

Jax's lips press into a thin line as he continues to stare at me.

I cross my arms and lift my chin. "Don't tell me you're going to hold me back and not let me ride Snarlhide."

He shakes his head. "Didn't say that, but you better get rid of your cockiness before you get on that backbreaker." He points at the big black bull that's kicking dust around in a circle.

My stomach fills with butterflies. They're nervous but excited. I admit, "I've been waiting for this. And I'm ready."

Jax's rugged smirk lifts his wrinkled cheeks. He pats my shoulders. "All right, then. Let's see what you got. My bet is you're off in two seconds."

"No way," I scoff, sure I'll stay on for all eight. If not all eight, then at least six or seven. There's no way Snarlhide's tossing me off like a rookie.

He chuckles. "We'll see, son."

In the adjacent ring, a newer rider gets thrown off a level-one bull. Jax shouts, "You're not going to make it, son. There's no point coming back tomorrow."

The ranch hands quickly rope the bull to ensure he doesn't charge the rider.

The guy takes way too long to rise, coughing as he gets to his feet. When he finally catches his breath, he says to Jax, "I'll get it, I promise."

Jax shakes his head. "No. Don't come back, son. This isn't a career for you. If I let you ride a bull one more time, you're probably going to end up dead or paralyzed."

"I won't," he argues.

"Consider it a blessing. You tried hard. I'm proud of you. But it's best if you get off the ranch now," Jax tells the guy.

Disappointment fills the rider's face.

I swallow hard, feeling bad for him, but Jax is right. He may sound like an asshole, but bull riding isn't something you mess around with. Wrong moves in the pen can land you in a wheelchair for life or in a casket.

I tear my gaze off the other rider, and focus back on Snarlhide. He's still kicking up dirt, which isn't anything new. I've had my eye on him since I started.

"Get him ready," Jax calls to his team.

Bucky and Matrix lasso him and push him into the chute.

Anxiety builds within me, but it's good. It makes me feel alive. I'm ready to conquer this bull, prove to Jax that I can do it, and move on to the next bull. Plus, I have no room to fail.

School's never been my thing. College isn't an option. This is the only dream I've ever had, and it's my ticket to success. I'm so close, I can feel it.

Once I master riding Snarlhide, there's only a few more bulls to conquer. After that, Jax will give me a spot on his team. And that's where the money and success lie.

The bull gets locked into the chute, and I step up the staircase, assessing the beast, my pulse beating between my ears.

Jax warns, "This one's been pissed off all day. You sure you want to do this?"

I grunt. "Yep. I was born to do this. Get Hellhorn ready. I'm riding him tomorrow."

Jax shakes his head. "You're about to learn a lesson about cockiness, son."

"Noted," I state, then swing my leg over the bull's back. I grip the braided rope and brace myself.

Bucky spits chewing tobacco on the ground, taunting, "Good luck, Wyatt. It's been nice knowing you."

I ignore him.

"Three, two, one," Jax roars. Then he releases the lever, and the gate disappears.

The bull explodes into the ring, jerks hard to the left, and I'm airborne. I slam into the dirt near the fence, tailbone first, and the pain lights up my spine like a damn firework. I'm pretty sure I just cracked my ass in half.

Dust suffocates me as Snarlhide kicks, trying to fight off Bucky's and Matrix's lassoes. Cornered between the bull and the fence, I cover my head, dazed, aching, and flat-out stunned by the sting.

"Get up, Wyatt!" Jax booms, pulling me out of my trance.

Even though it's painful, I somehow make it to my feet and to the other side of the fence. I get into the safety zone and lean against the rail, my ass throbbing like nothing I've ever felt before. The adrenaline pumping through me slows as I curse myself, staring at the bull who still isn't contained.

Jax steps next to me, chuckling. "Guess I should have put some money on that two-second bet."

I don't look at him. I can't.

Don't be a pussy, I tell myself.

As hurt as I am, I steel my resolve and lock my gaze on him. "I'm ready to go again."

He arches his eyebrow and moves his toothpick from one side of his mouth to the other. "Son, there's no way you're getting back on that bull today."

"I can do it," I tell him, so disappointed that I didn't even last two seconds.

"No. Go home and ice up. Luke is at the hospital since his wife is in labor, so he can't look at you. Have Macklin take some X-rays and send the report to me."

"Give me another shot. I'll do it," I argue, not wanting to meet with the PT and lose my shot at trying again.

"Not today," he sternly says, then points to my Bronco.

I clench my jaw as I glance at the bull one more time.

How did I let that happen?

"Get that cockiness out of you, and I'll see you back here on Friday."

I look at him in surprise. "Friday?"

"You're done for a couple of days. You're going to be pretty bruised and sore after that toss, so get into the ice tub. Now, go," he says sternly.

With disappointment searing through me, I obey. I spend the drive to the Cartwright ranch, grimacing over every pothole I can't avoid.

I pull up, and Ava rings the bell for dinner. I go inside with the others, sit down, and try to hide my pain.

"What's wrong, Wyatt?" Ruby asks.

Everyone's attention turns to me.

"Nothing," I lie, shaking my head.

She studies me. "You're wincing. Did you get hurt at practice today?"

Embarrassment washes over me. I avoid looking at Willow.

"Well, she asked you a question," Jacob interjects.

I clear my throat and lock my eyes with Ruby's. "Sorry, ma'am. I fell off the bull pretty hard. I'm okay, though."

She turns to Jagger. "You're doing barn duty for Wyatt tonight. You can trade with him one of your days."

"No, that's not necessary," I say, not meeting Willow's eye, hating that I'm not going to be alone with her tonight.

Jacob interjects once more. "I'm assuming that Jax told you to ice yourself tonight."

I turn toward him with a sigh. "Yes, sir, he did."

"Okay, then it's decided. Jagger, you're on barn duty. Wyatt, you're icing."

Like the rest of the Cartwrights, I don't dare say no to Jacob.

He orders, "Eat up, and we'll go to the therapy room after dinner."

"Yes, sir," I reply, still avoiding Willow's stare. I shove my mashed potatoes in my mouth, barely tasting them.

When I finally meet Willow's gaze, I'm hit with a wave of frustration and dejection.

I concentrate on my food, not engaging in conversation. I'm unable to get comfortable in the wooden chair because of the consistent throbbing of my ass.

After dessert, Jacob rises. "Let's get you in the ice bath, Wyatt."

"Have fun," Mason quips.

I ignore him as I stand, trying not to wince, and then follow Jacob through the house. We step outside into the warm early summer air.

He asks, "How many seconds did you last?"

Shame fills me as I admit, "Maybe one."

He chuckles.

"No offense, but I don't find it amusing," I grouse.

"Jax said you were getting cocky. Guess it was meant to happen."

"Sorry, but what does he want me to do? Go on the bull and be scared of him?"

Jacob stops. He pins his steely gaze on me.

I cross my arms and don't flinch, preparing myself for a lecture.

He asks, "When you came to me and wanted to ride, what's the first rule I told you?"

I grind my molars, cringing inside.

One of his brows curves upward, amused yet unimpressed.

I shift on my feet, and a sharp pain runs down the back of my leg. I clench my jaw to get through the sting, and admit, "Always respect the bull."

"Arrogance overshadows respect." He lets his lecture linger in the air for a moment and then makes his way into the therapy room.

I follow him, holding in my wince as I climb the porch steps and go inside. The wood creaks under my boots, and the ranch hands' voices echo around the room, bouncing off the metal tubs.

"Boss," Kit, a newer horse jockey with blond hair and freckles, booms, standing to attention.

"Kit. How's your ankle?" Jacob inquires.

"Should be healed up in another week," Macklin, the ranch physical therapist, interjects.

"Great. That tub free?" Jacob points to a tub in the corner.

"Yep. Something happen?" Macklin asks, looking at me.

I shake my head. "Nothing much. Just got tossed and need to ice."

Jacob grunts and exchanges an amused expression with Macklin.

"Well, get in," Macklin orders.

I carefully strip out of my jeans, clenching my teeth so hard at the pain, I think I might crack one. When I finally get them off, I step into the tub and dunk my body as soon as possible, knowing it's best to shock my nerves quickly and all at once. I lean back against the metal and close my eyes as my body turns cold and numb.

As I lie here, my thoughts circle back to what Jacob said.

Is he right about me being too cocky?

No. I always respect the bull.

Maybe I didn't as much as I should have?

The debate continues until the alarm rings. I open my eyes, push myself to my feet, and grab the towel off the hook. I step out and wrap it around my body.

"Let's get a quick X-ray," Macklin suggests.

"I'm fine," I state, wanting to get out of here and head over to the barn to catch Willow before she leaves.

"Do what he says," Jacob orders.

I sigh, then walk toward the X-ray room.

Macklin comes behind me, shuts the door, and directs me on how to stand, then says, "Don't move."

There's a click.

He makes me turn twice, then states, "Yep. You're going to have a big bruise for a while."

I grunt.

"Okay, all good on my part," he announces.

I return to the main room, and Jacob holds out a pair of sweatpants. "These will feel better than jeans right now."

I don't argue, and carefully slide into the sweats.

Macklin booms, "Your ass is intact. No fractures. You're just going to be sore for a while. I'd tell Jax to give you a week off."

"I'll be fine," I declare, still upset Jax told me to skip a day. The only way I'll make it on the main circuit is to practice and get through the levels. I pull my T-shirt over my head and then ask Jacob, "Am I excused now?"

"Yes. But you should listen to Macklin," he asserts.

"I'll take it under advisement. Thank you," I say to Macklin, then slide into my boots. Before anyone can say anything else, I move as quickly as possible and head out the door.

I make my way across the yard toward the barn.

Jagger steps past the wooden door, stating, "Just in time. How are you feeling?"

I groan, still embarrassed I got tossed so quickly and the entire family knows. "Still numb from the ice bath, but no biggie. Hey, I'm sorry you had to cover tonight. I'll take one of your days to pay you back."

Jagger shrugs. "No worries. What are you doing out here anyway? You're not moving too fast."

"I forgot my pocket knife in the barn. I'll be back in the house soon," I lie.

"All right. I have to start homework. I really can't wait until school's over," he says.

"Me too, bro," I agree.

He takes off, and I step into the barn, praying that Willow's inside. I walk down the row of stalls until I come to the one that's open, freezing at the sight before me.

She's brushing Vandal. He's wild and unruly. Everyone on the ranch thought he was impossible to break, but it took her coming to the barn and talking to him every day for him to eventually calm down enough to ride him.

Thinking back, that was the moment I knew Willow was special, but I still saw her as Jagger's little sister. Now, no matter how hard I try to return to that place, I can't.

I lean against a post. She doesn't see me watching, but I can't look away. Hay dusts her jeans. Several locks of hair have escaped her loose ponytail. The more I stare, the more I'm convinced she's not just taming her horse. She's taming every part of me I swore was untouchable.

My heart races the same way it does before I get on a bull.

She brushes him like she's got all the time in the world.

I watch her like an idiot. Flames dance across my previously chilled skin. And I realize I'm ruined. I've never wanted anything more than to be the one she touches so carefully, with so much certainty. Like I'm hers.

And God help me, I think I already am.

She slowly turns. Her breath hitches and her blues widen when she catches sight of me. Her voice barely rises above a whisper when she says, "I thought you weren't coming."

9

Willow – Age 15

y heart skips a beat, then picks up at double the normal speed. Heat blooms in my cheeks, spreading like wildfire with no relief in sight.

Wyatt drags his dark gaze down me in a slow-burning, dangerous way. It's like he knows my secrets.

Anticipation bubbles in my chest to the point I can only take shallow breaths. I shift on my feet, grabbing the nearest post to steady myself.

He teases in his drawl, "Why don't you have some more faith in me, sugar?" He steps forward too quickly and then tries to hide his grimace.

I wince. "How's your injury?"

"You mean my ass?" He cocks an eyebrow, and his dimples pop out.

Another round of fire crawls up my neck and into my cheeks. I bite my lip and glance at his sweatpants.

He steps closer, then does a half spin, taunting, "I think you're looking at the wrong part of me."

Flames of embarrassment engulf me. I stutter, "I-I...um..."

He chuckles, then glances toward the front of the barn and lowers his voice. He asks, "Is anyone else here?"

I shake my head. "No."

His expression turns more mischievous. "Good. I finally have you all alone."

Butterflies torment my insides, their wings fighting to escape my belly. I nervously giggle.

He studies me another moment, then looks around the barn, questioning, "What chores are left?"

"I just have to finish brushing Vandal and Quicksilver," I relay.

"I got Quicksilver," he declares, then steps in front of the stall next to Vandal's and tries to hide another wince. He reaches for the brush and opens the gate, moving slower.

"I can do it. You're hurt," I point out.

He grunts. "I'm not dead."

"Still..." I offer.

"I'm fine," he claims as he strokes Quicksilver's mane.

I study him for a minute, then return to grooming Vandal.

The quiet between us builds with the rapid elevation of my pulse.

I finish brushing Vandal, pat him on the neck, then step out of the stall. I lock the gate and return the brush to the metal shelf. Then I grab an apple and hold it out, cooing, "Here you go."

Vandal chomps on it, and I lean against the stall, staring at Wyatt.

He moves the brush in long strokes and then steps to the other side of Quicksilver. He tries to hide his discomfort but can't.

I blurt out, "So practice didn't go well?"

He pauses for a second, his jaw clenching.

I quickly add, "Sorry. I didn't mean to pry."

He resumes brushing Quicksilver and states, "It's okay."

Silence resurfaces.

He finishes, gingerly steps out of the stall, and locks the gate.

I grab an apple for Quicksilver and hold it out. He gobbles it like Vandal did.

Wyatt defeatedly mumbles, "I don't even know if I lasted an entire second."

Wyatt was so excited last night when he told us he moved up a level and was going to get a chance to ride Snarlhide. And I know enough about cowboys and their bruised egos. Wyatt's no different in that regard.

So I tilt my head, offering, "It's okay. You'll figure it out."

He looks away and grinds his molars.

I put my hand on his forearm and softly say, "Hey."

He slowly meets my gaze, and it tugs at my heart. It's the same expression he's had after encounters with his father. Shame, disappointment, and helplessness appears in his sharp features.

"Next time will be better," I offer.

He snaps out of it, nodding and puffing out his chest. "Darn right."

I beam. "Snarlhide will regret the day he set eyes on you."

Wyatt chuckles. "That's right, sugar."

My heart skips another beat.

He leans closer. His scent of sweat, dirt, and leather sinks into my skin, causing more chaos in my veins. He murmurs, "I'd say I'm sorry I got you reeled into doing barn chores all week, but then I wouldn't be able to have you all to myself right now."

All to himself.

A slow, fluttery warmth blooms in my chest. My smile explodes so big, it hurts. I don't think before I reply, "Now that you have me all to yourself, what will you do with me?"

Wyatt's surprise lights up his eyes, and his lips curve at the corners.

I'm mortified.

Did I just say that?

He takes his pointer finger, slowly slides it over my forehead and down my cheek, then pins a rogue wisp of hair behind my ear.

Tingles explode in the wake of his touch, and I gasp.

His challenging gaze turns lethal, filled with heat and possession and all the knowledge about things I've only fantasized about doing with him. He taunts, "That's a loaded question, Willow Cartwright."

My insides quiver, and I demand in a velvety rasp, "Tell me."

His lips twitch. His gaze roams over me again before landing on my mouth. He nonchalantly states, "Maybe instead of telling you, I should show you."

My mouth waters. Finding my courage, I step closer, and flirtatiously say, "Maybe you should."

Surprise and amusement are written all over his face.

I blurt out, "I'm not a child, Wyatt."

His expression sobers. He doesn't speak.

"I'm not," I insist.

"Trust me, sugar, I know you aren't," he replies in a haunted tone, continuing to stare at me.

I wait him out, my mind screaming for me to kiss him if he doesn't kiss me. Instead, in a cracked voice, I say, "I thought you liked me."

He scoffs. "You have no idea."

"Then what's the problem?" I ask, ready to crawl into the loft and never come down if he doesn't touch me soon.

He drags his knuckles over my jaw.

My breath hitches.

"If I kiss you, then I'm going to want more." His voice is like molasses slowly poured over gravel. It's thick and rough around the edges in all the right ways.

An ache so deep I don't know where it came from throbs between my thighs. Then he strips me bare with nothing but syllables.

"Hell, I already do want more, and I haven't even tasted your lips yet."

I swallow hard, square my shoulders, and lift my chin. I order, "Then kiss me."

He blinks a few times, like he's coming out of a deep sleep.

"Wyatt—"

He puts his fingers over my mouth.

My heart slams against my rib cage. My lips tremble against his warm skin. The scent of him flares hotter.

He closes the space between us, stating, "There's no going back once we cross the line."

My insides quiver harder, full of an electrical current buzzing more intensely every second.

"Do you understand what I'm saying?" he asks.

I nod. "Yes."

"I don't think you do," he claims, then brushes his fingers over my clavicle.

My heart tries to break free from my chest cavity. "I understand. I told you I won't tell anyone."

He stares at me.

"I promise," I tell him, knowing my father would kill me if he knew I was anything but friends with Wyatt. So would my brothers. In many ways, the men in my family are hypocrites. They have one set of rules for themselves and another for the females. We're supposed to be good and innocent, while they get to raise hell. But that's how it is, so I understand why we'd have to keep this between us.

At least for now, until I'm out of high school.

"That's not what I meant," Wyatt says.

"No? Then what did you mean?"

He licks his lips, then declares, "If you're mine, then you're *mine*, Willow."

A sense of giddiness overtakes me, but in a serious tone, I whisper, "I know."

"Do you?" He peers at me closer.

I stay quiet.

He continues, "It's going to drive me crazy hiding this from the others."

I nod. "I know. But it's okay. I'll be eighteen in a few years. Then we won't have to worry."

His smile taunts his cheeks. Surprised, he says, more to himself than me, "So you do understand."

I put my hand on his chest. Finding his heart beating as hard as mine is another surprise.

He covers my hand with his callused one.

Neither of us moves.

He takes his other hand and cups my cheek, tugging me closer to him. His hot breath merges with mine. He mumbles, "You're going to get me in trouble."

I softly laugh. "Maybe. But I'm worth it."

He grins. "I don't doubt that."

Another moment of heat expands around us.

"I want to be yours," I whisper.

His grin falls. He leans forward. His lips brush mine, and he warns, "Careful what you wish for, sugar."

"Willow!" Jagger bellows.

I jump back.

So does Wyatt. He cringes from pain.

My pulse skyrockets. I spin toward the barn door.

"Willow!" Jagger barks, then turns the corner.

"What?" I ask, unable to believe he just interrupted the most important moment of my life.

"Jesus, where's the fire?" Wyatt tosses out in an annoyed voice.

"Mom wants you to start your homework," Jagger relays in his big-brother tone, pointing at me.

"I already did it," I tell him.

"When?"

"When I got home. Not that you're my ruler and need to know," I snap.

"Then go tell Mom so she can stop freaking out about it," he orders.

"No. You go tell her," I fire back.

"Not my business," he claims.

"You sure made it your business when you came out here," I accuse, pissed he took away my kiss.

He grunts. "Didn't really have a choice."

"Whatever," I mutter.

He turns toward Wyatt. "Why are you still out here? I already did your half."

Wyatt grabs the brush. "Was just helping Willow finish up. Since it's my fault she's out here."

"Actually, it's her fault she can't skip rocks and made a bet she couldn't win," Jagger points out.

I put my hand on my hip. "Why do you have to be such an insuffer-able, boot-stompin' jackass?"

Jagger smirks. "Huge words. Did you spend some extra hours in vocabulary class this week?"

"Jealous since you can barely read?" I taunt.

"Please. I read just fine," he claims.

"Want me to get the phonics flashcards out again?" Jagger had the hardest time learning to read out of all of the siblings. Mom made him use flashcards longer than any of us, and he hated them.

Wyatt snickers.

"What are you laughing at? You had to do them too," Jagger reminds him.

"Not as long as you, bro," Wyatt says.

"Whose side are you on?" Jagger asks, his eyes turning to slits.

Wyatt holds his hands in the air. "I plead the fifth."

Jagger glances between us, as if we've done something wrong, and my stomach flips.

"We just finished and were about to head to the house. So you can put your panties back on now," Wyatt interjects.

"Are you wearing any? Dad says your bruise is gonna be a big one," Jagger quips.

Wyatt's face falls.

I mutter, "You don't have to be such a jerk."

"Sorry. That was low," Jagger quickly apologizes.

"It's fine. Let's get out of here," Wyatt says, taking a few steps toward the exit.

I don't move.

Jagger steps next to him, offering, "Want me to get a ring cushion for you?"

"Nah. I'm fine," Wyatt states, then continues moving forward. He gets to the end of the aisle and stops. He turns his head and declares, "Willow, you better get inside before your mom calls the rangers."

Disappointment, irritation, and anger toward my brother, heat my blood. I stomp past them and out of the barn. I head toward the house and run into Mason on the way.

"Mom wants you to do your homework," he says.

I fire back, "I already did it!"

He holds up his hands. "Jeez. I'm just the messenger. No need to be a little brat and have a temper tantrum."

"Ugh! Shut up." I push past him.

I get inside and go into the family room.

"There you are! How much homework do you have?" Mom asks.

"I already did it," I snap.

Her eyes widen.

"Don't disrespect your mother," Dad booms from behind me.

I jump from the sheer force of his voice.

"She's in a mood," Jagger states, walking into the room.

I glare at him.

"Don't harass your sister," Dad orders.

"Whatever. Anyway. Wyatt and I are going into town for a bit," my brother announces.

"For what?" I ask.

"None of your business."

"Answer the question anyway," Dad demands.

I smirk at Jagger.

He focuses on Dad. "Bonfire at The Waverlys'."

"You're going to Chelsea's?" I blurt out, feeling ill.

"Not talking to you," he replies.

"It's a school night," Mom reminds him.

He shrugs. "There are only a few weeks of school left, and I already did my homework."

"It's still a school night," I argue, sure I'll die if Wyatt goes to Chelsea's.

Dad assesses Jagger. "Do you have any tests tomorrow?"

"No, sir."

"What about you?" Dad turns toward the doorway.

"No, sir," Wyatt answers.

I glance at him, my insides shaking.

"Are you sure it's a good idea to go into town when you're all bruised up, Wyatt?" Dad questions.

Wyatt stands taller. "I'm fine, sir."

"But you're hurt," Mom interjects.

"They're big boys, Ruby. Let them go," Dad states, then points at Jagger. "Be home by midnight and not a minute later. Understand?"

"Yes, sir."

Dad looks at Wyatt. "I won't make your decision for you, but are you sure you're being smart right now?" He arches his eyebrows in challenge.

Stay home. Stay home. Stay home!

Wyatt keeps a stern expression and doesn't look at me when he claims, "I'm sure."

A knife slashes my heart.

Dad looks at him as if he doesn't believe him but only says, "Your choice."

"Let's get out of here," Jagger mutters, exiting the room.

I want to beg Wyatt not to go, but he turns and follows my brother out of the house.

The door slams shut, and my insides curl.

How could he go to Chelsea's?

He was going to kiss me.

He didn't.

But he was going to.

He still chose to go to Chelsea's instead of staying home with me.

"Willow, do you want to watch *Roped In* tonight?" my younger sister Paisley asks.

It's my favorite reality show, but I can't stomach any romance right now. "No. I'm going to bed."

"What? Travis is going to choose between Carley and Deserie!" she chirps.

"I don't care. Night," I offer.

Mom puts her hand on my forehead. "Are you sick?"

"No. Just tired. It's been a long day. Night." I hug her, then Dad, and climb the stairs.

I shut my bedroom door, slip my shorts and tank top on, and slide under the covers. I press my face into the pillow, replaying what happened in the barn. Whenever I get to the part where my brother interrupted us, I get angrier.

The room slowly grows dark with the sunset. The only light is from the quarter moon, which barely provides enough illumination to see by. I turn and look at my alarm clock.

11:45

Where are they?

He's with Chelsea.

Huffing out a breath, I get out of bed and go to the window. Staring out at the dark yard, I cross my arms, hating my unfair situation.

A minute before midnight, my brother's truck rolls through the gate. It stops in front of the house and the lights turn out. Jagger gets out of the passenger seat.

Wyatt opens the driver's door, but he moves slowly. Even in the faint glow of the moon, his pain is noticeable.

When they disappear under the front porch, I return to bed. A few moments later, I hear the creak of the guys walking down the hall and then their doors closing.

I slide farther under my covers and close my eyes, but I can't sleep.

A half hour passes and then my door opens. Wyatt's low murmur hits my ears. "You awake, sugar?"

My pulse leaps in my neck. I sit up in bed, whispering, "Yeah."

He carefully closes the door, creeps over, and points to the bed. "Slide over."

I obey, freaking out at the thought that we'll get in trouble but also shocked he's here.

He slides under the covers with a grimace.

"You're still in pain," I fret.

He faces me and puts both hands on my cheeks.

My breath catches.

The dim light coming in through the window makes his eyes look more all-knowing. I swear he can see every thought in my head.

My cheeks flame under his hands.

He moves his lips an inch from mine. "I didn't drink tonight."

"Is that why you drove?"

"Yep."

"Congratulations," I quip, still a little salty he went to Chelsea's.

His lips twitch. "Ask me why I rode over a bumpy dirt road with my ass bruised up and didn't try to drink away the pain."

The blood hums in my veins. "Okay. Why?"

He strokes his fingers over my face, pushing back my hair and not blinking, like he's in a trance. "I forgot to give you something. And I wasn't going to be intoxicated when I gave it to you."

My butterflies wake up. "Oh?" I hold my breath.

He studies me for so long that my entire body singes with the heat from his stare.

"Wyatt—"

He cuts me off with his mouth brushing against mine gently before parting my lips with his tongue. His hand slides to the back of my head, possessively holding my neck so I can't escape.

Not that I ever would.

His tongue rolls against mine like he's savoring me and has all the time in the world to do it.

I press my palm against his chest, feeling the rapid beat of his heart, but it's thumping harder than it was earlier in the barn.

"No way," he mumbles against my lips.

I kiss him more, then ask "What?" before diving back into his mouth.

He tugs me closer, answering, "No way you haven't kissed anyone before."

I still. "Why do you say that?"

He grins. "Because you kiss like you want me to forget my own name."

A ball of giddiness rolls through me. "I do?"

"Yeah. So give me some more before I have to sneak out of here," he orders, then tugs me tighter to him.

10

Wyatt – Age 20

Two Years & Seven Months Later

Christmas Eve

ucky spits his tobacco on the ground. The glint in his eye no longer shows doubt.

There's only respect.

This is it.

This is my ride.

Blackvein snorts and grunts.

Adrenaline floods every inch of my body, preparing me for what I've done fifty-six times in the last seven months.

Every time, Blackvein's bucked me off. Each time, I assess what I did wrong and come back to try again with more determination. Yesterday, I held on for seven and a half seconds. I was so close, I could taste victory.

So today's my day.

"You got this, Wyatt!" Willow cheers.

I glance over, feeling an extra wave of nerves. A cold gust sweeps the ranch, sharp and sudden. Her dark hair lifts with the wind, and she pulls her jacket tighter around herself.

This morning at breakfast, she made a big deal about needing to go to town for more gifts. She got her license but hasn't gotten a car yet. So I told the Cartwrights I'd take her to town to finish her Christmas shopping after practice. It worked like a charm, and now we have some time together, albeit not quite alone yet.

But there was another reason I was happy she came today.

I *need* her to see me master this.

She's rooted me on and picked me up on my bad days, so I want to prove to her, as well as myself and Jax, that I can do this.

"Ready?" Bucky asks.

I pull my glove on, grip the braided leather, and squeeze my thighs tight against Blackvein. I dig my spurs into him for anchor points and put my other hand in the air.

The gate flies open.

Blackvein rushes out, bucking in circles and trying to throw me off.

I grip the rope for dear life, and a cloud of dirt grows around me. My heart bangs into my chest, and I count inside my head.

One Texan.

Two Texan.

Three Texan.

Four Texan.

Five Texan.

Six Texan.

Seven Texan.

Eight Texan.

The horn blares.

Holy shit! I did it!

A new wave of adrenaline courses through my veins at the next test I face.

I have to get off him before he kills me.

Blackvein bucks, and I push off his body, making a clean escape and landing on my feet. I rush toward the safety zone as Bucky and Matrix lead Blackvein farther away from me so they can lasso him.

"Whoo hoo!" Willow cheers, jumping up and down next to Jax.

Pride swells on his expression under the wide brim of his hat. He chews on his toothpick and pumps his fist in the air. "Atta boy!"

"You did it!" Willow shouts.

My heart continues hammering like a war drum. My muscles twitch with fatigue and leftover fight. I exit the ring, just barely resisting touching my girl, who beams, making my victory that much sweeter.

Jax slaps my shoulders. "Now, that's the way to ride a bull!"

"Told you today was my day! When can I get on Whiplash?" I ask.

He chuckles. "Slow down, son. Enjoy your victory for a moment."

But I can't. I'm one level from the difference between an amateur wanna-be and a real rider who gets paid. I ask, "What about tomorrow?"

Jax chuckles again. "It's Christmas tomorrow. And besides, you gotta go a couple more rounds with Blackvein before you're ready for Whiplash."

"What? No. I'm ready," I insist.

He shakes his head. "You're not. You're close, but there's more to learn from Blackvein."

"Coach—"

"Don't argue with me. When you're ready, I'll be the first to tell you," he interjects in a don't-argue-with-me tone.

My adrenaline level plummets, and disappointment replaces it. I clench my jaw and look away.

I need to get into the big leagues. There's nothing else for me, and I can't live off the Cartwrights forever.

Willow puts her hand on my bicep. She softly says, "You did awesome. Don't worry. You'll be on Whiplash soon."

I meet her gaze, seeing nothing but understanding there. She's the only one who truly gets me.

"Listen to the little lady. Besides, nine times out of ten, sisters are right, and brothers are wrong," Jax claims.

I cringe inside, wanting to correct him about our relationship, but I know I can't. Over the last seven months, Willow and I have been all over each other. But I still haven't taken her virginity. I don't know why. I want to. Maybe it's the thought of what Jacob, or her brothers, will do to me if he finds out. But something keeps making me take my time with her.

It's getting harder, though. Every time we get close, I back off, but I have to force myself not to talk her into it.

Willow's lips twitch. "You're a very smart man, Coach. I'll remind

Wyatt of that when he forgets." She smirks at me, and my cock hardens.

My sassy girl's going to see who's in charge.

"You're close," Jax reiterates, then nods toward my Bronco. "Go on and get out of here. It's Christmas Eve. Enjoy your holiday."

"Merry Christmas," Willow offers.

"You too, little lady. Please keep him in line for me over the next few days. Don't let him party too hard. I don't need him coming back here with a hangover," he says.

She grins. "Don't worry. I'll make sure my brothers don't corrupt him."

"You do that," Jax states.

I groan. "Come on, Willow. Let's get going. Merry Christmas, Coach." I shake his hand.

He holds on to it longer than I expect, and tells me, "You did good, kid. A few more times, and you'll get your ride on Whiplash."

"Yes, sir," I reply, still not pleased he isn't my next ride but able to appreciate the eight seconds I stayed on Blackvein.

Jax adds, "You're close, Wyatt. Real close."

Excitement floods my veins. I try to stay cool, and nod. "Enjoy your holiday. Let's go, Willow." I hold myself back from touching her as I walk her to the passenger side. I open her door. Any gentleman would do it for a lady, so it's one thing I never worry about.

She bats her lashes and slides inside, and her face beams with happiness.

I feel the same. It's hard not to when I'm around her. We've figured out how to act around others and hide our affection for each other, but she makes me so happy. Every moment I spend with her, whether alone or with others, makes me feel giddy.

I get into the Bronco, start the engine, pull out of the gates, and slide my hand on her thigh. I turn toward her and waggle my eyebrows, stating, "Told you today was the day!"

She claps, chirping, "Yay!"

"I'm glad you were here to see it," I admit, and warmth fills my chest.

She beams brighter. "Me too."

I pick up her hand, kiss the back of it, then lace my fingers through hers. With one hand on the wheel, I refocus on the road. "Where do you want to go for shopping?"

"Oh, I had some other plans," she says.

I glance over at her.

She shoots me a coy smile.

A fluttery weightlessness dances under my skin. The space near my zipper disappears. I lean closer, lowering my voice. "Want to fill me in?"

She smirks. "Not really. You can return to the ranch but enter from the backside."

I cock an eyebrow. "Sugar, what do you have up your sleeve? And why do I feel like I'm in trouble?"

She bites her lip, and her cheeks flush.

I groan, muttering, "You're going to be the death of me."

She giggles and turns up the radio.

Christmas music blares through the truck, and she sings most of the way back.

I turn down several dirt roads and then get to the ranch's back gate. It's hardly ever used. I pull in front of it and park. "What now?"

Willow pulls a key out of her pocket and dangles it before me. "Duh. We unlock the gate."

I chuckle. "Okay, sugar."

She exits the Bronco, unlocks the gate, and opens it.

I drive through and stop.

She shuts the gate and puts the padlock back on before hopping back into the truck.

"No one will know we were here."

My curiosity is killing me. "And we're here because…"

She raises a brow. "Drive to Ashpost."

My pulse quickens. "The old cabin?"

"Yep."

"And what are we doing once we get there?"

She shyly smiles. "I'm giving you your Christmas present."

I stare at her blankly.

She tilts her head. "You don't want your present?"

"I didn't bring yours. I didn't know we were exchanging gifts right now."

She giggles and nudges me. "Don't worry. You can give me mine later."

"You sure?"

"Yeah. Unless you don't want your gift?" She tosses me a sad expression.

"Didn't say that, sugar," I answer with a kiss to her hand, then go through the woods on the dirt path until we arrive at the one-room log cabin. It was the first house the Cartwrights ever built several generations ago. The grass is higher than it should be. The faded exterior needs a paint job. A storm blew out all the windows but the one over the kitchen sink, and Jacob boarded that one as well, figuring it would eventually get destroyed when the next storm came.

I park the Bronco. "What now?"

"We go inside, silly."

I glance at the battered cabin, asking, "Didn't your dad say he was tearing this down?"

"It was our great-great-great-granddaddy's first home. Mom said Dad has to restore it and not rip it down," she announces.

"That's going to be hard. I agree with your dad. It's a safety hazard," I claim.

She leans closer and turns her head, challenging, "Are you scared to go inside?"

I scoff. "Of course not. I just don't want you to get hurt."

"Why would I get hurt?"

"There's a few spots in the floor that are rotting. And that's what I remember from several years ago when I was here last. Who knows what additional damage there is."

She touches my upper thigh, teasing, "Don't worry, Wyatt. I'll protect you from the floorboards."

"Cute."

"Come on," she urges, and flings open her door, sliding out of the SUV.

I follow suit, then step beside her on the porch, where a board snaps.

I jump back, pulling her with me. "Whoa!"

She curls into me and looks up. "Whoops."

"Willow, is there a reason we have to go in here? I can't guarantee you it's safe," I caution.

"Do you want your gift?" She widens her eyes and pretends to pout.

I sigh. "Of course. But I don't want you to get hurt."

"I won't. Come on. We just have to be careful," she insists, and takes a step forward, pulling my hand.

"Let me go first." I step in front of her and cautiously test each board, putting my weight on it before I allow her to. When we reach the door, I open it and step inside the dark room, ordering, "Don't come in yet."

"Why?"

"I need to make sure it's safe."

She scoffs. "I was here last week, silly. It's fine. The bad boards are marked, remember?"

I glance inside. It's so dark, I can barely see the red X marks on the wood. "Why were you here by yourself?"

"For your present."

"You shouldn't be out here by yourself," I scold.

She shuts the door, and the darkness surrounds us. She slides her arms around my waist and tilts her chin up. "Wyatt. Chill out."

"You could have gotten hurt. You—"

She puts her finger over my lips. "Stop freaking out. Now, tell me you want your gift."

I sigh, trying to relax. I have no idea what her gift is, but she obviously put a lot of thought into it. And no one's ever surprised me like this before, so as worried as I am, I'm also digging it.

She adds, "Please go back to being my cool boyfriend."

I chuckle, slide my arms around her, and cup her ass. "Okay, sugar. I'll be cool since I love you."

She gapes at me.

My heart pounds wildly in my chest and sweat beads on my forehead.

Did I just say that out loud?

Silence fills the tiny cabin. She holds her breath.

Don't be a pussy.

I slide my hands over her cheeks. "Aw, hell. I said it, and it's true. I love you, and I should have told you sooner." My pulse beats hard against my neck.

Time seems to stand still.

"Well, say something," I blurt.

She tugs my head toward her and kisses me. "I love you too."

I exhale dramatically and tease, "Damn near kissed the dirt, but it looks like we made it."

She laughs.

I kiss her some more.

She retreats. "Want your gift?"

"Yes. Please. The suspense is killing me," I admit.

She pulls a handkerchief out of her pocket. "I have to put this on you."

"Really? But it's already dark in here."

"Yep. Bend down so I can secure it," she orders.

I obey, and she covers my eyes with the cotton.

"Tell me if you can see anything," she says.

"Nope. It's blacker than night."

"Good. Now, don't move," she instructs.

"Be careful. It's too dark to see a lot of the X marks," I warn.

"I'm lighting a candle, so stop acting like a sissy," she teases.

I chuckle again. "All right."

Several minutes pass, and then sounds of Christmas music fills the room.

I hum along for two songs.

Willow says, "Okay. You can take off the blindfold now."

I tug at the handkerchief, blink a few times, and when my vision clears, my heart practically stops beating. I mumble, "Sweet mercy."

Candles are lit all over the cabin. A string of Christmas lights hangs over the oak mantel with garland. Willow's in nothing except a red and silver bra and matching panties. A huge bow wraps around her torso. She's got a Santa hat on, and her long, dark hair hangs in curls. Her back's against the headboard, and her legs stretch across the mattress, slightly bent at the knees.

My mouth waters. I swallow hard, unable to decide what part of her to look at.

She pins her blues on me. In a nervous husk, she asks, "Do you like your Christmas present?"

I grind my molars, unable to move, my cock throbbing in my denim.

She tilts her head, looking worried. "Was this a dumb idea?"

"What? No!" I reply, snapping out of my trance. I take two steps and sit down on the thin mattress. "You look... Damn, sugar. I can't even think right now."

Her lips twitch, and her gaze burns brighter.

I circle my fingertips on her stomach, unable to keep my focus on any one area of her body.

"You're making me nervous," she admits quietly.

Get a grip, I scold myself.

I lean closer to her and put my hand on her cheek. I brush my lips against hers and state, "You don't know how gorgeous you are, sugar."

I can sense her anxiety when she takes a deep breath and asks, "So, what do you want to do with your gift?"

I gape at her.

She arches her eyebrows.

"Be clear with me right now, because my brain isn't working well. At least, not the right one," I state.

She puts her hand over her smile.

I continue, "Are you telling me what I think you're telling me?"

She slowly nods, affirming, "Yeah."

My eyes widen, then my brain short-circuits for a moment. The muscles tighten in my jaw, hands, and thighs. It's like my body's trying to hold back, but it's barely working.

I swallow hard. "So, to be clear—"

"I'm giving you my virginity, Wyatt," she confirms.

My pulse pounds like a hammer between my ears. I stare at her.

She reaches for my hand and quietly asks, "Do you not want it?"

I shake my head and blink a few times. "No. That's not it."

"Then what is it?" Her question comes out shaky.

I stroke her hair for a moment to collect my thoughts.

"Wyatt?" She bites her lip.

"I want to make sure that you're 100 percent sure."

"I am."

"Are you? Because I don't want you to regret me."

She slides her hands over the sides of my head. "I could never regret you, Wyatt."

"No?"

"No," she firmly says.

Another moment passes, but then there's only one thing to do. I kiss her. It's slow. Deliberate. And deep. Because I've been starving for this.

She melts against me. Or maybe I'm the one who melts against her. Her breath hitches as my fingers tease the curve of her jaw, and she pulls at my shirt.

I put my arms up, and she tears it off me, then her lips return to mine with hunger. She reaches for my belt buckle, and I want to give in, but I grasp her wrist and pull back so she's forced to look at me.

"What's wrong?" she frets, out of breath.

"Sugar, we're not doing this quickly. I'm going to take my time so I can watch."

"Watch?" she asks.

I nod. "Yes. I'm going to watch you break for me. And when you cling to me, begging, I'm going to ruin you some more. You're never going to want another man inside you. You were already mine, but there's no going back after this. And I'm going to remember every moan." I tuck a lock of her hair behind her ear, then continue, "Every cry. Every way you scream my name."

She inhales sharply with her eyes going wide.

I push her back on the bed and cage my body over hers. I slide my tongue into her mouth and slowly tease her while gliding my knuckles over the curve of her stomach.

She whimpers in my mouth. Her body quivers under me.

"That's right, sugar. You're mine," I murmur, then rise off her, sitting up.

I pat my thighs, ordering, "Get up here so I can unwrap my gift."

11

Willow – Age 18

The glow of the candles and string of Christmas lights make Wyatt's expression rawer. He never takes his eyes off me.

The low flutter in my belly turns into a full-blown storm brewing in my core. It pushes deeper with every breath I take. My heart knows what's coming, or at least what I think it'll be like with Wyatt, yet it doesn't eliminate my nerves.

We've waited for years. I turned eighteen a few months ago and I thought we would have done it by now. Whenever we're together, and I think it'll happen, he pulls away and says we'll wait. At first, his restraint brought me relief. Now, it's driving me insane.

So the only thing I could think to get him for Christmas that meant anything was to give him me and show him I'm ready. So here we are, and it's finally going to happen.

His low, commanding voice rolls over me like honey laced with smoke. It's a demand that oozes over my skin. "Don't be shy or keep me waiting, sugar. The decision has been made, and I'm ready to open my gift." The heated war behind his eyes makes my pulse stutter.

I rise, and he reaches for me, but then pauses.

"What's wrong?" I fret.

"You started the pill, right?" he asks.

"Yes. I did months ago. You know that."

Even with my assurance, he still looks nervous.

I blurt out, "You're making me anxious."

He slowly exhales, stroking my thigh. "I'm not prepared. I don't have a condom."

"Why do we need a condom? I'm on the pill," I remind him.

He stares at me.

My stomach flips. "Wyatt?"

"If I got you pregnant—"

"You won't. I'm on the pill," I declare.

"Willow—"

"I'm not a child."

"I didn't say you were."

I point at him. "Then stop treating me like one."

"I'm not."

I scoff. "You are. I'm on the pill. Unless you have something I need to worry about catching, we don't have to use a condom."

Tense silence brews between us.

I put my hand over his, softening my tone. "Wyatt, do you want me or not?"

He groans. "You know I'm dying to have you, sugar."

"Then don't treat me like a child," I say, then add, "And don't treat me like a fragile virgin."

His lips twitch. "Fragile virgin?"

I nod. "Yeah. Don't pretend to be someone you're not."

He arches an eyebrow.

"You're sweet but arrogant. And I love that about you. So be yourself and take me how you want me."

He takes a deep breath, cocks a smile, then reaches for me, muttering, "Then get your sexy body over me like I told you to."

Relief envelops me. I giggle, sinking my knees on each side of his hips. Then I settle into his gaze, and the storm inside me resurfaces, twirling with anticipation.

He doesn't speak or move. He keeps his grip dominant around me. Every inch between us burns as he continues to showcase his discipline, making my thighs ache.

My virgin anxiety hits a high. "Wyatt—"

"Shh," he orders, grazing his thumb over my lips and assessing me until my skin is on fire.

It feels like he looks at me forever, and tension hangs heavy in the air.

He finally breaks it, muttering, "I want a photo, Willow. Can I take one?"

I take a shaky breath. "Of me?"

He grins. "Who else would I want one of?"

Another round of nerves hits me.

"It's just for me. I'll guard it with my life," he adds.

Stop being stupid.

Wyatt wouldn't show anyone.

"I know," I say, then kiss him, and reach into his back pocket, pulling out his phone.

"Sugar, you're my dream girl," he says approvingly.

Warmth spills through me like sunshine after a storm. "I am?"

He grunts and shakes his head. "How can you question that?"

I beam brighter.

He takes his phone, swipes it open, and snaps a photo, then stares at me for a minute.

"What?" I nervously ask.

He moves me off him, then rises. He directs, "Stretch out on the mattress for me."

I bite my lip and arch an eyebrow.

He leans down until he's an inch from my face, and in a low voice says, "I want to always have access to my present, even when you're not with me."

My ego skyrockets. "So you like my gift?"

He chuckles. "You have no idea."

"Good." I slide onto my back and pose in a few positions while he takes photos.

He turns it to video. "Tell me again what you're giving me for Christmas, sugar."

My cheeks heat. I pin my eyes on him, bat my lashes, and try to sound sexy, stating, "Me."

"Damn, darlin'…you're a whole wildfire."

My cheeks hurt from smiling.

"You want me to stretch that sweet little body of yours open, sugar?" he asks, his gritty tone so low it adds to the fire.

"Yes," I reply, my heart racing. Wyatt always talks dirty to me when we get intimate, and maybe I should be offended, but I never am. If anything, I crave more. Something about being the target of his words always makes me feel special.

He reaches for my thigh and slides his palm over it, slowly moving it closer to my torso. Then he gets right between them and makes a fist, pushing them open with his knuckles.

My breath hitches.

"Yeah. I think you want me in here," he teases, slipping the delicate lace to the side and taunting me with his finger.

I whimper.

"Is that a yes?" he asks, even though he knows he doesn't have to.

"Yes," I breathe, my chest rising and falling faster.

He steps back, his finger slick with my arousal, and keeps the camera aimed at me. "Ask me nicely to make you a woman while you pull at your bow. And use my name when you answer my questions," he orders.

My butterflies turn frantic. I slowly tug at the end of the red ribbon and ask, "Will you please make me a woman, Wyatt?" The bow turns to one long strand, and I toss it to the side of my body.

He unbuckles his belt one-handed, keeping his camera hand steady as he continues to film me. "This is what you want in you, sugar?" He pushes the denim over his ass, and the buckle slams on the wooden floor, echoing in the tiny cabin. He grips his shaft, giving it a few strokes.

My mouth waters. It's not the first time I've seen him naked, but it looks larger than ever.

Will it fit inside me?

Stop being a sissy.

I stick my chin out. "Yes. I want you in me, Wyatt."

He steps closer. "You want *me* to be the first to feel you tight, wet, and begging?"

My voice shakes. "Yes."

"I can't do it, Willow," he says in a guttural tone.

My heart stalls, and I gape at him. "Wh-why?"

His eyes turn darker. "I'm not breaking you in for others, my sexy girl. I'm ruining you for all other men if I take what you're offering me. Understand?"

I exhale a breath of relief. "Good. Only you, Wyatt."

"Forever?"

"Yes." I nod.

With a look of approval, he orders, "Then take your bra off."

I swallow hard, glancing at the camera.

"I need to see my gift forever, sugar," he reminds me, then adds, "Because there will never be another time like this. But don't worry, I'll re-watch it with you too."

My cheeks flare with fire.

He chuckles. "You don't know how sexy you are, Willow. I'm going to make you see it. Trust me. Now, be the confident girl I love, and take that bra off for me."

Courage fills me. I reach behind me, unclasp the hooks, and put an arm over my bust. I slide one arm out of the strap, then the other, and widen my eyes. Huskily I say, "You want this gone, Wyatt?"

His voice hums in the air. "Don't tease me. Or you'll pay for it."

I giggle, then dangle the bra on the side of the bed. I drop it on the floor. "Oops."

Wyatt's eyes flame, and his lips curve in a tight smile. His jaw twitches, and his gaze drops to my chest.

My nipples harden from his stare.

"That's it, sugar. Even your tits are begging for me," he rumbles.

"Yeah," I agree, breathless and aching for his hands on me.

He drags his gaze to my underwear. "Now, take off those panties and show me your beautiful pussy that I've been dying to break in." He repositions himself and the camera at the end of the bed.

A hundred thousand volts of pure electricity rush through my veins. I don't argue. I try to look sexy as I shimmy out of my panties. I hold them toward him on one finger. "Why don't you keep these?"

He groans. "Perfect, sugar." He snatches them away from me and holds them to his face. He breathes deeply and groans louder, muttering, "Love my gift."

Happiness and confidence surge through me. I drop my hand to my inner thigh and innocently ask, "What now?"

He studies me, then looks around the room.

I stay silent, unsure of what he's searching for.

He finally goes to the mantel, sets the phone on it, and points it toward the bed.

Nervously, I fret, "Is that still on?"

"Of course, sugar. You didn't think I would turn it off and miss recording this moment between us, did you?"

My chest tightens. "Ummm…" I swallow hard and bite my lip.

He sits on the side of the bed, caresses my thigh, and asks, "What's the problem?"

"Well…uh…"

"You don't trust I'll protect the video with my life?" he asks.

I shake my head. "No. That's not it."

He cups my face, bends over me, and kisses me for several minutes. Then he mumbles against my lips, "What's the issue, sugar?" He stares at me.

"What… What if I'm not good for you? Maybe we should record it another time?" I ask, letting my insecurities fly out.

He grunts, and the corners of his lips twitch. "That's not possible."

"It's not?"

"No." He says it with no room to argue.

I stay quiet, still worried.

He kisses me again, then says, "I'll make you a deal."

"What's that?"

"If you don't like the video, I'll delete it. But I promise you that you will," he says.

My nerves relax a little. "Okay. Um…"

He arches his eyebrows.

I blurt out, "How many videos do you have?"

"Of you?"

My stomach flips. "No. Of you with other girls."

His head jerks backward. "None, Willow. Only you."

"Really?" I ask, his response comforting me somewhat.

"Have I ever lied to you?"

I shake my head. "No."

A soft smile curves his lips. "Then don't doubt my truth. The only video I have is this one, and it's also the only one I'd ever want to watch."

Warmth floods my chest. "Good."

He sits up and caresses my jaw. "You're gorgeous. And this is the best present I've ever gotten, and there will never be anything that comes close to it."

I beam. "I'm glad you like it."

"Oh, I do," he states adamantly.

I laugh, and more of my nerves disappear.

He picks up my hand and wraps my fingers around his erection. His voice returns to a low croon. "Now, tell me again how badly you want me to be your first so I can take what I've been dying to claim."

I circle my thumb on the tip of his cock and declare, "Please take my virginity, Wyatt."

He lightly pinches my tit and grits through his teeth, "Tell me you need it, sugar."

"I need it. So badly," I add, squeezing my thighs together.

"That's my girl," he praises, then reaches for my hips. And in a swift move, he flips so he's on his back and I'm over him.

I gasp.

His hand grips my head, and his tongue slides against mine.

I flick deeper into his mouth, weaving my fingers between his thick locks.

His hand palms my ass.

I widen my legs, and he murmurs against my lips, "I'm in charge, sugar."

I freeze. My insides burst with light. He always has to say it when we have intimate time, and it always makes me feel high.

He grips my hips, pulls my lower body toward his face, and demands, "You better ride my face and show me how much you love me."

I giggle, then gasp when he sucks hard on my clit. I have to grab the old iron headboard to steady myself.

"I'm not playing, Willow," he warns, then repositions his hands on my hips and moves my lower body over his face, licking and sucking my pussy.

"Yes," he says on a groan as I take over, grinding over him just as he's taught me.

I never had anyone touch me before him, but it only took a month before Wyatt gave me my first orgasm. Since then, he's given me too many to count, all over the ranch in our secret spots.

He squeezes my ass, and slides his large finger inside me, sucking and flicking harder.

"Oh!" I whisper. My thighs quiver, and sweat pops out on my skin. I whimper louder and close my eyes, humming from adrenaline oozing in my cells.

Wyatt's tongue lashes against me. Wicked. Wild. Unforgiving.

My knees give out, and white light bursts behind my eyelids. I cry out, "Wyatt!"

He groans, gripping me harder and not letting up.

"Wyatt! Please!" I beg, so high I'm dizzy.

He doesn't release me, only sucks me with more force.

An orgasm like I've never felt before hits me. It shatters me to pieces, and I grip the headboard harder, unsure what's flying out of my mouth as I surrender to the adrenaline.

When the endorphins calm, Wyatt flips me onto my back, grinning like he always does, and slips his orgasm-covered tongue into my mouth.

Barely breathing, I hungrily kiss him back, loving every second of our bodies wrapped around each other.

"I need you, sugar," he claims in a rumbling, low tone.

"Yes," I breathe out, ready for everything I've fantasized about doing with him.

He slides to the side of the bed, pulling me with him and positioning me so I'm straddling his hips. His fingers lace into the hair on the back of my head, and the tip of his cock teases my pussy. He holds my hip so I can't push down.

I kiss him, but he retreats an inch from my mouth.

He demands, "Tell me to ruin your innocence and make you mine."

My core is throbbing, and my voice cracks when I say, "Ruin me. Make me yours."

A deep darkness floods his expression, sending a chill down my spine. He leans into my ear and murmurs, "There's only one man you're ever going to need, and it's me." He pushes me over him, entering me.

A stinging sensation engulfs my pussy, causing my eyes to water. I gasp out his name, but it's barely audible.

He strokes my head and locks eyes with me. "Don't tease me, sugar. I need all of you."

I blink hard as the stinging lessens.

There's more?

Panic tries to overtake me.

He sternly commands, "Relax, or I'll never fit."

"I am," I claim.

He chuckles. "You're as relaxed as Snarlhide the minute the gate flies open."

My lips twitch.

"There's my girl." He deeply kisses me and then mutters, "That's it. Just kiss me."

I obey, getting lost in everything Wyatt and all the feelings he evokes whenever he kisses me like I'm his everything.

He pushes deeper into me, and it's easier to take him, with less stinging.

We kiss for a long time, and I've never felt so filled, but my veins buzz with intense, loving energy. The stinging evaporates completely, and it's just Wyatt and me.

He eventually retreats, holding my head firmly, and announces, "I knew you were sweet, sugar, but, damn, you're filthy sweet."

My body pulses around the stretch of him, slick and aching. I arch my eyebrows, breathing hard, questioning if that's good or bad.

He grunts, relaying, "Grind those hips on me, and drive me a little crazier, darlin'."

I take a deep breath.

He holds my hips tighter, shifting me on top of him until I bury my face in his neck and declare, "This feels so good."

"That's an understatement, sweetheart."

The biggest wave of courage yet floods through me. My voice thick and laced with heat, I whisper, "Then don't breathe." I drag my mouth along his jaw, then add, "Because I'm not done with you yet."

His eyes flare. His guttural groan echoes around us and vibrates in his chest.

Somehow, I take him again, only deeper and harder.

He curses beneath me like he's already gone feral. "Shit. Are you trying to make me come begging, sugar?"

I smile as we kiss, shifting my hips faster.

He digs his fingertips into my ass. "Shit, baby. Ride me like I'm your bull. Show me who I belong to."

The words "You're mine" fly out of me, and a quiver runs through my core.

"Always." He grunts, meeting my gaze, then flips me to my back. "Fuckin' hell, Willow. You're wetter than a summer storm, and trying to make me come too soon," he accuses, then thrusts hard into me.

"Oh! Wyatt!" I scream, unprepared for the sheer force and unfamiliar sensation so deep in my body.

"My wet, sexy virgin's trying to take over the reins. But you're my bull to break, sugar. And we've done it sweet, so now it's time to show you who's boss," he declares, quickening his thrusts.

"Wy—" I blink fast, trying to keep focus.

He doesn't show me any mercy. He leans into my ear, breaths hot against my skin. "You're all sweet on the outside, but you aren't fooling me. I know you want to ride me rough. Don't you?" he taunts.

I reach for his butt and tug his cheek, lifting my hips to meet his thrust. "Yes!"

"Say please," he orders.

"Please!" I beg, adrenaline attacking me.

"Tell me to break you," he demands, his face beet red, his teeth gritted.

"Break me," I plead, my voice hoarse.

"Hold on, sugar," he warns, then thrusts so hard and fast inside me that it feels like he pushed through my stomach and into my throat.

I can't think or speak. For a brief moment it's painful, then a volcano of endorphins erupts, taking me so high, it's like an out-of-body experience.

I grip him tighter to me, turning into a rag doll under him, trembling as fiercely as an earthquake and unable to see anything but the blur of the Christmas lights.

I barely hear him shout, "That's it, sugar. Take it. Take all of it." He thrusts again, then grunts and grits out, "Don't stop. Don't you dare stop. Your fucking tight little body was made just for me. I'm right there!"

"Wyatt!" I breathe, drowning in my high.

He kisses me, stealing all the air I have left, then groans. He bellows, "Shit! I'm coming, baby. I can't stop it." His cock stretches me further, and I gasp.

Each thrust is wicked. They're hard, fast, and claim every inch of my body. And then he pumps fire inside me, like a hydrant out of control. He growls, "Jesus, Willow!" and buries his face into the curve of my neck.

Several minutes pass full of short, hot breaths, beating hearts, and tangled limbs.

He kisses my throat, makes his way to my jaw, then slides his tongue into my mouth.

I drown all over again, exhausted but happy.

He finally retreats and brushes the hair off my forehead. In a serious tone, he states, "My Christmas gift is never going to compete with yours."

I smile, then I laugh, and he laughs too. We stay in the cabin for several hours, kissing, cuddling, and enjoying every moment.

When we leave to return to the main house, one thing is even more clear.

Wyatt Houston was meant to be mine.

Now and forever.

12

Wyatt – Age 20

Four Months Later

"Hey," Willow's hushed voice floats through the air.

I spin, and a grin takes over my face. "Sugar, how'd you get back here?"

She glances behind her and then shuts the dressing room door. She leans against the wood, crossing one bare leg over the other and pointing her fringy, white cowboy boot to the side. She bats her lashes at me. "I wanted to say good luck."

My cock strains against my zipper. I tease, "Are you trying to make me lose my concentration coming in here wearing those shorts?"

She smirks, slowly grazes her fingers over the edge of the cut-off denim, and innocently asks, "These old things?"

I grunt and close the distance between us. I lean over her, stopping an inch from her lips, and warn, "Be careful, sugar. I might have to skip this event and pretend you're the bull I need to ride."

She breathlessly taunts, "Don't tease me, Wyatt."

I clench my jaw, debating about what to do with her.

She takes her hand and slowly inches it up my chest, one finger at a time. She gets to my neck and stops, grazing her fingertips over my Adam's apple.

I groan, then admit, "This isn't helping my dilemma."

"What's the problem?" She tilts her head.

I slide my hand behind her head, grip her hair, and tug.

She gasps, her eyes blazing with a fire I never want to extinguish.

I close the distance between our bodies and press my cock against her stomach, murmuring, "You know the rules."

She gives me another sly look, then slips her hands around my neck, gliding her thumbs behind my ears.

Tingles race down my spine. The little room left in my pants disappears, and I press closer, reminding her, "This is my first professional shot." I release her hair.

She smiles, her expression full of pride and excitement. "I know. I came to give you a good luck kiss."

My heart thumps harder against my rib cage. I accuse, "You're getting me all riled up, sweet thang."

She smirks again, then tilts her head to the side to get under the rim of my hat. Her lips barely graze mine, and she chirps, "Okay. Good luck." She ducks under my arm and reaches for the door.

I move over and pin her against the door so her back is against my chest.

Another tiny gasp escapes from her lips.

I murmur in her ear, "I think you can do better than that."

She glances at me over her shoulder, playing innocent, and asks, "But I know the rules. We wouldn't want to break them."

I grunt and slide my hand around her waist, then drop it between her thighs. Her back arches against me, and I skim two fingers under her denim and over her silk panties. "Who said we're breaking them?"

Pink flushes her cheeks. She licks her lips and states, "Aren't you right now?"

"Tell me the rule," I demand, pressing against her clit.

She murmurs, "No sex or messing around before you compete."

I circle my finger and kiss her neck. "Why?"

Her panties dampen. She closes her eyes and breathlessly answers, "You need all your focus to stay on the bull."

I increase my speed, asking, "Then why are you in here making my cock ache like a stallion left too long in the corral?"

"Ummm… I… oh, good lord," she whispers, her eyelids fluttering.

"What did you want, sugar? Me to think about you sitting in the stands with your pussy all slick and ready for me?" I slip my fingers under her panties and glide one inside her, repositioning my thumb on her clit.

She takes a shaky breath, and her hot exhale hits my chin.

"Answer me," I order. "Is that what you wanted?"

"I… I… I…" she whimpers.

I kiss her but don't let her put her tongue in my mouth. "That's what you wanted, didn't you, sugar?" I kiss her chin.

"Yes." She barely gets the word out, then whisper-shouts, "Wyatt!" Her eyes roll, and her body breaks against mine. But I know my girl. This is the appetizer before her real high comes.

I put my free hand over her mouth as I continue playing with her pussy, mesmerized as I always am whenever I make her come. I've memorized her different expressions, but they never grow old.

She grabs my thigh and digs her nails into my chaps, her muffled sounds echoing around us.

I growl, "That's it, sugar. You sit in the stands nice and wet for me. When I finish showing everyone in this town who the new champion is, I'm going to tear up your pussy until you can't walk tomorrow."

Another incoherent noise vibrates against my hand, and her knees give out, but I've got her pinned between the door and my body. She trembles harder against me, and her eyes close. She's right where I want her, about to spiral out of control.

I tear my hand out of her shorts.

Her eyes fly open, and desperation fills them.

"Naughty girls don't get rewarded," I taunt, sticking my fingers in my mouth to lick off her taste, which only tortures my cock more.

She stares at me, taking deep, hitching breaths.

I take my fingers out of my mouth, then spin her around to face me. I order, "Now, give me a proper good luck kiss."

Her lips curve into a sultry smile. She reaches for my cheeks, slides her tongue against mine, and sets my blood boiling for several minutes.

I force myself to retreat. "You better get out of here before we get caught."

"Okay. Good luck," she offers.

I puff out my chest. "The bull needs the luck, sugar, not me."

She grins, gives me one last chaste kiss, then rises on her tiptoes. Her breath teases my ear as she whispers, "Can't wait to celebrate tonight." Then she licks my earlobe.

A buzzer goes off. I glance at the digital clock on the wall, then groan. I squeeze her ass, mumbling, "Me either. Now, get out of here."

She retreats, pinning her dazzling smile on me, then steps aside.

I inch the door open, then stick my head out to make sure no one is around. I nod for her to go, and she disappears.

I shut the door and then take a glance at myself in the mirror, the adrenaline becoming more intense than ever before. I stare at my reflection.

Devil's Backbone is a goner.

I'm going to dominate him.

Eight seconds.

The air in my lungs turns stale. My nerves vibrate. I take a final look and then head for the door. I step outside the dressing room, and see Willow exit into the arena.

"There you are!" Coach Jax booms.

I spin toward him. "Had to get ready."

"Cutting it close," he scolds.

I ignore him and move toward the rider's exit. "It's all good."

"Wyatt," he calls out.

I freeze and turn back. "Yeah?"

He taps his head. "Use it today."

"I am. I will."

"Whatever you have going on in there, clear it out," he advises.

Panic hits me. Did he see Willow?

"I'm clear," I insist.

He puts his hands on my shoulders. "Forget this is your first professional ride. It's you, Devil's Backbone, and eight seconds. Nothing else matters. Understand?"

I let out a breath laced with relief. He didn't see anything. I nod. "Don't worry. I'm good."

"You've prepared for this your entire life. But don't get cocky," he orders.

I shake my head. "I won't."

He studies me a moment, then releases me and slaps my back. "Good. Go do your thing."

I nod and walk to the exit. I open the door, and the music from the arena surrounds me. I take it all in, with another shot of adrenaline kicking in.

I'm finally here.

The nervous anxiety builds in my stomach. I survey the stands, find the Cartwrights, and try not to keep my eyes locked on Willow's for too long.

It's not time for that, I reprimand myself, then refocus on why I'm here.

Bucky and Matrix are waiting for me. The rodeo clowns and pickup men are on their horses, ready to help protect me when I jump off the bull.

Devil's Backbone snorts in the chute, unhappy he's caged in and unable to escape. But he isn't just a bull. He's a legend stitched together from fury and muscle and a storm waiting to damage everything in its path.

His thick shoulders twitch with every breath. His flanks coil tight like a spring begging to snap. A low, guttural snort pushes out of him, then again, louder, with steam curling from his nostrils.

I step closer to the gate, meeting his wild, rolling white glare.

He slams his horns against the steel, and it isn't because he's scared.

He's pissed.

Devil's Backbone was never meant to be caged and contained. His hatred is hotter than Hell, and he's ready to punish me for even thinking I can tame him, much less dare to try.

A horn blows, and the clock turns to zero.

"Time to ride," Bucky booms, then spits tobacco on the ground.

"Hold tight with your thighs," Matrix reminds me.

I nod, slide my glove onto my hand, and step up. My heart pounds so hard, it could burst through my chest cavity. I sling my leg over the angry bull, and he snorts several times.

"Eight seconds. You got this," Bucky declares.

A drop of sweat drips down my chin. I grip the braided rope and push my hat tighter on my head. My knuckles lock, and all 800 pounds of Devil's Backbone shifts, full of pure muscle and his bad mood.

I don't blink. That would break my focus. There's only my breathing, the bull, and the brutal silence right before all hell breaks loose. It's nerve-racking but one of my favorite feelings.

"Ready?" Matrix asks.

Eight seconds.

"Cut him loose!" I order, squeezing my thighs against the beast.

The gate swings open, and Devil's Backbone's fuse is already lit. He charges out of the chute, bucking and circling, angry with the need for revenge.

One Texan.

Two Texan.

Devil's Backbone thrusts his hips high into the air.

I almost go flying but catch myself, squeezing my thighs tighter.

Three Texan.

Four Texan.

Five Texan.

The bull tries to toss me again, jerking toward the right.

I hang on, bouncing up in the air, and I lose my hat. The hot air hits my sweat-soaked hair, but I stay on the beast.

Six Texan.

He thrusts harder, trying to toss me off. I keep my eyes on his horns.

Seven Texan.

Eight Texan.

The horn blows, and the cheers of the crowd fill the arena.

I did it!

The rodeo clowns barrel at me.

Devil's Backbone dips low to the left, and I release my grip from the rope and kick my legs free. I push off, avoiding his horns and hooves, and land hard on the ground, rolling in the dirt.

The rodeo clowns slide between me and the beast, trying to distract him.

I rise and run to safety, stepping through the gate.

Jax slaps my back, growling, "Hell yeah, kid! That's how you take the purse!"

The purse.

Goose bumps pop out on my skin.

I was the last rider.

The purse is mine.

I open my mouth, but nothing comes out.

Jax chuckles.

The next half hour is a daze. The committee awards me a championship buckle and $30,000.

It's the most money I've ever had in my life. I stare at my check in disbelief.

"Wyatt!" The Cartwrights shout in excitement, circling me.

The next few moments are full of back slaps, hugs from the women, and me trying not to hold Willow too long or kiss her.

But I'm torn away from her before I know what's happening. Jacob, her brothers, and Jax drag me toward the exit and into the bar, along with Bucky, Matrix, and my teammates.

I'm not twenty-one, and neither is Jagger, but Jacob and Jax hand both of us a shot of whiskey and then a beer. The bar soon fills up with riders, their coaches, agents, and sponsors.

One person after another approaches me. Several agents, a few sponsors, and people I've never met all seek me out.

It's overwhelming but exciting. Jax stays with me the entire time, collecting their business cards and helping me handle the conversations.

The drinks keep flowing, and when Jacob finally says it's time to head home, it's dark out.

I grab my belongings from the changing area and slip into my other clothes. I reach for my phone and swipe the screen.

Shit.

Willow's sent me several text messages.

> Willow: I'm so proud of you. You were amazing!

An hour after that.

> Willow: I can't wait to kiss you all night.

An hour after that.

> Willow: I'm putting on your favorite thong. I'm leaving for our spot now.

A few hours later.

> Willow: I don't know why you aren't texting me. I'm leaving so I don't miss curfew and get grounded again.

A new text pops up.

> Willow: I'm going to bed. Night.

My gut churns. I click her name and hit the call button. It rings and goes to voicemail.

"This is Willow. Leave a message. Bye." The beep hits my ear.

I slur, "Hey, sugar. I'm coming home soon. Keep those panties on and go to our spot." I hang up and glance at the check one more time before putting it in my pocket.

Thirty. Thousand. Dollars.

Another rush of endorphins hits me as I exit the building and get into Jacob's truck. "Where are the others?" I ask.

Jagger answers, "Sebastian's truck."

"Oh yeah," I say.

"What are you doing with all that cash, hotshot?" Jagger asks.

Jacob interjects, "You should be smart with it and put eighty percent of it in your savings."

Jagger groans. "Don't listen to him. That's not the last purse you'll win. You should get that truck you want."

Jacob shakes his head, advising, "Be smart, Wyatt. Rainy days come often."

Jagger turns around. "What are you going to buy?"

I shrug. "Don't know yet."

"Think before you spend. One day, you'll meet a woman you'll want to marry, and the last thing you want is to bring her into a bad financial situation," Jacob adds.

Jagger rolls his eyes, then turns up the music.

He's right. Willow's going to need a nice ring.

I'm going to make so much, it'll make her trust fund look small.

The ride goes by quickly, with Jagger and I singing most of the way. When we pull up to the house, I get out and tell Jagger, "I'm going for a walk."

"Why?" he asks.

"Need to think for a bit," I state.

"Don't let Dad rain on our parade," he says.

"He's not. I need some time by myself," I insist, then walk toward the corral, taking my belt buckle with me.

Willow will want to see it, I'm sure.

I walk past the corral and onto the trail, then veer off toward the first guesthouse, whistling and ready to see my girl.

The closer I get, the more my happiness fades. The guesthouse is dark.

Maybe she's sleeping?

I step inside, call out, "Sugar, where are you?" and then turn on the lights.

It's pointless. She isn't here. The house is empty.

I text her.

> Me: Where are you?

She doesn't answer.

Damn it!

I race back to the house, step inside, and make small talk with the others, trying to find an opportunity where it'll be safe to look for Willow.

Another hour passes, and it's torture. I finally make my escape and sneak into her room. The full moon shines through her window. I slide into her bed and put my hand over her mouth.

She jerks and then glares at me.

I chuckle quietly. "Don't be mad."

The daggers in her eyes sharpen.

I remove my hand and kiss her.

She pushes me away. "Go to your room, Wyatt."

I tug her closer. "Is this any way to treat your champion man?"

"You mean my champion man who didn't have the courtesy to text me, and let me wait for him all night?" she spouts.

I stroke her hair. "I'm sorry, sugar. I didn't have my phone. There were so many people around trying to get my attention, and I didn't get your messages until we were leaving."

"Sure."

"It's true."

She glares harder, then blinks hard.

"Hey," I softly coo, sliding my hands on her cheeks. "I really am sorry. I didn't want to be anywhere but with you. It just happened, and I didn't know how to turn the situation around."

She bites her lip.

I drag my knuckles over her cheek and tease, "You did see me win, though, right?"

She cracks a smile. "Yeah. You killed it."

I waggle my eyebrows. "I did, didn't I?"

She softly laughs. "Yeah. You were amazing."

"That's because my girl got me all riled up and ready to kill before I got on that bull," I state.

She laughs again.

I grin, but then it falls. "I really am sorry." I slip my hand under the blanket and between her legs. "I'll make it up to you if you want to give me another shot."

She can't hide her smile but tries, declaring, "I shouldn't."

I graze the side of her panties, murmuring in her ear, "I've got thirty big ones to use to really make it up to you when we can get away for the night." I kiss her neck and put my face in front of hers.

Excitement erupts on her expression.

"Don't say yes all at one time," I tease.

She giggles. "Okay. You get another shot."

I wipe my brow. "Phew. I was about to go back to the arena and let Devil's Backbone stomp all over me to put me out of my misery."

"So dramatic."

I grin. "But I can't live without you, sugar. If you ever let me go, I'll have to do it."

She smirks.

I grip the sides of her panties and tug them down. "I think I have some unfinished business to attend to."

She puts her hand on mine. "Wait."

I still.

"Were there any agents or sponsors who want to work with you?" she asks.

I can't help but smile. I nod. "Yes. It was crazy."

She strokes my cheek. Pride shines in her eyes. "I knew you would do it. Which ones?"

I kiss her, rolling my tongue against hers and pulling her tighter into me. I murmur against her lips, "I'll tell you all about it later. There's more important things to do right now."

She giggles, and I move down her body, ready to have the only thing I crave in life besides riding bulls.

Her.

13

Willow – Age 18

Three Months Later

The boxes stare at me, waiting for me to make a choice, but I'm frozen.

Eight weeks late.

What if I'm pregnant?

Dad will kill Wyatt and be so disappointed in me.

At least I'm eighteen and graduated last week.

Doesn't matter. Dad will still kill Wyatt.

I swallow the lump in my throat. I glance behind me to make sure I'm alone, then toss a box in the basket. I scurry down the aisle, turn the corner, and run into Chelsea Waverly.

"Ouch!" she blurts, her gaze going straight to the basket that I rammed right into her stomach.

"Crap, I'm sorry," I offer, moving the basket to the side to hide the test.

There's no point. Her face lights up in surprise, then twists into the same excitement she always gets whenever she finds out new gossip.

It's just my luck that after not seeing her for over a year, I'd have to run into her today.

She chirps, "Well, well, well! Who's the guy?"

"It's not for me," I lie, my face heating.

"Sure it isn't," she retorts.

"It isn't," I insist.

She puts her hand on her hip. "Then who's it for?"

"None of your business."

She grabs the test out of the basket and smirks. "This is a good one. Quick and easy. You'll know immediately if you're knocked up."

Mortified, I snatch it back and brush past her, repeating, "It's not for me." I hightail it to the counter, but she follows me.

"Then tell me who it's for," she pushes.

I spin around and point at her. "You're being nosy and rude."

She shrugs and leans closer, as if we're besties. "I thought you were a Goody Two-shoes, Willow Cartwright."

My heart pounds so hard, it hurts my rib cage. The last thing I need is for her to spread rumors all over town.

I glare at her. "Shut your mouth, Chelsea. You don't know what you're talking about, and I'm not divulging my friend's name to you."

She lowers her voice. "You can tell me. I won't say anything to anyone. Promise."

"Sure you won't," I spout, then brush past her to the self-checkout. I quickly scan the box and put it in the bag, then reach inside my purse for my wallet.

Chelsea steps next to me, asking, "Is it for one of your sisters?"

Anger fills me. I shove my card into the machine, grab the bag, and hiss, "Don't you dare talk about my sisters!"

She holds her hands in the air. "Sorry."

I warn, "Keep running that big mouth, and I'll start mistaking you for the flies I swat on my porch."

She gapes at me.

I shove past her and exit the store, going directly to my car and slamming the door. I start the engine and then pull out of the parking lot.

My pulse takes a while to return to normal. When it finally does, the previous worries come flooding back.

Wyatt and I are toast.

How will Wyatt even take this news?

He's been gone for the last two weeks. There was a huge rodeo in Wyoming. Jagger went with him, so it's been hard for us to communicate except for the occasional text messages. He should be home tonight, but I'm not sure if I should even tell him I might be pregnant. He lost his ride, and Wyatt's normally in a better mood when he wins.

My stomach somersaults like a calf in a roping pen. I pull through our gates and park. I get out, and the sound of Jagger's diesel truck fills the air.

I turn, and my stomach sours even more. Jagger parks next to my car, and they get out.

"Willow. Anything exciting happening?" Wyatt asks, dragging his eyes over my body from under the shadow of his brim.

I might be having your baby.

All I want to do is dive into his arms and forget all our problems, but I can't. I reply, "Not much."

Another truck comes barreling through the gates. Dust floats in its wake, and Jax's face comes into view. He slams on the brakes and stops next to Jagger's vehicle.

"Great," Wyatt mutters.

"Long time no see," Jagger arrogantly offers.

"Don't you give me your shit," Jax orders.

I glance at Wyatt, quietly asking, "What's going on?"

It's not the first time Jax has been upset with Wyatt or my brother. They always seem to get into some trouble when they're at the rodeos, whether Wyatt wins or loses. Dad suggested Jagger stay home, but he couldn't stop him from going.

Jax flies across the dirt and comes to a stop in front of Wyatt, accusing, "Are you stupid?"

A hint of guilt crosses Wyatt's expression, but he puffs his chest and stands taller. "Meaning?"

"Don't you sass me," Jax snarls.

"What's all the commotion about?" Dad booms.

Wyatt clenches his jaw.

What did they do this time?

I glance at my brother, but his expression is neutral, and he has the same stance as Wyatt.

Jax turns to Dad. "These two prize idiots couldn't handle losing again."

Dad scowls at my brother. "I told you no more fights."

Jagger shrugs. "Assholes had it coming to them."

Rage turns Dad's face red. He pins a glare on Wyatt. "I thought I taught you to value your career."

"I do, sir," Wyatt insists.

Dad shakes his head, searing Wyatt with disappointment.

Jax growls, "Your agent pulled your contract."

"What? He can't do that!" Wyatt states.

I feel nauseous, and I put my hand over my stomach.

Jax scoffs. "Of course he can. I told you when you signed with him that he doesn't represent riders who don't take their careers seriously."

"I do take it seriously," Wyatt claims.

Jax jabs him in the chest. "How many times have I told you not to get into trouble?"

Wyatt stays quiet, grinding his molars.

Dad turns his scolding to Jagger. "I told you not to go with him. You two can't stay out of trouble. Now look what you've done."

"It's not his fault," Wyatt interjects.

"Oh, don't think I don't know you're just as much at fault," Dad seethes.

Wyatt takes a deep breath.

Dad adds, "You're acting like your father. I thought you wanted to be a better man than him."

My defensive instincts toward Wyatt kick in, and I blurt out, "That's not fair. He's not his father."

Dad whips his head toward me. "This isn't your business. Go inside, Willow."

I don't move.

"Now," he demands in a low tone.

I toss Wyatt a glance, but he's exchanging a look with my brother.

Damn you, Jagger.

"Way to go," I mutter, passing him and stomping into the house. I go into the family room and stare out the window.

"What's going on?" Paisley questions.

"Nothing," I answer.

"Don't treat me like a baby. You, of all people, don't get to do that," she whines.

I sigh. She's right. Being the youngest of the eight siblings means Paisley gets shafted a lot, left out of the loop much of the time. I'm only a few years older, and I know what that feels like, so I reply, "I'm sorry. Jagger and Wyatt got into another fight. Jax said Wyatt's agent canceled his contract."

Paisley's mouth drops toward the floor.

I refocus on the scene outside.

"Can his agent do that?" Paisley asks.

"Jax says he can."

The air conditioner is on, so the windows are shut. I can't hear anything, but Jax says something and looks even angrier than he did before.

Wyatt responds, and it only upsets him further.

The conversation goes on for a long time. Then Jagger comes inside alone.

Paisley and I run to the door. She asks, "Is Wyatt's career over?"

"Mind your own business," Jagger grumbles, and pushes the kitchen door open.

I follow him. "What did you do?"

He opens the fridge and grabs a gallon of milk. "Once again, not your business," he states, removing the cap. He drinks half the bottle.

"Use a glass, that's gross," Paisley gripes.

He gives her an arrogant look and takes another drink.

"Eww." She huffs in disgust.

"What happened?" I push.

"Stay out of it. Both of you," he warns, then brushes past us and into the hallway.

"Jerk," I call out.

"Yep. Sue me," he responds, climbing the stairs.

I return to the window, and my mouth turns dry. Jax says something else to Wyatt, gets into his truck, and then takes off.

Dad continues to lecture Wyatt.

It feels like forever until they part ways. Dad comes into the house, and Wyatt stomps off, disappearing behind the barn.

Paisley asks, "Is Wyatt's career over?"

"That's his choice," Dad says, then asks, "Where's your brother?"

"Upstairs," I reply.

"Jagger! Get your ass down here," Dad shouts. Then he lowers his voice. "You two give us some privacy."

Paisley rolls her eyes, then goes into the kitchen. I slip out the front door and head toward the barn just in time to see Wyatt on his horse, trotting across the field toward the woods.

I go into the barn, saddle my stallion, Sassy, and run him until I catch up with Wyatt. I yell, "Hey! Wyatt!"

He turns his head and slows.

I pull up next to him.

He drawls, "Hey, sugar."

"Where's my kiss?" I tease.

He barely smiles but leans over and gives me a quick one. "You doing okay?"

I nod. "Yes. What about you?"

He clenches his jaw, keeping his gaze on mine. "I messed up."

I deeply inhale. "I kind of caught that. But you'll be okay, right? You always are."

He swallows hard.

My anxiety hits a high. "Wyatt?"

"Let's go to the lake, sugar. We'll talk there," he says.

The worst feeling I've ever had comes over me. Silently, I nod.

Wyatt makes a loud clicking noise, and the horses move forward.

We don't speak as we ride through the thick trees. The sun peeks through in several spots and then shines brightly when we exit the foliage and approach the lake.

We dismount from our horses, and Wyatt ties them to a nearby tree. Then he grabs my hand, kisses it, and steers me toward the log on the shore.

We sit, and my stomach churns as I ask, "What's going on?"

He takes a moment to gather his thoughts, digging his toe into the sand.

"Wyatt?"

He finally meets my gaze. "I really messed up this time."

I just stare at him.

He adds, "I'm sorry."

I put my hands on his face. "It's okay. We'll find you another agent."

He closes his eyes for a moment, then releases a long breath. "It's not that easy, Willow."

"Then explain it."

He stares at the water, grinding his molars, then picks up my hand, rubbing his thumb over it. He declares, "Jax said he's moving me to the Tennessee team."

My pulse shoots up so fast that I get dizzy. "What? He can't do that!"

Sounding despondent, he says, "If I don't go, I have no spot on any team."

"Then we'll find you one!" I insist.

Wyatt takes off his hat and puts it on the log next to him. He pats his thigh. "Come here."

I rise and move to his lap.

He strokes my hair.

"Don't worry. We'll find you another team."

"It doesn't exactly work like that, Willow," he claims.

"Why not? This is Texas," I remind him.

He tugs me closer to him. "I can go to Tennessee and still compete. If I find another team, I'll start at the bottom."

My anxiety eases a bit. I knew there had to be another option. I reassure him, "You'll move quickly up to where you are now. You're too good!"

He grunts. "I lost the other day."

"It's okay. You can't win every rodeo. You'll win the next one," I insist.

He sighs, shaking his head. "I don't think you understand, Willow."

"Then fill me in," I state.

He studies me, running his thumb over my jaw, then gives me several chaste kisses. He retreats and says, "If I go to Tennessee, I keep my ranking. I can win back all the money I lost, and earn my spot back on the Texas team."

The hairs on my arms rise. I angrily mutter, "I'm going to kill Jagger."

Wyatt insists, "It's not his fault."

"There's no way on God's dusty earth that isn't true, and you know it!" I declare.

In a stern tone, Wyatt claims, "I'm my own man, Willow."

"Jagger's always making you bet!"

"He doesn't make me do anything! Like I said, I'm my own man, and I make my own decisions."

My insides quiver. I glance at the water, blinking hard.

He can't go to Tennessee. Wyatt belongs on our ranch.

I'm going to kill Jagger.

I shake my head, asserting, "You can't go to Tennessee."

"I don't have much of a choice," he reminds me.

I blurt out, "I think I'm pregnant!"

Wyatt stiffens, his face going pale.

Tension builds between us. Birds chirp, the gentle breeze blows across the water, and my heart feels like it's dying. The longer we sit in silence, the more freaked out Wyatt looks.

"Say something," I whisper.

He opens his mouth, then shuts it and swallows hard.

"Wyatt?"

In a low, guttural tone, he says, "I thought you were on birth control."

"I am."

"Then how are you pregnant?" he questions.

Anger, irritation, and fear of him leaving assail me. I retort, "It's not one hundred percent effective, and you know that, Wyatt Houston!"

"Don't get nasty with me, Willow Cartwright," he says in the same tone.

I blink hard. "You don't get to do this."

"Do what?"

"Blame me."

"I'm not blaming you!"

"Are you sure about that? Feels like you are," I claim. I try to get off of him, but he tightens his arm around me.

He tugs me into his chest and holds my head against him. "I'm sorry. I'm not blaming you for anything. You know I love you."

My heart calms slightly. I sniffle. "I know you do."

"So give me a minute to process this, okay?" he says, hugging me tighter.

I don't say anything.

He finally speaks. "We need to get a test."

"I got one at the store."

"Where is it?"

I retreat from the safety of his chest and meet his gaze. He's trying to look calm, but his worry is obvious, and it freaks me out. My insides quiver, and I reply, "In my car."

"Okay. As soon as we're back, you need to take it," he asserts.

"I will."

"Good."

A moment of silence builds between us.

I blurt out, "If you go to Tennessee, I'll come with you."

His face falls. "How?"

"What do you mean?"

He chuckles sarcastically. "What would I say? *'Hey, Jacob. I knocked up your daughter. And I'm moving her to Tennessee to live in a bunkhouse with a bunch of other cowboys even though there's a no-women-allowed rule'?*"

The earthquake in my stomach intensifies. "We'll get another place."

"With what money?" he asks.

"You've won a lot," I point out.

His expression shutters, and he looks away.

Dread claws at me. My voice trembles as I ask, "How much did you lose gambling?"

He takes a minute, then finally meets my eyes. "Almost everything."

I gape at him.

He closes his eyes. "I'm sorry. We just got carried away. I didn't realize how much I'd lost until the following day."

My anger flares. I accuse, "How could you not have known?"

His voice drops into the low octave he saves when he's mad. He admits, "We were drinking a lot."

My eyes turn to slits. I hiss, "I told you Jagger shouldn't go with you!"

"It's not his fault."

"Stop defending him!" I cry out.

Wyatt's face darkens. He insists, "I'm my own man, Willow."

I stay quiet, glaring at him.

"Don't look at me like that," he says.

I look away, taking deep breaths.

He takes his finger and turns my chin so I can't avoid him. "I'll win it all back, Willow. I promise."

I don't say anything.

He adds, "But you understand why I have to go to Tennessee, right?"

Reality hits me. If he stays in Texas and has to start over, it'll take forever for him to earn what he could in Tennessee. So I say, "I have my savings. I'm sure it'll be enough for a down payment and maybe six months' worth of rent. You'll have some money to cover us after you win a few times, and I can get a job."

He scoffs. "You have college in the fall."

My pulse pounds between my ears. "I'll try to transfer somewhere out there."

He scrubs his hands over his face. "You had to apply last year. I'm sure the universities already have their freshman solidified for the fall."

"Then I'll take a year off. I can start next year," I suggest.

"No way."

"Why not?"

He groans. "Willow. You can't take off for a year. Besides, the only way I'm allowed on the team is if I live in the bunkhouse. Jax already told me the stipulations," he announces.

I cry out, "What if I'm pregnant?"

A fresh wave of tension detonates between us, sharp and undeniable.

"Wyatt!" I cry, my voice cracking.

He tugs me into him, murmuring into my hair, "Let's find out the situation before we freak out."

I pull back so he can't avoid me. "But what if I am? You'll still go?"

"I-I don't know."

"What do you mean you don't know?"

He shakes his head. "Willow, babies cost money."

"Really? I didn't know that," I bite out sarcastically.

"Well, I'm going to need to make money quickly," he points out.

Scared, I take several breaths, and ask, "So when would you be back?"

He stares at me, jaw ticking.

I barely get out, "You'd never come back?"

"No! Of course not! Don't say crazy things that aren't true!"

I relax a little, but it's short-lived.

Anger darkens his features. "You think I wouldn't take care of our baby?"

"I didn't say that."

"Sounded like it."

"I didn't mean it that way," I say.

The wind picks up, and a gust blows between us.

He rises and holds out his hand. "Let's go find out."

Nausea hits me again. I swallow down bile as I take his hand, and he leads me to the horses.

We ride back in silence, and every step toward the house increases my anxiety. When we're at the end of the trail, he directs, "You go first. I'll take care of Sassy. Tie him to the post and then go take the test. I'll meet you upstairs."

I silently follow his orders, and soon find myself peeing on the stick. I put the cap on it, take it to my bedroom, and wait.

Wyatt finally comes inside. He sits on the bed and asks, "Well?"

I pick up the stick off my desk and hand it to him. "I can't look."

He takes it, stares at it, and says, "It's just a dash. What does that mean?"

I grab it from him, glance at it, and relief fills me. "Oh thank God!"

"No baby?" he questions.

I shake my head. "No!"

He grins. "Phew. That was scary."

"Right?"

"Yeah."

"Okay. So you don't have to go, then, right?" I ask.

He gives me stricken look.

"Wyatt, you don't have to go. You can work your way back up and everything will be fine," I insist.

"You don't understand."

"I do. It's just money!"

He grunts. "Easy for you to say."

"What does that mean?"

"Look around, Willow. You've got it all. I've got nothing," he claims.

I shriek, "You have me!"

"Shh!" he reprimands, and pulls me closer. "I wasn't referring to that."

I deflate.

"I have to go," he states.

"Wyatt—"

He puts his finger over my mouth. "I'll go and earn my spot back."

I move his finger. "You can do that here."

"No, I can't. If I don't go, I might never get it back," he declares.

"That's a lie!"

"It's not! You and I both know anything can happen at any time," he reminds me.

It's true, but I also know Wyatt. And why isn't he being his normal cocky, assured self right now like he always is when it comes to riding?

"I love you," he declares.

Tears fill my eyes. "Then don't go."

He sighs and pulls me into him. "I have to."

I grasp at straws. "Then take me with you."

"I already told you the rules," he replies.

I jerk out of his hold. "Why don't you want me with you?"

A bored expression crosses his face. "Don't be crazy. Of course I want you with me, but you can't go."

"You aren't trying very hard for a man who says he wants me with him," I accuse.

His eyes turn to slits. "You're acting like a child."

I huff. "Me? You're the one who gambled all his money away and now wants to leave me."

He jerks his head backward. "Is that what you think?"

I shut my mouth, my heart racing faster.

For several moments, we stare at each other. He finally breaks, asserting, "I have no choice. I have to go."

"You do have a choice. If you go, I'm not waiting around for you," I warn.

He stands and looks down on me. "Is that the way it's going to be?"

"If you choose money over me? Yeah. It is," I say, tears spilling down my cheeks.

He studies me another moment with a challenging look, but I don't flinch. He finally replies, "I don't want to leave you, but I can't stay here. I'm sorry you can't understand the position I'm in, sugar."

A knife slices my heart, and I snap, "Don't call me sugar ever again."

He takes heavy breaths for what feels like forever, then ends up saying nothing. He turns, and walks out of my life, taking my heart and soul with him.

14

Wyatt

Present Day

The daggers from Willow's glare sink deeper into me. I try not to stare at her, but I can't help it. My cock's aching, my blood's vibrating through my veins, and every second she spends loathing me, I hate myself deeper.

A sharp, metallic, and unmistakably nostalgic clang fills the air, tearing me out of my obsession with Willow.

"I'll get it," Alexander's son, Wilder, cries out, jumping up and grabbing the receiver off the wall. "Hello, Cartwrights."

I glance at Willow again, but she won't look at me.

"Hold on a second, he's right here. Wyatt, phone for you," Wilder relays, holding the receiver out.

"Who's calling me here?" I glance at Jagger.

He shrugs.

"Maybe it's the police station," Willow mutters.

"Maybe it is," I retort, just to get under her skin, then grin at her.

She glares at me harder.

I push my chair back, rise, and go over to the phone. I grab it from Wilder and answer, "Hello?"

A gritty, old cowboy's voice comes across the line. But he doesn't just speak. His gravel-packed and sun-dried tone scrapes into my ear. It's the sound of dust-choked trails, too many cigarettes, and years of hollering over the wind.

It's a voice so ingrained in my memory that I sometimes hear it in my sleep. But now, there's a deeper rasp in his throat, like barbed wire dragging over pavement. Yet somehow, his low drawl stretches vowels like molasses on a cold morning.

Like always, when he talks, it's not just conversation. It's history. Grit spun into a voice born of broken bones, busted boots, and more regret than he'd ever admit.

It's been years since I've seen him, and after our last encounter, I never thought I'd speak to him again.

He booms, "Wyatt, I heard you made quite the commotion coming into town this time."

My chest tightens. Jax McCoy was clear he was finished with me. No more coaching. No more advice. No more bailing me out of the consequences of my bad decisions.

I turn toward the wall to avoid the stares of the Cartwrights, and quietly admit, "Surprised you're calling me."

He starts to chuckle but ends up coughing. I hold the phone several inches from my ear, cringing from the harsh sound. When he finally calms, he declares, "I think it's time we talked, son."

Son.

I used to be okay with him calling me that. Now, it turns my gut rancid. I stare at the crawling vine pattern on the wallpaper. My tone is as sour as my gut when I reply, "What about?"

I can hear his arrogant smile. "Best we speak of these things in person. Don't you think?"

My heart pounds hard against my chest. Besides Jacob, Jax was the closest thing I had to a father. But he was also my coach, and I disappointed him.

It wasn't just when he moved me to the Tennessee team that got us to where we now reside. Years of stirring up trouble, making bad decisions, and not listening to him, finally led him to release me from his teams.

But my years of looking for his approval are over. At least, I thought they were. Yet the slow boil of need perks in my stomach, and I loathe it almost as much as I hate Willow detesting me.

The Cartwrights always preached to forgive and forget, yet I've never been good at it. Whether I was right or wrong, Jax tossed me aside. Maybe I deserved it. Maybe I didn't. But he knew I had nothing except riding and the Cartwrights, and he tried to take both of those things away from me.

Luckily, after he kicked me off his teams, the rival team in Tennessee was happy to sign me. But now I have nothing, and the last thing I want to do is go back to Jax with my tail between my legs.

He taunts, "What's wrong, son? Bull caught your voice in the dust?"

I clear my throat. "I'm pretty sure there's nothing for us to talk about."

"Ah, but there is. From what I hear, you've got nowhere to go. All the connections you made won't touch you."

The air grows thick around me. I growl, "You know nothing about my business, so stay out of it."

He chuckles. "Don't get your panties in a twist."

Irritation fills me. "What do you want?"

"Seems to me that you don't have a lot of options right now. We'll talk when you get here."

Confused, angry, and curious, I close my eyes and grit my teeth, hating that he's right.

What does the old man want?

"I'll see you in an hour," he says, and hangs up before I can say anything else.

Frustration coils in my gut. I hang up the phone, take a moment to collect myself, and then turn.

Jagger asks, "Who was that?"

The saliva in my mouth evaporates, and the sour taste intensifies. "Jax."

Jagger arches his eyebrows. He's the only one who knows the full story about what happened between Jax and me. He asks, "Really?"

I nod. "Yes."

The phone rings again. I reach for it. "Cartwrights."

"Need to talk to Willow," Jax demands.

My eyelids instantly lower to slits. "What for?"

He asserts, "It's none of your business, son."

I anxiously glance at Willow, then say to her, "Jax wants to talk to you."

She's surprised at that, but she stands and steps toward me. She avoids my gaze and takes the phone from me. In a sweet voice, she answers, "This is Willow."

I stare at her.

She pretends not to notice me, but a flush rises in her cheeks. She listens and then questions uncomfortably, "What do you mean?"

What does he want with her? I wonder.

She glances at me uneasily and states, "I'd rather not."

Though the way she's looking at me isn't positive, just having her attention on me causes a new round of chaos in my pants.

Her expression turns hard, and her tone matches it when she says, "Not to be disrespectful, but that's a bad idea, Jax."

What is?

I pin a questioning look on her.

She glares harder at me and then turns toward the wall, shaking her head. She must cave to his request because she sighs and tells him, "Okay, I'll see you in an hour."

A spark of hope lights in me, but I don't know why.

Willow hangs up but doesn't move for a moment, releasing a deep breath.

A little too eager, I question, "Are you coming with me?"

Exasperated, she answers, "Yeah, apparently I am."

I attempt to hide my excitement as I ask, "What does he want?"

She shrugs. "How do I know? And I thought he wrote you off."

The silence of those behind us is deafening.

Shame fills me as I stare at her.

She softens but doesn't apologize. "You don't have any idea what he wants?"

"No." I shake my head.

"Well, this ought to be fun," she snarks, then retakes her seat at the table.

"If Jax wants to see you, it has to be good news," Jagger says, and I wish he'd shut up.

Everything he's saying today seems to irritate me, whether it's about his sister or my old coach. They're both sore spots, and his comments are just rubbing salt in my wounds.

Willow smirks. "Maybe Wyatt owes him money too, and he wants to collect."

I blurt out, "I told you I'd pay you back, and I will."

"Sure you will," she mutters.

"He will. Stop being nasty," Jagger scolds.

"Stay out of my business," Willow reprimands.

He replies, "Then get over yourself."

"Jagger..." I warn.

"Enough," Jacob interjects.

Everyone goes quiet.

"Finish breakfast," Jacob orders.

Within a few minutes, normal breakfast conversation resumes. We finish eating, but I'm not paying attention to what's going on around me.

The last time I saw Jax, he made it clear he never wanted to see me again. He's not the type to have a change of heart. So I'm not sure why he's insisting I go to his place.

And why does he want Willow to come?

I hold the dining room door open for Willow, teasing, "Didn't know you and Jax were buddy-buddy."

She turns a scathing look my way. "You've got a lot of nerve."

I chuckle. "I was just teasing. You don't have to get so upset."

"Just keep your comments to yourself, Wyatt." She pushes past me and into the foyer.

I follow her, put on my jacket, and step out into the cold, blistering air.

I pace near the porch. Jax is the last person I thought would be on that line. And I can't help but feel like I'm stepping into a trap.

Willow finally comes out, bundled up, and continues to ignore me. She trudges through the snow and over to an SUV.

I hold out my hand. "Give me the keys."

She scoffs. "No. I'm driving."

The snow blows around us. "It's bad out. You should let me drive," I insist.

"I'm more than capable of driving through snow. Now, get in or I'm leaving you," she warns, then opens her driver's door, and slides into the seat. She slams the door hard.

I begrudgingly get in the passenger side, then drawl, "You've lost your manners, sugar."

"Don't call me sugar," she spouts, and turns on the engine.

Her perfume flares inside the cab. I slide the seat toward the back with a groan, confessing, "You always smelled so damn good. Are you trying to punish me more?"

She doesn't look at me, keeping her eyes on the road ahead of her, her fingers gripping the wheel as she accelerates. She orders, "Stop acting like I mean something to you."

"You do. Always have and always will," I assert.

She scoffs. "Can you stop saying stuff like that?"

"You mean the truth?"

She blinks hard, staring at the snowy road.

I turn toward her and question, "So you're never going to forgive me?" My voice is as hollow as my heart feels.

She floors it through the gate a little too fast, and the SUV skids.

"Whoa, slow down," I say.

"Don't tell me what to do," she replies and then turns the music up louder so neither of us can hear the other speak.

I turn it down. "Willow—"

"Don't start with me, Wyatt. Just don't," she says, her voice shaking.

I freeze.

She blinks rapidly, keeping her attention on the road, and an ill feeling attacks me.

I soften my voice. "I'm sorry."

"I don't want to hear it," she says with more control.

I study her for several moments and then decide to honor her wishes. "Okay."

A long time passes. The roads are treacherous, and I hate sitting in the passenger seat while she drives. My job is to protect her, not let her navigate the snowy conditions.

Willow finally asks, "You really have no idea what Jax wants?"

I shake my head. "No. You don't either?"

"Nope." She cautiously glances at me, inquiring, "When did you talk to him last?"

The pit in my stomach grows. I grind my molars, breathing for a few moments, and then I answer, "A couple of years ago. We were up in Montana."

"And?" she pushes.

"I don't want to talk about it," I state, then turn to look out the window.

She scoffs. "You're really something else."

I look back at her. "What does that mean?"

She keeps her hands tightly gripped on the wheel. "It means that whenever anything gets tough, you run or you don't talk about it. You hide from it."

I grunt. "Where's this coming from?"

She huffs. "Really?"

"I'm not looking to fight, Willow. Let's not talk right now," I assert, leaning back in my seat and tipping my cowboy hat over my face.

"Freaking typical," she mutters.

I remain silent, trying to calm the shaking inside me. My last encounter with Jax is as fresh as if it were yesterday. No matter how much I try to push it away, I can't.

His wrinkled, sun-worn face is clear as day in my mind. The disappointment in his expression as he wags his finger at me. His crackling voice announcing, *"We're done. Don't ever reach out to me again."*

The more I try to push it away, the more insistent it becomes. Hurt and guilt eats at me.

The car slows, and I peek out from under my cowboy hat. As the gate comes into view, I put my seat back up and adjust my hat on my head.

Memories of thousands of practice sessions and hours spent on the ranch pummel me. It's bittersweet, and as much as I want to lean into it, I also want to run.

Willow parks where we always used to. I get out of the SUV, and she jumps out before I can come around and open her door.

Jax is on the porch, leaning against a post, finishing his cigarette. He snubs it out, curls his fingers in the air, and orders, "Let's talk inside." He turns, opens the door, and disappears before we get there.

I grit my teeth and close my fist, wishing I could redo a lot of things in my past, but I can't. I never thought I'd hear from the old man again. When he gave up on me, it wasn't with an emotional statement one could take back. It was a true declaration and position of finality.

Which is why this is so nerve-racking. Plus, I don't like not knowing why he insisted on Willow being here, even if I do like getting to spend time with her.

I motion for Willow to go first. She stomps past me up the stairs, and I follow. We step inside.

Jax stands in his kitchen, pouring a cup of coffee. He locks eyes with Willow. "Darlin', how have you been?"

"I'm good," she says in a neutral tone, the questions I'm sure she has, barely being held back.

"Coffee?" he offers.

"No, thanks."

He finishes pouring the hot liquid into the mug, takes a few sips while staring at me, then finally sets it down.

"Wyatt. Didn't know you were going to be in town."

"That makes two of us," I drawl.

He points at the table. "Let's sit down."

My anxiety gets worse, but I don't argue with him. I pull a seat out for Willow, but she ignores it and selects another one.

I sit next to her and direct my question to Jax. "What's this about?"

"Glad we're going to avoid the niceties," Jax quips.

I bark, "Sorry. Did you want them?"

"Wyatt!" Willow scolds.

"What? He brought us here, and now he wants to play games. I don't have time for this," I argue.

A quiet laugh rumbles from his chest.

"Glad we can amuse you," I mumble.

A wicked grin curls his lips.

"Cut the games, Jax. Why are we here?"

"Wyatt," Willow reprimands again.

I glance at her, insisting, "I'm not a kid anymore. He needs to tell us why we're here." I pin Jax with a challenging gaze. "Spit it out. I've got work to do."

He arches his eyebrow. "Oh? What work is that?"

Embarrassment and shame wash over me. I try not to let it show, but my defenses rise. I snarl, "Is this what this is? You're going to rub it in my face that you know I'm in a bad situation with my career?"

He grunts. "No, I'm going to offer you an opportunity."

"What do you mean?"

His wicked grin pulls wider, slow as honey and twice as dangerous. It tugs at one side of his mouth first, trying to hold back. Then, it spreads, full and cocky; the kind of smile that knows it's trouble. His eyes glint, sharp and steady, like he's got all the time in the world to wreck your plans and enjoy every second of it.

I force myself not to shift in my seat. My pulse bangs against my brain.

He says, "The way I see it, you don't have any options right now."

"Once again, you don't need to state the obvious," I growl.

He points at me. "That mouth of yours has always gotten you in trouble."

I take my cowboy hat off and put it on the table, then run my hand through my hair. "Jax, what is it that you want?"

He leans closer. The rasp in his voice grits deeper. "It's not what I want. It's what I'm going to offer."

The hairs on my arms rise. I clench my jaw, cross my arms, and sit back. I put my ankle over my knee, cautiously asking, "And what would that be?"

Arrogantly, he states, "Well, Willow owes me a favor."

My head jerks toward her. "Why do you owe him a favor?"

"None of your business," she hisses.

"It is my business, so explain," I declare.

"No, it's not your business," she insists.

I turn back toward Jax. "Explain."

"Seems like the little lady doesn't want you to know her business. I'd rather we keep it between her and me." He winks at her.

I curl my fists tight. "I swear to God..."

He holds up his hand. "Calm down."

I take a few breaths, waiting.

He doesn't answer, the tension growing.

I finally slam my fist on the table. "Tell me whatever it is you want, Jax. I'm not into your games. Why am I here?"

"Ah, that's what I wanted to see."

"What are you talking about?"

"I wanted to see if you still had it in you."

"Had what in me?" I firmly demand.

He drawls, "The drive. The fire. The thing that makes you a bull rider."

"Of course I have what makes me a bull rider. Why wouldn't I?" I question, stepping into his trap.

"Well, you've made some dumb choices lately. Makes me think you don't want to be a rider anymore," he claims.

"Okay, I'm done here." I rise and move toward the door.

"Get back here," Jax orders.

I whip around. "I don't take orders from you anymore, old man."

"Sit down," he asserts in his no-nonsense tone.

I stay where I am.

"Wyatt, sit down," Willow softly orders.

I glance at her.

"Please, sit down," she says, and points at the chair.

I still don't move. My heart pounding, I press her for an answer. "I want to know why you owe him a favor."

She sighs, confessing, "He helped me solidify my last big rider. I told him I'd owe him one, that's it."

I don't speak. I don't like her owing anybody anything, and especially not Jax. Once, I had nothing but good feelings and respect for him, but now, I'm not so sure.

"Sit down so I can tell you why you're both here," he demands.

I don't look at him, continuing to stare at Willow.

"Please, just sit down," she says, exasperated.

I realize that as much as I want to leave, I'm also curious about what he wants from me, and especially Willow. So, begrudgingly, I move back to the table and take a seat.

15

Willow

Wyatt finally sits. I anxiously tap my fingers on the table, waiting for Jax to tell us why we're here.

I knew the day would come when Jax would call in his favor. I never imagined it would involve Wyatt, though.

When I made the deal, I needed to sign that rider. Jax was the only one who could convince Beau Hart to sign with me. It was worth making a deal with Jax.

Unfortunately, two months later, Beau got bucked off a bull and fell the wrong way. He had several operations, including on his hips, which ended his career.

And I'm no fool. The deal I made with Jax sticks, even though my rider can no longer compete. So I ask, "Can you get to the point?"

"Do I have to spell it out?" Jax asks, his lips twitching. He glances at Wyatt, then me, the crinkles around his eyes intensifying.

My instincts kick in, and everything becomes clear. Panicked, I declare, "No."

"You don't have a choice," Jax reminds me.

"Hello. Someone want to fill me in?" Wyatt whines.

Rolling my eyes, I turn toward him and huff. "He wants me to be your agent."

Wyatt jerks his head backward.

Jax chuckles. "Well, don't look so shocked. I'm surprised you haven't already begged Willow to sign you."

I focus on Jax. "I only sign serious riders, and you know it."

He nods. "I do." He points at Wyatt. "But he's still got a lot left in him. Since he's down to his last chance, I bet he's going to take things a little more seriously this time, and won't make you regret it."

I scoff. "I wish you could guarantee me that, but you can't. So I still owe you, but I'm going to pass on this one," I state, trying to get out of it.

Jax chuckles louder. "Now, come on, darlin'. You know you don't get to pick what favor you owe me."

"Don't call her that," Wyatt snaps.

Jax's amusement grows as he turns to Wyatt. "Ah, forgot how you always had a sweet spot for her. And why is that?" He gives him a knowing look.

My gut churns.

Does he know?

He can't.

No one knows.

Wyatt's eyes turn to dark slits.

Jax continues to assess us in his arrogant, all-knowing way.

Heat fills my cheeks.

Jax makes circles with his finger between us. "There always was something going on between you two, wasn't there?"

"No, there wasn't," Wyatt denies.

I'm grateful for his effort to fool Jax, but the words sting. Wyatt was my everything, but the minute I told him I could be pregnant, he bolted. He could have taken me but refused. The only thing important to him was success and money. So I wish his denial didn't hurt, but it does. It makes his actions match his words.

Jax taunts, "Sure you weren't."

"You're mistaken," I say, voice unsteady.

Jax glances at me, and I feel like a kid caught with my hand in the cookie jar. My cheeks heat further.

He puts his forearm on the table and leans closer to Wyatt. "You always were the most talented of all my riders."

"No shit," Wyatt says, then turns toward me. "Sorry, excuse my language."

"Well, don't hold back on account of me," I mutter.

Jax chuckles, then says, "Okay. I'll pretend nothing was going on between you two, especially since Willow seems to hate you right now."

I close my eyes and shake my head, wanting to die on the spot.

How does he know?

Wyatt retorts, "You better watch yourself, old man. You're stepping in a corral you have no business being inside."

Jax just grins.

Get off the topic.

I declare, "Jax, I'm not going to be Wyatt's agent."

"You owe me," Jax reiterates, his face taking on a stern expression.

My gut flips.

"Willow's not going to be my agent, and I'm not going to be your rider," Wyatt states.

"Ah, but you are going to be. You have no other choice."

"That's not true," Wyatt claims.

Jax arches his eyebrows. "Then tell me what choice you have. Who's knocking down your door right now?"

The question hangs in the air. Wyatt grinds his molars, not flinching under Jax's challenging stare.

"Go on, spit it out," Jax taunts.

It makes me feel bad for Wyatt. I know he got himself into his own mess, but he is a really good rider. I know how hard he worked to get where he is.

He just shouldn't have acted so stupid.

Stop feeling sorry for him, I reprimand myself.

The longer the silence builds, the tension wrapping around us, the more my heart hurts for Wyatt.

"I thought you retired. What are you now, eighty?" Wyatt scoffs.

Jax chuckles again. "Not quite, but I'm going to come out of retirement just for you."

"Nah, you can stay in it," Wyatt says.

"Jax, I still owe you a favor, but I'm not going to be Wyatt's agent," I repeat.

"You can and you will," Jax demands.

"You don't understand." My words come out almost pleadingly.

Jax crosses his arms and sits back. "Then tell me the real issue. And don't say it's because he's not a serious rider."

Silence fills the air.

Jax lowers his voice, and his lips curl again, making me nervous. "Do you think I'm a dumb cowboy? There were several instances where you were in Wyatt's changing room over the years. I never said anything. I didn't tell your dad. I didn't tell your brothers. Hell, I didn't tell anyone."

My stomach twists, and I glance at Wyatt.

He keeps his attention pinned on Jax, his jaw locked tight.

Jax continues, "I know you two were together. You might not be now, but you'll just have to get over that. This is happening. So wrap your heads around it."

Panic spins inside me.

Wyatt finally meets my gaze.

Jax smiles. "Now, come on. Get over whatever lovebird squabble you have. It's time for us to make some money. This is going to be my last run, and you're not going to disappoint me this time." He focuses on Wyatt.

Wyatt scowls at him, accusing, "You weren't the only one disappointed."

Jax arches his eyebrow in surprise. "Really? What did I do? I trained you. I placed you in the right rodeos. I made sure you had everything you needed. I even kept your little secret from everyone."

Wyatt stays silent.

Jax points at him. "You screwed it up. You made the decisions that led you here."

Wyatt grunts. "Then why do you want me back on your team?"

"Ah, see, that's the thing," Jax says, the curve of his lips arcing more.

I put my hand over my stomach, still reeling that Jax knew about Wyatt and me.

Jax drops a bomb. "There is no team. We're going independent."

Wyatt scoffs. "We'd be at zero for sponsorships."

Jax shrugs. "So? You've got nothing now. You're already at zero."

"Not if I join a team," Wyatt points out.

I speak up. "Jax, with all due respect, I have a team. You know how my business runs. This doesn't fit my model."

The wrinkles around Jax's eyes deepen. "Willow, you're one of the best agents I've seen. You're still learning, but there's no doubt you've got the gift. And I know this doesn't exactly fit into your business plan, but you'll figure it out."

"Please, I can refer you to some other agents that would be better for this."

He shakes his head. "No. You're going to do it, Willow. And, Wyatt, you're not going to disappoint either of us this time."

Wyatt says nothing. Anger radiates from him. His fist clenches near his thigh. He declares, "I'm not doing it."

"You are. You have no other choice," Jax reiterates.

"You don't know that," Wyatt asserts.

Jax nods toward me. "Ask your girlfriend."

"Don't call me his girlfriend," I blurt out.

Jax holds a hand up. "Apologies. Ask Willow. She'll tell you. The pool isn't that big. You're out of options besides this one. Isn't that true, darlin'?"

My gut rolls over and over and over, as if somersaulting down a snowy hill.

Wyatt doesn't move.

"Go ahead, turn toward her and ask," Jax challenges.

Wyatt still doesn't say anything. He scoots his chair back, rises, and says to me, "I'll meet you in the car when you're done with this." He moves toward the door.

"I didn't say you were dismissed," Jax calls out.

Wyatt flings open the door. The cold air rushes through the small space.

Jax barks, "Practice starts tomorrow at noon. We'll give the bulls some time to warm up."

Wyatt disappears and slams the door shut.

I sit there, my heart racing, as my mind tries to figure out how to get out of this.

"There's no point hurting that pretty head of yours, darlin'. This is the favor you owe me."

"Jax, please," I beg.

"Sorry, I won't change my mind."

"Why me? A million other agents probably owe you favors," I declare.

He nods. "That's true, they do."

"Then why me? Please, pick another one," I plead.

He leans closer. "I can't. That boy owes both of us something."

"He doesn't owe me anything."

"Ah, but he does," Jax insists.

I shake my head. "No, he doesn't."

Jax takes another sip of coffee, then says, "He owes both of us, and we're going to get what we're owed."

"He doesn't owe me anything," I repeat.

Jax takes another large swig of coffee and sets his mug down. "Do you know what I lost when I finally kicked him off the team?"

"No. What did you lose?"

"Let's just say it was more than money. And I know he's still got it in him, but this is his last chance. So, if anyone is going to profit from him, it will be me. Hopefully, he's smart enough to save himself this time."

"Another agent—"

"Won't get the sponsors on board the way you will," Jax interjects.

"That's not true. Other agents can get the sponsorships," I argue.

Jax shakes his head. "They won't work for him as hard as you will."

"I don't even like him anymore," I point out.

Jax shrugs. "Not my problem." He leans across the table. "I know sweet spots may burn, but they don't disappear. So I know you'll work harder than anyone else will for him."

Embarrassment steals my words.

Jax insists, "You'll get it done. I know you will."

"No, I won't. Please. I'll owe you two favors. Just don't make me his agent."

"Sorry, Willow, it's done." He rises, picks up his coffee mug, and takes it to the sink. He turns on the water and rinses it out.

Dread swallows me whole.

Jax turns off the water and puts the mug on his dish rack.

"Tough Rider and Roughneck Armorworks are looking for riders to sponsor. They might be a good place to start." Jax winks.

"How do you know that?" I question.

"I know everything." He grins.

I glance at the rounded logs in the ceiling.

"Don't worry, you'll get your money's worth for the work you put in. Besides, I heard he owes you quite a bit from last night."

I rise and put my hand on my hip, attempting one final time to get out of this. "This isn't okay, Jax. There are a dozen other people who could be his agent. You already said you know… Well, you know that we have a past. Please, I don't want to work with him."

Jax replies, "Which is why you deserve to make money off of him."

"I don't want to make money off of him," I claim.

Jax shrugs. "Sorry, I do, and you're going to help me. Now, is there anything else we need to talk about?" He gives me a this-conversation-is-over look.

My insides quiver. I cave, realizing there's nothing else I can say. I push the chair in and leave the house without another word. The cold air hits me in the face, slapping me several times until I get to the car.

Wyatt's in the driver's seat.

I open the passenger door since it's the closest. "Get out of the car, I'm driving."

He barks, "No, I am. So get in, or I'll leave you here with him." He turns on the engine.

Infuriated, I slide into the seat and slam the door. "This is my car. You don't have the right to make decisions on whether I'm driving or not."

He reaches over me to grab my seat belt, and his familiar scent flares around me.

I push at him. "What are you doing?"

He turns his face and slides his hands over my waist with the seat belt.

I stiffen, holding my breath.

The click of the buckle is loud in the otherwise quiet car.

His breath hits mine, his lips an inch from my mouth. "Did you convince him that this isn't happening, sugar?"

My pulse skyrockets. Tingles race down my back.

I spout, "What do you think?"

Disappointment fills Wyatt's face. He leans back and shakes his head. "I don't know what the old man's thinking."

"What happened the last time you saw him?" I demand.

Wyatt shifts into drive and accelerates down the driveway. "A lot of stuff that shouldn't have."

"Like what?"

"I told you before, Willow, I'm not going to talk about it." He squeezes the steering wheel as he passes the gate.

"I have a right to know," I claim.

He grunts. "Yeah? What gives you that right?"

"The fact that I'm your agent now."

He glances at me. "I haven't agreed to let you be my agent."

I sarcastically laugh. "One, I don't want to be your agent. Two, we have no choice unless you die or a bull paralyzes you. So unless one of those two things happens, I'm pretty sure I have to represent you, even though I'd rather crawl into a grave and let them pour dirt on me."

His lips curve. "Really? You'd rather be down there just clawing through the dirt, trying to get out?"

"Yep."

He leans his head closer, asking, "What would you scream?"

Butterflies flood my stomach. "What?"

"If you were in a grave trying to get out? Would you scream the basic 'help!' or something else?" he asks.

I open my mouth to answer, then shut it.

Don't fall for his charm again.

"I don't know. Stop asking me strange questions."

"You're the one who brought it up," he points out.

"No, I didn't."

"You did. You said you would rather crawl into a grave and let them pour dirt on you than represent me," he argues.

"Ugh, shut up," I say, crossing my arms and looking out the window.

"Suit yourself, sugar." He chuckles and turns up the music. We drive down several back roads.

After a few minutes, he turns the music down. "You really want to know what happened between Jax and me?"

I uncross my arms and turn toward him, softening my tone. "Yeah."

"Fine. I'm sure you're going to find out anyway. However, I'm fairly certain you can guess what happened. You want to take a stab?" he asks.

I shake my head. "No."

He turns his gaze back toward the road, taking several deep breaths, then admits, "I gambled my World Championship belt away."

My head jerks backward, and I gape at him.

He continues, "Jax was so proud of it. He never could earn it himself, and I think the next best thing for him was when I won it."

"Wyatt Houston! Why would you do that?" I scold.

Shamefaced, he quietly says, "Because I owed people money. Why else would I do it?"

I stare at him, shocked into silence.

He adds, "I was in debt pretty bad, Willow. I needed the money. The guys I borrowed from weren't the type you don't pay back."

I swallow hard, my heart racing faster. Gambling has always been part of the Texan lifestyle that I know. My family owns a race horse business. My brothers got the itch to place bets when they were barely ten. Wyatt was right in it with them, but he never seemed to listen to my father's warnings about being a "smart gambler." Not that I know if such a thing really exists. The way I see it, you either win or lose. Smarts don't really come into play.

Wyatt takes a deep breath and adds, "Jax loved that belt. He warned me not to gamble with the men I borrowed from, but I didn't listen. It was just like his warnings not to get into bar fights or drink too much."

I take all of it in, imagining all the scenarios Wyatt's describing.

He continues, "He was on his last straw with me. When they came after me, the only thing I had of value was that belt, so I went and pawned it."

I gasp. "You pawned it? They probably gave you pennies on the dollar. That was pure gold."

I can almost see the guilt and shame pouring from him when he mutters, "You don't even want to know what they gave me."

I study him closer. My pulse beats so hard, it makes me dizzy. I can't help but ask, "What did you get for it?"

Wyatt clenches his jaw, and it twitches. He finally meets my eye. "A thousand dollars."

My eyes widen in shock.

"Yep. I thought you were going to feel that way," he says, then focuses once more on the road, slowing down to take a curve.

"That belt has to be worth at least $20,000 on a bad day," I remind him, stunned he'd sell his World Championship belt.

Wyatt's nostrils flare. He tightens his fist around the wheel and then glances at me. Self-loathing coats his words as he declares, "Now you know the big secret about why Jax McCoy hates me. And the truth about how far I've fallen."

16

Wyatt

"What did Jax want?" Jagger asks when I walk into the barn.

"You don't want to know," I mumble, still pissed and contemplating whether I'm going to go through with it or not.

Jagger puts a saddle away and then asks, "Well, go on. Don't keep me waiting."

I grumble, "He claims he's going to coach me again."

Jagger's eyes widen. "Really?"

I nod. "Yeah, except I'm not allowed to join a team. Jax wants to go independent."

Jagger whistles. "That kind of sucks, doesn't it?"

"Yeah, it does," I state, my hand curling into a fist. It's been a long time since I competed without the backing of a team. Now, I'm going to have to fight for every penny I make.

"You're going to do it, right?"

I shrug. "I don't know. It's putting your sister in a bad situation too."

Jagger's eyes narrow. "What do you mean?"

"Did you know she owed Jax a favor?" I question, unhappy Willow owes anyone anything, especially him.

Jagger steps closer. "No. What for?"

"Some rider he helped her secure."

"Oh. That sounds like Willow."

"She shouldn't be making those kinds of deals," I seethe.

"What's the big deal? You know how this industry works. She has to fight for her riders just like every other agent."

I cross my arms, insisting, "It's not smart for her to owe men anything."

Jagger chuckles. "She's not doing anything out of the ordinary. You're just upset she owes Jax."

I try to get fresh oxygen into my lungs, but my anger is too stifling. I repeat, "She shouldn't do that."

"Good luck stopping her," Jagger taunts.

I stare at Butterscotch, a beautiful golden Palomino with a white tail. Jacob gave her to Ruby for her birthday a year before I left.

Jagger cautiously asks, "Am I correct to guess that Jax wants Willow to be your agent?"

My gut twists. I bitterly confirm, "Yep. He's calling his favor in."

Jagger pumps his arm in the air. "Yes! I told you she'd do it."

Anger heats my blood. "This isn't anything to celebrate. She only agreed because she owes him and has no other choice."

He scoffs. "That's just semantics. This is great news. Stop being such a downer. You'll be back on top in no time with Willow as your agent and Jax coaching you."

"You aren't listening. She doesn't want to represent me. She's being forced to. And, honestly, I don't think it's a good idea for me to do this anyway. Jax and I are long past the point of anything we can fix."

Jagger crosses his arms. "Don't be stupid, bro."

"How am I being stupid?" I question.

He glances around and then lowers his voice. "I know you better than anyone else. You and I both know you're close to being out of options."

His words hang in the air. I look away, clenching my jaw, knowing he speaks the truth.

"Quit digging your heels in the dirt, and get it done," Jagger prods.

I glance back, restating, "I don't want to put Willow in that situation."

Jagger waves off my concern. "Willow will be fine. She's going to make a ton of money off you, so don't worry about her. And it'll be way more than that $60,000 she had to shell out last night."

The disappointment I felt after Willow had to bail me out of jail returns. I curse myself for starting the fight and destroying the bar so badly. It's the worst damage I've ever caused.

Jagger peers closer and pushes, "Something else wrong?"

I shake it off. "No."

He pats me on the shoulder. "Well, congratulations. You're back. I knew everything would turn out for you."

I point out, "I haven't agreed yet."

He groans. "But you will. So stop being a dramatic sissy. Let's talk about more important things. Where do you want to go to celebrate tonight?"

I arch my eyebrows. "Probably best if I cool it a bit."

He scowls. "Don't let one bad situation ruin our Saturday night."

"I didn't know we had agreed to go out," I say.

"Since when do I have to make plans with you?" he questions.

I stay silent.

"Is there something better you want to do?" he asks.

Willow's face flies into my mind the same way it used to when we were hiding our relationship. I always preferred to be with her, but the guilt about lying went hand in hand with my desire.

Yet things are different now. When we hit the town, we drink too much, women tend to swarm around us, and he gets laid, while I'm trying to fill the void his sister created.

But now she's in front of me again. There's no way I want any woman coming near me unless it's her.

"Be ready by eight o'clock," Jagger orders and then ducks out of the stall.

I spin. "Jagger—"

"There she is, the new representation," Jagger crows when Willow enters the barn.

She glares at him. "You're so annoying."

"I told you, you were going to represent him," he boasts.

"Jagger, shut up," I interject.

He eyes me with disdain. "Don't tell me your soft spot for her is back."

Another round of guilt assails me. As much as Willow and I hid our relationship, he did always allege I took her side too often over his.

He glances between us. "You two are super testy today. I'll see you at eight, Wyatt," he says, then disappears.

Willow steps closer, and my pulse starts to rise.

"Hey," I cautiously offer.

She looks at me, opens her mouth, then snaps it shut.

It's the same look she'd give me whenever I'd go out with Jagger and leave her at home. Back then, I had the best of all worlds. Or so I thought. Today, I'd give anything to make different choices and stay home with her every night, even if it meant the Cartwrights knowing about us.

I force myself not to touch her. "What's wrong?"

She shakes her head, and her expression hardens. "Nothing. Can you go to my dad's office with me? We have to go through contracts."

"Willow, I don't know if we should be doing this."

"Doing what? This is nothing more than a business arrangement," she states, stabbing me in the heart.

I study her.

"Don't look at me like that."

I glance around to make sure nobody's around and step closer, closing the gap between us. I put my hand on her cheek. "Listen, I know—"

She ducks out of my grasp, lecturing, "The only way this is going to work is if we keep it professional. I'm going to settle my debt to Jax, and you're going to make good on your debt to me. That's it. Understand?"

Reality sinks in. I open my mouth to speak, but she cuts me off.

"Please, don't even try. I don't need this to be harder than it is." Her eyes plead with me to follow her wishes.

I cave. "Okay."

"Thank you. Can we go look at the contracts now?" she questions.

My heart sinks. "Sure."

We leave the barn and go back to the house, walking in silence. We pass a couple of her siblings, nieces, and nephews before we get to be alone in the office. She shuts the door and then sits down in her dad's chair.

I sit across from her and jokingly say, "So official." It comes out awkward, and I shift in my seat.

She nods with a sad expression. "Yeah, it is."

A world full of hurt and regrets blooms between us.

Wanting to move past the discomfort, I clear my throat and ask, "Okay, what have you got for me?"

She opens a folder and slides the first set of papers toward me. "This is a contract for you and Jax. Do you want me to go through each point?"

"No. I trust you. No matter how much you hate me, I know you'd never screw me over," I state.

"I don't hate you, Wyatt," she admits.

Hope soars in me. "You don't?"

A tiny curve forms on her lips, but she reminds me, "Don't get all excited. Nothing's changed."

I contain my excitement and pick up a pen. "Where do I sign?"

She puts her hands over the paper, advising, "Wyatt, you should read contracts. My dad always told you that, and there's a reason for it."

"Is there something in this I need to know about?" I question.

She sighs, picks up the paper, goes to page three, and sets it in front of me. She points to the payment clause.

I glance at it, and rage fills me. I exclaim, "That backstabbing crook. First, he refuses to let me join a team, and now this?"

She nods. "Yep. He's going to make sure he gets his money out of you."

"For how long?" I question.

She doesn't say anything. She releases a slow breath, staring at me.

My blood boils hotter. I boom, "Forever? There's no clause to lower it?"

She shakes her head. "Nope. These are his terms."

I stare at the number on the paper, then mutter, "You have to be kidding me, Willow."

She gives me a sympathetic look. "I'm sorry, but I'm not. You don't have to sign this. I'm sure somebody will pick you up."

"They won't," I say before I can even think about it.

She tenses at the certainty in my tone.

I swallow the lump in my throat. Then I admit, "I think we both know I'm pretty washed up at this point."

"You're not washed up, but you're going to have to make a lot of changes, Wyatt."

I glance at the bookcase and the trophies of horses from different races the Cartwrights' have won. I mumble, "I wish things were simple like they used to be."

Willow asks in the tender voice she used to use with me all the time, "How?"

I lock eyes with her, my pulse racing faster. "You know. Before I screwed everything up?"

She stays silent.

I lean closer and add, "If I could go back to when you and I were sneaking around, and my life was full of promise, I'd do it. I'd return to before I screwed us up and redo it all."

She blinks hard, then looks away.

I reach across the desk and put my hand over hers. "I mean it. I would, Willow. I'd be a better man and do everything differently."

She meets my gaze for a brief moment.

I stroke my thumb over her knuckles.

She pulls her hand back, sighing wearily. "Let's not talk about it, Wyatt. I can't go through this back and forth every day. The past is the past. Let's leave it there and hope that Jax keeps his mouth shut."

I blurt out before I can stop myself, "Well, that's the worst thing I ever heard."

Her eyes widen. "Don't tell me you're going to say something to my family?"

"No, of course not," I assure her.

"Then why would you say that?"

"I mean, if he told your family... I don't know. It just seems silly that we hid all those years," I state.

She reminds me, "I said we could come clean numerous times."

I close my eyes and take a deep breath, my insides shaking.

"Yeah, I remember. I was too big of a coward, though," I confess.

She puts the pen down and pushes for answers I'm sure have been plaguing her for years. "Why is that? What were you so scared of?"

"Well, that's a loaded question, sugar," I tease.

Her expression doesn't break, demanding answers from me.

Another lump forms in my throat. I clear it and sit taller. I reveal, "I didn't have anything to offer you."

"What are you talking about?" she asks.

"What was I going to do? Go up to your dad and say, *'I want to marry your daughter, but I have no money. I've spent it all on stupid stuff'*?"

Her eyes widen. She inhales sharply.

"Why do you look shocked?" I question.

"Marry me?" she whispers.

Anxiety and nerves overpower my stomach. I put my hand over hers. "Did you not think that's what I always wanted? How could you not? You were my life. The only other thing I had was bull riding. I wanted to marry you back then, and you're still the only woman I can ever envision committing my life to."

Her lip trembles, and she blinks hard. She manages to get out, "It's in the past. If you wanted that, you would've done it."

I insist, "Willow, it wasn't that easy."

"Why? Why wasn't it easy?" she demands.

"For one, you were in high school still," I point out.

Her eyes turn to slits, and she angrily says, "I was graduating. You were twenty-one. I was eighteen. We could have done anything. I could have gone with you. But you didn't want me there. Did you?"

"I told you I had to live in the bunkhouse," I remind her.

"It doesn't matter, Wyatt. I could have gone with you. If you had stayed for more than a second, we could have figured it out. But instead, the minute I told you I might be pregnant, you ran as far away from me as possible." A tear drips down her cheek, and she swipes at it.

Guilt bombards me. I open my mouth, but nothing comes out.

She looks away and shakes her head. Voice cracking, she quietly states, "I don't want to keep going through this, Wyatt. The past is the past."

I assert, "The hardest thing I ever did was leave you. Even though we got into that big fight, I could barely get in the truck and leave."

"Yet you did! You left and didn't call for over a month!" she accuses, her eyes red with rage and hurt.

A storm brews inside my chest. I confess, "I didn't know what to say. I thought it would be best to focus on work and let you cool down."

My statement angers her further. "Let me cool down?"

I try to stay calm and focus on keeping my tone steady. "Yes. But you didn't call me either. And you didn't take my calls."

"You mean the calls where you left me voice messages where I could barely hear you slurring over the sound of music and girls around you?" she hurls back.

My pulse bangs between my ears. My heart pounds so hard, I think it'll rip out of my chest.

She shakes her head, asserting, "The only way this is going to work is if we keep it professional, so promise me you're going to keep it professional between us."

The last thing I want to do is be professional with Willow.

She adds, "I owe Jax a debt, and as stated, you don't have a lot of other options. Now, I need to finalize this contract with you to fulfill my debt to him. So, can we please focus on business?"

Everything sinks in. How badly I hurt her. Why she's never going to forgive me. And how my sins aren't redeemable.

When I can't handle looking at her broken gaze any longer, I cave. "Okay."

She looks more than relieved at my agreement. Squaring her shoulders, she puts her finger back on the contract in the payment section, and says, "This is the only thing that's not normal. Are you going to sign?"

There's no debate. I've burned too many bridges and sunk too many ships. This is a final gift, if anything, even though Jax wants to rip me off.

I sigh. "Yes. I'll sign."

She gives me an approving nod, then turns to the page with the "sign here" flags.

I take the pen she offers me and then scribble my signature.

As soon as I'm done, she puts the stack of papers aside and pulls out another contract. "This is your contract with me."

"Am I paying you double?" I tease.

Her face turns serious. "You're paying me triple until I get my sixty grand back. I don't care if it comes from you or my other two riders. However, once it's paid, my fee will revert to normal terms. And it's the only way I'm taking you on, Wyatt."

I don't even glance at the paperwork, saying, "Sounds fair to me."

She turns the page and taps it. "Sign here."

I sign it and ask, "Is there anything else?"

She reveals, "Expect meetings next week with sponsors."

"Okay. Anyone I need to be aware of?"

"No, but I'll make sure they're lined up. I need you clean, presentable, and sober. And for the love of God, *do not* show up with bruises or cuts on your face. Do you think you can stay out of bar fights between now and then?"

My ego tanks. She shouldn't have to ask me that question and not know the answer. I sit taller in my chair. "Yeah, don't worry."

"Okay. I'll let you know when the meetings are set up." She rises.

I do too, nervous energy filling me.

She steps past the desk, and I grab her wrist.

She stops and swallows hard, glancing up at me.

"Thank you, Willow."

She doesn't say anything, just nods.

I open my mouth again, but nothing comes out.

She tilts her head. "Are you going out with Jagger tonight?"

I confess, "I don't want to."

"But you are?" She arches her eyebrows.

"If you tell me to stay here with you, I will," I state, and mean it.

The Willow I knew shines through for a moment, and I almost see a smile, but then her face hardens again. "Make sure you and Jagger don't do anything stupid tonight. We can't risk any negative press with sponsorships on the line."

"I'll be on my best behavior," I tell her, a little bummed that she didn't ask me to stay.

She studies me another minute.

I hold my hand up. "Cowboy's promise."

She glances at it, then a soft laugh escapes her. "That doesn't make me feel any better."

I grin. "I promise you I'll be good. You don't have anything to worry about."

"Good." She takes another step.

I step in front of her again. "Hey."

She glances up. "What?"

I shouldn't ask it. I have no right to ask anything about her life, but I can't help it. "Are you seeing anybody?"

She opens her mouth but then shuts it. Her eyes turn to slits. "It's not your business if I am."

"Willow—"

"No. You lost the right to know anything about my personal life when you left."

"I know. But if you give me another chance—"

"There is no other chance regarding us on a personal level. I will put my effort and energy into making sure your career gets back on track. You do your part. I promise you I'll do mine, but that's where it ends, Wyatt. I'm not going down this road with you again. Do you understand?" she declares with a finality that breaks me.

I stare at her, unable to answer.

"Wyatt, I need you to tell me that you understand," she implores hoarsely.

I shake my head and release her. "I'm sorry, sugar, but I'm never going to be able to agree to that."

I walk out of the office, needing air, trying to contain my emotions that feel more chaotic than ever.

17

Willow

Monday

The house is bustling with my huge family. Every holiday is a little hectic, but Christmas and New Year's have more excitement than the rest of the year.

But this isn't a normal holiday. It took me three years to enjoy Christmas again after Wyatt left. Now that he's back, the bitter taste I finally got rid of has returned.

My only saving grace is that Jagger's made sure to keep Wyatt away all weekend. They're off on whatever adventure grown men call fun, and honestly, I'm relieved.

I need the space to breathe and pretend the last few days haven't ripped open old wounds I swore were long healed. So, instead of having fun with my family, I'm burying myself in preparations for the New Year's Eve rodeo on Thursday.

Contracts, sponsor decks, travel itineraries, and riding schedules aren't doing much to distract me. It all reminds me of Wyatt. Every time my mind drifts to him, I dive deeper into work, trying to drown in it. Unfortunately, I keep grabbing a life raft to keep me from going under, and then I have to try to forget about him all over again.

Phoebe is the one person who takes my mind off Wyatt. When I'm not working, we're giddy over her engagement, obsessing over wedding dresses, bridal shoes, and bouquets.

And it's ironic. At one point, I thought I'd be Wyatt's wife. Now, I'm scrolling through endless photos of lace trains and champagne fountains, and it's the only thing keeping me from spiraling into dangerous memories of my past with Wyatt. And I hate how he's the only man who still has the power to set my skin on fire by merely looking at me.

"Are you sure you don't want to come with me to the florist on Wednesday?" Phoebe asks, holding her tablet up to show me the different designs the local flower shop posted on Instagram.

I smile, forcing my voice steady. "You don't need me hovering while you and Alexander pick out flowers. Besides, I have meetings scheduled all week. Sponsors don't woo themselves."

Phoebe arches a brow. "I know, but you're my ride-or-die. Planning a wedding is supposed to be fun, you know."

"Who's not having fun?" I question, sipping my coffee and adding, "I'm having a blast. And it makes me happy to see you and my brother so happy. And out in the open." I wink, referring to the secret romance they had, even though I knew something was up between them.

She narrows her eyes at me playfully. "And what about you? You've been working yourself into the ground lately. You need something— or some*one*—fun too."

I try to deflect, saying, "My kind of fun is making sure everything is ready for this rodeo."

Phoebe sighs dramatically. "You're impossible sometimes." She scrolls to another image of a floral arch. "I don't understand why Alexander keeps telling me to look at venues instead of having the wedding here. The view at the lake is perfect for sunset photos. But I swear, if one cloud ruined my pictures, I might throw a full-on bridal tantrum."

I chuckle. "You'll be stunning no matter what. Alexander will be too busy staring at you to notice if you're inside or outside."

Phoebe's cheeks heat. She swipes the screen and lowers her voice. "But seriously, Willow, look at this dress." She holds the tablet out. "I know I said I wanted simple, but this one? The beading, the train… Do you think it would be too much? I'm kind of in love with it."

I study the photo. The dress is stunning, a perfect balance between classic and dramatic. "It's gorgeous, Phoebe. If you feel amazing in it, you should wear it. Alexander won't know what hit him."

Her smile goes soft, dreamy, and excited.

She gushes, "That's exactly what I want. I want him to lose his breath when he sees me walk down the aisle."

I reach over and squeeze her hand. "He will!"

She admits, "I never thought I'd get married."

"That makes two of us," I mutter.

"You will," she insists.

I shrug. "Doubt it."

All the dreams I used to have of marrying Wyatt pop into my mind, and I blink hard.

Phoebe's expression shifts, a hint of hesitation creeping in. "Speaking of men… Can I ask you something?"

I stiffen slightly and then force a nonchalant tone. "Of course."

She glances around to make sure we're still alone, and her voice drops to a curious whisper. "Is there something going on between you and Wyatt?"

My stomach clenches. I blurt out, "He's going to be more trouble for me than a snake in a sleeping bag."

"I didn't mean client-wise." She arches her eyebrows.

Panic hits me, and all I can do is lie. "No. Nothing is going on. Why would you insinuate there's anything besides the trouble he's created for me?"

She studies me for a moment, then says, "Every time his name comes up, you get this look."

I scoff. "He's a pain in my booty, that's why."

She's not convinced. "Willow—"

"Phoebe," I cut her off softly, managing a weak smile. "It's business. That's it. He's a rider trying to earn his place back. That's all."

She pauses, then holds up her hands in surrender. "Okay. If you say so. I'm here if you need to talk."

"I know." Guilt fills me. When I called her out about my brother and her, she confided in me. I don't know why I'm not doing the same when I trust her.

Because my history with Wyatt is staying in the past.

"My lips are always sealed," she reminds me.

My chest tightens. I force another smile. "And I appreciate it. But really, it's just business."

She lets it go, switching back to another dress design, but I feel her gaze flick back to me, as if she doesn't quite believe me. And if I'm honest, I don't entirely believe myself either.

Nothing is happening between Wyatt and me, no matter what he says.

The way he left the office after signing his contract hasn't left me feeling very reassured about that, though.

"Let's find you the perfect shoes," I say quickly, eager to change the subject. "If you're going to make Alexander's jaw drop, you might as well do it from head to toe."

Phoebe grins, letting me off the hook for now. "Oh, you know I already have a Pinterest board full of options. Sparkly, strappy, and dangerously high. Nothing I would normally wear, but, hey, it's my wedding!"

"It is, and I say go for it!" I gush.

She adds, "My feet may hate me, but it'll be worth it for the photos."

Before I can say anything else, my phone buzzes with a text. I glance at the screen.

Jericho: Colt and I are on our way.

I stand, my stomach twisting into knots. I haven't had the patience to deal with them and Wyatt, and like always, Wyatt seemed to step first in line. I sigh. "Duty calls. Idiot one and idiot two are on their way to my office."

Phoebe winks. "If you need to scream afterward, I'll have wine waiting."

"And that's why you're my bestie!" I tell her, then leave the house and drive to town.

When I get to my office, Jericho and Colt are already seated across my desk, wearing the same sheepish expressions from Christmas night.

The weight of their actions still hangs between us, heavy and thick. It's a storm refusing to break, and I won't let it stop me from taking action.

"Let's get this over with," I say flatly, dropping the paperwork onto my desk.

Jericho rubs his palms together. "You're still mad."

My voice is calm but clipped. "Sixty thousand dollars' worth of mad. Sign here, initial there." I point to each stickered section without elaborating.

Colt leans forward, studying the contract. "This says you're taking three times our normal payment until the debt's paid off."

I lift my chin and square my shoulders. "Correct. Until I recover the sixty grand from prize money, sponsorships, or your personal funds, I take triple."

"What about Wyatt? He started it," Colt whines.

"He's on the same contract, but it's not your business, is it?" I point out, still upset that my two best riders ruined an establishment.

Jericho's eyes turn to slits. "You're representing him?"

"It's not your business," I repeat sternly.

Jericho grinds his molars.

I tap the paperwork, ordering, "Sign."

Colt begs, "Can't you take double? That's not leaving us with much."

"No. I can't. You should have thought about that before you destroyed another working man's livelihood," I lecture.

They exchange a glance, hesitating, but then sign.

Jericho sets his pen down first, his tone tight when he says, "Seriously, Willow. This Wyatt situation… Do you really think adding him to the team is a good idea?"

Colt leans in to add sharply, "It's bad enough you're entertaining it.

But if you take him on, you're risking the entire agency and team. He's toxic."

"This has nothing to do with you two. Stay out of it," I fume.

"The hell it doesn't," Jericho snaps. "Every time his name shows up in a headline, our sponsors get nervous. You know how small this circuit is. If he screws up, it doesn't just stain him. It stains the entire team."

Colt pipes in with, "You think every sponsor isn't watching him? Now they'll be watching you too. And the second they smell instability, they'll pull their money. So if you bring him in, you're rolling the dice with all our futures."

I clench my jaw, refusing to let them rattle me, not ready to reveal Wyatt's riding as an independent.

Let them squirm after what they did.

I declare, "I know exactly what's at stake."

Jericho laughs bitterly. "Do you? Because from where we sit, it looks like you're making decisions with your heart, not your head. And that's a problem."

A wave of anxiety crashes over me. I fire back, "I'm treating him like any rider who wants to rebuild. He's earned at least that much."

Colt scoffs. "Earned it? Plenty of riders out there who've worked their asses off don't get this shot. But he does? Because he grew up on your ranch?"

I relax, realizing they weren't referring to our secret relationship. But I keep steel in my voice. "I know exactly what he's done. But it's *my* decision. *My* agency. You don't like it? You should have thought about it before you made Christmas into a fight club. And if you don't like my decisions, you're welcome to walk."

Jericho's eyes narrow. "You think you're untouchable because you built this place? Don't forget the basics. If you lose your credibility, we all lose opportunities. If you drag his mess in here, you're gambling with more than just *your* name."

Colt interjects, his voice dark. "Let's not pretend Wyatt won't self-destruct again. That's what he does, Willow. He burns everything down around him. He won't think twice about including you in the flames."

I exhale through my nose, steadying myself. "You don't need to like my decision. You just need to respect it."

Tension swirls around us, crackling like a live wire. No one speaks.

Jericho's jaw clenches.

Colt's fists curl against his thighs.

Finally, Jericho exhales sharply. "Fine. Do what you want, Willow." He rises.

Colt follows, scowling. "Don't say we didn't warn you. When he crashes, don't expect us to stand by quietly."

"Noted," I say coolly.

As they push back from the desk, the door swings open. Like clock-work, fate twists the knife.

Wyatt steps in.

His dark gaze sweeps the room, locking on me instantly. Heat coils low in my stomach at the sheer weight of his stare. He doesn't glance away when addressing Jericho and Colt. "Gentlemen."

Jericho's lip curls. "Houston."

Colt folds his arms, his voice dripping with hostility. "Didn't realize you were already making yourself comfortable."

"Didn't realize you still had anything to say that mattered," Wyatt replies smoothly, his voice calm but razor-sharp.

I step in quickly. "Don't."

The tension between the three of them sits on the edge of exploding.

No one moves. The testosterone saturates the air as thick as smog.

Jericho shifts, his eyes never leaving Wyatt's. "Just remember, Houston. Some of us earned our place here without needing second chances."

Wyatt's smirk sharpens, dark and unapologetic. "And yet here I am, still standing."

"Enough!" My voice cuts through like a whip. "All of you, except Wyatt, out!"

Jericho and Colt finally move, both shooting Wyatt one last glare before brushing past him.

As they exit, Wyatt doesn't move an inch. "Always a pleasure," he drawls, voice laced with venom.

The door slams, distilling their tension and creating a new one.

And the tension between us is even thicker. Too many minutes pass of Wyatt dragging his gaze over my body.

"You enjoy poking bears, don't you?" I say dryly.

Wyatt shrugs. "Just making conversation."

I sigh internally.

I'm cursed. Every time I think I'm prepared to face him, he chips away at my defenses, utilizing that Wyatt Houston charm, and catching me off guard again.

His gaze slides over me again, like a slow caress, lingering on every curve.

It's like nothing's changed, and my body still belongs to him.

It doesn't, I tell myself.

"You're staring," I force out, trying to steady my breath.

"Hard not to," he replies in a rich and dangerous drawl.

"Don't start," I warn.

He steps closer. "It's been years, Willow. You expect me not to notice every damn inch of you?"

My heart trips. I take a step backward, but I keep my chin high. "We're here for business."

He murmurs, "Business. Right. But don't pretend there's nothing left between us."

I clear my throat and gesture toward the chairs. "Two sponsor meetings today. Sit."

He stretches his long legs as he takes a seat, looking entirely too comfortable. He could own the place, and it's something I used to love about him.

Today, it really irritates me.

His gaze drops to my crossed legs, his stare practically scorching my skin. My breath catches and my pulse shoots higher.

My body suddenly remembers every wicked thing he's done to it. It betrays me the same way it used to when we were together.

"So let's talk business," he says, giving me a reprieve from memories I'd rather not dwell on.

I push a folder at him. "We're meeting with Roughneck Armorworks first. Tough Rider is after them."

"What's the chances of securing a platinum sponsorship?" Wyatt questions.

"Not sure. I'll feel them out to see what their budget is, but there's no guarantee they'll give us anything," I remind him.

He clenches his jaw.

The front door opens, and Brent Wallace, Roughneck Armorworks' VP of marketing, booms, "You in here, sugar?"

Wyatt's eyelids lower to slits. His jaw clenches and fists curl tight.

"Behave," I mutter, then rise. Brent's no different from most of the male contacts at the companies that offer sponsorships. But as long as I secure the deals for my riders, I suck it up.

I meet him at the door and offer a sweet-sounding, "Happy Holidays."

"You too, sweetheart." He pulls me into a hug.

Wyatt interjects in a cool voice, "Mr. Wallace. Nice to meet you."

Brent pulls back. "Call me Brent. And I have to say, we're impressed with your riding, Wyatt," Brent says, shaking Wyatt's hand.

"Thank you, sir," Wyatt replies.

"Please. Let's sit," I suggest, motioning toward my conference table.

We all take a seat.

Before I can speak, Brent says, "I don't have tons of time. The grand-kids are coming over tonight. But I wanted to meet you in person, Wyatt. You've always had a strong track record."

Wyatt nods. "Appreciate that. I'm just focused on getting back to where I should've been all along."

Brent tosses me a glance I can't decipher, and I'm immediately on guard. He looks at Wyatt and states, "The footage from your last two events speaks for itself. You're riding sharp. Confident. But you know why we're cautious."

"Because of my past," Wyatt answers directly, no hesitation. "I own it. And I won't pretend it didn't happen. But I'm not that man anymore. I'm here to ride and represent any sponsor that's willing to take a chance on me the way I'm taking a chance on myself."

I can't help the small flicker of pride that swells in my chest at how steady and earnest he sounds.

Brent replies, "That's good to hear. But you're a risk, Wyatt. Hopefully a calculated one if we decide to back you. This vest launch is a significant milestone for us. We've invested millions of dollars. We want a face that represents strength, safety, and stability."

Wyatt meets Brent's gaze head-on, declaring, "And that's what I'll give you. I'm not just here for a second shot. I'm here to build something lasting."

Brent nods slowly. "When's your next ride?"

Wyatt looks to me for help.

I clear my throat. "We're figuring the schedule out."

Brent raises his eyebrows.

"We should have it solidified in the next week," I add.

He nods and points at Wyatt. "If you handle the pressure and stay on track, we'll revisit this after your next competition." Brent extends his hand.

Wyatt shakes his hand. "Fair enough. I appreciate the consideration."

I interject, "Before you leave, I have one question."

"What's that, sugar?" he asks.

Wyatt shifts in his seat.

The hairs on my arms rise, but I don't look at him. I say to Brent, "You said you want the face for your vest. I assume you're looking to offer a rider a platinum sponsorship deal?"

Brent chuckles. "Always going in for the kill, aren't you, darlin'?"

I put on my sweetest smile, cooing. "Gotta do well for my riders."

Brent nods. "You guessed right, sugar."

I do a mental fist pump. I need a platinum sponsor for Wyatt as soon as possible. So I smile bigger. "Perfect. Then I'll put you at the top of the list."

He chuckles again and rises. "It was nice meeting you, Wyatt. Willow, tell Jacob and Ruby I said Happy Holidays."

"I will. Thank you for taking the time to meet with us," I reply.

He pulls me in for another hug, and when he releases me, we walk him to the door just as Tough Rider's director, Candace O'Hearne, parks her SUV.

She gets out, exchanges niceties with Brent, and within minutes, we're sitting across from her in my office.

She flips through Wyatt's portfolio as she speaks.

"Your stats are excellent. And I won't lie, the media loves a comeback."

Wyatt gives a small, easy smile. "That's because everyone loves a good story. I intend to give them one."

She adds, "We've been following you closely."

She doesn't have to come out and say that they know about his recent troubles.

"Wyatt's had a few hiccups," I admit.

She nods. "Yes. We're interested, but we're cautious. Our bull rope launch is a high-visibility campaign. Image matters."

Wyatt states, "I understand. I've made mistakes, but my focus now is entirely on my riding and proving to sponsors like Tough Rider that I'm worth the investment."

I lean in slightly. "He'll deliver exciting rides and a professional media presence at every event going forward. The sponsors who get in early on Wyatt's rebuild are going to reap the rewards."

Candace smiles thoughtfully. "You make a strong case, Willow. And, Wyatt, you're saying all the right things. Corporate's intrigued. But they want to see you under more pressure. When's your next ride?"

"We're solidifying the schedule this week," I quickly inform her.

She studies Wyatt.

He blurts out, "I'll make sure you don't regret me."

Candace closes the folder. "Fair enough. We're watching. After your next ride, let's have another meeting."

She rises, shakes our hands, and leaves.

Wyatt groans. "This is going to be harder than I expected, isn't it?"

"You're a bigger risk than they let on."

He sighs and steps in front of the window, crossing his arms.

I keep to myself that he's a risk that might cost me everything.

18

Wyatt

*B*efore my mind can spiral into another round of what-if scenarios, Willow's phone buzzes. She glances at it, her expression unreadable, but the second she answers, I hear Jax's voice on the other end.

He booms, "Got good news. Just landed Wyatt a slot for Whispering Junction's Boots, Bucks & Mistletoe Rodeo."

My adrenaline level spikes.

Did I hear that right?

Willow's voice pitches high, sharp with disbelief. "That's not possible. The entry deadline has passed."

This is my chance!

I lock my gaze on her, my chest tightening, and I order, "Put it on speaker."

She rolls her eyes but obeys.

"Full rider slot. Promoter owed me a favor," Jax explains.

Willow rubs her temples. Her shoulders tense, and hesitation creeps behind her eyes. She's calculating every angle, and it makes my nerves stand on edge. She says, "Jax. He can't ride in the show."

"What are you talking about?" I blurt out.

Jax adds, "Don't be ridiculous. I've got a few days to sharpen him up."

"No. This isn't happening," Willow snaps, harder than a bull's horn to the ribs.

The words hit me like a fist. I jerk back, caught off guard, not just by the tone but by the finality in her eyes.

Jax's voice crackles from the phone. "Willow, don't start."

She fires back, "I'm not starting. I'm ending it. Wyatt isn't riding. He's not ready. Not mentally. Not physically. He hasn't competed in months."

I stare at her, trying not to explode. "I can handle it," I insist.

"No, you can't," she fires back.

"He'll be fine," Jax interjects.

Willow points at me. "You're not just out of practice, you're reckless. You got into a bar fight two nights ago. You're nursing a swollen face and a bruised ego. That doesn't exactly scream rodeo-ready."

"You think I can't ride anymore?" I grind my teeth.

She doesn't even flinch. "I think you're too much of a wild card. You want to prove something? Fine. But not at Whispering Junction. Not when we have major sponsors considering you."

I huff. "Which is why I need to ride. You heard them. Until they see me ride again, they won't make any offers."

"You aren't ready," she repeats.

It takes everything in me not to raise my voice. I wonder where the girl is who used to believe in me wholeheartedly.

"I'm not asking for your blessing, Willow. I'm going to ride."

She looks at me like I'm already the failure she predicted. "Then find another agent. I won't let you put my career at risk."

"She's serious," Jax mutters through the speaker, mostly to me, but Willow hears him too.

She asks, "Do you realize how much drama this adds? We're barely getting the sponsors to stay open-minded."

Jax counters, "Drama sells, Willow. You know that. Besides, you know how to keep him in line."

She glances over at me. I know that look. She's reading me, searching for any sign that I might self-destruct and take her with me again.

"Wake up, Willow. He needs this. *We* need this," he pushes.

She snaps her head toward the phone, venom in her voice. "You know nothing about what I need."

"Then fill me in," Jax orders.

She declares, "I need to know my riders are focused."

"I am," I claim.

She continues, "They need to be sober, not out every night drinking until God knows what time."

"Seriously? You're holding me going out with Jagger over my head?" I hurl.

Jax states, "You're overreacting, darlin'."

Willow scoffs. "Don't even get me started on you, Jax."

"Meaning what?" he growls.

"I don't need my career to implode because some bull-headed cowboy thinks a rodeo slot will magically fix his life."

After a moment, I try again, this time softer. "Willow—"

"No. You're not riding. Not under my name," she asserts, cutting me off before I can finish.

"I'll see you at practice tomorrow. You're riding," Jax states, then hangs up.

Willow's eyes flame.

I stare at her, splintering apart, piece by piece. My voice drops into something dark and bitter. "You're doing this to punish me."

She crosses her arms like a goddamn judge at sentencing. "No. I'm doing this to protect what matters. The only thing I care about right now is that my riders don't end up in a cell, the hospital, or the morgue."

"And what about me?" I ask, hating how hollow the question sounds as it leaves my mouth.

She meets my gaze. Hers is flat, cold, and unreadable. She spouts, "You? You're a complication I should've left behind a long time ago."

Her words sting, but hell if they're not fair. I deserve her doubt. I've given her every reason to question me. But this is my shot. And I'll be damned if I don't take it.

With certainty, I tell her, "I'm ready. I can do it." I look her right in the eye and add, "You may not trust that yet, but I do. And I'll prove it."

She exhales, her chest rising and falling. "Don't push me, Wyatt."

I warn, "Don't deny me my opportunity. I'll be ready, and you know it."

For the first time in too long, I see it. The flicker in her eyes. The part of her that still believes in me. Even if she doesn't want to.

She turns to leave. But I can't stop myself.

My next words chase her, smooth like silk, sliding straight through her defenses. "You can pretend all you want, Willow. But we both know neither one of us wants to be denied."

She freezes.

Her back stiffens, breaths coming short and fast.

Bullseye.

This isn't over. Not even close.

Barely above a whisper, I state, "I'm riding that bull, sugar. And I'll be damned if you're not riding me again soon too."

She swallows hard and glares at me.

I leave her office, and go over to Jax's place, where I get thrown off the bull so many times, I have to sit in an ice bath half the night.

The next morning, I beat the sun to her office. I couldn't sleep. Hell, there was no point in trying. My brain wouldn't shut off. Her scent was still burned into my nostrils. And the scared look in her eyes when I left haunted my thoughts. I spoke the truth yesterday, and nothing she could say or do would lead me to ever believe otherwise.

And the lack of sleep gave me wisdom about how I could win her back. So I sit behind her desk like I own the place, ready to go to war with her.

When she finally walks in, her eyes narrow the second she sees me. She snaps, "You're early. Make yourself comfortable."

I kick my feet off the corner of her desk and stand. "Couldn't sleep. Thought I'd check on my favorite agent-in-denial."

"I'm not in denial."

I take a step toward her, keeping my voice low and steady. "You are. But you'll be out of it soon. I know you, Willow Cartwright."

She folds her arms, raising her chin high. "You don't know me like you think."

I move closer, breathing her in, letting every ounce of my restraint pull tight. "I know every inch of you, sugar. Every breath. Every murmur. Every part that still belongs to me."

Her breath hitches. She chokes out, "I told you business only, and I meant it."

I close the last few inches between us. My hand hovers near her waist, not touching but close enough. I can feel the heat rolling off her. "You're a liar."

Her head jerks backward.

I chuckle. "I'll prove it."

"Yeah? How?" she hurls.

"One kiss. That's all it would take. One kiss, and you won't be able to deny you still love me," I taunt.

Her lips part. But nothing comes out. She glances at my mouth with eyes full of fear and want.

I take it as her answer. I walk forward, one step at a time.

She's forced to move backward with my stride until her back is against the wall. Her eyes widen.

I graze my thumb across her cheek, mumbling, "Do you have any idea how many times I've watched our videos?"

Her cheeks flush bright red as she gapes at me.

"You thought I'd delete them?" I chuckle, but it's laced with nerves. I admit, "They're my prized possessions. The only things I'd never pawn or destroy. They're what kept me going all these years."

"Wyatt—"

"Shh," I order, putting my finger over her lips.

She stills.

"You gonna stop me?" I ask, my breath mingling with hers.

She blinks hard but doesn't move.

I lower my finger and press my lips against hers.

It's not gentle. It's a violent thunderstorm with seven years of anger, lust, and unfinished business crashing between us.

Her gasp melts in my mouth as I deepen the kiss. My tongue sweeps against hers, claiming her the way I always did.

She tries to fight it, but only briefly. Her hands fly to my chest, pushing me, then gripping the cotton of my shirt. She drags me closer, as if she hates herself for needing it but can't stop.

I press her harder against the wall, my thigh slipping between hers. She arches into me with a soft, desperate moan that shreds my control.

My hand slides into her hair, yanking her head back just enough to drag my mouth down her neck. I push her blouse to the side, exposing the curve of her collarbone and kissing her skin.

"Damn you, Wyatt," she breathes, barely able to speak.

"I've already been damned, sugar," I growl against her throat, teeth grazing just enough to make her tremble. "Might as well enjoy the fire."

I kiss her again, harder this time, vowing to make her remember this moment every time she tries to pretend she's over me.

She kisses me back with the same fury, her nails digging into my shoulders, hips grinding against mine, and I swear she wants to set me on fire and burn with me.

Her breath comes in sharp gasps when we finally break apart, foreheads pressed together, our bodies still tangled in heat.

"I hate you," she whispers, lips swollen, eyes glazed with want.

"No, you don't," I murmur, brushing my thumb over her mouth. "You hate how badly you still want me."

She doesn't deny it, and that's the real danger.

This kiss isn't just heat.

It's a warning shot.

"Still think we're finished?" I taunt.

She closes her eyes.

I mumble against her lips, "We're far from finished, sugar." I kiss her again, then step back. "I'll see you in a few days."

She tilts her head in confusion, still breathing hard.

"I'm staying at Jax's to train. I'll see you at the rodeo," I tell her, then exit her office before she can argue.

For the next few days, sharp stings cut through my thighs the second I swing my leg over the gate and land on the other side. My muscles scream. My back tightens. Every step I take fans the flames licking my insides.

"Damn, Jax," I curse under my breath after every ride.

He's been working me harder than I ever remember. Every morning, predawn drills. Every afternoon, drills. Every night, drills. Mounting, dismounting, balance training, core work, strength exercises, repetition until my muscles tremble and the ice bath feels like heaven and hell rolled into one.

It still doesn't touch the soreness.

Sooner than I know it, Whispering Junction's Boots, Bucks & Mistletoe Rodeo is in full swing. The holiday lights flicker against the clear, bitter air. The packed arena rumbles with laughter, shouts, and the unmistakable boom of country music vibrating throughout the grandstands.

The limp I caught two days earlier is more pronounced tonight, but I force myself to keep moving.

I shouldn't even be here, but there's no way in hell I'm letting those cocky riders near Willow without me around.

And I'm not losing my opportunity to prove to Willow I'm worth her time and effort—professionally or personally.

For several minutes, I scan the rider area before I see Willow. She stands next to Jericho, Colt, and the others on her team. All of them are decked out in their gear, chatting and throwing smug looks around the arena like they own the place. She's smiling at something one of them said, but when her eyes catch mine, her face tightens.

Nothing has changed. She still doesn't want me here.

Hell, none of her riders do. They barely tolerate my presence, but I don't give a damn.

Jax appears at my side, slapping a hand on my back. I wince but keep my mouth shut.

"Gear up," he orders.

Willow storms over, fury flashing in her eyes. "He's not riding."

"Stay out of this, Willow—"

"Jax, are you serious? He's injured. He's limping. He's in no condition to ride."

Jax crosses his arms. "It's his decision."

She whips toward me, voice tight. "You'll get tossed off in three seconds flat. That's not going to prove anything to sponsors."

I glance between them. "If I don't ride, I'll never get another shot."

"You'll ruin your career if you get thrown. They'll see you as weak, reckless—"

"Or they'll see me as a man who doesn't back down," I cut in, then add, "I have to prove I belong. To you. To them. To everyone who fired me."

Willow shakes her head in disbelief. "This isn't the way. You're not ready."

I firmly state, "I'm riding." Ignoring Willow's glare, I ask Jax, "Where's my gear?"

He replies, "Trailer."

Without waiting, I limp off toward the trailer, every step hammering my joints, but the fire in my chest drowns out the pain. I step into the dressing room, wincing.

The door flings open behind me. Willow barrels into the room, shutting the door. She shouts, "You've got more dust than sense between your ears!"

"It's my only shot."

"Wyatt, listen to me." Her voice cracks, her hands fisting at her sides. "You're not thinking clearly. If you get thrown, no one will sign you. This isn't the way to fix your career."

I pull on my chaps, trying not to show any pain in front of her. "If I win, you're spending New Year's Eve with me."

"What?" she scoffs.

I grin. "To celebrate."

"The only thing you're doing is ruining your career and heading to the hospital, maybe in a body bag. You have no chance to win in the condition you're in, and you know it," she claims.

I grunt. "Then you shouldn't have a problem taking my bet."

She stays quiet.

I fasten my gear. "So it's settled. If I win, I get what I want. A deal is a deal."

She narrows her eyes. "And if you lose?"

"If I lose, you can decide what you want. Anything. I'll owe you. But I'm not losing, so don't think too hard, sugar."

Her jaw tenses, and she exhales sharply. "You're impossible."

I step closer so she can't miss the emotions and intensity behind my words. "I have to do this, Willow. For the agents who fired me. For every stupid mistake I've made. And for you. So I can start paying you back."

Her throat bobs as she swallows. She insists, "This isn't the way to pay me back."

"Sure it is. But don't forget our bet," I remind her, waggling my eyebrows.

She shakes her head. "You better not get hurt."

I flash her a crooked grin. "Sugar, that's always a risk." Before she can argue again, I step past her and out into the arena.

The chanting vibrates around me, and the world fades to just me and the beast I'm about to ride. Adrenaline ignites in my veins. I lower myself onto the bull. His muscles coil like loaded springs. My grip tightens around the rope.

Jax leans into the gate. "Make this count."

"I intend to." I give the signal to Bucky.

The gate flies open.

The first jump jerks my body forward. The second nearly snaps my spine. I grit my teeth, locking every muscle, riding with pure instinct.

One Texan.

Two Texan.

Three Texan.

Fire shoots through my sciatica.

I nearly fall off but grip the rope harder.

Time stretches into an eternity.

Four Texan.

Five Texan.

Another shot of fire races through my spine.

Six Texan.

Seven Texan.

The bull twists hard left, then bucks high, snapping into a spin that tests every bit of my strength.

Somehow, I stay on him.

The buzzer blares.

I fly off the bull, landing hard but rolling out of the way before the beast charges past.

The arena erupts in cheers.

I run to the safety zone, adrenaline masking the pain. When I'm out of danger, it wears off.

I limp toward Willow as the announcer shouts my score. The crowd roars.

She runs to me, fury and relief mixing with excitement in her expression. "You idiot."

I grin. "Be ready at six tomorrow. And pack an overnight bag."

Her eyes narrow. "Wyatt—"

"You made a deal. I held up my end. Hold up yours."

"I never said I agreed." She fights a smile, but the shimmer in her eyes tells me another story.

"You didn't say no," I remind her, grinning bigger, and knowing she'll follow through.

And for the first time in a long while, I know I'm back in the game, but not just with my career.

19

Willow

New Year's Eve

Che morning of New Year's Eve hits like a sledgehammer. I'm jittery. Not from coffee or lack of sleep but from something worse.

Anticipation and dread mix with more than a touch of desire, which I keep trying to shove down so far it gets tangled in my rib cage.

Today is the day.

Why the hell did I agree to Wyatt's stupid bet?

I didn't.

Well, not technically...

I pace my bedroom, my feet lightly slapping against the hardwood floor as I try to figure out what to wear. It's not like we're going to a gala or even some wild New Year's bash.

But knowing Wyatt? He could say we're grabbing dinner and then end up stealing a plane and flying us to Mexico.

Which, to be fair, almost happened once.

I can't help but smile at the memory.

It was right after Wyatt's first big win in Montana. Sponsors were sniffing around, and he hadn't yet learned how to say no to anything or anyone.

I was almost eighteen, and giddy in love.

He'd come home and told me to pack a bag, add my bikini, sunscreen, and passport, and meet him by the truck.

I'd felt the rush of excitement I always got whenever he'd surprise me with secret getaways. I'd asked where we were going.

He'd winked and said, *"Trust me. And tell your parents you're staying the weekend at Ginny's."*

Ginny had become my excuse when I'd wanted to go places with Wyatt overnight.

The next thing I knew, we'd been on a puddle jumper to San Diego, where a new buddy of his had a pilot license, a questionable plane, and a taste for adventure. Two hours later, Wyatt's hand had been wrapped around mine as we'd crossed the border in a rental car with no GPS, two bottles of tequila, and no real plan besides "find a beach and get lost."

We'd ended up in some sleepy fishing village on the Baja coast, eating grilled octopus from a vendor on the pier, barefoot and drunk on each other. He'd danced with me under a string of lights and kissed me so hard, I'd forgotten my name. That night, he'd made love to me in a bed with no frame, in a room that'd smelled like salt and citrus, with crashing waves as our only witnesses.

The next morning, we'd gotten caught in a rainstorm on the way back. The rental car had gotten stuck in the mud, as did our shoes. We'd had to hike barefoot up the road while laughing so hard, I'd nearly peed my shorts. It was the stupidest, most reckless trip I've ever taken.

To this day, it's still the best weekend of my life.

I curse under my breath and yank my robe tighter around my waist.

Stop taking trips down memory lane.

I'm not going.

I lost the bet.

My phone buzzes.

> Wyatt: Ready for tonight, sugar?

I stare at the screen. My thumbs hover over the keyboard, but then I drop the phone on the bed with a frustrated groan.

No, Wyatt. I'm not ready.

Not for you.

Not for your half-cocked smile and those sin-dipped eyes.

Not for the way you limp around now, like you didn't start a bar fight three days ago, and still think you can ride bulls like your body is made of Kevlar.

He shouldn't even be out of bed, let alone going anywhere.

Yet, here I am, nervously counting down the hours until I get to sneak away with him, just like the olden days.

I ignore his dozens of messages and calls. To pass the time, I spend the afternoon pretending to be busy.

I play with my nieces and nephews. Then I reorganize a perfectly organized closet. I scrub already-clean counters. I even try to make banana bread, which ends with flour everywhere and a loaf that comes out like a brick.

Jagger walks through the kitchen, lifts a brow at my failed attempt, and says, "Remind me never to piss you off if this is your idea of victory baking."

"Victory?"

"Wyatt's win," he boasts, grinning like an idiot.

I throw a towel at him just as Georgia walks in.

He dodges it and tells Georgia, "Teach her some baking skills, for the love of Texas!" and laughs his way out of the room.

Eventually, the sun sets, and I'm out of time. I dress slowly, pulling on jeans that hug my hips, boots that click confidently with every step, and a top I shouldn't be wearing. It's a deep burgundy with an open back, thin straps that whisper trouble, and a clingy fit. I throw a plaid wrap around my shoulders.

Like that will keep Wyatt from staring at me.

A soft knock rattles my door, startling me.

"Willow," Wyatt's deep, rich, unapologetic drawl calls through the wood.

I stand frozen for a second. Then, I open the door, trying to breathe normally.

It's the Wyatt I spent my teenage years obsessing over. All rugged charm and crooked temptation, dressed in dark jeans and a black button-down that he didn't bother to button all the way. His rolled sleeves show off his forearms, tattoos, and bruised knuckles. And he wears a glint in his eye that promises chaos.

"You're still limping," I say, arms crossed, the butterflies going to war inside my stomach.

He grins. "I'm just standing here."

"You shouldn't be going anywhere."

"Aw. You worried about me, sugar?" he teases.

I glare at him. "No. I'm worried about myself. If you collapse on the sidewalk, I'm not dragging your ass back here."

He chuckles, stepping into my space. "Then I guess I'll have to stay upright. For you."

Don't fall for him again.

"Cut the cowboy charm. Where are we going, Wyatt?"

He steps back, that grin still playing on his lips. "You'll see."

I grab my purse and coat. "What am I supposed to tell my family? That I'm sneaking off with the guy I haven't spoken to in years until he ruined Christmas and then kissed me like he owned every memory I ever had of him?"

Horror fills me when I realize what I just said. My cheeks flame with embarrassment.

He savors his win for a moment, then states, "I'm telling them we have business to attend to."

My brows lift. "On New Year's Eve?"

"Sure. We're meeting the head of a corporation in Dallas tomorrow morning. Bright and early," he adds with a wink.

"And I'm just supposed to tell them I'm with you?"

He nods, all wolfish confidence. "Yeah, sugar. Let them know you're with me. You're my agent. Remember?"

My stomach flutters.

Damn him.

He leads me downstairs. We walk into the living room, and my chest tightens like it's caught in a vise.

Jagger's sprawled on the recliner with a beer, watching football. Dad's got his glasses low on his nose, reading something on his tablet. Mom's folding napkins and putting them on the coffee table like it's a competitive sport.

All three look up at once. All three narrow their eyes when they catch sight of me with Wyatt.

I clear my throat. "Hey. Wyatt and I have to head out for the night."

"Ace!" Wilder and Isabella shout.

Ace darts between us and through the other door. Wilder and Isabella are quick on his heels.

Jagger sits up, brows furrowed. "Where the hell are y'all going? It's New Year's Eve. The party starts in a few hours."

Wyatt slides right into the conversation, smooth as whiskey. "Sorry. We have to miss this one. We've got a meeting tomorrow morning in Dallas. There's a new sports drink brand looking for a rider."

He really thought this lie out.

Dad lowers his tablet. "On New Year's Day?"

I nod, too quickly, falling right back into the old way Wyatt and I used to tell tall tales to my family. "Yeah. Apparently they're from Europe. Don't do the whole 'holiday' thing like we do."

"Since when don't Europeans party on New Year's?" Jagger prods suspiciously.

"Like you know anything about European business people," I point out.

He scrunches his face, as if he's trying hard to figure out how anyone would want to meet on New Year's Day.

My stomach flips faster.

Wyatt adds, "They're on a tight marketing timeline and have to find someone. It was the only time that worked in their schedules."

Mom lifts a skeptical brow. "And they want to meet with you two specifically?"

Wyatt flashes that grin that should be illegal. "They're interested in sponsoring a few of Willow's riders and potentially building a training partnership. Willow thought it was best to bring me. It's a big opportunity."

Jagger makes a face. "Still weird. On a holiday?"

Guiltily, I add, "New year, new deals. Besides, if it pans out, it could be major for the team too. We'd be the first to land them stateside."

Dad grunts. "Guess business doesn't sleep."

Mom looks between us, fretting, "Are you staying at Sebastian and Georgia's?"

Wyatt answers before I can. "No. The company got us rooms at a hotel."

Mom waves us off. "Well, drive safely. And swing by Sebastian and Georgia's on the way home. You can bring back her pie dish."

"Pie dish?" I question.

"Yes. She forgot her favorite one. Remember?" Mom reminds me.

I faintly remember Georgia whining about her dish. I quickly state, "Sure."

Dad's already back to his tablet. "Make it worth it, kids."

My heart pounds so hard, we could have just pulled off a heist. I follow Wyatt outside, and he opens the passenger door to his old truck.

I slip into the seat.

He leans in, close to my face, and murmurs, "Told you they'd buy it, sugar."

I push him away. "Don't get cocky."

He grins, shuts the door, then limps to the driver's side.

His truck still has the same leather seats and the dent in the back fender. As we cruise past familiar roads, butterflies start to beat their wings harder inside me.

I glance out the window. "Why are you driving toward Devil's Wash?"

He quickly glances at me from the corner of his eye. "Aww, you're taking the fun out of it."

We pass the old bar, the grocery store, and the diner we used to sneak off to when no one was paying attention.

Then he veers left at the fork toward Pecan Hollow.

Panic and memories rush me all at once. "I thought we were going to Devil's Wash."

He chuckles. "We gotta eat, sugar."

"Eat? Where? Everything's packed on New Year's Eve," I point out, on a racetrack rushing down memory lane.

His maddening smirk grows. "Don't think I forgot your favorite restaurant."

I stay silent, my heart skipping a beat.

He proudly states, "Magnolia & Oak."

"Wyatt, we'll never get in tonight. Are you nuts?"

He chuckles deep in his throat. "You should know me better than that." He pulls down another street, then parks in front of the restaurant.

The valet greets us by name, but I can't remember his, not because it's been too long but because I can't think. Wyatt's got me spinning with memories I tried to bury.

"Carlos. How's your family?" Wyatt asks, fist-bumping the valet.

Carlos grins. "Getting too big for their britches. Great ride the other day."

"Thank you." Wyatt slips him some cash and says, "Take care of my baby."

I stifle a laugh. I forgot how proud he was of the truck he bought when he won his first rodeo.

He holds the door open for me. "After you."

I step into the warmth. Christmas lights glow around the restaurant, and memories hit me hard.

Us laughing until we cried.

His hand on my thigh under the table.

That night, we licked sugar off each other's fingers and laughed over stolen sips of wine, pretending we weren't already burning at the edges.

"Welcome," the hostess chirps, tearing me out of my thoughts. She leads us to a private corner booth. Red and green candles flicker on the tabletop. The scent of truffle oil and roasted peaches lingers in the air. A plate of chocolate-covered strawberries waits for us.

"You remembered," I murmur.

His eyes darken. "I remember everything."

An electric tension simmers between us, fiercer than a lightning strike. One spark and I'll lose my resolve not to burn with it, so I try not to look at Wyatt, scared he'll see I'm losing my ability to keep our boundaries.

A petite woman with gray-streaked auburn curls approaches. Her apron has *Margo* embroidered on it and her smile is wide and warm. She's aged but not too much.

"Evening, y'all. Happy New Year's Eve. Haven't seen you two lovebirds in years," she says, placing two leather-bound menus on the table.

I blink hard, feeling a rush of emotions.

Wyatt grins, sliding an arm along the back of the booth behind me. "Surprised you remember us."

Margo beams. "Of course I do. It's rare we get such a gorgeous couple in this booth without a reservation made months ago."

"We got lucky," I murmur.

"Mm-hmm." Her eyes twinkle like she knows something I don't. "Can I get you two started with something to drink?"

Wyatt glances at me, then at the wine list.

I raise an eyebrow. "You don't even like wine."

He shrugs one shoulder, cool as sin. "I'll take the pinot noir. Whatever bottle you recommend."

Margo laughs. "If memory serves me right, the last time you two were here, you got caught giving her sips of your wine when she was underage."

Wyatt leans in just enough to brush my arm. "You do have a great memory. And this is Willow's favorite place, and she's legal now. So please bring your best bottle."

My face warms.

Margo practically swoons. "Well, I'll be right back with two glasses and a bottle. It's silky, not too dry, and pairs perfectly with our signature short ribs, in case you were wondering."

"That's exactly what I was gonna order," Wyatt says, handing her back the menu without looking at it.

I smirk. "Since when do you eat short ribs without barbecue sauce?"

He nudges me gently with his knee under the table. "Since you taught me what bourbon glaze reduction means."

Margo grins. "That comes with roasted root vegetables and herbed polenta, but if y'all want to mix and match, we've got creamed kale, maple carrots, smoked gouda mashed, or truffle mac."

I glance at Wyatt. "You decide. You're the wine expert now."

He fakes deep thought. "Let's do the short ribs, sub the polenta for gouda mashed. And add truffle mac on the side. For her."

Why does he have to remember everything?

I shift in my seat.

He murmurs, "You underestimate me. But I remember everything about you."

"Sounds good. I'll be right back with your wine," Margo announces, scribbling on her notepad before walking away.

As soon as she's out of earshot, I glance at him. "Pinot noir?"

He picks up the empty wineglass. "Tastes better when it's across from you."

Over wine and the best short ribs I've had in a decade, I ask the question that crumbles our walls. "How did everything get so messed-up? You had everything."

"I didn't have you." He pins me with a regretful look.

"You know what I mean," I insist, trying to brush past his statement, and wanting to know the truth.

He swirls the wine in his glass like he actually knows what he's doing. He doesn't. But he always tried to do what he thought would make me happy.

I study him over the rim of my glass.

Ten minutes pass, and he doesn't eat or drink.

I wait him out.

He finally speaks, the words coming out low and raspy. "I remember the moment everything changed. It was a Tuesday." He smirks without humor. "That's the part that kills me. Not even a dramatic day. Just a Tuesday."

I stay silent.

He continues, "I was sitting in a hotel room outside Rock Springs, ice on my knee, trying to decide if I was more pissed that I lost another ride or that the pain didn't scare me anymore. I used to ride for something. For pride. Legacy. For... Well, you." His voice hitches, but he swallows it back. "But that night? I rode because I didn't know how to be anything else."

I exhale slowly.

He looks at me, eyes darker than I've seen in years. "It all slipped through my fingers. Sponsors bailed. Agent dropped me. The phone stopped ringing. Friends no longer were anywhere to be found. And the worst part? The silence wasn't just in the arena."

He leans forward, resting his arms on the table. "It followed me home. Echoed in every room. I kept thinking, *This isn't how it was supposed to go.* But I couldn't tell anyone. Couldn't call you."

"You could've," I whisper thickly.

He shakes his head. "You never picked up when I tried."

"I told you why."

He scrubs his face. "Yeah. I understand that now, but I didn't then."

My hand tightens around my wineglass. The hurt creeping up my throat, screaming it has unfinished business.

My will to keep my wall up dissolves. I admit quietly, "I tried to forget. I wanted to bury every memory of you. So I went to work. Built something. Traveled. Dated guys who had zero risk of breaking my heart because they didn't even know how to touch it."

His eyes flicker, and that old storm of jealousy and possession arises.

My lips tremble. "None of it worked. I'd see a worn leather cowboy hat and think of you. Someone would call me 'sugar' and I'd want to punch them in the throat."

He softly chuckles, but it fades fast.

I look away. "You were everywhere, Wyatt. And nowhere. All at once."

Silence folds over us, but it isn't empty. He grabs my hand, caressing the back of it. It's slow and gentle, with the same desires of long ago brewing under the surface.

He murmurs, "Tell me this doesn't feel the same."

Warning bells ring. My mind tells me to pull back. But I don't.

I can't.

I squeeze his hand. And he's right. It does feel the same.

We don't kiss in the restaurant. Not because we don't want to. But because the heat in the air is too thick, and maybe we both know once we start, we won't be able to stop.

So we drink wine and smile across the candlelit table like nothing happened. As if our story never ended, and there's hope for us.

For the first time in years, I can't help but wonder if somehow our love survived the wreckage.

20

Wyatt

argo asks, "Did you save room for dessert?"

I hand my card to her, saying, "Add dessert to go, please."

Willows's face shows her surprise, but it's quickly taken over by a flicker of anxiety.

I squeeze her hand and ask Margo, "Do you remember our favorite?"

Her gaze dances between Willow and me. "Bourbon pecan with a side container of extra whip?"

"Bring two containers, please," I state, grinning.

Willow stiffens next to me.

I slide my hand between her thighs under the table.

Don't worry. I remember what you love.

"Coming up," Margo replies.

Willow squeezes her legs together and smiles at Margo. "Thank you."

Margo nods and turns, but not before throwing me a wink over her shoulder.

"Careful, cowboy. That charm might get you in trouble tonight," Willow teases under her breath.

"Lucky for you, sugar, I brought enough charm and bad ideas to last well into the New Year," I boast, dragging my thumb slowly across the inside of her wrist, right where her pulse thumps hard.

Willow smirks. Another hit of nostalgia pummels me. It's the same look that used to drive me wild and make me do reckless things just so I could see more of it.

Margo sets a brown bag full of dessert on the table. She puts the check next to it.

I scribble my name on the receipt, slide my card back into my wallet, and stand. I place my hand on the small of Willow's back.

She doesn't fight me. Instead, she leans into me the same way she always did. The scent of her shampoo flares around us, eliminating any possibility of me staying a gentleman tonight.

I guide us through the cozy restaurant and out into the cold.

Fresh snow falls in lazy spirals under the glow of the streetlamps. My boots crunch against the sidewalk, and the sound of her heels keeps pace with my heart. Everything around us sparkles. Christmas lights adorn every building, wreaths hang in every window, and the holiday music plays in the bar next door.

It all makes me nervous as hell.

Christmas was always our special time. Willow gave herself to me for the first time at Christmas, and it was the best present I ever received.

For years, it was the gift that kept giving, then it was gone without warning.

I want my gift back.

Emotions I haven't allowed myself to feel in years lodge in my throat. I glance at Willow and note how she's the same yet different.

She's prettier than I remember.

How is that possible?

Her dark hair spills over her shoulders like she just stepped out of a movie. Pink flushes her cheeks, and she looks up at me like she's pretending she's not feeling what I am, but those eyes say everything her mouth won't. Her blues turn almost hazel, glowing under the streetlamps, seductive yet innocent, flickering with nerves.

After all these years, it still rattles me like it used to.

She has no idea how much power she holds over me.

She pulls her wrap tighter. It curves snugly around her waist, showcasing her ass, triggering my pulse several notches higher. Her jeans mold to her hips, and I swear she wore them on purpose to torment me. It's the kind of outfit that leaves just enough to the imagination, causing a man's blood to pump hotter.

Snippets of our history flash in my mind, one scene at a time. All involve intimate moments between us that I'm determined to experience again.

A gust of snow darts at us, making it harder to move forward. Willow leans closer to me, and I do my best to shield her from the harsh flakes, holding her head against me. My palms sweat despite the thick snowflakes falling everywhere. I forge ahead, leading her toward the truck, my hand gripping the curve of her waist, our breaths visible in the chilly air.

Every step I take reminds me of a gamble I can't afford to lose. She hasn't let me be this close without being angry since I got back. But I'm not a stupid man. I know I haven't yet earned back a permanent spot in her life. So I debate about how to get one. By the time I get to the truck, my heart's wildly thumping against my rib cage, and I'm running on instinct.

I open the passenger door but don't let her climb in. Instead, I turn her toward me, sliding my hand into her hair. My voice comes out low, "Willow. Wait a minute."

The holiday lights cause her features to glow, reminding me of the night she gave me her virginity. Her lips slightly part. The pink flush on her cheeks from the cold deepens. She arches her eyebrows, holding her breath.

God help me.

Before she can duck away from me, I lower my lips to hers. This kiss is different from yesterday's. This time, I take my time, slow and deliberate, reclaiming everything sacred I stupidly lost a long time ago.

To my surprise, she doesn't fight me. She leans into our kiss.

All the aches I've carried since I left resurface. With each shot of pain, I continue to taste her, holding her tighter. My tongue coaxes hers, hungry with all the words I never said and regrets I'll live with forever. My hand curls in her hair, with just enough tension to keep her as close as possible.

She breathes in sharply, then her lips part wider, and I deepen our kiss.

Every whimper and flick of her tongue, I savor. She relaxes more and more until there's no resistance, just a sweet surrender she doesn't even realize she's offering.

Her breathy moan hits my ear. She shivers against my chest, and the cold disappears. She fists my shirt, clawing at my chest, pulling me closer. And I don't know who's been starving more. Me or her.

Her body melts against mine. Her hips shift subtly, as if her subconscious is already giving in to everything her mouth won't admit. Then she moans louder, and it shreds every bit of control I have left.

I move her over two steps so we're in front of the passenger door, then pin her to it.

My breath turns ragged. I nip her bottom lip, then soothe it with my tongue, tugging her hair tighter.

Her hands roam under my jacket, taunting me.

She gasps. "Wyatt—"

"No," I growl roughly against her mouth. "Not a goddamn word, Willow. Not yet."

Her knees wobble.

I grab her thigh, hooking it around my hip without asking, grinding into her, letting her feel exactly how hard I am. I drawl against her lips, my voice thick with need, "Damn, I missed the way you fit me, sugar."

She barely gets out between kisses, "How am I supposed to be smart when you kiss me like this?"

I chuckle, then say, "You're not. So stop trying."

She softly laughs, then kisses me back with a new ferocity, gripping my shirt tighter.

When I finally tear my lips from hers, I'm out of breath. I keep my face close, warning, "No matter what's happened in the past, you're mine. Deep down, you know it."

She blinks several times, her eyes glistening in the holiday lights.

With my pulse pounding between my ears, I move her to the passenger seat, peck her on the forehead, and order, "Get in, sugar."

She doesn't resist. She never could when I kissed her like that.

I shut her door, hurry around the truck, and get in. I start the engine and pull away from the curb.

Thick silence crackles with tension during the short ride to the motel. My fingers flex around the steering wheel, and I steal glances at her every few seconds.

She chews her bottom lip, staring out the window, but it's frosted over. The only thing visible is the blurred glow of the lights on the buildings.

Knots pull tighter in my gut. My pulse is louder than the rumbling engine. I squeeze her hand and assert, "Stop trying to figure out how to get rid of me tonight."

She slowly turns and meets my eyes.

I tease, "I know you don't want to have to beg me for a New Year's Eve kiss."

She breaks into a smile, and laughs. "You wish."

I kiss the back of her hand, then refocus on the white road. After several miles, the run-down motel finally comes into view. I park near the front office, and leave the engine on.

I clear my throat, forcing a grin to mask my fear. "Stay put. And don't go making a run for it. I ain't chasing you through snow in cowboy boots."

She smirks. "That might be fun to watch with your limp."

I warn, "Don't test me, sugar." I climb out and head into the office. My nerves gnaw my insides.

The same clerk from years ago is still behind the desk. He's greasier than a plate of fairground fries, but he doesn't ask questions. He never did.

I hand him cash, sign the form, and pocket the key to room number eight. It's the same room we used to sneak off to when neither of us wanted to be found.

I return to the truck, park farther down, and nod toward the row of doors. "Secured good old room number eight. The lobby still smells like smoke and bad decisions. Just like we left it." I wink.

Nerves stamp across her face, flaring hotter.

I lower my voice, coaxing, "Relax, sugar."

Her gaze darts to the room, then back to me. "Maybe we shouldn't relive bad decisions."

"We weren't a bad decision," I firmly state, my heart racing faster.

"Weren't we?" she questions.

"No," I assert.

Pressure swells in my chest, seizing my breath until it's sharp. I lean over and kiss her on the cheek, and declare, "I'm going inside. Nothing bad ever happened there. No matter what choices we made in the past, that room was always filled with love."

She blinks hard and scrunches her forehead.

The thud in my heart bangs against my rib cage with more force. I take the biggest gamble of my life and add, "That's what I want, Willow. I want to make love to you all night, ringing in the New Year and figuring out how to move forward. So I'm leaving the keys in the truck. You can join me or leave me. It's up to you, but I hope you come inside."

She arches her eyebrows and holds her breath.

I hop out of the truck before I lose my nerve, grab the bag of dessert, and tease, "You don't get to keep the dessert or the whipped cream if you don't keep me."

A soft, barely audible laugh flies out of her mouth.

I wink. Adrenaline builds in every one of my cells. I shut the door and move toward the building, but every step I take away from her is a shot of dread.

My hand fumbles with the lock. I eventually shove the door open, and a brick of memories hits me.

The room has barely changed. The lilac paint and matching faded floral wallpaper are the same, but both are peeling now. The comforter is worn thinner. A groan from the heater makes me jump, and dry air pushes out of it.

Get a grip.

On the oak table, next to a coffee-stained armchair, sits a tiny plastic Christmas tree with blinking red and green lights. Gold tinsel wraps around its base, and a gold foil star sits on top, but it's bent.

A yellow glow from the decades-old lamps makes everything look dingier. But when we were kids, we didn't care. It was our safe haven where we didn't have to hide or keep our voices down.

I should have brought her to a nicer place.

Where is she?

I sit on the bed, my forearms on my knees, staring at the tan carpet. The original texture has long faded into a patchwork of threadbare spots and flattened fibers. Soil marks shade the high-traffic areas.

The loud tick of the clock echoes in my ears as the minute changes.

She's going to drive off.

What am I doing?

I can't let her leave without me.

I jump off the bed and reach for the door right as it opens. The wood bangs into my head. "Ooof! Hell's bells!"

"Oh my! I'm so sorry," Willow frets.

She came in!

Relief overshadows the pain.

I rub the spot. "Damn near knocked the cowboy outta me!"

"I'm sorry," she repeats, tossing me a sympathetic but semi-amused grin.

I blink through the throb in my forehead, and my grin explodes. "Hell, sugar. If it's for you, I'll take a concussion and call it foreplay."

She bursts out laughing, then puts her hand over her mouth.

It's all it takes to release the tension.

Her laughter trails off, and her gaze darts around the room. "It's... um..."

I chuckle. "Guess they still have their Christmas spirit."

Her smile gets bigger as she does a more thorough scan.

I offer, "I should have taken you to a nicer hotel. This is dingy, isn't it?"

She bites her lip, and her gaze does another lap around the room. She admits, "I don't remember it being this umm..."

"Beat up?"

"That's one way of putting it." She turns, grinning at me.

A spark of tension reignites, but it's the hottest it's been all night.

A lot of our best moments were in this room. Intimate, private, unforgettable memories, and they all come barreling at me. And the walls seem to come alive, as if they remember every kiss, every whispered promise, every time we swore this wouldn't be the last.

I glance at the bed, wondering if it'll rise and devour me whole. I take a few deep breaths and then blurt out, "Maybe we should go somewhere else?"

She arches her eyebrows, then closes the gap between us, putting her hand over my heart. In a sultry voice, she coos, "Wyatt Houston, I'd swear on my granddaddy's grave that you're more nervous than I am right now."

I take another pull of air and admit, "I guess I am. I don't want to mess everything up with you again."

Her pink tongue darts out of her mouth, slowly grazing her lip. She gives me a look that's always gone straight to my pants.

Tonight is no different. My belt buckle feels heavy, and my nerves shift into a state of desperate need. I wrap one arm around her waist, the other around her shoulder, palming the back of her head. I lock eyes with her, grazing her lips as I grit out, "You think we should go somewhere else, sugar?"

She doesn't say anything, just stares at me, her eyes wide and bright.

The need inside me builds, ready to explode. My thumb finds its way under the hem of her sweater, grazing the soft skin near her spine.

She shudders, and her breath hitches, but she doesn't step away.

I kiss her jaw, then murmur against her ear, "You remember this room and all the good times, don't you, sugar?"

Her body arches with the smallest shift, but it's the answer I need. Her hot breath sparks a tingle on my chest.

I sink my hand under her jeans. My lips brush the shell of her earlobe. "I used to spend nights dreaming about dragging you back here, laying you out on this creaky old bed, and reminding you why you love to beg me." I palm her ass cheek.

She whimpers, "Don't."

"Don't what? Don't talk about the way you used to cry out my name? Don't touch you like I already know where you're aching?" I ask, tone dark and husky.

"Wyatt," she warns, the sound barely a whisper, her fingers grasping my shirt.

I dip my head until our lips nearly touch, challenging, "Tell me I'm wrong. Lie to me, and I'll stop."

She doesn't answer. Just trembles in my arms. Her breath mingles with mine, and her gaze flicks down to my mouth.

It nearly kills me, but I've never been so ready to die.

This time, I'm not looking for a night of fun.

I'm looking for a second chance. I'm after a lifetime to prove to her I'm the only man for her, the only one who's ever counted.

And I'm going to make sure I'm the last one she ever has to bet on.

21

Willow

Wyatt's dark eyes challenge me to lie to him so this doesn't go any further.

I should, but I can't. My skin buzzes with longing and anticipation, and I'm way past the point of having any control over this situation. It ended the moment I got in the truck with him.

The atmosphere between us thickens, heavier than it was on the ride over, denser than it was in that damn jail cell, and more electric than it's been in seven years.

Blood rushes hot in my veins. The scent of cheap soap and pine-scented cleaner hangs in the air, stifling any remaining discipline I may have to make a good decision.

Wyatt doesn't flinch. He stands in front of the door, with his rugged stare, daring me to bolt.

My chest rises and falls too quickly. I blurt out, "Are you going to say something?"

He tips his head slightly, a teasing twinkle appearing in his gaze. He taunts, "I was trying to let you breathe first."

"I'm not sure I've done that since I saw you in your cell."

He swallows, his jaw twitching, not missing a beat. "If it makes you feel better, I haven't since I saw you glaring at me through the bars."

A laugh stumbles out of me, unsure and too high-pitched.

He steps closer, peering at me so intensely, my bones feel like they've caught fire.

What am I doing here with him?

We aren't kids anymore.

This is going to end in disaster again.

I shift, needing something to do with my hands, but all I've got is the hem of my wrap and a fast-dissolving grip on my sanity. "Wyatt—"

"Don't." He closes the gap further, his voice low, not tearing his gaze off mine. "Don't give me the speech. Not right now. Not after that truck ride. Not after what I felt when you touched me."

"I didn't touch you," I claim, but it's a lie, and we both know it.

A wicked, slow, dangerous grin curls his lips. He drawls, "Sugar, you grabbed my shirt like you were trying to rip it off and leave me to freeze in the snow."

Heat scorches through my chest and runs straight between my legs.

I cross my arms. "You're imagining things."

He steps so close, the toes of our boots touch. He shakes his head. "No, I'm not. And trust me, I've imagined plenty of things about you, Willow, so I know fantasy versus reality."

Butterflies resume the war they've been fighting in my belly since Christmas night. Every time they destroy a red flag, another one appears to replace it.

This isn't a smart way to start the New Year.

I tilt my chin up. "You think a few sweet words are going to undo what you did?"

He drops his voice lower, sending a wave of shivers down my spine. "No. I think one more kiss might, though."

Brutal silence expands around us until the air in my lungs turns stale.

I don't want to forgive him, but I want him.

God help me. I still want him.

It's the same problem I've had since the day I realized Wyatt was no longer a big brother figure anymore.

His hand lifts. His rough fingertips skim my jaw. "You're still the most beautiful thing I've ever seen."

I should shove him away and spew every curse at him that's been festering in my chest for years. Instead, I whisper, "You still talk too pretty."

His lips twitch. "Want me to shut up?"

Eight seconds pass and then the ability to jump out of the way of a moving train no longer exists. Years of pain and longing come to a halt.

His mouth crashes into mine with the force of a storm, and the winds are too ferocious to fight.

And there's nothing sweet about it this time. It's hard, deep, filthy, and full of everything we can't take back.

His hand slides into my hair, tilting my head back as he takes more.

My arms go around his shoulders, gripping him for dear life. I kiss him back, sinking into everything that's Wyatt, and remembering how good it feels to be the object of his insatiable hunger.

He breaks the kiss just enough to challenge, "Still want me to stop?"

I breathe against his lips, "Shut up, Wyatt."

A low growl vibrates in his throat. He moves me backward, pinning me to the peeling wallpaper. Every inch of his thick, demanding hard-on fights his denim, pressing against my stomach. He yanks my hair.

My eyes flutter with borderline dizziness.

His mouth trails down my neck while his fingers unzip my jeans. He mumbles, "You still smell like warm amber, jasmine, and sin, all ready to rope around me forever."

"You still talk in cowboy riddles."

"And you still clench your thighs when I say something dirty."

I smile against his lips, then slip my tongue back into his mouth, fumbling with his shirt.

He reaches behind his neck and tears it off, displaying a bruised abdomen more ripped than it was seven years ago.

I wince, staring at the purple and yellow marks.

He tilts my chin up, forcing my gaze back to his. "Don't worry, sugar. My cock and tongue still work just fine."

I stifle a giggle, feeling giddy and drunk, even though I'm not inebriated.

He nips at my ear and murmurs, "I got extra whipped cream, and I remember how to use it."

Bolts of adrenaline shoot to my core. I squeeze my thighs together.

He grunts, grinning. "I told you." He slides his hand under my jeans and over my panties.

I sharply inhale, my insides quivering, sinking into his familiar—and missed—possessive touch. I press my hand to his chest over his heart. It beats furiously under my fingers, reminding me how broken he left me. So I whisper, "I hate you."

"I know."

"I really do."

"Then punish me," he growls, grinding his erection against me and sliding two fingers past my panties. "Scratch me up. Ride me like you're trying to forget me."

Arching into his hand, I groan and pull his mouth back to mine.

He turns us and moves toward the bed without breaking our kiss. Our boots hit the floor, followed by my shirt, his belt, then my jeans. He peels them off, and his voice comes out slightly angry, stating, "I'm taking my gift back." He pushes me on the bed and kneels between my legs.

Gift?

I tense. "Wyatt—"

"Don't, Willow," he warns, then glances up, breathless, eyes ablaze. "I remember everything about you. Every sound. Every taste. Every goddamn look you ever gave me in the dark. And then you ripped it all away. But I didn't say you could have it back. So I'm reclaiming it as mine."

I suck in a breath, thighs trembling under his hands.

He leans in, dragging his tongue up my inner thigh. "I'm gonna take my time, so sit back and say some prayers, sugar."

My voice cracks. "Wh-why?"

"Because I'm not walking out of this motel room until you're as limp as I am and have no more reservations about us." He moves his tongue to the tip of my slit, his hot breath buzzing against my skin.

My hands dive into his hair. I curl my fingers, tugging, and admit, "I hate how much I missed that mouth."

An amused promise barrels out of him. "Then let me remind you how much you need it." He drags his tongue slowly against me, sinfully circling exactly where I'm already aching.

Every flick pulls a gasp from deep in my chest. The quiver in my stomach intensifies, and every nerve I have swells with anticipation.

He murmurs against me, "And, sugar, I ain't stopping until you lose your voice crying out my name." His mouth ravages me like he's starving.

"Wyatt!" I call out against my will. My fingers tangle in his hair, gripping for dear life as I grind my trembling pussy against his face.

He groans, tightening his fingers around my hips. He flicks his tongue until I'm spent, then kisses my inner thighs.

I take ragged breaths.

He taunts, "You always sounded so goddamn sweet when you begged. Let's hear it again, sugar." His mouth latches back on my pussy, and a round of adrenaline sits ready to detonate within me.

"Wyatt! Oh God… Please."

"That's it," he coaxes, pressing his tongue so firmly to my clit, it makes my hips jerk.

"Wyatt!" I whimper, my legs shaking. My heart pounds so hard, I swear the walls echo with it.

"I've been dreaming about your taste since you stole it from me," he snaps, voice tight with hurt. He circles his tongue, pulses it, then flattens it, repeating the cycle over and over.

I fall apart under his mouth again, arching my back and clenching the thread-bare comforter.

He relentlessly flicks, mercilessly owning every drop of my pleasure.

My back bows higher, and I cry out, shattering with an all-consuming pressure so great that I squirt my arousal all over him.

"That's my fucking sugar," he praises, sticking his tongue in my hole and lapping up every ounce he can.

I moan, shaking through it, trying to catch my breath, feeling delirious.

He finally lifts his head and then crawls up my body. His mouth hovers over mine, smelling like my orgasms. "I'm not done," he warns, tone guttural, erection taunting my pussy.

I pull his face toward me, kissing him the same way as I used to, with no reservations, hate, or regret. It's just Wyatt and me, two lovers who were separated from each other for too long.

His hand slides under my back, arching me to him as he shucks his jeans. Then he's fully pressed against me, bare, thick, harder than ever before. He pushes between my thighs.

I gasp.

"Sure you can still handle me?" he teases, brushing his lips over my cheek.

My heart pounds in my throat, craving the things he can do to me. "I'm not scared," I lie.

His grin turns wicked. "There's my girl."

He drives into me in one long, deep thrust.

I choke on a moan, rocking my hips while straining to take all of him at once.

"Damn it, sugar," he barks, pushing my thigh higher, sinking deeper, then withdrawing slowly before slamming back inside.

It pulls another cry from my throat.

"Don't tell me to be nice," he growls.

"Don't you dare," I manage to get out.

Our rhythm turns brutal, but it's honest, built on years of unsaid things and bodies that never forgot how perfectly they fit together.

The headboard hits the wall, banging so hard, it should break the drywall.

My pussy clenches once, then spasms. My nails dig into his shoulders, then score down his back.

He groans, low and feral. "You feel even better than I remember."

"Harder," I gasp.

"Fuck," he mutters, then gives me what I want, pounding into me with a new intensity.

It's rough and dirty. It's everything we were and everything we could have been if he hadn't left or maybe if I had taken his calls.

He braces on one arm. His other hand slides between us, finding my swollen clit with precision.

I cry out, my breasts squishing into his chest as waves of endorphins slam into me. My entire body goes taut, shuddering against his.

A bead of his sweat drips on my cheek. He licks it, watching me unravel, and scolds, "You don't take gifts back, sugar."

Guilt hits me, but it mixes with anger. I stutter, "Y-you l-left."

He grits his teeth, thrusting harder, barely hanging on, and lowers his face an inch from mine. "You didn't take my calls and avoided me every time I came back to town. But that's over now. I'm taking my gift back forever."

I blink hard, trembling with adrenaline.

His jaw clenches. His hips stutter. Then he buries his cock deeper, keeping his stare on mine, and his low, guttural moan shakes along with his hard frame before he collapses over me.

Our ragged breaths compete with the ticking clock and the beating of our hearts. Neither of us moves, tangled in each other, coated in sweat and years of unfinished business.

I clear my throat. "Wyatt—"

"Don't," he warns, rolling off me and pulling me onto his chest.

I curl into his warmth.

He strokes my ass as the silence stretches.

The little Christmas tree blinks red and green, and reality hits me.

What have we done?

A tidal wave of emotions floods my soul. I stare at the cheap tree, trying to ignore the tear sliding down my cheek.

"Still hate me?" he asks softly, the words coming out rough with a hint of fear.

I take a moment to try to figure out why this is so hard, then finally whisper, "No. That's not the problem."

He runs his hand up my spine as he turns his head and buries his nose in my hair. He inhales deeply, asking, "Then what is?"

I look up to his handsome face.

His dark eyes search mine, his cockiness evaporating. He takes his finger and wipes my wet cheek.

More tears fall. I accuse, "You left me, Wyatt, without even a proper goodbye. You broke something in me I never knew could break."

He nods slowly. "If I could go back and beat the shit out of that kid, I would. But I can't, Willow."

I quietly study his stubble and the new scar on his chin.

He offers, "In fairness, I didn't see any other way."

"I could have gone with you," I remind him.

He scoffs. "And given up everything you worked for?"

"I could have transferred, and you know it."

He sighs. "And what would I have told your father? *I'm in love with your daughter but have nothing to offer her?*"

"That wasn't the truth," I protest.

"It was. I thought I'd make something of myself and come back for you, but all I did was lose you."

The heater kicks on, breaking the silence that's settled in the room in the wake of his words. It pushes a wave of soap, pine, sweat, and arousal around us.

He laces our fingers together, asserting, "I meant it about my gift."

My stomach flips. I bite on my lip, pinning my eyebrows together.

He rises and lifts the covers, ordering, "Slide under."

Not knowing what else to do, I obey.

He slips in next to me, and demands, "Turn over."

I glance at him, my lips twitching with amusement. "You want to cuddle?"

"Yep. And I want to wake up beside you and pretend, for a few hours, that I didn't mess this up beyond repair."

The hairs on my arms rise. I bite my tongue, afraid of what might come out of my mouth.

"You're supposed to say it's not beyond repair," he states in a flat tone, his gaze narrowing on mine.

Guilt, hope, regret, and fear all plague me. I kiss him on the lips and quickly turn onto my side, pushing my back into him.

He sighs into my hair, tugging me closer and holding me tighter. He kisses my cheek, then the back of my neck.

I close my eyes and pretend that none of this ever broke, wishing it were easy to move forward without any worries.

But I know what Wyatt's capable of. I've experienced how easily he can break me, and there's no way to forget it.

He strokes my jaw, kisses behind my ear, and says, "You're not keeping my gift from me anymore, sugar."

I close my eyes and inhale his scent. I eventually fall into a deep sleep where I dream of a world where Wyatt and I live happily ever after, and the last seven years never happened.

I don't know how long I'm asleep before his hot breath hits my ear as he coos, "Wake up, sugar."

I blink a few times. The dingy room and the green and red blinking lights on the tree come into view.

I'm at the motel.

With Wyatt.

I freeze, except for my rapidly thrumming pulse.

He flips me onto my back, caging his hard frame over mine. His stern expression looks as tough as his voice sounds. "You almost missed it."

I swallow hard. "Missed what?"

The corners of his mouth curve up. "This." He closes the gap and kisses me with fervor.

I pull him closer, kissing him back, unable to stop it if I tried.

He finally retreats, breathing hard, and mumbles, "Happy New Year, sugar." He shifts me onto my side, wraps his body around mine, and returns to kissing my neck.

I reach for his wrist, lift his hand to my lips for a kiss, then snuggle closer, pretending again that everything is perfect between us.

22

Wyatt

Willow's body, warm and pressed up against me, pulls at my heartstrings. I hadn't forgotten how soft she was, but reality is way better than my imagination. Her hair's sprawled over my chest, and my thigh is wedged between hers. Our bare skin's a mess of heat under the cheap motel sheets, and her steady breathing kept my wild nerves calm all night.

I never want to move. I stare at my beautiful woman, continuing to spoon her, loving how perfectly her body still fits with mine. And I wonder how we could ever part again.

A soft moan escapes her lips. She shifts her hips, slow and sleepy, into my semi.

It's all it takes. My cock hardens, and I yank her ass closer to me, slipping into her wet heat.

Her eyes fly open, and her mouth forms an O as her whimper collides with my groan.

I grip her hip, kissing her neck and thrusting at a snail's pace.

"Wyatt," she breathes.

"Morning, sugar," I say hoarsely.

A low, needy moan rattles in her chest. She pushes her ass into my thrust, trying to get me deeper.

"That's it. Ride me like I'm the bull you need to tame."

She curls her legs, taking more of my cock inside her, continuing to moan.

"Jesus," I mumble, licking her earlobe as I clench my arm around her and circle my fingers on her clit. I bury my erection inside her, only moving a few inches back before I fully thrust into her again.

"Oh," she whimpers, digging her nails into my forearm and thigh.

My lips trail behind her ear. I confess, "I missed you."

She pushes against me the moment I pull back. She whimpers my name, the sound raspy and thick with sleep.

"That's it, sugar," I praise, adrenaline building so fast in me, I have to grit my teeth to stop from coming too soon.

She rolls her hips in a circle while I thrust. A faint quiver racks her. She clenches around my cock like she wants to break it.

"You feel so damn good," I whisper, dragging my mouth over the top of her spine and forcing myself not to rush.

She arches and gasps, "Oh God."

I groan into her shoulder. "I've been dreaming about this. About you."

She moans, and I add more force. Her nails scrape my skin.

I lose control. It's worse than coming too soon. I admit into her ear, "I'm so in love with you. More than I ever was before, and I didn't think that was possible."

Just like that, the high crashes. Her entire body tenses up.

My gut sinks. I thrust a few times to get us back to where we were, but it's pointless.

She shifts forward, pulls off of me, and sits up. She drags the sheet with her like it's armor.

My hand hovers behind her, frozen. "Willow?"

She doesn't turn around. "Don't say stuff like that."

I sit up. "Why not? It's the truth."

She wraps the sheet tighter around herself and then turns toward me, glaring. "Because you always ruin it, Wyatt."

My chest caves in. "I—"

"All my Christmases have been ruined since you took off. Did you know that? You left, and every year, I fake smiles for my family, because none of it's been the same without you," she hurls.

I shift closer. "Mine were horrible too. But I didn't know you still loved me. I thought you never would again. But now I know you still do. And I'm going to make it up to you."

Her laugh is hollow. "You can't make up for seven years of heartache. You walked away like I didn't matter."

I reach for her. "It wasn't like that, and you know it."

"No? Sure as hell felt like that," she fumes.

Anger hits me, taking me by surprise. I assert, "You need to take a bit of the blame here."

She jerks her head backward. "I have to take the blame?"

I nod. "Yeah. I called you. You never took my calls."

She shouts, "You were drunk!"

"You never answered. You avoided me any chance you got," I say in the calmest tone I can.

"You broke me!" she states.

"You don't think I was broken?" I ask.

Tense silence fills the air.

Her lips tremble.

I take a breath and admit, "You weren't the only one who struggled, sugar. And I'll take responsibility for my role in this, but you aren't innocent."

Her eyes fill with tears. She looks away and wipes her face.

I scoot closer and wrap my arm around her. I insist, "It doesn't matter anymore. All that matters is we still love each other. And this time, I won't fuck it up, and that means you won't have a chance to either."

She shakes her head, then turns back to me, eyes glassy. "I can't go down this road again. I can't sneak around and lie to my family only to get torn apart the second you get scared or your career takes off and you bolt."

I clench my jaw. "I didn't leave because we had a pregnancy scare. I left because I didn't know how to stay."

She laughs while crying. "You didn't know how to stay? I thought I was having your baby, and you didn't even ask me if I was okay."

My chest tightens. I take eight breaths, then confess, "I won't lie. I didn't know how I would ever be a good dad, but that isn't why I left. I needed to make something of myself before I could be the man you deserved. And you ended up not being pregnant."

"So that made it right to just bolt before I woke up the next morning?" she accuses.

My voice breaks. "I'm sorry. I shouldn't have been stubborn and left without making things right with you."

She wipes her cheek. "Which is why you'll do it again when push comes to shove."

"No, I won't." I move to sit closer to her. "Tell me you don't still love me."

She stares ahead, staying silent.

"Stop fighting us." I press a kiss to her shoulder, then her neck. I reach for her chin to turn her toward me.

She twists away, climbing off the bed and grabbing her clothes. "I'm sorry, Wyatt. But I can't do this again."

"Willow—"

"No more motel rooms. No more secrets. No more pretending we're the same people we used to be and that our love survived the explosion." She pulls her jeans on.

I get out of bed, emotions raw and on full display when I say, "We're not pretending. This is real. And our love did survive."

She throws her shirt over her head, then tightens her wrap. She brushes tears from her cheeks. "I have to go."

I step in front of her, blocking the door. "Take a breather, Willow."

"I'm not doing this again, Wyatt. I'm an all-or-nothing woman, and you already showed you can't handle that," she declares.

"I'm all-in. I always have been," I insist.

She scoffs. "We hid from my family for three years. You call that all-in?"

Shame fills me as I stare at her.

Her chest rises and falls as heavy as a marathon runner's. She seethes in a trembling voice, "You think I didn't want to scream our relationship from the rooftops? That I was yours? I had to lie to everyone I loved and pretend you were just my brother's best friend. I had to act like I hadn't already given you everything."

I swallow hard around the lump in my throat as guilt strangles my lungs. "I'll admit I was afraid of ruining my friendship with Jagger. But what stopped me was losing your dad's respect. I wasn't enough. Not yet. But I did want to become a man good enough for you."

She shouts, raw and painful, "You were enough! But you didn't think I was enough for you. That's the real truth."

"Not true."

"Then why didn't you stay and fight for us?"

I cautiously step closer to her. "The past is the past, Willow. I can't undo my mistakes. But I'm fighting for you now."

She shakes her head, eyes filled with glassy betrayal. "It's too late."

I reach for her, but she sidesteps me, grabs the keys, and yanks open the door. The morning's chill blasts past the door, biting my skin.

She pauses on the threshold. "You can't love me the way I need you to. And I can't keep letting you halfway in."

"Willow—"

"I'll be in the truck." She steps outside and slams the door.

For a moment, I stand still, naked and stunned, the scent of her still clinging to my skin. The echo of her heartbreak pounds louder than my own, and I don't know how to fix this.

The sound of my truck's engine pulls me out of my trance.

I dress quickly. My jeans feel like sandpaper, my boots too stiff. Nothing fits right, whether it's my clothes or my damn life.

When I get to the truck, she's already in the passenger seat, arms crossed and eyes aimed straight ahead.

The whole ride back is cold and silent. The snow has stopped falling, but the roads are super icy. I barely look at her, but I don't need to. I feel her and our regret the entire time.

We pull through the gates at the Cartwright Ranch. The holiday lights twinkle across the front porch, their brightness muted by the ice.

I turn off the engine. "Willow—"

"Don't start," she warns as she gets out of the truck.

I follow her into the cold, up the porch, and inside.

The aroma of bacon and cinnamon floats around the house. The same happy chaos that's always present in the Cartwright residence hits my ears.

She trudges into the family room, and everyone's there. Jacob and Ruby, Jagger, Ava, and the rest of the crew.

"We're home," Willow announces in a flat tone.

Ruby looks up from the table where she's working on a puzzle with the grandkids, and smiles. "How was Dallas?" she asks.

Willow stiffens, and woodenly answers, "Fine."

"How was the meeting?" Jacob asks.

Willow glances at me with guilt, then shrugs. "We'll know more in a few weeks."

"They made you ruin your New Year's Eve and can't even tell you if they want you or not?" Jagger spouts.

Willow's face flushes pink. "That's how it works, Jagger."

"Really?" He cocks his eyebrows.

Fuck this.

No more hiding.

She turns to leave, but I reach out and grab her arm, spinning her toward me. I confess, "We didn't go to Dallas."

Her eyes widen. "Wyatt! Don't."

"It's about time you all know the truth," I continue, not tearing my eyes off hers.

No one speaks. My pulse rattles between my ears.

Panic fills Willow's expression.

I take a breath and then look at the only two people who matter at this moment besides Willow. I stand taller and tell Jacob and Ruby, "I'm in love with your daughter. Have been since my eighteenth birthday."

Gasps fill the room. Jacob's eyes turn to slits. Ruby's mouth drops open in shock.

Jagger blurts out, "Ha, ha. Funny."

"And she loves me too," I continue, gaze back on Willow. "Even if she won't admit it."

Jagger stands up so quickly that his chair tips backward. It crashes with a bang against the wood floor. His voice is sharp with anger. "You aren't kidding, are you?"

I lock eyes with him. "No. I love her. Always have. Always will."

Willow pulls her hand from mine and takes a step back. "Wyatt—"

"Tell me you're joking," Jagger booms.

I shake my head. "It's not a joke. I'm in love with your sister."

Ruby clears her throat. "Willow? Is this true?"

Willow looks at me in question.

"It's okay. Tell them," I push.

She swallows hard, then looks at Ruby. She nods, confirming, "Yes. It started when I was fifteen. But it's in the past."

"It's not," I insist.

She looks at me, and her lip quivers.

A thick silence blankets the room. No one moves. The Christmas tree twinkles behind us, completely out of place in the emotional wreckage of Willow's and my life.

Jacob finally speaks up. "You hid this from us for years? Went behind our backs and lied to our faces?"

I lift my chin and tug Willow close to me. "It's my fault, sir. I should have come clean back then. Don't blame Willow."

"Damn right, I'm not blaming her," he snarls, his gaze burning with anger and betrayal.

My stomach drops, but I don't flinch. "I know it was wrong to hide it from you."

Willow blurts out, "It wasn't just Wyatt's fault. I lied too."

"He was older than you," Jacob states, standing slowly and towering over the room while pinning me with a look so sharp, I have to force myself not to stagger.

"Dad, it's not all his fault," Willow repeats.

"You loved her?" he questions.

"I still do," I answer.

"And you left her." He says it as a statement, not a question.

"I did." I don't try to excuse it. The facts are the facts with Jacob.

Jacob turns to Willow. "And you took him back?"

Her throat bobs. "I didn't."

Hurt stabs me in the chest. I look at her. "Don't lie anymore, Willow."

Jacob walks toward us. "Do you love him?"

Willow's eyes glass over. Her shoulders stiffen, and for a second, I don't think she's going to answer.

When she does, it's barely above a whisper. "Yes."

That one word is both a balm and a bomb. Because before anyone else reacts, I hear boots pounding across the wood.

Jagger barrels toward me. "You son of a bitch!" His fist cracks against my jaw.

Someone screams.

My head snaps to the side, and stars burst behind my eyelids. I stumble backward, slamming into the wall.

He lands another punch before I can recover. Blood spurts everywhere, and pain radiates down my neck and jaw. But I don't try to defend myself. I deserve every blow he wants to give me.

"Jagger, stop!" Willow screams.

The other Cartwrights shout, and Sebastian and Alexander try to pull Jagger off me.

Mason leans against the couch with his arms crossed.

Jagger's too angry to stop. His third punch connects with my stomach, knocking the wind out of me. Then his knee drives into my ribs.

I gasp and double over.

He grabs my shirt, and spittle flies at me as he snarls, "You lying bastard! How dare you touch my sister!"

"I love her!" I manage to grit out, blood leaking from my mouth.

"Jagger, stop!" Willow screams again.

"Enough!" Alexander orders, pushing between us.

Sebastian tugs Jagger backward with both his arms locked behind his back.

"Let me go!" Jagger bellows, still thrashing.

"Jagger, enough!" Jacob's voice thunders through the house.

Silence descends.

Jagger's chest heaves. Blood stains his knuckles. His wild eyes remain primed with rage, betrayal, and disbelief.

Willow steps toward me, fretting, "Are you okay?"

I wipe my mouth, breathing heavily, the metallic taste thick on my tongue. I don't look at her. I keep my gaze pinned on Jagger. "I didn't plan it. I tried to stop it. But I couldn't. I couldn't stop loving her."

Jacob steps between us. "You didn't just love her. You hid it. From all of us."

"I know," I rasp, my jaw throbbing and already swelling.

Jacob turns to Willow. "You should've come to us."

She trembles. "We were young and stupid. Don't be mad at us."

"I'm not mad at *you*. I'm mad at *him*," he firmly states, then turns his gaze back to me.

"It's not just his fault," Willow states.

Jacob points at me and continues, "You broke my trust, Wyatt. And that isn't earned back easily."

"I know. I'm sorry for that. But I'll earn it back. Whatever it takes," I vow, my voice ragged.

"Don't make promises you can't keep," Jacob warns coldly.

"I'm not," I say, dragging my gaze to Willow. "But I've always loved her. I never stopped. And I'm not letting her go this time."

The Cartwright brothers all give me deadly looks. Ruby holds a hand to her mouth, her gaze darting between Willow and me. The grand-kids have disappeared into the kitchen, and every adult stands frozen like the damn room might split in two.

Jacob finally breaks the silence. "You want to prove something, Wyatt? Then don't just say it. Show it."

I nod, bloody and raw. "I will."

Jagger breaks free from his brothers. He gives me a final angry look and then stalks off, muttering, "Unbelievable."

Willow stands rooted to the floor. Her hands tremble and her lip quivers. But her gaze stays locked on mine.

The hatred is gone. Hurt and confusion have replaced it.

But I'll take hurt and confusion over hatred any day.

Jacob points to the door. "I think it's best if you find somewhere else to stay."

"Dad!" Willow exclaims.

"It's okay. I'll be at Jax's. But I'm not leaving you," I insist, my stomach in knots.

"Jacob, let's not overreact. Wyatt doesn't have to move," Ruby asserts.

"He lied to us. He snuck around with our daughter behind our backs," Jacob points out.

"It's okay, Ruby," I say.

"Don't speak right now," Jacob orders.

I shut my mouth, trying not to wince from the pain.

Ruby tries again. "Jacob—"

"No. Wyatt, I'm not saying you aren't welcome here ever again, but right now, you can't stay here," Jacob declares.

"I understand."

"Dad—"

"No. And I'll remind you that this is my roof you're still under," he asserts.

"It's fine. I'll call you later," I say to Willow, then look at Ruby and Jacob. "I really do regret not being up front with you years ago."

Jacob's eyes narrow further. He crosses his arms, as if holding himself back from hurling himself at me.

Ruby steps forward. "Let me at least clean you up before you go."

Jacob grinds his molars.

"Thank you, ma'am, but it's best if I go. I appreciate all your hospitality," I offer.

She gives me a sympathetic look.

I step in front of Willow, kiss her forehead, and reiterate, "I'm only at Jax's. I'm not leaving."

She bites her lip.

I nod and leave the house, more determined than ever that Willow's going to stay mine.

23

Willow

W
hat just happened?

Damn, Wyatt.

My pulse still thunders in my ears, drowning out everything but his deep voice repeating that he loves me.

He told everyone.

My family stands frozen in the living room. The Christmas tree glows softly, but all the warmth has been sucked out of the air.

Mom's hand rests on Dad's arm, her gaze locked on me. My siblings stare at me in shock.

Hurry up and process it.

I can't believe he told them.

Phoebe's gaze is the one I try to avoid. I lied to her. I shouldn't have, so the guilt swelling in my throat is ten times worse when it comes to her.

The sound of the screen door shutting hits my ears, and a wave of panic assaults me.

He can't leave.

I tell myself it's so he has to face the music at my side, but I'm lying to myself again.

"Wyatt isn't leaving the ranch," I blurt out, stepping toward the door.

"Like hell, he isn't," Dad booms.

"Jacob," Mom warns.

I turn my head, declaring, "He can stay in one of the guesthouses."

"No," Dad states.

"Yes. He can," Mom says with authority.

He looks at her in surprise. She rarely goes against him.

Regardless, I don't have time to waste. I run out the door, crying out, "Wyatt!"

He turns, his truck door already open.

I leap off the last step and go skidding on the ice, landing hard on my butt. I wince. "Ouch!"

Wyatt slams his door shut and rushes toward me. "Willow! Are you okay?" he asks as he reaches for me.

I allow him to help me, grabbing his hand.

He yanks me up and tugs me into him. Worry fills his swollen face. "Are you hurt?"

I tilt my head. "Emotionally or physically?"

His lips twitch. "Let's start with physically."

"My butt will live," I declare.

He rests his hand over a cheek, his dark eyes flickering with amusement. "That's good news."

My smile doesn't last long, replaced with a grimace. "You might need to stick your face in the snow."

He grunts. "I'll be fine."

"That was a suicide mission in there. Why did you do that?" I ask.

He doesn't flinch. "Tell the only people I've ever cared about I'm madly in love with you and aren't going to ever fall out of it?"

Excitement competes with irritation for the most dominant emotion. "Wyatt—"

"Don't lecture me, Willow. It was time to come clean. I meant everything I said, and nothing is going to stop me from winning you back. So maybe you can stop trying so hard to push me away?"

My insides quiver. I swallow hard, with the recurring debate restarting in my head.

"I love you. Now, tell me why you came out here," he orders.

My anxiety grows. I open my mouth, but nothing comes out. The wind kicks up, and I shiver.

He pushes a lock of hair behind my ear and pulls me closer. "You're going to freeze out here."

"Don't stay at Jax's. Stay in one of the guesthouses," I say.

I can tell my suggestion shocks him, but his lips curl. "I'd love to stay, sugar, but I don't think that's a good idea right now."

"It is," I claim.

"Your father thinks otherwise, and I'm pretty sure your brothers do too," he reminds me.

"I'll take care of them," I assure him.

He studies me in silence for a moment.

"Why aren't you saying anything?" I question.

His gaze drifts to my lips, then back to my eyes. He demands, "Tell me you still love me, and that's why you want me to stay."

I take several deep breaths.

"I'm going to stay at Jax's," he states.

I swallow hard, every nerve frayed. "You're my rider. I need you to have a roof over your head. So stay in the Butterfly House."

His timbre soft and dangerous, he asks, "Is it only because I'm your rider?"

My need to be honest barrels past my caution. "I don't know what this is, Wyatt. But I know I want you to stay so we can talk…when I can think straight."

He shakes his head slowly. "Your dad doesn't want me here. We can talk somewhere else."

"I'll handle my dad. Stay. I'm going to get your things." I attempt to step back, but he holds me firmly to him.

He looks at me intently. "I love you, Willow. And I don't have any doubts about what this is between us. I don't think you do either."

"I…" I blow out a breath of air.

"Why do you really want me to stay?" he pushes.

My heart slams against my rib cage.

He tries to arch his eyebrows at me, but his face is too swollen. "Give me something, sugar. I just need something, and I'll fight to stay on this ranch and deal with your family, who now hates me."

"They don't hate you," I claim.

He takes several breaths, slowly exhaling. He slides his hand on my cheek. "I'm waiting."

My demons fight my heart, trying to get me to lie to him, but my heart wins. "I still love you," I tell him quietly.

Time stands still. Wyatt says nothing, just stares at me.

"I'm going to get—"

He cuts me off when his mouth lands on mine. His arms tug me closer, so no space exists between us, and he kisses me until I lose my breath.

He pulls away, grinning. "Okay. I'll stay."

I softly laugh, then push his chest, warning, "Don't think this means things are back to the way they were."

"No, ma'am," he says, his expression turning serious.

Giddiness fills me. "Okay. I'm going to get your things."

His brows lift. "What guesthouse do you want me in? Butterfly or Stallion?"

I shrug. "Which one do you want?"

"Butterfly's closer to the main house," he muses.

I can't help but smile. "Don't get me into more trouble, Wyatt."

"I'm just saying," he taunts with a wink.

I laugh, shaking my head. "Don't go anywhere."

"I'm not, sugar."

I return to the house and attempt to head to the stairs, but I can't get past the living room.

My father demands, "What do you think you're doing?"

I apprehensively step into the room.

The air is thick with Cartwright rage. My father's eyes lock on mine, hard as iron.

I rarely defy my father. But I lift my chin and announce, "To get Wyatt's bag. He's staying in the Butterfly House."

His face reddens. "The hell he is."

"Don't make a mountain out of a mole hill," I argue.

"He's got a lot of nerve staying on my land," Dad states.

Mom snaps, "Jacob! This is our home. Our ranch. Wyatt is family. You aren't kicking him off the property!"

Mason chimes in with, "He's got a funny way of treating a family member."

"Shut up, Mason!" I bellow.

"Kind of incestuous if you ask me," he adds.

"You're disgusting and super immature," Phoebe interjects.

"Agreed," Georgia adds under her breath, glaring daggers at him.

"Keep out of this," Mom warns my brother.

Dad scowls at her. "That boy lied to us for years, going behind our backs."

"So did our daughter. He didn't do it alone," she reminds him.

Guilt assails me. But there's nothing I can do about the past. I blurt out, "We aren't kids anymore."

Dad turns his disapproval on me. "This is my roof you live under."

"Then I'm leaving with Wyatt," I proclaim before I can even think about it.

Dad's eyes widen.

I remind him, "I only moved back home because my apartment got infested with roaches and I didn't have time to find a new one since I've been traveling so much. But it seems like I should have left sooner because you must have forgotten I'm an adult now."

Dad's face flushes red and hardens.

Mom steps between us. "No one is going anywhere. Wyatt can stay in the Butterfly House. Willow, you're not moving out right now. End of conversation." She pins a look on Dad.

He looks like he wants to argue but doesn't.

"Thanks, Mom." I rush out of the room, up the stairs, and into Wyatt's room. I shove his clothes into his bag, grab his toiletries, and run down the stairs.

Dad stands near the landing with his arms crossed.

"I'm sorry we lied, but you're going to have to get over it," I state.

"Watch your mouth, young lady," Dad warns.

I sigh. "Dad, I'm sorry. I hope you forgive us soon." I kiss him on the cheek and bolt out the front door.

Wyatt's standing in the cold next to the passenger door.

"Why aren't you in the cab? It's cold out here," I remind him.

He grabs the bag from me and slings it over his shoulder. Then he opens the door. "I'm fine. Get in."

I don't argue, hopping into the truck. He shuts the door, tosses his bag in the back, and gets into the driver's seat. He starts the engine and then turns toward me, asking, "How bad was it?"

I cringe and hold my fingers an inch apart. "Only a bit."

"I'm sorry."

"A little warning would have been nice," I say.

He chuckles. "No way you'd have let me tell them."

I stare at him, fighting myself. I've always wanted to be with him, no matter how much I told myself I was over him. Now that our secret is out, maybe we have a real shot.

But what if we don't?

His face falls. "Stop worrying, sugar. Things will only move forward with us this time."

I offer a tiny smile.

He slides his hand in my hair and leans closer. "Trust me."

I quietly reply, "Okay."

He matches my soft grin and pecks me on the lips. He releases me and asks, "Are you sure your dad isn't going to shoot me in the night if I stay on the ranch?"

I shake my head, wincing. "Nope."

He chuckles and pulls forward, passing the barn and turning down the snow-covered dirt trail.

I add, "Don't worry. My mom put her foot down."

"Oh?" He glances over, arching his eyebrows.

"Yep. You know how she's always had a soft spot for you."

"She stood up to Jacob? For me?"

"Yep."

"Well I'll be," he says, taking another turn.

The small, pale-blue guest cottage appears, nestled among ice-covered trees. Snow blankets the roof several inches thick. Holiday lights match the ones draped across the ranch. The wooden sign with "Butterfly House" carved on it is unreadable due to the snow.

Wyatt pulls near the porch and parks the truck. He turns off the engine. "I'm glad you're coming in with me."

"I am?"

"Why else did you hop in the truck?"

"You told me to."

"Since when do you do anything you don't want to?" he questions, a wicked grin on his face.

I nervously laugh.

He picks up my hand and kisses it. Then he gets out of the truck, tosses his bag over his shoulder, and comes around to my side to open my door.

I hop out, and he takes my hand, leading me up the porch.

I glance behind me.

"We don't have to worry about anyone seeing us. They all know," he reminds me.

"Oh. Yeah. Right." My gut flips.

He opens the door and motions for me to go inside.

I step into the warm, cozy house.

"Remember when we were here last time?" Wyatt asks, glancing around at the white beadboard walls, wood-burning stove, and tiny kitchen.

Memories of us sneaking into the guesthouse hit me. I smile, inhaling the cedar scent that always hangs in the air, and stare at the butterflies covering the main wall.

He shuts the door with a finality that echoes in my chest. He tosses his bag on the couch and closes the distance between us in two strides. He drags his molten gaze over me and runs his knuckles over my jaw.

I'm hit with another stab of fear.

What if he hurts me again?

I whisper, "This doesn't mean anything."

Amusement fills his expression. "You know that's a lie, sugar."

My anxiety mixes with the tingle in my core.

He murmurs, "Okay. If it doesn't mean anything, then why did you go to bat for me with your parents?"

I open my mouth, but nothing comes out.

He moves closer, and his chest touches mine. "I meant what I said, Willow. I'm not going anywhere. I'm not ever letting anything come between us again."

My heart races faster, and I take a deep breath.

He cups my face, stroking his thumb over my lips. "I'm going to need your cooperation."

"My cooperation?"

He nods. "Yeah."

"For what?" I raise my eyebrows.

He leans down and kisses behind my ear.

I shiver.

He murmurs in a low growl, each word a hot brand on my neck, "To help me with this." His mouth trails from my earlobe down to the sensitive spot where my pulse hammers in my neck.

I gasp. My hands fly to his shoulders, my nails digging into his hard muscles.

He walks me backward until I'm pressed against the wall, his thigh sliding between mine, parting them. His hips grind against me, slow and deliberate. His erection pushes into me, making my pussy ache.

His lips brush mine, his breath fanning over my mouth. He adds, "I'm going to spend my life trying to make up for every second we wasted." He kisses my jaw.

I whimper.

He pulls back just enough to keep me wanting, then drops his hands to my hips, squeezing possessively as he drags me closer. His voice turns darker, edged with a roughness that weakens my knees. "I guess I need to remind you again who this body belongs to."

A knocking sound slams into the silence. The door bursts open. Jagger storms in, eyes wild. "Why are you still on the ranch?" he bellows.

"Jagger, stop!" I demand.

Wyatt straightens, shifting between me and my brother like he's ready to take a bullet for me. "I'm not leaving. Not unless Willow's coming with me."

"Dad told you to go," he snarls.

"Jagger, enough! He's staying!" I shout.

His gaze darts to me. "You've got to be kidding me!"

I lift my chin. "I'm not!"

Jagger points at me. "Go home, Willow."

"Don't tell me what to do," I snap back.

"Houston and I have some unfinished business, don't we?" he seethes.

"Jagger, go away!" I order.

"No. He's right. Take my truck to the house. I'll call you later," Wyatt says calmly, locking eyes with me.

"What?"

"Go on."

"Why? So you two can kill each other?" I ask in horror.

"He dug his own grave," Jagger mutters.

"Jagger, stop it! Wyatt's your best friend!" I remind him.

He grunts, nostrils flaring. It reminds me of a bull before a rider tries to mount him. "He should have thought about that before he took advantage of you behind my back!"

I step in front of Wyatt. "He didn't take advantage of me."

"Of course he did," Jagger insists.

Wyatt demands, "Willow, go to the main house."

I glance up at him. "You're already bloody and swollen. I'm not going to let him beat you up anymore."

"Who said I'm letting him beat me up? He already got his freebie punches in," Wyatt claims.

I'm horrified at this situation. "So you're both going to be bloody, bruised, and broken?"

"No. Just Wyatt," Jagger states.

I snap my head toward my brother. "Stop it! You're being childish."

Jagger points at me, his eyes blazing, roaring, "You're my little sister. He's supposed to be my best friend. There are consequences."

"We've already paid for our mistakes," I blurt out, my anger rebuilding, but this time only at my brother.

He scoffs, then shakes his head.

Tense silence fills the air for several long seconds.

Wyatt's low tone sends a chill through me when he says, "Willow, please leave."

I look up at him again. "This isn't all your fault. I lied and snuck around too. You weren't in a relationship all by yourself."

Wyatt's lips twitch. "No. But Jagger and I have to talk without you here."

"*Relationship*. Jesus," Jagger mutters under his breath.

I jab my finger in his chest. "Yes, Jagger! Relationship! And I love him, so stop being a jerk! Wyatt and I are adults. You don't get a say in this."

Another moment of tension builds, and my cheeks heat as I realize what I just said. I force myself not to look at Wyatt.

He cuts the silence first, begging, "Please go, Willow."

I glance at him again.

"It's fine. I'll call you after your brother and I finish," he assures.

"Oh, we're finished," Jagger mumbles.

"You're such a hypocrite," I toss out at him.

He jerks his head backward. "I'm the hypocrite?"

"Yes."

He snorts. "Why don't you fill me in about how I'm the hypocrite?"

"Gladly. You run around town, fucking anyone you want and never commit to any of them. You have a different set of rules when it comes to others than you do for yourself," I declare.

He gives me an arrogant look. "Doesn't make me a hypocrite."

"Fine. Makes you an idiot," I say.

"Spoken from the prize idiot herself," he retorts.

"Don't talk to your sister like that," Wyatt warns darkly.

Jagger turns his angry gaze on him again. "Don't tell me what I can say to my sister."

"I can and I will," Wyatt states.

Jagger steps forward. "Oh yeah?"

Wyatt moves me out of the way. "Yeah. Now, I think we have some things to say, and it's best if Willow isn't here. Do we agree?"

Jagger glances at me, then turns his scowl back on Wyatt. "Agreed."

"I'm not leaving so you two can beat the crap out of each other," I insist.

Jagger crosses his arms. "I already beat him up."

"Because he didn't try to fight back," I point out.

Jagger scoffs. "I'll let Wyatt try again if he wants."

"Stop it!" I say loudly, but Jagger isn't listening.

"Let him show me what he's got," my brother taunts.

"Jagger!"

"I'll be right back," Wyatt says to my brother, then slides his arm around my waist and moves me toward the door. "I need you to take the truck to the house."

"Wyatt—"

"Willow, I'm not going to ask again," he says forcefully.

I freeze, taken aback by his tone.

He releases a deep breath and tries again, softer this time. "Please. Go to the house. I promise I'll call you when we're done talking."

"You're only going to talk?" I ask, panic rushing through my veins.

"That's my plan. What about you?" he asks Jagger, looking at him.

My brother just stands there, silently stewing in anger.

"Jagger!" I exclaim.

"Yeah. We're just talking," he answers gruffly.

I stare at him.

"Go on. Get out of here," he adds.

"Promise me there won't be any fighting," I say.

He begrudgingly agrees. "No fighting. Now, leave."

I glare at him and turn back to Wyatt. My voice catches. "P-please don't fight."

"I won't. Promise."

I add, "But if Jagger comes at you, beat the crap out of him."

"Like he could," Jagger mutters.

Wyatt chuckles. "Will do." He opens the door and then leads me to the truck. He yanks the driver's door open and gives me a quick kiss.

I don't want to leave, but I follow his wishes, my stomach in knots. Jagger rarely gets angry. So I want to believe they won't fight, but it's a hard pill to swallow.

Especially since I've never seen him this mad.

24

Wyatt

illow leaves in my truck, and I go back inside the Butterfly House. Tension coils in my muscles, and my banging pulse competes with the ticking of the clock.

Jagger hasn't moved, but it's obvious that he still wants to tear me apart. His arms are tightly crossed over his chest, feet planted shoulder width apart, and a menacing scowl pointed right at me.

I lean against the wall, taking a similar stance. Now that I've confessed to the Cartwrights and let Jagger take his punches, I'm not going to let him take any more blows without fighting back.

And I'm not apologizing for loving his sister.

"You want to start talking?" he snarls, low and lethal, eyes narrowing.

I don't flinch, keeping my gaze locked on his for several minutes before replying, "What do you need to know, Jagger?"

He steps closer, his face flushing an angry red, his boots grinding on the wooden floor. "Why don't you start with how long you've been sneaking around with my little sister?"

Every muscle in my body flexes. I've called Jagger brother for as long as I can remember. I crossed a line with him, and him knowing the time frame of my betrayal won't help him to forgive me.

He demands through gritted teeth, "How long, Wyatt?"

A sour taste floods my mouth. I admit, "Years."

"I got that. I want exact details," he pushes.

"Like we said in the house, it started on my eighteenth birthday," I declare.

His eyes widen, a firestorm of fury. His voice cracks with betrayal so deep, it rattles my bones. "You weren't making bets about skipping stones that night, were you?"

I stand straighter, steeling myself. "No. Nothing had really happened yet, but it's when it started."

"What does that mean?" he demands, more rage flaring on his sharp features.

"I hadn't kissed her. I almost did, but I stopped myself," I confess.

His eyes are red balls of rage as he hisses, "You should have been smart and not taken advantage of her."

I release a heavy sigh. "I loved her. I loved her before I kissed her, and what's done is done." The words scrape out of me low and raw.

He lunges for me, grabs my shirt, and slams me back against the door. He snarls, his breath hot and furious on my cheek, "Don't you fucking say that to me! Bros before hoes, Wyatt. That was the code."

Anger like I've never felt explodes within me. I shove him away, my muscles screaming with the need to smash my fists into his face. But I somehow contain myself. I warn, "Don't you ever call her that again!"

"You know what I mean!" He stumbles a step back, boots skidding.

I roar, "I don't care what you meant! Don't you dare even think that about her ever again!"

He laughs. It comes out sharp and bitter. "Oh, I hit a nerve? Are you gonna protect her honor now? Where the hell was that protective instinct when you decided to use her and then skip town?"

The words cut deeper than any bull's horn ever could. Wrath churns in my chest, black and acidic. I hurl, "I've never used Willow. And you know why I had to go to Tennessee. But it seems you forgot the role you played in that mess."

He grunts. "Oh, so it's my fault?"

"You took the first punch," I remind him.

His gaze darkens. "How long have you been waiting to use that against me?"

"I haven't. But don't act like I wanted to go when you know damn well I didn't," I fume.

He stalks forward until we're nose to nose. "So you lied to me for years, looking me square in the eyes without even flinching while you snuck around with my sister right under my nose?" Every word drips with venom.

My pulse roars in my ears. I state, "I never wanted to hurt you. It wasn't personal, so don't make it that way."

He barks a humorless laugh. "Not personal? You've got to be kidding me!"

I scrub my face and groan. "What's between Willow and me isn't going to go away, Jagger. And it has nothing to do with you."

"Like hell it doesn't!" he shouts.

He grinds his molars, scowling harder.

I lower my voice, adding, "You're going to have to get over this. Willow and I have already proved that what's between us is too strong to fade."

A hint of amusement fills his expression. He arches his eyebrows. "You honestly expect me to accept this?"

I drag in a breath so ragged, it feels like knives in my lungs. "I don't expect anything."

"Bullshit! You think you can come back here and pick up where you left off, and we'll all just welcome you with open arms as Willow's what...boyfriend?"

I shake my head. "No. I'm going to marry her."

His eyes widen. "Marry her?"

"Yes. At least that's what I want. But I haven't asked her yet. She's only just started to forgive me."

His jaw clenches so hard that the veins in his neck bulge. His eyes are dark and empty, a deep well of rage. He seethes, "You know what the worst part is about this?"

I brace myself. "No. Go on and tell me."

"Right around the time you left, I knew something had happened to Willow. I didn't know what or who caused it, and she wouldn't tell me. Now it all makes sense. It was you, Wyatt. You hurt her."

I flinch, the words sinking deep into the cracks of my soul. I nod, gritting out, "You think I don't know that?"

He shakes his head slowly. "The only thing I know is that you never gave a shit about anyone besides yourself."

"Spoken from the king of selfish himself, but good to know. Got anything else to say?" I snarl, hurt barreling at me fast as a racecar.

He scoffs. "Don't turn this on me."

"Just calling what I see."

We stand there, breathing like bulls in a chute, every second stretching until it feels like the world's going to snap.

Finally, I demand, "You done?"

His eyes flash with anger. "Not even close." He jabs my chest. "You hurt her again, and I will finish what we started tonight."

I let out a cold, humorless laugh, tasting dried blood on my lips. "You can try. But you got your free shots, Jagger. Next time you lay a hand on me, I'll fight back, and this is your only warning."

He doesn't move, hatred coating his expression.

As big as my ego is, pain hits my heart. I soften my tone. "You've always been my brother. That hasn't changed in my eyes. So take the time you need to get used to this. I'm not disappearing. Willow's mine and I'm hers."

A tense silence settles between us for a few beats.

Then, in a softer but sharper-than-a-blade tone, he replies, "I loved you like a brother."

My throat tightens so much, I almost can't breathe. "I know. And I hope things will go back to normal between us down the road."

His jaw tics, and he grunts. "Don't count on it." He stalks past me and flings open the door.

The cold air rushes into the cottage, but it doesn't touch the hot anger or suffocating hurt.

Jagger slams the door, and I go to the window, my heart still pounding hard. He trudges through the snow, gets into his truck, and drives away.

"Fuck," I mutter under my breath, wishing things would have gone differently, but knowing it's an impossible desire.

I stare out the frost-covered glass for a long time. The war inside me continues, and I finally step away and mumble, "I gotta get off this ranch."

I pull out my phone and text Willow.

Me: I need to go to Jax's.

Willow: Why? You don't have to worry about my parents. They agreed that you can stay in the Butterfly House.

I smile.

Me: Are they really okay with me staying on the ranch?

Willow: Yes.

A touch of relief hits me.

Me: That's good, because I meant, I need to go to Jax's to work out. I didn't mean as in to move there.

Willow: You're still injured.

Me: I need to go, sugar, but I'll be fine.

Willow: You need to rest.

Me: You know how I handle things.

She doesn't respond.

> Me: Can I see you when I'm back?

Dots bounce on the screen for several seconds. Then they disappear.

I wait, feeling like my heart's going to explode.

> Willow: I might be washing my hair.

I chuckle.

> Me: You have no idea how much I missed that response.

Again, she doesn't text back.

> Me: So I can see you then?

> Willow: Okay.

I sigh.

> Me: Good. I'll let you know when I'm back.

> Willow: Please be kind to yourself.

My heart soars. She's breaking down some of her walls, and it feels like old times.

> Me: You can kiss me and make me feel better tonight.

> Willow: Maybe if you're good.

> Me: I'm always good.

Willow: That's debatable. Did you and Jagger make up?

My pulse shoots back to the sky.

Me: Not exactly.

Willow: I'll talk to him.

Me: Might be best to let him cool off a bit.

Willow: Did you two get physical?

Me: No. I promised you we would only talk.

Willow: You kept your word?

Me: Of course. When have I ever gone back on my word?

Nothing from her.

Me: Name one time.

Willow: Sorry. You're right. I was just worried.

Me: Don't be. I'll see you tonight.

Willow: Drive safe.

Me: Will do.

I shove my phone in my pocket and dip out into the bitter cold. I push against the wind as I make my way toward the main house. After a miserable walk, I jump in my truck and start the engine. I drive past the gates and carefully make my way to Jax's.

He steps out on the porch when I pull up in front of his place.

I turn off the engine and exit the vehicle.

"We don't have practice today," Jax states.

"I say we do," I assert, and limp toward the pole barn that houses the workout equipment.

Jax follows behind me. "You have to rest your body."

I snort. "That's rich coming from you when you almost killed me the last few days."

"Which is why you need to rest now. Go home. We'll restart training after the weekend," he says.

"I'm good. Go back inside your warm house and do whatever it is you do, Jax." I yank open the barn door, grinding my molars as pain shoots through my shoulder.

"Wyatt, it's not a suggestion. Get your ass back in your truck and get out of here before you hurt yourself so badly you never ride again," Jax orders.

I turn to face him, spouting, "I'm fine. I'll still earn you money, so go mind your own business, old man."

He reaches beneath his tightly-woven, tan canvas jacket, pulls out a pistol, and points it at me. "I said you're not working out today."

My adrenaline kicks up several notches. "What in the seven hells are you doing, Jax? Do you have a death wish?"

"You might if you don't get out of my barn and back into your truck," he warns, his gaze deadly serious.

"So you're going to kill your bread and butter?" I ask, but my heart races faster. Jax has never pulled a gun on me before. Maybe he's going senile.

His smoke-laced voice takes on a lethal edge when he states, "I suggest you don't stay to find out."

I don't move.

He clicks the safety off.

"What the fuck, Jax!" I boom, worried he's going to shoot me.

He nudges the gun toward the door. "Out. Now."

I study him for a few more seconds, then realize he's crazy enough to shoot me. So I mutter under my breath, "I need to have you seen by a mental health professional."

He grunts. "Make my day. Don't come back until Wednesday like we discussed."

"With this type of treatment, I may never return," I threaten.

He scoffs. "Keep on running your mouth. I'll shoot you in the ass on your way out."

"Crazy lunatic," I mumble, trudging across the yard and opening my driver's door. I get inside, take one last look at Jax, then speed past him and onto the road.

What now?

The only other place to work off some steam is at the Cartwrights' gym. And I can't go back there right now.

I drive around, unsure where I'm going, until the racetrack comes into view. Goose bumps pop out on my skin, and I'm hit with the shot of endorphins I get before I think I'm going to win big.

"Not a good idea," I tell myself while pulling in and parking the truck.

I sit, staring at the building, with my chest tightening.

Don't go in.

I just need to kill some time.

I've got the feeling.

I'll just place a small bet. I'll give the winnings to Willow to pay her back faster.

Bad idea.

Trying to talk myself out of it doesn't work. I open the door and limp through the parking lot and into the racetrack.

Races across the world appear on the televisions. Smoke circles the air, suffocating my lungs. Regulars chatter and drink.

I glance around, taking it all in, the high of anticipation growing. It's the same thing I always experience whenever I'm in a casino or at a racetrack.

I should get out of here.

No. I'm going to win.

Willow wouldn't approve.

She'll be happy when I pay her back faster.

I read the numbers on the sports screens, then take a seat at the end of the bar.

"Well, look who the cat dragged in," Bo Caruthers, the longtime bartender, announces.

I slap his hand, admitting, "Been a long time. How've you been?"

"Good. The kids keep me busy when I'm not here. Still drinking whiskey?" he asks, reaching for the fifth.

The expressions on the faces of the Cartwrights when I came clean about me and Willow, haunt me. Especially those of Jacob and Jagger.

I nod to Bo.

Bad idea.

Willow's beautiful face appears in my mind.

"Actually, I'll have a beer," I state.

He sets down the bottle of whiskey. "You sure?"

I hesitate, glancing at the bottle.

Bo fills a shot glass and sets it in front of me. "On the house." He pulls a frosted mug out of the cooler and pulls the lever on the keg.

The foam rises until it's at the top. He puts the mug next to the shot glass. "Hell of a ride you gave the other day."

"Thanks." I glance at the shot, take a mouthful of beer, then wrap a hand around the cold mug.

"No!" a lady screeches.

I glance over my shoulder.

She scrunches her face, pounding on the table. "No! No! No!"

"Stop hitting the furniture, Lucy. It's not going to give you a win," Bo reprimands.

She glares at him, then plops onto the seat, staring at the screens, shaking her head.

Sweat forms at my hairline. The sense of dread I feel whenever I lose creeping up on me. For some reason, I can't take my eyes off her.

"Five minutes before she's begging Johnny for another loan," Bo mumbles, but he might as well have screamed it.

Disgust over my past bad decisions hits me. The last time I lost a big bet, I begged my bookie to lend me more money, and he refused.

What am I doing here?

"Wyatt!" a deep voice bellows.

I turn, and the hairs on my arms rise.

Jeb Smoody, a former classmate and guy Jagger and I used to hang out with, stumbles toward me. He used to be the "cool kid" in our class. Now, I barely recognize him.

He's at least fifty pounds heavier, sporting large rolls under his too-tight T-shirt. Three stains stretch down the right side. His hair spikes in every direction and is in desperate need of a cut, just like his beard. He plops down on the stool next to me, slurring, "Well, I'll be, if it isn't the famous Wyatt Houston!"

"Jeb. It's been a long time," I offer.

"Too long. Now that you're all famous, you don't have time for us little people," he teases.

I chuckle.

Bo points out, "You can't call yourself little anymore, Jeb."

He pounds his hand on the wood, ordering, "Bring us a round."

I hold my hand in the air. "I'm good. Just got a drink." I tap my mug.

He points at the shot. "Why's that sitting there?"

I glance at the shot of whiskey. Heat crawls up my neck. I try to distract him. "What have you been up to?"

He motions to Bo to bring him a whiskey, and scratches his head. "Living the dream. I'm down two hundred today, but I'm about to win it back. Put another grand down to sweeten the pot."

"That's good," I reply, but my gut screams he's going to lose his ass.

Bo puts the shot down.

Jeb picks it up and holds it in front of me. "To the good old days."

Swallowing back bile, I pick up the shot and clink it against his glass.

He downs his, then waits for me to take mine.

"You take mine," I offer.

His eyes me warily.

"For good luck," I add.

He grins, grabs it, and shoots it back.

There's no way I'm getting out of here if I start drinking whiskey.

"What bets are you placing?" Jeb asks.

I glance at the boards, staring at the odds. I open my mouth, then shut it.

I picture Willow's face again.

"Well?" Jeb pushes.

My chest tightens.

A roar fills the bar.

"About time!" a fifty-something woman cries out in excitement.

More people cheer.

A rush of adrenaline flows through me, almost making me dizzy.

Just one bet, then I'll leave.

One will lead to two.

This isn't the way to be anymore.

"Well? What will it be?" Jeb questions.

I glance back at the boards, fighting my demons, assessing the odds.

A new race starts. More cheers fill the room, so loud that they compete with my pounding heart.

"Looks like a lucky streak finally arrived," Bo claims.

Jeb slaps his sweaty palm on my back. "What's your take, Wyatt? You feeling lucky and going for the 40 to 1?"

I refocus on the screen, my mouth watering, heart hammering, and adding up how much I need to bet to pay Willow in full.

25

Willow

The sound of muffled voices hits my ears. I tiptoe past the kitchen and almost get to the staircase.

"Where do you think you're going?" Ava asks.

I close my eyes on a sigh, then turn back. "Going to take a nap."

She smirks. "Ha! That's funny! Get in here. You've got a lot of explaining to do!" She opens the kitchen door.

My stomach sours with dread.

"It's best to get it over with," Ava reminds me, beaming brighter.

"Stop gloating. It's a bad look on you," I mumble, stepping past her, knowing she's right. Avoiding my family means it'll only be worse when I finally do spill the beans.

The minute I step into the kitchen, the conversation stops dead. Coffee mugs hover in midair while spoons clang against the ceramic.

Every set of eyes locks on me like I'm a wanted criminal; the women who know me better than anyone else, staring me down.

"Sit," Mom orders in a clipped voice, her hand gesturing to a stool at the massive island.

Phoebe's eyes widen with sympathy. Georgia's look matches Phoebe's, soft and almost motherly. It only adds to my guilt.

I don't argue, and pull the seat out, plopping onto it and leaning over the cold granite counter.

It's my oldest sister, Evelyn, who starts the attack. Her honey-blonde hair's twisted into a perfect bun, and her blue eyes pin me with Cartwright intensity. She doesn't bother to hide her excitement, asserting, "You've got a lot of talking to do."

I silently take in the situation, debating how to get out of it quickly.

Ava sits next to Evelyn, crossing her arms over her chest. Her posture's so rigid, she could compete with a nun.

Paisley fidgets on the edge of her stool, her gaze darting between me and our mom like she's watching a bull buck in slow motion.

My mom arches her eyebrows.

"Mom—" I start, but she holds up her hand, her silver bangles clinking like tiny gongs announcing my doom.

"I want the truth, Willow. All of it. Every last scrap," she demands.

My mouth goes dry. I swallow, tucking my hair behind my ear. "I... Wyatt and I..." I trail off, hating how shaky I sound. The shame of years' worth of secrets weighs on my shoulders.

"You and Wyatt..." Evelyn prods, pursing her lips and leaning closer.

Silence looms, and there's no way to get out of it.

I collect my thoughts and then start again. "We were together. A long time ago."

Phoebe's eyes soften further, making my guilt explode.

I give her my best "I'm sorry" expression.

"How long?" Mom questions.

"I was fifteen."

Ava gasps. "Fifteen! You lost your V-card when you were fifteen?"

"Ava!" Mom reprimands.

My cheeks heat. I glare at her. "Seriously?"

"So it was serious between you two?" Evelyn asks.

I clench my fists in my lap, blinking hard. I open my mouth, but a tidal wave of emotions attacks, and I can only nod.

Mom's lips press into a thin line, her eyes filling with a storm that makes me feel six years old again. "How could you not tell me, Willow? You know how much we all love Wyatt."

I flinch. "I know. I just… I couldn't. Plus, you saw how Jagger reacted."

Evelyn has never sugar-coated anything in her life, and today isn't the day she's going to start. She states flatly, "So you thought it would be better to lie to us all."

I argue, "I didn't want Jagger to be mad at Wyatt."

Ava huffs. "He would have gotten over it."

"Really? Does it seem like he'll get over it?" I ask, my heart aching at the thought that our relationship might destroy their friendship.

Ava gently adds, "This isn't about Jagger's feelings, Willow. They'll work it out."

"Will they?" I question again, unsure it's possible.

Mom says, "Give it some time. Those two have always been as thick as thieves. I'm sure they'll work it out."

"I'm not so sure about that. Did you see Jagger try to kill him?" Paisley points out.

Mom waves her hand in front of her face. "Cowboys will be cowboys. Like I said. Give it some time. I know your brother. He'll make peace with it."

My heart pounds so loud, I'm convinced they can hear it. "I hope so."

"So why did you two end it?" Ava asks.

Pain shoots through my heart. I take a minute before I answer, "He went to Tennessee. He didn't see how he could stay under the terms Jax gave him. And he wouldn't let me go with him and switch colleges."

"Thank the Lord for that," Mom declares.

"It would have been fine," I assure.

She scoffs. "You wouldn't have the career you've built."

"Says who?" I question.

"There's no other program in the country that fast-tracks agents. It would have taken you fifteen years to be where you are right now," she points out.

I don't say anything.

Was Wyatt right not to let me go with him?

"So you really loved him?" Paisley asks.

I suck in a shaky breath. "Yes. I loved him. More than I should have."

Georgia's gentle voice pierces the air. "And do you still?"

I don't know how to answer that without detangling all the ropes tied up in my chest. I finally croak, "I think so."

"Think so or know so?" Evelyn asks, arching her eyebrows.

"I…" I take a deep breath and slowly exhale, blinking hard.

Phoebe's hand wraps around mine, warm and grounding. She soothingly says, "You don't have to figure it all out right now."

Evelyn snorts. "Yes, she does. Wyatt's not just here for a quick visit. He's staying, and she now represents him. And from the scene in the living room, I'm pretty sure he's head over heels for her."

Butterflies have a party in my stomach while anxiety swirls around it.

She adds, "You can't lead him on when he's been in love with you since he was eighteen."

I whip my gaze at her. "I'm not leading him on. I'm trying to figure it out, okay? I haven't seen him in years, and it's all… It's all just…"

"A mess?" Ava supplies, her teasing tone edged with concern.

"Exactly," I sigh, deflated.

Mom's eyes narrow, sharp and unyielding. "What happened when he left, Willow? Why didn't you tell us then?"

"Because it was humiliating. Jax insisted that he move to the Tennessee team. And Wyatt needed to chase his career. So we got into a huge fight, and when I woke up the next day, he was gone."

A hush settles over us, thick and heavy.

Phoebe's thumb strokes over my hand. "Oh, Willow."

Tears well in my eyes. I choke out, "I thought I'd die from the pain. But I survived. I moved on. I built something for myself. And now he's back, and I don't know how I'm supposed to handle it."

Evelyn leans forward, her gaze unwavering. "So what do you want?"

I blink at her. "What do you mean?"

"What do you want, Willow?" she repeats, tone softening just a hair.

"Do you want him gone? Do you want to give him a chance? Do you want us to run him off the ranch with pitchforks?"

A startled laugh escapes me, but it turns into a sob halfway through. "I-I don't know wh-what I want," I stutter.

Ava rests her chin on her fist. "Well, you better figure it out, because that man looks at you like you hung the moon."

"Don't remind me." I groan, slumping over the counter and pushing my face into my forearms.

Mom's voice cuts through the thick air, calm but lethal. "You do realize you pushed for him to stay here, right? And you're going to see him every day?"

The pit in my stomach grows deeper. "Yeah. I know."

"Do you think you two can just be friends?" Paisley asks.

Evelyn scoffs. "Oh, please. That man would crawl across broken glass to get her back, and it's not to be friends."

"Evelyn," Mom warns.

But Evelyn's not backing down. "I'm serious. He's either here to fully win her back or ruin her life again. There's no halfway with Wyatt, and you all know that."

Mom sighs, exasperated. "Willow, Evelyn is right. You need to decide how you want to handle him. Because if you don't, he'll decide for you. And while I love Wyatt, you're my daughter. If he's not what you want, then don't go back down this road with him."

She's right. I have to fully jump in or get out now.

My pulse beats faster between my ears.

Silence follows, growing more nagging with every second. I shift, with every eye in the room on me, waiting for me to tell them my decision.

But I can't. My brain's a tornado of heartbreak, anger, and a shameful undercurrent of want. And I don't want to be a woman who leads a man on only to break his heart.

I rise off the stool. "I need to figure this out on my own."

Evelyn's gaze is soft, but she firmly states, "Then you'd better get started. Because the longer he's here, the deeper this will cut if it's not what you really want."

Mom rubs her temples, adding, "Willow, I let him stay because he's family. But if he hurts you again, I will throw his ass off this ranch so fast he won't know what hit him."

That finally gets a tiny smile out of me. "Thanks, Mom."

Georgia graces me with a small smile. "We're here for you, Willow. Whatever you decide."

Ava points a finger at me. "But don't you dare lie to us again. Because we'll find out."

Paisley softly reminds me, "We love you and have your back."

"Thanks. I love you all too," I choke out, grateful I have such a loving and supportive family.

I move toward the door. "I'll talk to you later."

"Wait!" Ava calls out.

I turn back, arching my eyebrows.

"How bad do you still want him?" she taunts.

My face feels like it bursts into flames. "Shut up."

"Scale of one to ten," Evelyn prods.

"Eight," I admit before I can stop myself, then correct, "Nine."

"Liar!" Evelyn smirks.

I don't admit it's a ten.

A collective gasp fills the kitchen, followed by hoots of laughter.

"You're so screwed," Ava sing-songs.

Evelyn grins. "Or maybe you'll *get* screwed. There's a difference."

"Evelyn!" I reprimand, but there's no heat behind it.

She shrugs innocently. "What? Someone had to say it."

Mom sighs, pinching the bridge of her nose. "Enough. Go cool off, Willow. And remember what I said."

I nod and then quickly escape the kitchen, practically running up the stairs. I throw myself on my bed, every nerve ending sparking, every thought tangled up in Wyatt, every fear as alive as it's ever been.

Several hours pass, but the afternoon drags. I spend most of it pacing my room, peeking out the window at the ranch entrance every five minutes, and praying Wyatt's truck will appear.

By the time the sun starts to slip behind the rolling hills, the house is bustling again. The kids thunder through the halls, the smell of roasted chicken and mashed potatoes fills the air, and the kitchen hums with chatter.

I look at my phone again.

> Me: Are you coming back soon?

There's no reply.

My nervousness ticks higher.

The dinner bell rings, and I leave my room. I descend the stairs, picking at the edge of the banister, and listen to everyone laughing.

Where is he?

Worry eats at me. Wyatt's injured, whether he wants to admit it or not. He needs rest. But I know him well enough to know that no matter how bruised and sore, he'll work out until his bones are on the verge of breaking if something is bothering him.

And I gather his talk with Jagger didn't go well.

Dinner starts without him. I sit at the far end of the table, pushing food around my plate, barely tasting a thing. The room echoes with jokes and stories. The only ones not engaging are Dad, Jagger, and me.

Ava gives me a sidelong look and murmurs, "You gonna eat that or just play with it?"

I force a smile. "I'm not hungry."

She arches an eyebrow. "You were always a terrible liar."

I ignore her and stand, gathering my plate. "I'm going to the Butterfly House."

Paisley's eyes go wide. "At night?"

"It's not like the butterflies are going to mug me," I deadpan.

I avoid Dad's narrowed gaze.

I scoop a generous portion of chicken, mashed potatoes, and roasted carrots onto a new plate, adding a warm roll and a slab of butter. I wrap it all in foil and then tuck it under my arm.

"Feeding the enemy?" Jagger asks snidely.

I glare daggers at him, snapping, "Don't."

He scowls, giving me the same betrayed look he wore when he arrived at the Butterfly House.

I slip out the door.

The evening air bites with cold. Stars prick the dark sky. A sliver of the moon appears over the hill. Each breath clouds in front of me. My boots crunch across the frost-tipped grass as I cross the wide yard and head down the path to the guesthouse.

When the holiday lights come into focus, I pause, my heart hammering.

His truck isn't here.

Disappointment stabs deeper than I expect. I grip the plate tightly as I open the door. I set it on a bench and pull out my phone.

My thumbs hover over the keyboard. I type *Where are you?* Then I delete it. I try again. *Dinner's waiting,* but erase that too.

Finally, I send a message.

> Me: Brought you a plate. Are you okay?

I watch the screen until I get the "delivered" message. A moment later, the three dots pop up like a lifeline, but then they disappear. I stare at the screen, a chill seeping through my jacket, even though the cottage is warm. The phone's glow becomes a spotlight on my desperation.

Memories slip in like ghosts. I'm fifteen again, lying in bed, clutching my phone, waiting for his good night text. I stare at my ceiling with butterflies tumbling in my stomach, full of anticipation and worry. Then I scroll back through every sweet thing he said to me, rereading his promises until I fall asleep with the phone pressed to my chest.

How pathetic am I now?

It's a decade later, and I'm doing the same damn thing, clutching my phone like it's my last hope, and hanging on every dot that pops up on the screen.

Disappointed in myself, I sink onto the couch, wrapping my arms around myself. Then, just like when I was fifteen, I scroll back through our texts from earlier today.

> Wyatt: Can I see you when I'm back?

"I should have stayed inside and washed my hair," I grumble to myself.

My phone pings. My heart jumps so violently that I almost drop it.

But it's just a weather alert about a winter storm warning.

"Great," I mutter, stuffing my phone back into my pocket. I glance at the plate, the foil still tightly wrapped.

I drag myself back to my feet, and pace near the indoor planters. The tiny white flowers glow like stars from the holiday lights. My boots scuff against the wood floor. I rub my arms, my mind spinning, and going nowhere good.

Maybe he regrets coming here.

Maybe he's already trying to leave.

Maybe he realized seeing me again was a mistake.

A sudden memory slices through me. We had snuck into the Butterfly House, and Wyatt lifted me onto the counter, kissing me like the world was ending.

God, I'd been so sure he was my forever.

I lean against a potted lemon tree, dragging my finger over the smooth bark. The scent of citrus fills my nose, but it doesn't calm the storm inside me.

Damn you, Wyatt.

I reach for my phone again. My fingers flying over the keyboard.

> Me: I'm worried. Please tell me you're okay.

The silence that follows is deafening.

I text Jax.

> Me: Is Wyatt still there?

Jax: He left as soon as he showed up.

My stomach dives.

Me: When?

Jax: Earlier. Noon maybe.

Where the hell is he?

I go back into our text messages, and freeze.

The three little dots are hopping along the screen.

Wyatt: I'll be home soon. Can you meet me at the guesthouse?

I take a shaky breath. Several minutes pass before I reply.

Me: Okay.

Wyatt: Sorry you were worried.

Me: Where were you?

Wyatt: Nowhere good. We'll talk when I get back.

I jerk my head backward. Nausea hits me just like it used to when Wyatt would go out with Jagger and leave me home.

Tears well, hot and useless, blurring my vision. I blink hard, refusing to let them fall.

I can't do this again.

Why did he have to come back?

My phone pings again. My breath catches, but it's just a low battery warning. I bite back a sob. I've never felt more foolish.

Wyatt will never change. I was stupid to think he was at Jax's all this time.

What did he mean when he said he was nowhere good?

Lights beam into the window. A truck engine dies, and not long after, a door slams.

My shoulders droop. I stand, knowing there's only one truth left.

I can't do this anymore. Wyatt's the same boy he's always been.

I've ridden on his merry-go-round. The only place it goes is around in circles.

And it's time I got off for good.

26

Wyatt

My breath turns to vapor in the midnight air. Acid creeps up my esophagus, brutally burning. I sit in my truck with my hand on the door.

Through the semi-frosted glass of the cabin window, I see Willow standing there with a sad expression. Even with the distance and darkness, I see it.

Don't be a coward.

I shove the door open. The hinges screech loudly, mocking me. My legs feel like lead as I force myself out and limp across the crunchy lawn.

Willow pins her gaze on mine, hers blazing with fierceness.

My steps stutter at that look. I've always hated disappointing her. I know I screwed up again tonight, but I had to make a decision. I wish

I could hide it from her, but just like I was done hiding our relationship from the Cartwrights, I can't pretend tonight didn't happen.

I've become the man I never wanted to be. It's clear as day to me now. And now that I see it, I can't escape it. So I'll tell Willow the truth. She deserves honesty. But it'll be the nail that shuts the coffin on us. Once she knows my truth, there won't be an us anymore.

My insides rearrange themselves. I grit my teeth and step on the porch, trying to breathe. Everything I've ever wanted was so close, yet there's no one to blame for screwing it up but me.

"Be a man," I mutter, and turn the knob, opening the front door. I softly say, "Hey."

"Don't," she warns, her voice shaking with anger.

I ignore the coward in my head, ordering me to run. Instead, I step farther inside and shut the door. I peel off my hat and grip the leather tight.

"I can't do this again," she blurts, breath ragged. "I can't, Wyatt. I won't watch you destroy yourself again."

"I know," I rasp. My voice cracks under the weight of everything I've done.

She throws her hands up. "No, you don't know! You have no idea what you did to me! You think you can show up with those sad cowboy eyes and I'll melt into a puddle at your feet? That I'll forget all the nights I worried myself sick? Or cried over you? And that I'll just want to return to that?"

"I don't want you to forget," I force out. My chest tightens until I can barely breathe.

She glares harder at me. "Don't patronize me."

"I'm not."

"You are. Don't you dare!" she hurls.

I stay quiet, fighting emotions I was taught a man doesn't show. I struggle to put the words together so I can be honest with her.

"Let me guess. You were out drinking and having a good old time. Did you meet someone fancy?" she spouts.

I jerk my head backward. "What? No. I've never done that to you, nor would I want to."

She scoffs. "Sure you haven't."

"Willow, there's never been another woman and never will be," I insist.

Hurt flares hotter on her expression. "I don't believe you."

I step closer, trying to stay calm. "I've never looked at another woman when I've been with you. Not once."

She blinks and turns her head.

"Look at me," I order.

She refuses.

Not hiding my nervousness, I state, "There is something I need to talk to you about. But it sure as hell doesn't involve another woman. And I need you to look at me before I chicken out and hide it from you."

She slowly turns to face me.

I fight to not look away, adding, "I don't want to lie to you."

Her anger burns, but curiosity flickers alongside it.

My heart pounds so hard that I think it'll break my rib cage.

"Just spit it out, Wyatt."

I collect my thoughts, confessing, "I have a problem."

She sarcastically laughs and crosses her arms. "Tell me something I don't know, Wyatt."

My pulse ratchets up. "Jax wouldn't let me work out. So I ended up at the racetrack. There were 40 to 1 odds." The admission tastes like acid.

Her lips part, but no words come out. She swallows hard. In an almost inaudible tone, she asks, "How much did you lose?"

"I was going to try to win back everything I owed you. I could have. I had enough cash."

Her face pales, and her lips quiver.

I continue, "I had the cash out, Willow. I was seconds away."

Her mouth opens, closes, then opens again. "Why are you telling me this?"

"Because I didn't do it, but I have a problem," I choke out. My throat burns like I swallowed glass.

She turns her head slightly, furrowing her forehead.

I admit, "I was about to place the bet. But all I saw was your face and the emotions flashing across it. Anger. Sadness. Disgust. It was all directed at me."

Her eyes widen.

"Then I saw my father's drunk, worthless face. And I knew I was just like him. That I'd become exactly what I swore I'd never be."

She takes a slow step back, but instead of running, she sinks onto the sofa.

I sit next to her, unable to not get all of it out. "I left the track. I drove around, not knowing where to go. So I pulled over. Decided I have to change. And I know I'm going to lose you over this. But I can't just change for you. I have to change for myself. So I searched for a Gamblers Anonymous meeting online. I drove back to town to the church and went inside. I… I stood in front of a dozen strangers, and I told them…" I wrinkle my nose, breathing like a bull.

She puts her hand on mine. "What did you tell them?"

I blink several times before croaking, "My name is Wyatt, and I'm an addict."

Her breathing goes shallow.

I look away in disgrace.

She orders, "Wyatt, look at me."

I take a few ragged breaths and then slowly meet her eyes.

She asks, "You did that?"

I nod, shame flooding every inch of me. "I'm so goddamn sorry. I'm not the man I want to be. I'm not even sure if I'm fixable. But you needed to know the truth."

The tension turns so heavy, I can barely swallow. The clock ticks on. The fridge hums. A branch rattles in the wind, tapping against the window.

She doesn't scream. She doesn't bolt. Instead, she stares at me like she's seeing me for the first time. Her chest heaves with quiet, broken breaths. "You really didn't place the bet?"

I shake my head. "No. I swear on my life."

A single tear slides down her cheek. She doesn't wipe it away. She reaches out a trembling hand and sets it on my shoulder, fingers curling into my shirt.

"You're not your father. You never were," she says softly, voice cracking.

I close my eyes, fighting the tears stinging my lids. I argue, "I sure as hell do a lot of the same things."

She scoots closer, sliding her arm around my shoulders. "No. Only a few. And if you admit you have a problem, then you're one hundred steps ahead of where he ever was."

I open my eyes, and she's looking at me like there might be something in me worth saving.

For the first time in years, I let myself believe there might be. But then I remember what I'm losing. I choke out, "I'm sorry. I never wanted to hurt you. I shouldn't have come back here. I shouldn't have tried to win you back."

She inhales sharply.

I look away, trying not to cry.

Sounding hurt, she asks, "You don't want me anymore?"

Her question hangs in the air, raw and bleeding.

I look back at her. "Of course I want you. You're all I've ever wanted."

"Then why would you say that?"

I admit, "I'm confused."

"About?"

I blurt out, "How can you even look at me after what I just told you?"

"You don't think I already knew you had a problem?" she asks.

The hairs on my arms rise. "You knew I had a gambling problem?"

She bites her lip and tilts her head, sympathy softening her gaze.

"I hate that pity-filled look," I mutter.

She puts her hand on my chin and holds my face in front of hers. Sternly, she states, "It's not pity. And it takes a lot to admit you have a problem and need help."

"But how can you still want me?"

She jerks back, eyes wide with hurt and fury. "How can I still want you? Wyatt, I've *never* stopped wanting you! Not for a day. Not for a second. Even when I hated you, I wanted you so badly, it made me sick."

Her confession slams into me harder than any bull ever could. I reel, chest heaving. "I'm a mess, Willow. I'm an addict. I almost threw everything away again tonight. You deserve someone better. Someone who isn't always one bad night away from blowing it."

She shoves my shoulder, surprising me with her strength. "Better? You think I want *better*? I don't want some perfect man who's never struggled a day in his life. I want *you*. I want the man who told me the truth tonight, who's trying to *be* better."

I blink hard, fighting the sting in my eyes. "You don't know what you're saying."

She throws her hands up in the air. "Don't you dare tell me what I feel, Wyatt Houston. Don't you ever decide for me again. You've done that too many times already."

It's another punch straight to the ribs. I argue, "I'm not deciding anything for you. But I don't want to bring you down with me."

She scoffs, eyes blazing. "Bring me down? You think you're so powerful that you could ruin me? I've already survived you once, Wyatt. And I'm still standing. I know what I want."

My heart thunders. "What do you want?" I ask, scared of the answer but desperate to hear it.

She leans closer, eyes locked on mine. "I want *you*. All of you. Even the broken parts. Especially the broken parts. Because I'm broken too, Wyatt. Neither of us is perfect. But when we're together, we make each other stronger."

I want to believe her. God, I want to. But the shame claws at me. "You don't understand—"

She grabs my face, palms warm against my cheeks. "No. *You* don't understand. Tonight, you chose not to place that bet. You chose *me*. You chose *us*. You chose *yourself*. And that's all I need to know."

Her words slice right through my fear. My voice comes out raw. "For the first time in my life, I realized I don't want to live this way anymore. I don't know why I didn't see it before."

Her gaze softens, filling with so much love that it shatters me. "That's good, Wyatt. I'm proud of you. I know it had to be hard for you to walk into that meeting. And I love you more for it."

A sob catches in my throat. I bury my hands in her hair, pulling her face to mine. "How can you still love me?"

She lets out a shaky breath. "Because I never stopped. And because you're worth it. You always have been." She kisses me, gently at first, then fiercely. Like every emotion we've bottled up for seven years pours out through our lips.

When we break apart, we're both panting. I rest my forehead against hers, and whisper, "I'm so sorry."

She shakes her head, tears shining in her eyes. "I don't want your apologies, Wyatt. I want your promise."

I pull back just enough to look her in the eyes. "What promise?"

She grips my shirt so tight, her knuckles turn white. "That you'll fight for yourself. That you'll fight for us."

I swallow hard, heart hammering. "I swear to you, Willow. I'm done gambling. I'm done running. I'll do whatever it takes to be the man you deserve and the one I want to be."

She lets out a choked laugh, tears slipping down her cheeks. "Good. Because I'm all-in, Wyatt. I won't let you push me away this time. And I won't push you away. My mom made me realize today that I can't be half in."

"She did?"

"Yes. Right before she told me she'll kick your booty off the ranch if you hurt me again."

I crack a smile. "That's fair, but I'll make sure that doesn't happen." I hold her against me, breathing in the scent of her shampoo and warm skin.

She clings to me, and nothing feels better, but doubt claws at me. I reveal my fear. "What if I screw up again?"

She pulls back just enough to cup my face. "Then we'll deal with it. Together. One day at a time."

Emotion bubbles up inside me. "I don't deserve you."

She kisses me hard, shutting me up. When she breaks the kiss, she shakes her head. "Stop saying that. *I* get to decide what I deserve. And I deserve *you*."

I bury my face in her neck, breathing her in. "I love you, Willow."

She wraps her arms tighter around me. "I love you too. I always have."

For a long time, we hold each other. The world outside could fall apart, and I wouldn't care. She's here. She's mine. And I'm hers.

Eventually, she pulls back, eyes searching mine. "We need a plan."

I blink. "A plan?"

She nods, fierce and determined. "If you feel like you want to gamble, tell me. I won't judge you. Just no more secrets."

My throat tightens. "Okay. I'm going to keep going to meetings."

"Did it help?" she asks.

I shrug. "I don't know. But I think it helps to talk to others who have the same urges I do. It was kind of a relief, to be honest. To know I'm not the only one. Is that messed-up?"

She shakes her head. "No. Not at all. But we're in this together, Wyatt. You're not alone anymore."

A sob catches in my throat. She holds me tighter, grounding me. For the first time in years, the crushing loneliness lifts. Hope sparks in the darkness.

I pull her onto my lap, wrapping my arms around her. She curls into me, and I admit, "I missed you so damn much."

She shivers. "I missed you too."

We stay like that for a long time, tangled together, listening to each other breathe. My hands drift over her back.

Her fingers thread through my hair, teasing my scalp like she used to when we were teenagers sneaking around the ranch. She pulls back, her eyes still wet but determined. "Promise me one more thing."

"Anything," I vow.

She softly says, "Don't shut me out. No matter how ugly it gets."

I nod. "I promise."

She kisses me again, slow and deep. The taste of her floods every broken piece of me with light.

When we part, she cups my face. "You're not alone. You never were."

I squeeze her so tight, I'm afraid I'll hurt her. "And I'm never letting you go again."

She lets out a soft laugh, and a tear falls. "Good. Because I'm not letting you go either."

I kiss her, pouring everything I can't say into it, knowing that the time for me to step into who I am as a man is here.

There's no going back. I know what I want, and it's a life with Willow. But not just any life.

A life we both deserve.

27

Willow

Warmth cocoons me. Wyatt's leather and earth scent mixes with that of our faded arousal from the hours of sin we engaged in. Exhaustion pulled me under not long ago, but I flutter my eyelids, drifting awake, hazy and dazed. It's the kind of half-sleep that's filled with dreams created from memories.

Shadows dance from the faint light spilling through the cracked door. The cream-colored walls adorned with pastel butterflies, make me smile sleepily.

My overly-sensitized body still hums faintly with pleasure. From behind me, Wyatt kisses my shoulder, then his lips travel down my spine.

I try to roll onto my back, but Wyatt takes his callused hand and pushes my thigh into the air. He moves his face past my butt, then glides his tongue across my pussy to my clit.

I gasp, already trembling.

His tongue slowly circles my most intimate place, tasting every part and dipping in and out of me.

I glance down, and the top of his head peeks from between my thighs. I try to reach for it, but the rumpled sheets, secured to the headboard, wrap around my wrists. There's enough slack to move my arms several inches from under the pillow, but not any farther.

The tip of his nose grazes my clit, and his hot breath teases me. His stubble scrapes the inside of my thigh.

I whimper, my heart skipping, then pounding furiously. I close my eyes, pushing my face into the fluffy pillow, moaning with a raspy, almost hoarse tone.

He licks slow, thick strokes with tongue.

A muffled "Oh!" escapes me. I arch my back, pushing my body into his face, and grip the sheets.

He groans against my damp skin, sending another shock wave through me.

My hips jerk off the bed. I gasp, a strangled sound that barely makes it past my lips, "Jesus, Wyatt."

He chuckles, his hand squeezing my thigh, strong fingers biting into my flesh with possession. He flicks his tongue, then plunges deeper with a ruthless rhythm that strips my brain of every coherent thought. A sob tears out of me as he sucks hard, his nose nudging my swollen clit with more force.

I grasp the sheets tighter, drowning in a mix of memories and my current reality, of what it's like to be restrained by Wyatt.

He grunts, the sound dark and feral, and slides his hand up my thigh, repositioning his palm on my calf, and pushing my legs wider.

"Oh God!" I shout.

His teeth graze me, sending zings through my entire body. Adrenaline flows everywhere he touches, waiting to spill over and consume me.

"You're so damn sweet, sugar," he growls against me. He flicks his tongue back and forth sideways instead of up and down, and all hell breaks loose in my body.

I shatter, convulsing against his mouth, my toes curling so tight they cramp. "Wyatt... Oh God."

Like always, he doesn't show me mercy. His mouth and hands own me, and the high makes me dizzy.

"Look at me, sugar," he orders, tone deeper than the night.

I blink hard to focus, lifting my face out of the pillow and meeting his stormy gaze. The black in his pupils swallows the faint brown surrounding them. For the grand finale, he drags the tip of his tongue along my slit, so achingly slow, more incoherent cries fly past my lips.

His deep chuckle vibrates against me.

"Are you ready for the main event?" he questions.

I try to catch my breath, my words lost to the thundering pulse between my ears.

He flips me onto my back, then crawls up my body, smirking with a devilishly cocky grin. He pushes my thigh up toward my chest, and thrusts inside me in one hard, brutal stroke.

"Yes," I cry out, barely audible, as pleasure tears through me.

He pulls back, then sinks deeper, until his hips press flush against me. His eyes stay locked on mine, dark and hungry, as if we haven't been tangled together several times since before we even got into the bedroom.

My breath comes out in ragged bursts. I twist my hands around the sheets, increasing the tension.

He notices, and his lips twitch. He thrusts hard, and I moan, trembling. He places his hand over my mouth, muffling my cries, and lowers his lips to my ear.

His tongue swipes my earlobe, then he hisses, "Goddamn, you're tight," his jaw flexing against mine.

"Mmm," I moan, wrapping my free leg around his waist and digging my heel against his ass, trying to take him deeper with a furious and desperate upward thrust.

"Naughty girl. I'm in charge," he reminds me. Then, in punishment, he slows his movements, rolling his hips so every inch drags along my raw nerves.

I bite down on his palm, and wickedness flashes across his face.

"So you want to play like that?" he taunts, then moves his hand to my wrists, stretching them into the air as high as they can go.

"Wyatt," I cry out against his hand.

His thrusts turn frantic, pounding into me so hard, I spiral and see stars. The bed creaks beneath us, the headboard knocking the wall in a rhythm that matches the explosiveness of my pounding heart.

His hand moves from my mouth to my throat. His fingers brush under my jaw, then land on my pulse.

More unrecognizable syllables tear from me, lost in my haze of need.

"You feel what you do to me?" he rumbles. He thrusts harder, deeper, hips grinding against mine until more stars burst behind my eyes.

"Kiss me," I beg.

His lips slide against mine, wet and hungry. We kiss like we're drowning, like we're each other's oxygen, our tongues tangling in the darkness.

I dig my nails into the part of his hand I can reach, my arms still straight in the air.

He grunts into my mouth, a tremble running through him. He repositions my thigh over his shoulder, changing the angle.

"Oh my..." Another round of adrenaline attacks me. I shudder violently beneath him.

He's relentless, coaxing me into an extended high.

My body obeys him, splintering apart, my back arching, moans ripping from my throat.

Every muscle spasms around him, failing to lock as he rips his cock out of me before pushing back inside.

His jaw twitches next to mine before he lets out a strangled roar, his movements becoming savage. Then he groans, "Fuck, sugar," as he spills inside me. Heat floods me, leaking on the bed as he continues to thrust through his orgasm.

When it's over, he collapses over me, his ragged breath in my ear, his weight pinning me to the mattress.

He carefully unties my wrists while kissing my neck. As soon as they're released, I wrap my arms around him.

Wyatt's sly grin widens as he catches his breath, his sweaty hair falling over his eyes. He skims it back, revealing a boyish sparkle in his eyes that makes him look eighteen again instead of the sin-soaked man who just ruined me.

"Damn, sugar," he drawls, low and ragged, gaze roaming every inch of me like he's etching me into his memory.

I nervously laugh. "What?"

"It's official. I'm adding a warning label on you: *Too Hot to Handle Without Fire Insurance*." He waggles his eyebrows.

I let out a loud laugh that bubbles through my exhaustion. "Fire insurance?"

He shifts so his weight presses me deeper into the mattress. "Yep. And maybe a waiver of liability. Pretty sure you broke my hip." He winks.

I snort, my chest shaking with laughter. "That's rich, Houston. You're the one who nearly split me in half."

He plants a quick, hot kiss on my lips, charming mischief twinkling in his eyes. Then he glances over his shoulder at the glowing red numbers of the digital clock.

The humor drains from his face. He groans, scrubbing his forehead. "I don't want to leave, but I've gotta get out to the barn."

I blink, every muscle twinging with a satisfied, spent ache. I whine, "Noooooo! Stay in bed with me." I wrap my arms tighter around him.

He chuckles and ducks out of my grip. He slides off me and then rises. "Sorry, sugar. Gotta earn my keep. Can't let your daddy think I'm free-loading."

I prop myself up on my elbows, hair spilling around my face like a curtain. "Don't be silly. Stay in bed. My brothers can handle everything."

He slips into his worn jeans, tugs a T-shirt over his head, then leans down, bracing a hand on either side of my head. His gaze, a mix of stubbornness and hunger, sears into mine. "That's exactly why I need to go. I'm not hiding from them. It's best if they get used to us sooner rather than later."

I want to argue, and pull him back into bed so we can hide under the covers until the rest of the world ceases to exist. But his tone is too adamant, and I know him too well. So I groan loudly, pouting, "Aw. You're no fun."

He chuckles as he leans over to kiss me. "I'll show you who's no fun later." He grazes the tip of his finger over my nipple.

I whine louder.

"Get some sleep, sugar," he orders, then slips out the door, his boots pounding on the wood down the hallway.

I drop back onto the bed, rolling to his empty side. I inhale his scent on the sheets. It doesn't take long before sleep drags me under again.

But I don't sleep long. It's only a few hours before I wake up smiling, throat dry, and muscles deliciously sore.

I get up, go to the window, and peek across the snowy yard, but I can't see the barn from where the Butterfly House sits.

I wonder how my brothers are treating him.

Doubt they've gotten over it.

I glance at the clock. Breakfast isn't for another two hours, so I throw on yesterday's jeans. I dig into Wyatt's unpacked duffel and pull out one of his long-sleeved thermals. Putting the shirt on, I slip into my boots and then run my fingers through my locks.

I glance in the mirror. My hair's still a mess, but there's no time for a fashion show on the ranch. I step out on the porch.

The bitter cold bites at my cheeks. The snow's crusty surface sparkles under the sharp sun. Frost glitters on the barn roof, giving the impression that diamonds hide beneath the thick blanket. Holiday lights still glow, as the darkness hasn't completely faded.

I make my way across the ranch, heading toward the barn. As soon as I step inside, warm air tinged with the scents of hay and manure flares in my nostrils. My brothers' mocking laughs rumble in my ears.

My irritation sparks. Wyatt can handle them, but it's not fair that he takes all their wrath on his own. And knowing my brothers, they'll try to make him pay for his lifetime of sins that don't even have anything to do with me.

I turn the corner to see Wyatt holding a pitchfork. He scoops horse shit into a wheelbarrow. His dark hair's damp with sweat, sticking out in spikes past the brim of his cowboy hat. His worn T-shirt, covered in dirt and God knows what else, sticks to his torso.

Jagger leans against a stall door with his arms crossed, scowling. Mason, Sebastian, and Alexander have similar stances.

Jagger drawls, "Well, look at that. Bull-riding bad boy's got a new specialty in grade A manure."

Mason adds, "Got some under the snow in the corral that needs to be picked up after this."

Wyatt doesn't react to their taunts. He keeps working, jaw set tight, eyes locked on the pile he's shoveling.

Unlike Wyatt, anger explodes from me. I shout, "Enough!"

My four brothers freeze. Even the horses' restless shuffling goes silent.

I storm forward, planting myself between Wyatt and my brothers.

Wyatt looks at me, ordering, "Go back inside the house, Willow."

I place my hands on my hips. I clear my throat and demand, "Stop being dicks. This is the new reality. Wyatt and I are together. We're adults, so deal with it."

"You weren't an adult when he took advantage of you," Jagger snarls.

"This again? You've got to be kidding me!" I exclaim.

"You were fifteen!" Jagger roars.

"You're such a hypocrite! You lost your virginity to Camile Henderson when you were thirteen!" I point out.

His eyes widen in shock.

My other brothers snicker.

"Yeah. Don't think I didn't know like the rest of the school! So don't you dare act like Wyatt forced me to do anything I didn't want to do."

"Willow—" Wyatt starts, but I cut him off.

"No! Let's get this over with once and for all." I point at my other brothers. "Do you have anything you want to get off your chest? Because I don't have to discuss my personal life with any of you. But this is your one chance to say whatever you want. After you're done having your temper tantrum, this is over. You're going to accept that Wyatt and I are together, and things are resuming as normal."

"Normal isn't you with him," Jagger seethes.

"Get over yourself!" I hurl, crossing my arms and glowering at him.

Silence falls over us. A horse neighs, breaking the tension for a moment, then it resumes.

I turn to Wyatt and point to a pile of manure. "You missed a spot."

The corner of his mouth lifts into a crooked grin. He replies, "Guess I need to get that." He scoops the pitchfork under the pile and tosses it in the wheelbarrow.

I grab another pitchfork and step next to him.

"What are you doing, sugar?" he asks.

"Showing you I've still got skills," I tease.

Jagger groans. "Yuck."

"What's yuck?" I snap.

He wrinkles his nose. "You two flirting."

"Get over it," I order, then I toss the pitchfork aside, step in front of

Wyatt, and throw my arms around his shoulders, saying, "I think you forgot my kiss."

A choked laugh breaks from his chest. His grin expands.

"I'm out," Sebastian mutters. He moves toward the door.

"Fun's over. Me too," Alexander adds, following him.

I rise on my tiptoes, pressing my fingertips behind Wyatt's neck, and kiss him like we're alone.

"Gross," Mason grumbles.

I ignore him.

"Okay. Enough," Jagger spouts.

I continue to kiss Wyatt as he tries to pull away, then I retreat. A tad out of breath, I spin to face Jagger. In a firm tone, I assert, "Don't be stupid and let this ruin your friendship. Wyatt's not the only one to blame. And I won't have you disrespecting my man."

Jagger wrinkles his nose.

Mason pushes off the stall door. He grabs the pitchfork. "Jesus, Willow. You don't need to be so dramatic, but you made your point. Just stop kissing him in front of me."

I don't move.

He turns toward Jagger. "Are you planning to stand around, or are we getting this barn done before the next ice age?"

Jagger shakes his head, muttering curses I can barely hear, then grabs a shovel and moves to the next stall.

The four of us fall into a rhythm. The barn echoes with the sounds of metal scraping on wood, the dull thump of manure hitting the wheelbarrow, and the occasional neigh of a restless horse. It reminds me of the time when Wyatt and I had barn duty after he pretended to lose to Ava while skipping stones.

I catch Wyatt glancing at me every time we pass each other in the narrow aisle. His dark eyes soften, a flicker of heat smoldering under the exhaustion of working on little sleep. He brushes my hip once when we maneuver around the same wheelbarrow, and it sends a jolt through me that I can't hide.

"Damn it," Jagger mutters, slamming his pitchfork into a pile with a little too much force, causing straw to fly everywhere.

I arch an eyebrow. "Problem, big brother?"

He glares at me, cheeks red, then at Wyatt. "You really think this is going to work? You two?"

Wyatt straightens, chest rising and falling with heavy breaths, eyes locked on Jagger. "It's not even a question. I told you before, and I'll tell you again. I love her."

A hushed standoff ensues, the two men staring one another down.

I grip my pitchfork so hard, my knuckles crack. My pulse rises again.

Wyatt adds, voice hard as granite, "I'm not losing again what I stupidly lost once before. So either get over it or keep throwing your shit with the horses.'"

Mason lets out a low whistle.

Jagger's jaw tics. Then he shakes his head and scoffs. "Fine. But if you fuck this up, I'll break every bone in your body."

Wyatt grows serious. "I wouldn't expect anything less."

Jagger jabs his pitchfork into another pile.

We work through the stalls in tense, stubborn silence that eventually fades into something familiar. My brothers start to banter again, insulting each other about who smells worse or who's more incompetent with a pitchfork. Slowly, they include Wyatt in the conversation.

I wipe sweat from my forehead with my sleeve, catching my breath. Wyatt leans on his shovel, watching me with dark eyes that flicker with pride and relief. He teases, "Nice form. Have you ever thought about joining the rodeo shit-shoveling team?"

A warmth curls inside me. I roll my eyes, but a grin tugs at my lips. "Says the man who's missed his target twice already."

Mason groans. "Oh God. Here we go again. More flirting."

I smirk at him, feeling the happiest I've felt in years.

Jagger clears his throat. "You two done making eyes at each other? We've got two more stalls."

Wyatt and I exchange a quick look, a shared heat that no one can mistake. Then we get back to work.

For the next hour, we move like a team. The barn starts to resemble something livable again, with manure cleared and fresh straw spread. By the time we finish, the breakfast bell rings.

Wyatt leans his pitchfork against the wall, wiping sweat from his brow. "Well, sugar. Think we earned some food?"

I laugh, breathless, my heart thumping in a way that has nothing to do with the physical labor.

Jagger groans. "It's so weird hearing you call her 'sugar.'"

"Sorry," Wyatt offers Jagger with a shrug and a grin.

Jagger shakes his head and leaves the barn, but he doesn't have the same angry air he did earlier.

Wyatt leads me out of the barn, where morning sun slices through the chilly air.

The bell rings again, and the kids all yell, "Breakfast!"

When Mason and Jagger are far ahead of us, Wyatt steps closer, murmuring, "Thanks for saving my ass in there."

I meet his gaze under the shadow of his brim, teasing, "Don't make me regret it, Wyatt Houston."

"Never again, sugar," he vows.

And for the first time in years, I believe him.

28

Wyatt

One Month Later

There's a funny thing about routines. You never realize you're building one until it's got you by the throat. And Willow's got me tighter than a bull rope in the final seconds of an eight-second ride.

I'm loving every second of it. The tighter she pulls, the more I crave. She could suffocate me with her schedules and meetings. All I feel is her love and the direction I'd been missing in my life. Or maybe I didn't want it because she wasn't attached to it. But I'm finally a peaceful, happy man.

Jax has me on another rope. Every day this past month has been a blur of bruised knuckles and two-a-day practices until my thighs scream.

Between the grueling workouts, I have endless meetings with Willow about cleaning up my reputation. Whatever she advises me to do, I agree to, and so far, it's working.

But good things never come easy. I've had to toss my ego aside so I can crawl out of the grave I dug for my career. After the train wreck at The Buck and Bruise, I had doubts that any sponsor would touch me. But Willow secured the deals with Tough Rider and Roughneck Armorworks. With two contracts in hand, there's enough to keep me in the circuit so I can make my big comeback. Only this time, I'm determined not to screw it up.

Sometimes, I pull up to the Butterfly House and dwell on my life like a lovesick fool. I lean back in the driver's seat, knowing Willow's inside, and wonder how she's still with me.

Sooner or later, she'll come outside, either in tiny pajama bottoms and goose bump-covered legs or skinny jeans made to haunt a man. She'll cross her arms over her chest to keep herself warm, rasping, "Could hear your truck a mile away. You plan on coming in sometime tonight? Or should I put dinner in the fridge for leftovers tomorrow?" Then she'll toss me a smile.

Sometimes, we don't make it inside the house. I'll pull her into the truck and try to put the last orgasm I gave her to shame. Too often, dinner goes cold, and we eat it under damp sheets.

Every morning, I get up at the crack of dawn, making sure I earn my keep. Willow whines when I get out of bed, but I never stay. I'm still trying to prove to Jacob and the rest of the Cartwrights that I'm a man who's worthy of her.

This morning is no different. I'm hunched over the workbench in the barn. The cold bites my fingers as I retie a loose knot in Spitfire's lead. Mason's somewhere outside, cussing loudly at the tractor that won't start. Jagger and Alexander are in the corral. Sebastian went back to Dallas with Georgia.

The wood door creaks, and Willow's voice floats over to me. "You're gonna freeze your ass off out here, Houston."

I grin. "Thought you liked my ass cold. Builds character."

She snorts as she steps closer, and her warm-amber and crushed-jasmine scent that's always made my knees weak envelops me. She teases, "Not sure your ass has ever had character."

"You've forgotten." I stand up slowly, facing her fully. I turn, pushing out my hip. I boast, "This is class A character."

She rolls her eyes, but her cheeks pink up. "Is that what we're calling it?"

"Sugar, this ass is a national treasure. You just forgot how lucky you were to admire it," I tease.

"Don't confuse me rubbing balm on your bruises as admiration," she fires back with a smile, batting her eyelashes.

"I was referring to the years you spent tracing it with those sweet hands. Don't pretend you didn't honor every inch," I taunt.

Her cheeks turn beet red. She laughs. "You're impossible."

I tug her toward me, and palm the back of her head, tilting it. "Did you miss me?"

"Always," she replies, her smile softening.

"I'm leaving later." The words come out heavy.

"So am I," she states, the humor gone from her expression.

"It's going to suck not seeing you," I add, wondering how I'll survive being away from her.

She nods. "Agreed."

Jax got me into a rodeo in Arizona. Willow's riding team will be at one in New Mexico. It'll be the first time we've really been apart since I got back.

Mason's voice booms, "Don't worry. We'll keep you entertained."

I look over my shoulder. "What do you mean?"

He grins. "You didn't think Jagger and I would let you have all the fun, did you?"

My pulse beats faster. I cock an eyebrow. "What are you talking about?"

"Just what I said. But you're in the back with Jagger. I'm calling shotgun," he claims.

"I'm confused," I admit. Things have been better between us, but they aren't the same. Mason and I are on better footing than Jagger and I.

Mason grabs a tool from the chest and then points at Willow. "Explain it to him. I don't have time to dummy things down." He steps outside.

"Jagger is coming with me?" I question.

She shrugs. "Sounds like it."

"Did you arrange this?" I ask.

She shakes her head. "No."

A hint of anxiety pricks at me. Back in the day, I would have given my right foot for Jagger to go on the road with me. But things are different now.

I'm different.

It's like Willow can read my mind. Worry fills her expression at our shared concern. "You're going to have to tell my brothers. Probably best to discuss it before you leave."

I take a deep breath, holding it in as I grind my molars. It's not that I didn't know this day was coming, but the shame and disappointment in myself are still fresh wounds.

I'm a gambling addict. That means no casinos. No racetracks. No bets on the side while sitting at the bar. The thirty-five days of Gamblers Anonymous meetings I've attended have taught me a lot. Yet there's still so much I need to learn and come to terms with.

It's been easy staying on track at the ranch. I go about my daily routine and come home to Willow at night. Even though I go to the meetings, I'm not jonesing to place a bet like most of the members.

Now that I'm going on the road, and Willow won't be there, waiting for me, it's another story. And nothing is engrained in the Cartwrights more than gambling. After all, they own a racehorse business.

"Breathe, Wyatt," Willow orders gently, stroking my cheek.

I release air I didn't know I was holding.

"That's it," she teases, smiling.

"I think I need a kiss," I say, leaning closer.

She gives me a good one, and I tighten my arms around her.

The alarm on her phone goes off, and she groans into my mouth before retreating. "I've got to get ready to leave."

I sigh.

She tilts her head. "I can tell my brothers for you, if it's easier for you."

I shake my head and take a deep breath. "No, sugar. I'm a man. That's something that needs to come from me."

Her lips twitch. "And what a man you are." She waggles her eyebrows.

I pat her ass, warning, "Get out of here before I strip you out of your clothes and spread you out on the hay."

She kisses me again, then begrudgingly exits the barn.

I finish working on Spitfire's lead, going through different ways to tell Jagger and Mason. When I finish, I put the tools away and step outside.

Jax pulls through the gate and parks near the corral. He gets out and struts over to the others.

"No time like the present," I mutter, my heart racing and chest tight. I slip on my gloves and duck against the wind. I push my way toward where the horses are being trained. When I get there, I lean against the rail, hating the chaos clawing inside me.

Dawn's barely cracked, the sky bruised purple on the horizon. My breath mists white as I exhale. My nerves shoot higher and higher as I watch Jagger and Mason saddle the colts, who snort clouds in the air while their back muscles bunch with restless energy.

Don't be a pussy.

Jax asks, "You ready?"

"All packed," I answer.

"Good. It'll be like old times, right, boys?" he crows with his smoke-cracked drawl.

Jagger turns to me with a mischievous expression. It's the first time since finding out about me and Willow that he's looked at me with anything resembling the way he used to look at me. He announces, "I'm ready."

Tell them.

My blood pumps hot, and my pulse pounds between my ears.

Mason shouts, "Booker! Come take the horses inside."

The new ranch hand replies, "Okay, boss."

"I'm showering before we go," Mason says.

"No shit. I'm not riding all the way to Arizona smelling any of you," Jagger states.

"You got coffee?" Jax asks.

"Of course. Mom can warm some breakfast up if you want," Jagger offers.

Jax nods. "Lead the way."

The three of them move toward the house. My anxiety builds as the opportunity to tell them dwindles.

Jagger looks over his shoulder and teases, "Are you coming, or are you gonna miss the rodeo?"

I can't go without them knowing. I'll end up wrecking myself all over again and dragging Willow down the hole with me.

I blurt out, "Stop."

They all turn, looking at me in question.

Say it. Don't be a coward.

A sound like gravel rattling around a steel drum fills the air. And I realize the noise came from me when I cleared my throat.

Mason arches a brow. "What's got your boxers in a twist?"

Jax's eyes narrow, the wrinkles around them deepening.

"Wyatt?" Jagger prods.

I swallow hard. My pulse kicks into a brutal gallop. The horses behind me seem to sense it, neighing loudly.

"I need to tell you something." The words scrape my throat raw.

Mason teases, "What is it, buttercup?"

I laugh, but it sounds awkward, making me more nervous.

Jagger's eyes harden, and his voice is sharp when he asks, "Is this about Willow?"

I shake my head, gaze fixed on the trampled dirt under my boots, then I raise my eyes to his. "No. This is about me."

A gust of wind whips across the corral, slapping my back. I almost chicken out, only getting out "Never—" before cutting myself off.

I swallow hard, clenching my jaw.

The three men wait.

My pulse pounds harder. I finally blurt out, "I've got a problem."

Jax's focus is lasered on me. "Spit it out, son."

I drag in a shaky breath. The shame is thick enough to choke me, but I reveal, "I'm a gambling addict."

Jagger laughs. "Funny."

"It's not a joke," I say seriously.

Time seems to stand still. Even the horses go silent. The only sound is the whisper of the cold wind as it blows by.

Jagger comes closer, his boots crunching on the ground. "I'm confused," he says.

I lift my head higher, meeting his stare. My gut twists like a bull's spine when he's trying to buck off a rider. "I have a gambling problem. A bad one. I've lost more money than I want to admit. There's nothing I haven't bet on. Bulls, cards, horses, sports teams I know nothing about, even stupid things like which rider would get thrown first."

Mason mutters a low curse, scrubbing a hand over his face.

Jax's glare drills into me like a branding iron.

Confessions pour out of me as fast as blood from a fresh cut. "It's a big reason why my sponsors dropped me. Why my life's been circling the drain. But I'm done. No more. No racetracks, casinos, or stupid bar wagers. And I'm swearing off whiskey too."

A moment of thick silence descends.

Mason's gaze looks like it wants to slice me open. "You serious?"

I nod, throat burning. "I have to be. I can't keep living like this. I won't."

Jagger mumbles, "Damn, Willow."

I snap my gaze to his. "Why are you damming her?"

He shakes his head and groans. "Should have known she'd convince you of something so you'd change."

"What are you talking about?" I hurl, anger building quickly.

He continues, "You don't have a problem. Don't listen to her."

"Willow didn't know until I told her. *I* realized I had a problem. *I* took myself to the first meeting over a month ago. *I* sat her down and told her I'm an addict."

Jagger gapes at me.

"It's true. I can't control it when I start, so I'm not betting ever again," I explain, disgust with myself burning in my stomach.

Mason declares, "Christ, Wyatt. You should've told us sooner."

"I was too ashamed," I admit, my voice splintering.

Jax pins me with his steely gaze. "So you're getting help?"

I nod. "Yes, sir. I started attending daily meetings a month ago. I just wanted you all to know why I won't be indulging in anything I used to while we're on the road. And I'll probably find a meeting to attend once we get there."

Jagger takes a bit to process it, looking like he wants to either punch or hug me.

I stay silent, my chest tightening so bad, I think it might collapse in on itself.

Mason steps beside him, his eyes glassy in the cold morning light. "You better keep hold of this, Wyatt. 'Cause I'm not watching you destroy yourself or our sister."

"I got this," I assert.

Mason nods. "Okay, then. We'll stick to beers on the road."

Relief fills me. "Thanks."

Jax finally moves, placing a heavy hand on my shoulder. "You mess up, you come talk to me. Are we clear?"

I nod, a sob lodged so deep, it doesn't stand a chance of escaping. "Clear."

Jagger shakes his head, his voice coming out rough. "All right, you stubborn bastard. Let's get cleaned up so we can hit the road."

I let out a strangled laugh, eyes burning from more than the wind. "Sounds good."

We make our way toward the house, but Jagger hangs back with me. We're almost to the porch when he quietly says, "You could have told me."

"I just did."

He adds, "Before today."

I stop walking.

He turns toward me, eyes locking on mine.

"I know I've been giving you shit about my sister, but I still have your back."

Appreciation for my oldest friend sends warmth through me. "Thanks. Good to know."

"So no betting at all?" he questions.

"None," I answer.

He stares at me for a moment, then questions, "But we can still drink beer?"

I chuckle. "Yeah. I only have a problem with whiskey. It makes me think I'm invincible and that the odds are in my favor."

Jagger grins. "Whiskey's overrated these days anyway."

I offer, "I'm okay if you drink it around me."

He shakes his head. "Nah. Don't tell anyone, but the headaches the next day are starting to kill me."

I grunt. "Isn't that the truth."

He slaps me on the back. "All right, then. Get your dirty ass inside and shower. We have to get on the road. You have a rodeo to win!"

29

Willow

Six Months Later

Warm August air kisses my skin. Male cicadas sing their summer song, calling their mates. They fly around in groups, their prominent eyes set wide apart, transparent wings, and stout bodies flittering across the fields.

The louder they get, the antsier I become. It's been fourteen days, six hours, forty-three minutes, and some odd seconds since Wyatt and I were in the same state, let alone the same bed. Between his rodeos and my team traveling for competitions, we've been two shooting stars going opposite directions in the same sky.

My heart aches. We've survived six months of this crazy routine. His winning streak has been unreal. Headline after headline, buckle after buckle, he's on the longest streak any rider's ever had. And I couldn't be prouder of him.

Every time I tell Wyatt how amazing he's doing, he tells me that the best part doesn't involve victory. He claims it's knowing that every time he wins, he can come home to me.

I always tell him that if he loses, he's still to come home.

He'll put his fingers over my lips and remind me, "We don't say that word," which always makes me laugh.

The deep rumble of a diesel truck hits my ears, growing louder. The Butterfly House is far from the main gate, but I scan the dark drive, looking for the cloud of dust that I know is coming.

My heart does a two-step when his truck slice through the trees. I press a hand against my belly, trying to calm the nervous fluttering, but it's useless. The second I see the familiar silhouette of his truck, every bit of resolve I've built up to stay cool shatters.

I dart down the porch steps and run toward the truck. The gravel crunches, his tires spitting up pebbles. I get past the summer garden, and the truck stops hard enough to jolt.

The door flies open, and Wyatt jumps out. He runs toward me, boots heavy, hat casting dark shadows over eyes that burn like wildfire. He growls, "Sugar!"

I leap into his arms, and he lifts me off the ground, spinning me. Unable to contain my excitement, a squeal escapes my mouth. I wrap my legs around his waist.

He chuckles. One large palm cups my ass, and the other splays across my back.

I grip his broad shoulders, and our mouths connect, our lips and tongues pressing together. I kiss him deeply until I'm out of breath.

He mumbles against my lips, "Goddamn, sugar. Two weeks. I thought I was gonna lose my mind."

"I know. I missed you terribly," I tell him, my arms locking tighter around his neck. The heat of his body merges with mine, and the chaos inside me calms.

He kisses me again, then retreats. "I should park the truck properly and turn the lights off."

I laugh, realizing we're in the middle of the dirt trail that leads to the driveway. I release my legs and find my footing.

He leads me to the truck and opens the passenger door. "Hop in, sugar."

I obey.

He gets into the driver's seat and then accelerates down the path, stopping in front of the guesthouse that has been our home for the last seven months.

We get out, and he sweeps me off my feet.

I giggle, holding on to his shoulders, and kiss him some more.

He carries me up the steps, each press of his mouth more feral than the last. He slams the front door with his boot, then sets me on the counter. He puts his hands next to my hips and leans in an inch from my face. A wicked glint flicks in his eyes. "You smell like summer and sin. Damn, I missed you!"

I inhale his intoxicating scent, running my hand through his hair. "I'm the one who missed you."

"Then what are you going to do about it?" he challenges, his grin matching his gaze.

Giddy, I bat my eyes, teasing, "Why, Wyatt Houston. Do you have naughty thoughts on your mind?"

He licks his lips, glancing at the low-cut neckline of my sundress. He declares, "I'm not letting you out of my sight tonight. You hear me?"

"Loud and clear, cowboy," I say, biting my lip.

He tosses his hat on the table. It lands with a thud. His mouth claims mine again, hands rough, hot, and greedy as they slide under my dress.

I arch into him, aching for everything we couldn't do while we were apart.

He slides a finger past my panties and groans. "You're already wet. Jesus, sugar. How long have you been melting like this?"

"Since you jumped out of that truck," I admit, then return to kissing him.

He breaks the kiss only long enough to mumble, "Those two weeks felt like two lifetimes."

My fingers dive into his hair, pulling him back to me. "Same. It was torture."

"Let's stay naked the next few days," he suggests.

I laugh. "I'm game."

"Good. Let's start now." He shoves a finger inside me.

I gasp.

A knock rattles the door, cutting through the haze. We both freeze, breathing heavy. We look toward the door.

"Don't answer it," I whisper.

Another sharp knock echoes around us.

Wyatt doesn't move except to say, "We need to be farther away from the main house."

"Y'all better have clothes on!" Jagger booms from outside.

Wyatt groans, pressing his forehead against my collarbone. "That brother of yours has the worst timing."

I remind him, "He's your bestie."

He grunts but removes his hand from under my dress.

"Noooo," I whine.

He sucks on his finger with a groan, then shouts, "Keep your pants on for a hot minute, Jagger." Lowering his voice, he says to me, "Save that fire for me. Let me see what he wants and then I'll get rid of him."

"Please," I beg.

"On it, sugar," he says, then opens the door.

Jagger pushes inside past Wyatt, wearing his usual shit-eating grin. "Well, well. You two look cozy."

I roll my eyes with a smile. "Get to the point, Jagger."

His eyes dance. "Heard your team won today. Figured you'd want to know Wyatt took the purse at the rodeo too."

My chest swells with pride. "Yes, I know, Einstein."

Wyatt shrugs with infuriating nonchalance, but his grin betrays him. "Rode that bull like the devil was on my tail."

"Damn straight you did," Jagger boasts.

I jump off the counter and step next to Wyatt. "I bet you did! I'm so proud of you!"

Jagger clears his throat dramatically. "Well, if you're done making moon eyes, Mom wants you to head over for dinner tomorrow. Sebastian and Georgia are coming in town for the week."

Wyatt slings an arm around my waist, tugging me close. "We'll be there."

Jagger's eyes narrow on Wyatt. "Better be. And keep your hands to yourself. There will be children present."

"I won't make promises I can't keep," Wyatt shoots back with a smirk.

Jagger mutters something under his breath as he walks off. The second the door shuts, Wyatt picks me up again. "Where were we?"

"Think we were about here," I tease, tugging him down for another hungry kiss.

The hours blur after that. Clothes become casualties of war, littering the floor. The bed springs creak under the rhythm of our bodies coming together. His name becomes a mantra on my lips. When he finally collapses beside me, both of us slick with sweat, the silence is thick with more than just exhaustion.

Our love has grown roots, deep and lasting.

Wyatt's hand strokes lazy circles on my stomach. "I've been thinking."

"That's dangerous," I tease.

He chuckles, but it fades quickly. His eyes meet mine, dark and serious. "I've been winning big. I put most of it in savings, like I promised. I have more than enough now to buy that land I told you about."

My breath catches. "You're serious?"

He nods. "Yes. And I know what I want to do with it."

"Build the house you keep sketching out?"

He pauses.

Nerves fill my belly. "What is it?" I sit up.

He sits up too, announcing, "I want to start a bull riding school."

I gape at him, then ask, "You don't want to ride anymore?"

Something flickers over his expression, but I can't pinpoint it. He declares, "I still like it, but I don't think I love it anymore."

I'm shocked at his admission. "Really?"

He tugs me onto his lap. "I don't like being away from you."

My heart skips a handful of beats. I coo, "Aw. I don't like being away from you either."

He cautiously says, "I can't stay on the circuit forever. We both know that."

"You have a few more years in you at least," I assert.

He shrugs. "I don't know. I think it'd be awesome to go out on top, and right now, that's where I'm at."

"I can't disagree with you. But won't you miss it?"

"Sure. But I'd rather be here with you. I can teach kids, keep them safe, and give them the tools I never had. We can make a real life."

Warmth floods me, spreading from my chest outward. I caress the side of his head. "We don't already have a real life?"

He stares at me intensely, and my butterflies kick up again. "What?" I ask.

"You're always going to have to travel some with your career," he asserts.

"True. But it's not too horrible. And I'm not looking for a new career, Wyatt."

He chuckles. "Simmer down, sugar. I'm stating a fact."

"Okay," I agree, not sure where he's going with this.

He says, "Someone has to be home with the babies. So if I have a school, I can be here while you're on the road."

"Babies! Who's pregnant?" I blurt out.

He grins. "No one yet. But once I make you my wife, I fully plan on knocking you up as much as possible."

I gape at him, my heart pounding wildly.

"Now, don't act like you don't want kids. I know you do. Besides, you'd be a great mom," he claims.

"Ummm…thanks."

"Did I just freak you out?" he asks, his lips twitching.

I shake my head and release a breath. "No. This is just a super-serious conversation."

He nods, his expression serious. "Yes. But it's best we talk about this, right?"

"Yes," I agree.

He kisses me. "Okay. So do you think I should put an offer on that land?"

I blink hard against a flood of happy tears.

"I didn't mean to make you cry, sugar," he says, holding me closer.

I sniffle. "You're not. I'm just happy."

"Me too," he murmurs in my ear.

I lift my face to his, trying not to smile. "So…"

"So?" He arches his eyebrows.

The butterflies in my stomach have a full-on war. I tease, "When are you making me an honest woman?"

He chuckles. "You'll know when you know."

I bite my smile.

He kisses my forehead, admitting, "I need you to help me with the paperwork for the school. Permits. Taxes. All that shit I don't understand."

I laugh. "Of course I'll help."

"You're the best thing that ever happened to me," he declares.

"You're the best thing that's happened to me too," I reply.

We make love until we're breathless, then we do it all over again. The next morning, the sun filters through the gauzy curtains. Wyatt's sprawled across the bed with an arm draped possessively over my waist.

I trace the scar on his shoulder, remembering how it tells a story of a bull he conquered and the mistake he survived.

He stirs, pulling me closer. "You keep touching me like that, sugar, I'm never going to let you get out of this bed."

"Wyatt?"

He turns and pushes a lock of my hair behind my ear. "What's going on in that pretty head of yours?"

"Were you serious last night? About the school and giving up riding?" I ask.

His expression turns solemn. "Never been more serious about anything."

"You'll be an amazing instructor," I offer.

He grins. "Thanks."

I add, "But you'll be an even more amazing father one day."

A smile explodes on his lips, and he cages his body over me.

I squeal.

He pushes my thigh toward my chest, slides inside me, and declares, "That's the plan, sugar. So let's practice making those babies."

30

Wyatt

One Day Later

$\mathcal{I}$ try to get a grip, reminding myself that I've climbed onto two-thousand-pound angry bulls, been flung to the ground like a rag doll, and survived my father's wrath.

I curse myself at the thought of him.

I take a deep breath, wipe my sweaty palms on my jeans, and stare at the dark-mahogany door. It's as solid as the man behind it. Jacob's voice rumbles inside, and each second I stand here feels like an hour.

He has to give me his blessing.

What if he doesn't?

I have my shit together now.

What if it's not good enough yet?

I shift my weight, scanning the room to buy time. Framed photos of winning horses, large gold medals, and members of the Cartwright family line the walls. Other pictures boast family vacations, holidays, and kids at various ages.

Nostalgia hits me when I glance at the ones with Jagger and me. Then one catches my attention, and I can't look away. It makes my heart skip a beat. Willow's sixteen, her hair's wild, and her smile is brighter than the sun.

She's going to be my wife.

Only if Jacob gives me his blessing.

Anxiety creeps through me.

Maybe I should do this in a few months.

I don't want to wait any longer.

Stop being a pussy.

He still hates me.

No, he doesn't.

Since I told Jacob I'd snuck behind his back with his daughter for several years, things haven't been the same between us. I want to get back to the way we were, but I'm not sure that will happen.

Get it over with.

Several more excruciating seconds pass before Jacob calls out, "Come in."

I take another nervous breath, and turn the knob.

I'm met with the stern expression I remember from childhood. His brows furrow. "Wyatt. You okay?"

No. I'm about to piss myself.

I nod. "Yes, sir. Do you have a minute?"

His head tilts in curiosity as he waves me in. "Sure. Come on in."

The air conditioner is on, but the air feels heavy and too warm. Sweat pops out on my skin.

"Wyatt, is something wrong? You look sick," Jacob says, studying me.

Jesus. Stop freaking out.

I take in the oversized wooden desk, worn leather chairs, and aged oak paneling. My pulse only creeps higher.

"Sit," Jacob orders, motioning at the chair across from him.

I obey, perching on the edge like a teenager about to get his ass chewed.

Jacob waits for me to speak.

I scold myself again, then sit back, trying to get comfortable. I blow out a shaky breath. "I, uh, wanted to talk to you about Willow."

His gaze sharpens, and suddenly, I'm not a grown man anymore. I'm the poor, scrappy kid who used to get into trouble with his sons. Firmly, he prompts, "What about Willow?"

My heart tries to escape through my throat.

"Well, spit it out, son," Jacob demands.

I blurt out, "Sir, I want to ask for your permission to marry Willow."

He goes absolutely still at my pronouncement.

It's not the reaction I imagined, and it throws me off. My heart slams so hard against my rib cage, I try not to wince. I rush to fill the silence. "I realize I've made a lot of bad decisions in my life. But since I returned, I've worked hard to redeem myself."

Jacob lifts on eyebrow.

A bout of nausea hits me.

I continue babbling. "I was an idiot to destroy The Buck and Bruise, but I paid Willow back. I stopped drinking whiskey, and I uh..." I release an anxious breath.

"You what?" he questions, leaning closer.

The same sense of shame I felt when I told Willow and the others tries to pull me under. I swallow hard, pushing forward. "I've stopped gambling. I attended Gamblers Anonymous meetings every day for a few months, but now I only go once a week. I'm not sure if I really need to go anymore, but I figured it doesn't hurt."

Jacob doesn't speak, and his silence doesn't help my nerves.

My mouth turns dry. I try not to flinch under his stare.

I add, "I also saved my winnings over the last seven months. Well, besides paying Willow back and buying her a ring. I found some land that would be good for a riding school, and I'm going to put an offer on it."

"Riding school?" Jacob questions.

I nod. "Yes, sir. I've had a good run, but I think it's time to hang up my boots. Willow will always have to travel for her career, and we can't both be on the road when we have a baby."

"Is she pregnant?" he asks in a rumble.

"No! Sorry. I suppose I didn't express that correctly. But we want a big family. When she's gone, I'll be here. And going out on top is the best. I can get off the road, head up the school, and have a team of coaches who travel."

He just stares at me.

"Please say something, sir," I beg.

He leans back, pushing his fingertips together, keeping his intense gaze on mine.

An eternity passes before he says, "Do you think the land you're looking to buy is enough?"

My chest tightens. "I think it'll be enough to start a school. I can expand it down the road."

His lips twitch, but his tone remains flat. "You remember the Ashpost cabin?"

"The one where…" I stop myself from saying *where Willow gave herself to me.*

"Where what?" Jacob questions.

I clear my throat. "The one where your great-great-great grandaddy settled?"

"Great-great for me," he corrects.

"Oh. Yeah. Sorry."

He takes another moment to assess me.

I force myself not to shift in the seat.

He finally discloses, "Ruby and I decided that plot of land is yours. It's in the family trust. It sits on ten acres, and ironically, Willow's ten acres butt up to it. You can turn the dirt track into a private entrance for your students. The only stipulation I have is that you keep one of the cabin's existing walls and the fireplace if you decide to rebuild. If you don't want to put your house on that spot, then you'll have to restore it as a guesthouse. If you don't, Ruby will string me up next to you when the bulldozers arrive."

I gape at him.

I heard that wrong.

With a smirk, which is a rare thing for him, he waits for me to speak.

I sit taller. "Sorry, sir, but I'm not sure I understand."

"What isn't clear?" he prods.

I blurt out, "Did you just say you put those ten acres in my name?"

"Yes."

Shock and vulnerability have me worrying I might tear up. I shake my head, stammering, "I-I— What?"

Jacob's expression softens. "You got shafted by your blood kin, son. And Ruby and I have always considered you as one of our own. So you've been in the trust since you were twelve."

My mouth drops toward the floor.

He chuckles. "Don't think I've ever seen you look so shocked."

I close my mouth, staring at him, blinking hard, and trying to process everything. My eyes want to betray me, so I look away for a moment, taking deep breaths.

How is this possible?

He continues, "If you prefer to buy the other plot of land you mentioned, that's okay too. The trust always owns the land so that no one can squander it away. You're not the only Cartwright to get in too deep when gambling."

I swallow a lump in my throat and then turn back toward him. Shame still weighs heavy on my heart, but I inquire, "I'm not?"

"No. So, the ten acres are yours to do with as you please. However, every acre will remain in the family; the trust stipulates that it'll pass to your future heirs. If you have none, then it'll go to another one of my grandchildren. Just don't forget about the wall and fireplace. I prefer we both keep our balls." His eyes twinkle.

My laugh comes out choppy.

Willow.

I lift my chin. "Sir, does this mean I have your blessing to marry Willow?"

His eyes narrow again.

Is he going to say no?

I swallow the bile creeping up my throat.

He leans closer. "Willow's her own woman. She'll have to make that decision. But as long as it's what she wants, then yes. You have both Ruby's and my blessing."

Giddiness fills me. I blink hard. "Thank you, sir. I'll take good care of her."

"I'm counting on it. And I'm happy to hear about the changes you've made, Wyatt. Don't stop moving forward."

"I won't, sir."

His eyes flicker with mischief. "I assume you bought a ring?"

"Yes, sir."

He holds his hand out.

I chuckle, finally relaxing, and pull it out of my pocket. A three-carat, round diamond with a halo around it and a hidden halo underneath is cradled by two thin white gold bands lined with tiny diamonds, and there's a slight V where they meet the hidden halo. No matter which way I turn the ring, the brilliant gems sparkle.

Jacob picks it up and whistles. "That must have set you back a pretty penny."

"Willow's worth it, sir," I proudly declare.

He studies it further, then hands it back to me. "She'll love it."

"I hope so," I state, shoving it back into my pocket.

Jacob grunts. "If a woman can't appreciate that ring, she doesn't deserve one." He rises.

I follow.

He steps around the desk and pulls me into a manly hug, slapping my back. "Glad you finally grew up, son."

His words mean more to me than any ever have. "Thank you, sir."

He steps back. "When are you asking her?"

"Now that I have your blessing, I'm asking her tonight."

He grins. "Great. And just so you know, she's as stubborn as her mother, but she has a heart bigger than Texas. Both those things will grow the longer you're married."

I laugh again. "Noted."

I leave his office, and spend the rest of the day preparing to propose to Willow. And now that Jacob told me about the land, my idea is even more perfect.

When it turns dark, I pull out my phone.

Me: You home soon, sugar?

Willow: About to pull onto our road.

Me: I took a walk and ended up at the cabin. My ankle is hurting. Think I overdid it when it was already sore. Can you pick me up?

Willow: Ashpost?

Me: Yes.

Willow: I didn't know you hurt it.

Me: Didn't want you worrying about a little twinge.

Willow: Sounds like more than that.

Me: I think the walk did it. I'll be okay. Just don't think I should walk back.

Willow: No, don't move. I'll be there soon.

Me: Thanks.

Nerves have me pacing as I glance around the cabin, taking in the weary bones and stone fireplace in the glow of the lights I strung everywhere. Memories flood me of when Willow and I first tore open each other's hearts, souls, and bodies.

I turn the lights off, and wait until Willow pulls up.

I text her.

Me: Can you come inside? I need some help getting off the couch.

Willow: Should I get my brothers?

Me: Nah. I just need a good pull to get on my feet.

The muffled sound of her SUV door shutting hits my ears. Anxiety rolls through me as I kneel on the floor.

The front door opens. She flicks the switch, and the string lights turn on.

"What's—" Her mouth drops open and her eyes start to water. She blinks, but a tear escapes.

My heart hammers hard, and I swear it shakes the old floorboards beneath my knees. I grab her hand, softly greeting, "Hey, sugar."

The corners of her lips curve. "Hey, you." Her blues shine brighter, and then a huge smile erupts on her face.

It helps calm me. I chuckle my nerves away, knowing this is the most important moment of my life, and I'm staring at my future wife.

I kiss, then caress her hand, feeling emotions I've only ever felt for her. I rise as tall as I can and start, "You're the only woman I've ever loved. You've helped me become the man I want to be. There's no one I could imagine spending my life with besides you. I don't just want you for the rest of my life, sugar. I need you so I can breathe. So please. Say yes and become my wife. I promise you I'll adore you until the day I die." I open my other hand.

Another tear rolls down her cheek, competing with the bling of the diamond. She inhales sharply, staring at it.

"You can touch it if it helps you say yes," I joke, but I'm suddenly worried she might say no.

A laugh bursts from her. She steps closer, tosses her arms around me, and beams. "Yes! Of course I'll marry you!" She kisses me.

Happiness fills me to the point I might burst. I kiss her back, holding her tight.

She slides her hand into my hair and presses her body against mine.

I retreat from our kiss, stating, "You better slip it on, sugar, because the rest of the night, the only thing you're wearing is this diamond."

She laughs as more tears fall.

I slip the ring on her finger, relieved it fits perfectly, feeling more alive than ever.

She's the only one I've ever wanted. Seven months ago, I never thought we'd get here, but we did. All the years of heartache and pain have finally come to an end. Now, the only thing ahead of us is a lifetime of love.

EPILOGUE

Willow

Three Months Later

A gentle autumn breeze floats across the yard, complementing the ambiance of the soft, instrumental music. Bright leaves rustle in the oak trees, glowing from the hundreds of clear lights strung around their branches. Our friends and family sit in white chairs, facing the Ashcroft fireplace and the original wall on which it was built. It's the only part of the cabin remaining. It roars with flames, and floods the area with the scent of the cedar logs burning in it.

Wyatt stands in front of it, his dark eyes locked on mine, full of love and compliments I don't hear but see. His new, shiny brown boots and cowboy hat match his tan suit. The W on his gold belt buckle gleams with pride. I gave it to him on the second Christmas we were together. He told me he wanted to wear it on our wedding day, and I loved the idea.

Jagger stands next to him in a matching suit, grinning as cockily as ever. Phoebe is on the other side, waiting for me to arrive and take my spot next to her. I'm relieved that Wyatt and I decided to have only one person on each side of us.

Dad holds his arm out, his eyes bright. "Ready?"

I hook my lace-covered arm through his and smile. "Yes."

The music changes to an acoustic country song, written by an up-and-coming band in our hometown. Wyatt and I saw them perform one night when we were out. I raved about how much I loved the singer's voice.

Wyatt contacted the band the next day. He asked them to write something for our wedding. They made him tell them about our relationship so it would be personal and meaningful. Then he surprised me and took me to a bar to hear them sing the song. I was immediately in love with it, and said I wanted to walk down the aisle to it.

Wyatt had chuckled and said, *"I guess I'm going to need them to write another for our first dance, then."* Which he did. We've listened to the songs so many times that I can recite the words in my sleep, but they never grow old.

Every time we play the songs, my heart skips several beats. Today is no different, but it leaps in my chest, wanting nothing more than to officially tie itself to the man I've loved since I was fifteen.

As soon as I take my first step down the aisle, Wyatt's lips twitch and then quickly burst into a huge grin. I force myself not to run toward him.

The delicate lace skirt on my boho wedding dress swishes across the runner. There's a slight chill in the air, blowing against my naked back, but my blood runs hot.

The singer's voice reminds me of warm honey, oozing romance and sacred love.

We get to the end of the aisle, and Dad kisses my cheek. He murmurs in my ear, "You'll always be my little girl."

Tears well in my eyes. I nod, and he steps in front of Wyatt, leans toward him, and says something I can't hear.

Wyatt's expression turns serious, and he nods.

Dad pats his back and then takes his place next to Mom. She's already dabbing her eyes.

Wyatt places his warm, callused palms in mine and squeezes. He mumbles, "Jesus, sugar."

I smile bigger, and the world goes quiet. We exchange our vows, pledging to spend the rest of our lives together and support one another in good times and bad. It's the most important moment of my life, but it passes in a blur. Before I know it, the officiant declares, "By the power vested in me by the great state of Texas, and in the presence of your family and friends, who have gathered to witness this moment, I now pronounce you husband and wife. You may kiss your bride!"

Applause echoes around us, and I lose my breath. Wyatt puts his hand on the back of my veil, and his lips melt against mine in a possessive, needy masterpiece of desire. The crowd explodes into cheers and whoops.

When he pulls back, I declare, "I'm Mrs. Wyatt Houston now."

He chuckles, keeping my face close to his, and boasts, "Damn right you are, sugar. Don't ever forget it."

* * *

Quick note from Maggie Cole

Thank you so much for reading Holiday Rider. I really enjoyed writing this Second Chance Holiday Cowboy Romance.

And don't worry! You don't have to say goodbye to Willow, Wyatt,
and the rest of the Cartwright family.

Jagger's story is up next in Holiday Heir and you won't want to miss
it. You've seen glimpses of him throughout the first three books, and
this secret baby romance is going to tug on all your heart strings!

And did you know that you can grab your paperbacks, ebooks, and
audio at a deep discount by visiting Maggie's personal bookstore?
https://maggiecolebookstore.com/

MAGGIE COLE

Jagger's story is up next in Holiday Heir and you won't want to miss it. You've seen glimpses of him throughout the first three books, and this secret baby romance is going to tug on all your heart strings!

And did you know that you can grab your paperbacks, ebooks, and audio at a deep discount by visiting Maggie's personal bookstore? https://maggiecolebookstore.com/

CAN I ASK YOU A HUGE FAVOR?

Would you be willing to leave me a review?

I would be forever grateful as one positive review on Amazon is like buying the book a hundred times! Reader support is the lifeblood for Indie authors and provides us the feedback we need to give readers what they want in future stories!

Your positive review means the world to me! So thank you from the bottom of my heart!

CLICK TO REVIEW

MORE BY MAGGIE COLE

For exclusive collector's editions, autographed books, and discounted paperback and audio visit Maggie's bookstore at www.maggiecolebookstore.com

The Cartwright Family - Holiday Billionaire Novels

Holiday Hoax - A Fake Marriage Billionaire Romance

Holiday Hire - A Billionaire Single Dad Nanny Romance

Holiday Rider - A Second Chance Cowboy Romance

Holiday Heir- Jagger's Book-coming November 1, 2026

The Underworld

Bride By Initiation (Sean Jr. and Zara)

Bride By Coronation (Fiona and Kirill)

Bride By Ritual (Brax and Valentina) - January 1, 2026 or possibly sooner

Mafia Wars - The Ivanovs & O'Malleys

Ruthless Stranger (Maksim's Story) - Book One

Broken Fighter (Boris's Story) - Book Two

Cruel Enforcer (Sergey's Story) - Book Three

Vicious Protector (Adrian's Story) - Book Four

Savage Tracker (Obrecht's Story) - Book Five

Unchosen Ruler (Liam's Story) - Book Six

Perfect Sinner (Nolan's Story) - Book Seven

Brutal Defender (Killian's Story) - Book Eight

Deviant Hacker (Declan's Story) - Book Nine

Relentless Hunter (Finn's Story) - Book Ten

*** If you're looking for Dmitri and Anna's love story, the book that created the Ivanov and O'Malley families, then grab book six of It's complicated: Secret Mafia Billionaire - Book Six

Mafia Wars New York - The Marinos

Toxic (Dante's Story) - Book One

Immoral (Gianni's Story) - Book Two

Crazed (Massimo's Story) - Book Three

Carnal (Tristano's Story) - Book Four

Flawed (Luca's Story) - Book Five

Mafia Wars Ireland - The O'Connors

Illicit King (Brody)-Book One

Illicit Captor (Aidan)-Book Two

Illicit Heir (Devin)-Book Three

Illicit Monster (Tynan)-Book Four

***Club Indulgence Duet** (A Dark Billionaire Romance)*

The Auction (Book One)

The Vow (Book Two)

***Wilted Kingdom Duet-** (A Dark Bully Romance)*

Seeds of Malice-Book One

Thorns of Malice-Book Two

***It's Complicated Series** (Chicago Billionaires)*

My Boss the Billionaire- Book One

Forgotten by the Billionaire - Book Two

My Friend the Billionaire - Book Three

Forbidden Billionaire - Book Four

The Groomsman Billionaire - Book Five

Secret Mafia Billionaire - Book Six

***Behind Closed Doors** (Former Military Now International Rescue)*

Depths of Destruction - Book One

Marks of Rebellion - Book Two

Haze of Obedience - Book Three

Cavern of Silence - Book Four

Stains of Desire - Book Five

Risks of Temptation - Book Six

Brooks Family Saga

Kiss of Redemption- Book One

Sins of Justice - Book Two

Acts of Manipulation - Book Three

Web of Betrayal - Book Four

Masks of Devotion - Book Five

Roots of Vengeance - Book Six

ALL IN BILLIONAIRES

The Rule - Book One

The Secret - Book Two

The Crime - Book Three

The Lie - Book Four

The Trap - Book Five

The Gamble - Book Six

STAND ALONE NOVELLA

JUDGE ME NOT - A Billionaire Single Mom Christmas Novella

ABOUT THE AUTHOR

Amazon Bestselling Author

Maggie Cole is committed to bringing her readers alphalicious book boyfriends and fiercely strong heroines.

She's been called the literary master of steamy romance. Her books are full of raw emotion, suspense, and will always keep you wanting more. She is a masterful storyteller of contemporary romance and loves writing about broken people who rise above the ashes. Her books can often be found hanging out in the top 100, even years after publication.

Maggie lives in Florida with her son. She loves tennis, yoga, paddle-boarding, boating, other water activities, and everything naughty.

Her current series were written in the order below:

- All In (Stand Alone Billionaire Novels with Entwined Characters)
- It's Complicated (Stand Alone Billionaire Novels with Entwined Characters)
- Brooks Family Saga- A Dark Family Saga – Read In Order (Each book has different couples)
- Behind Closed Doors-A Dark Military Protector Romance – Read in Order (Each book has different couples))
- Mafia Wars (Stand Alone Novels with Interconnecting Plot and Entwined Characters)
- Mafia Wars New York (Stand Alone Novels with Interconnecting Plot and Entwined Characters)
- Mafia Wars Ireland (Stand Alone Novels with Interconnecting Plot and Entwined Characters)
- The Underworld (Next Generation Mafia Wars Secret Society with Stand Alone Novels with Interconnecting Characters)
- Club Indulgence Duet A Dark Billionaire Duet – Read in Order (Same Couple)
- Wilted Kingdom Duet-A Dark Bully Billionaire Duet
- Interconnecting Plot and Entwined Characters)
- The Cartwright Family - Holiday Billionaire

Click here!

Hang Out with Maggie in Her
Romance Addicts Reader Group
Maggie Cole's Romance Addicts

Follow for Giveaways
Facebook Maggie Cole

Instagram
@maggiecoleauthor

TikTok
https://www.tiktok.com/@maggiecole.author

Complete Works on Amazon
Follow Maggie's Amazon Author Page

Book Trailers
Follow Maggie on YouTube

Feedback or suggestions?
Email: authormaggiecole@gmail.com